The Storytellers

Metamorphosis

BY *ROBERT MERCER-NAIRNE*

POETRY
> *Mercer-Nairne in Malta*
> > illustrated by Marisa Attard
> *On Fire*
> > illustrated by Marisa Attard

PLAY
> *The Arrow*

NOVELS
> *The Letter Writer*
> *Like No Other*
> *Warlord*
> *The Storytellers*

NON-FICTION
> *Notes On The Dynamics Of Man*
> *A Paper (Monograph)*

The Storytellers

Metamorphosis

Robert Mercer-Nairne

a novel

GRITPOUL, INC. · WASHINGTON · USA

First edition 2015

ISBN-13: 978-0-9748141-5-5
Library of Congress Control Number: 2014910585

Published in the United States of America by Gritpoul, Inc.,
2025 First Avenue, Penthouse A
Seattle, WA 98121-3125
www.gritpoul.com

Interior Design and Typesetting: Danscot Print Ltd, Scotland
Cover Design: Larry Rostant
Author Photograph: Christine Muscat-Azzopardi

Printed in Canada by Friesens Corporation
10 9 8 7 6 5 4 3 2 1

The paper used in this publication meets the minimum requirements of the American National Standard for Information Sciences – Permanence of paper for Printed Library Materials ANSI Z39.48-1948

For
Jimmy Wales
knowledge is the first step

Part One

CHAPTER 1

"MUDD!" The editor's voice shot out of his sanctum like a white ball, sending the office reds into a momentary frenzy of activity. That's how the news day started. George Gilder believed in firing a starting gun, just to get the juices of his idle sons-of-bitches flowing again. He'd been there; knew the score. After a night of booze and smoke that passed for journalism, one needed a propellant just to remember what the hell one had been chasing down the day before.

Harvey Mudd had a splitter. A protracted session with a disgruntled politician, whose blood must have been at least 90% alcohol, had yielded nothing beyond the bile of the perennially passed-over. James Callaghan, who had become Prime Minister following his colleague's unexpected resignation, was looking vulnerable. Inflation was in double figures, unemployment rising and his party had lost its majority in the House of Commons, forcing him to deal with a minority group. Labour had been in power for eight of the last twelve years and the party, like the country, seemed to have become ungovernable. There was a growing smell of rot. Callaghan was no slouch, having held all the top offices of state, but even a top dog must tire eventually. The age-old game of trying to identify the next *primus inter pares*, an egalitarian notion that fooled no one, was in full swing.

Mudd had not exactly chosen journalism, but rather it him. A story in his university paper *Protest!*, exposing a scam in the college kitchen, had earned him a prize. In a drunken moment, the head chef, with whom he had struck up a carousing friendship in his favourite watering hole, the Lord Nelson, had bragged about a holiday in Tenerife, all expenses paid, courtesy of a local butcher. When Roray – the chef – had been fired for erratic timekeeping, they agreed to stick it to the butcher, whom Roray said was a nasty piece of work, as well as to the now ex-head chef's replacement, whom Roray liked even less.

Under the guise of smoothing things between the butcher and the new man, Roray set up a meeting and recorded the whole encounter. The recording was pretty terrible, with the sound of Roray's jacket obscuring most of what was said, but Harvey had taken a punt under the headline *Moo-Cow Madness – Are We Paying For More Than Meat?*, with an article questioning his college's purchasing procedures. He'd been hauled before the principal to justify his claim and even though the scratchy conversation hardly proved his case, the explosive denials from the butcher, plus a cursory look at the kitchen accounts, persuaded Principal Harris that all was not well, elevating Harvey from scholastic oblivion to journalistic hero.

A £10 prize had been awarded by the *Oxford Mail*, a local daily, and an internship offered on graduation, which Harvey readily accepted, for want of anything else to do. Eight years at the paper had passed quickly and it even seemed he had some aptitude for the work. Several pieces exposing minor instances of local authority corruption eventually brought him to the attention of George Gilder, the editor of the great national newspaper *The Sentinel*, who offered him a position on the political desk.

'The best place for your talents, Mudd,' Gilder had intoned.

'Politics and malfeasance are irresistibly attracted.'

Harvey had never thought of himself as a moral crusader. In fact, he hadn't thought much about morals at all. As a boy he had dreamed of becoming a mining engineer. A branch of the family had emigrated to America and his namesake had founded the Cyprus Mines Corporation, ending his days with a reputation for civic leadership and a California college being named after him. What had fired the young boy's imagination was the fact that ancient Cyprus had been famed for its copper, but he had never quite grasped how a Los Angeles-based company could have revived the trade at the start of the twentieth century. More interested in ancient galleons than in modern mining techniques, and with no affinity for mathematics, his dream had eventually collapsed around him.

Being brought up in a modest terraced house in London's East Shoreditch by a mother with a vivid imagination and keen, if conservative, interest in the world was no barrier to fancy. 'Take from no one' was his mother's mantra. Earn your own way and think for yourself. His father had died when Harvey was twelve, of a heart attack, and his mother survived on her husband's modest pension, paid faithfully each month by the bank where he had been a junior clerk, supplemented by several cleaning jobs. Her *bête noire* was socialism. A trick to turn men into vassals, she called it, using their own labour. It was a long time before Harvey had the faintest idea what she meant.

Another unusual aspect of his young life was opera, although it seemed perfectly normal to him at the time. His mother, who was part Italian, had a passion for it and whenever she could, they would stand at the back and soak up Rossini, Bellini, Verdi and anything else she could scrounge a cheap ticket for, even Wagner and Strauss. As the sounds filled his head with love and anger, sorrow, deceit and vengeance he came to marvel at the human condition. Gradually it dawned on him that what he wanted to mine was people, not copper, and no science degree would be required. But how one might go about such a thing and earn a living from it was quite beyond him. So cluttered is a young man's head when he is starting out that it wasn't until he had been working at *The Sentinel* for several years that he realized he had found what he was looking for. The epiphany upset him. Suddenly there was something he didn't want to lose.

"Sit, Mudd."

George Gilder's habitually brusque manner belied a fierce loyalty towards those he had decided to take under his wing.

"So how are you seeing things?" the great editor continued.

It was only ten in the morning and Harvey still wasn't seeing much. Whenever he found himself in George Gilder's office he felt either inadequate or guilty of some unspecified misdemeanour. Was his boss's question personal, a forerunner to 'and when are you going to start justifying my faith in you?' Or was it about the workings of the office which could best be described as an anarchic circus of the high-blown and scatological, with *The Sentinel*'s editor its ringmaster?

"It can't go on, Mudd. Change has to come, one way or another."

"Yes sir," Harvey agreed, without any clear notion of what he was agreeing to.

The view of St Paul's Cathedral from the editor's office always gave him a lift. Wren's masterpiece had somehow survived German bombs but would not exist had the capital escaped the conflagration of 1666 when a fire in Thomas Faynor's bakery on Pudding Lane had spread, engulfing almost all of mediaeval London's wooden houses.

"Yes, we need a fire, Mudd," he continued as if reading his junior's distracted mind, "to clear away the tangled undergrowth that is choking this great nation of ours."

Harvey felt relieved. Any reference to 'our great nation' removed him from the frame. George Gilder was a patriot and *The Sentinel* his mouthpiece. Great nation talk usually presaged some line of attack against the establishment's shortcomings and Harvey realized he was about to be given a mission.

"There's someone I want you to go and see. Here's his card."

"Is there an angle you would like me to develop?"

"Just listen to what he has to say, Mudd, and then follow your instincts. When you think you have something, come and see me."

That was it. George Gilder was waving him out. Taking one last look at the mighty cathedral dome, he turned and left his editor's office, awake, excited and alive.

*C*HAPTER

S HOREDITCH had passed through many guises. In the seventeenth century, Huguenot silk weavers had established themselves in the district, one of the many groups to find sanctuary in London from persecution at home. After textiles came furniture-making and all the while the neighbourhood supported a thriving theatre trade. But by the end of the nineteenth century, the locality was best known for crime, prostitution and poverty. The Blitz that spared St Paul's was merciless to East London and by the end of the war, hardly a house escaped redevelopment. Utilitarian apartment blocks, the brainchild of government planners with limited budgets and weary imaginations, replaced the friendly terraced houses German bombs had missed.

But even in the bleakest landscapes miracles can be found. One such was a neat little row of terraced houses on Buttesland Street across from Aske Gardens, a small patch of green with a cluster of trees and a playground. On three floors, two windows across, with a basement, number 71 had been Harvey's home all his life. His grandparents had lived there when his parents moved in, but had died soon after. Now, surrounded by a hotch-potch of blocks, the sixteen or so houses that made up the terrace were keenly sought after. His mother had been approached by agents many times, but apart from playing them along for devilment, never thought to sell.

Sometimes he would walk home from the office. At other times, especially when it was wet, he'd take the Northern Line from Bank to Old Street, all of two stops, and walk from there. But the office was not where George Gilder wanted his journalists to spend their time, unless they were filing a story.

'You are reporters,' he would growl, 'so get out there and report. No one's interested in what goes on here.'

On the way home he would pass Bache's Street, where a thriving brothel once stood, and imagine the girls entertaining their wealthy Mayfair clients: West End boys and East End girls, the closest the classes came to mixing. Neil Tennant and Chris Lowe hadn't written their song yet, but a little bit of what they fancied doubtless did the classes good.

"That you, Harve?"

"Just me, mother."

Harvey closed the front door behind him. Their invariable routine pleased them both. Sylvia, his mother, was less of a dynamo these days, with fewer cleaning jobs. The money he now brought in made her work unnecessary, from a financial point of view, but she enjoyed getting out. He never thought once about leaving, in spite of her chiding him that he wouldn't get a girl until he had his own place. She had looked after him when it mattered. Now it was his turn to look after her.

"Good day then?"

From her perspective, days were good unless proved otherwise. She was optimistic by nature.

"Yes, I think it was."

"Well surely you must know?"

Harvey moved to the kitchen. It was still early enough for a cup of tea. He hadn't wanted to contact the man on the card right away. He just knew that from the moment he did a chase would be on. If George Gilder smelled a story it was sure to be a big one.

"What do you make of things?" he called out as he watched the kettle boil. Then, remembering his bafflement in the corner office, he added, "In the country, I mean."

"Just don't get me started, Harvey. It's a mess. The unions are running the country now, or ruining it, more like. I blame the bosses. They never say you can't have that pay rise, we can't afford it. The union just has to whisper the word 'strike' and the bosses cave. It's Labour to blame. The unions are their paymasters, right? So the government doesn't lift a finger. Wages go up and prices go up, so wages go up some more and prices follow. It's a joke, Harve, a bad joke, that's what it is. They're supposed to govern not just sit around saying yes, to get re-elected. How about some of that angel cake, dear?"

Harvey returned from the kitchen with the cups of tea and two slices of the cake.

"George Gilder wants me to meet someone."

"Who?"

"I don't know," he said, taking the card from his pocket and handing it over to his mother.

"Mr Peter Betsworth," she read out, "and a telephone number. Not very informative. It's quality print and paper, though."

His mother noticed things like that.

"Seen that girl again?" she asked, changing the subject to something more interesting.

Harvey was never sure if his mother's interest in his limited love life was benign or defensive, so tended not to talk about it. But he had met this woman, Frances Graham, at a cocktail party. Something about her had got right into him and he couldn't help mentioning it. Her face was serene and her laughter sounded like bells. They had talked about opera and Italy, where she had family. She was quite out of his league, of course, and married.

"No. And I don't suppose I will."

"Never sell yourself short, Harvey. You're as good as anyone."

"Anyway, she's married."

His mother just shrugged.

"Nature doesn't know that," she said.

They sat, as they often did, on the sofa, watching the evening news on Sylvia's small, black and white television set. The world could seem a profoundly dismal place when viewed through this narrow window. After the 1973 Yom Kippur War against Israel, which a number of Arab states had started and then lost, an oil embargo was launched against the West by Arab oil producers. Prices rose across the board, the stock market crashed and inflation was running at 24% by 1975 before slowly starting to fall back. Since the Second World War, there had been a consensus. Whether right of centre or left of centre, governments had not interfered with the unions and management was expected to engage in what was known as 'free collective bargaining', which usually meant that under threat of strike, labour negotiators extracted a little more from management at each pay round. Like lobsters in slowly-heating water, industry failed to notice the deathly path it was on. With the oil shock of 1973, the water suddenly got much hotter and even government began to see the problem.

Faced with rampant inflation, workers demanded large pay rises, which their union bosses felt obliged to pursue and company management to accept. The government urged pay restraint on the public sector, whose wages it had to pay out of taxation or borrowing, and attempted to hold the line at 5%. But when Ford, after a surprisingly good year, settled for a 17% increase in 1978, strikes spread across the country.

"That'll do it," asserted Sylvia tartly, with a certain grim satisfaction, as the newsreader informed the nation that tanker drivers, members of the Transport and General Workers' Union, planned to 'go slow' in support of a 40% pay claim. "The coalminers brought down Heath," she said. "You see what no oil will do to this government."

As if to compound the bad news, the weather forecast that followed offered up nothing but unremitting cold. Harvey looked at his watch. It was 9.30 p.m.

"I'm just going to make a call," he told her.

In the hall he pulled out the card and dialled the number. He didn't expect anyone to answer, but couldn't resist trying. The line rang briefly, clicked and rang several times more before a man answered.

"Betsworth." The voice was crisp, business-like and took Harvey by surprise.

"Er, I'm sorry to be calling so late. George Gilder of *The Sentinel* suggested I contact you."

"Who am I speaking to?"

"Mudd, Harvey Mudd, of *The Sentinel*," he repeated.

"Yes, Mr Mudd, I have been expecting your call. Shall we meet?"

"Certainly. I could meet you tomorrow."

"Excellent. The bridge in St James's Park, say at ten. You know it?"

Harvey had to think for a moment. St James's was the park closest to government. At one end Buckingham Palace, at the other, Horse Guards, the Foreign and Commonwealth Office, Treasury and Cabinet Office. Now bridge, bridge – yes there was a bridge, across the lake.

"I believe so, yes."

"Good. Tomorrow then."

The line went dead.

"I'm going out for a quick walk before turning in," he called out to his mother from the hall.

"Very well, dear," she called back. "Wrap up warm."

He put on his thick overcoat and wound a scarf tightly round his neck. Outside, light snow flurries swirled past the pavement lights. Occasional Christmas decorations in windows gave the streets a festive air, incongruous against the mountains of bagged rubbish that were piling up in every corner because the refuse collectors were on strike for higher wages. At least the cold suppressed the smell of rotting waste. But he loved his city, in spite of it all. What things it had witnessed since being founded on the banks of the River Thames two thousand years ago by the Romans. Wars, plagues, fire, but somehow it had gone on growing, a testament to what people, pursuing their own interests, can achieve. Its population had fallen back since the world war, but was still over 6 million with more than 300 different languages spoken.

He had been born just after the great deflagration and so was spared being sent off into the countryside to live with strangers, a well-intentioned policy, invented by bureaucrats to save the city's children from German bombs. The heartache caused was invisible and so the policy was never questioned until many years later. At the same time, in Germany, bureaucrats were sending Jewish families by the thousand, and eventually by the million, to death camps where work would set them free. There was something about the 'state' that frightened him. Its capacity for cold-blooded efficiency, in simple things – like sending millions of men from this war-front to that, or millions of families from their homes to somewhere else, all at the stroke of a pen, – was surely diabolical.

Perhaps there were worse things than the near anarchy gripping Britain now, although it was hard to think so. When the Conservatives had briefly been returned to office, Edward Heath, the new Prime Minister, had attempted to curb union power. But the miners took him on with strikes in 1972 and 74, forcing the government to introduce a three-day working week to conserve fuel. He called an election to bolster his position, but the result was inconclusive and the long-standing Labour leader, Harold Wilson, was eventually returned to power. Now Wilson, too, had gone, leaving Callaghan the poisoned chalice.

As he turned into Haberdasher Street, he came upon three youths huddled outside the off licence, which had just closed, handing what looked like a bottle from one to the other. A large black woman, with late-night shopping bags, walked past from the other direction and cussed them.

"What's your problem, sister?" one of the boys taunted, which seemed mild, but Harvey hurried on quickly, avoiding eye contact. His was a mixed area and none the worse for that. As he walked, he turned over in his mind what the mysterious Peter Betsworth, if that was his real name, might have to say. There was certainly a growing mood in the country that things had to change.

When he came back into the front room his mother was asleep. The television flickered away and he turned the volume down. She would wake soon and take herself off to bed. With her head tilted forward and her face reflecting the ebb and flow of the pale light from the screen, he found himself thinking, just for a moment, about the time when she would not be there.

CHAPTER 3

S t JAMES'S PARK looked grey. A watery sun was failing to free its frosted trees and probably wouldn't succeed any better on that day than it had on all the previous ones, stretching back to an autumn Londoners had forgotten. Strands of mist furrowed the lake's water top, will-o'-the-wisps, entreating passers-by to join them. Unimpressed, ducks and geese stood huddled together like spinsters around a dance floor, content to watch, their playfulness long drained. The cold, invisible, penetrated everything. Winter was in control.

Harvey had passed from Westminster along a path christened Birdcage Walk by locals after King James I, on his accession in 1603, ordered the marsh there drained to form a landscaped park with an aviary along its southern edge. But the park took its name from an ancient hospital for lepers, dedicated to St James the Less, which once stood nearby. The narrow lake that Harvey now hurried by, his coat pulled tight, gathered water from the little River Tyburn before it spilled into the Thames near Downing Street.

The village of Tyburn had been a short distance north, close to where Marble Arch now is, once a place of execution. The first recorded was in 1196 when William Fitz-Osbert, a charismatic champion of London's poor, had his limbs pulled off by horses before being hung there for stirring up trouble, along with nine of his accomplices. In 1537, Henry VIII used Tyburn to dispatch a number of those opposed to his suppression of Catholicism. A clever innovation, allowing for multiple hangings, increased the popularity of the spectacle considerably. On a June summer's day in 1649, a delighted crowd was treated to twenty-four simultaneous killings: twenty-three men and one woman. The last official lynching to take place at Tyburn was of John Austin, highwayman, in 1783. The maintenance of order was seen by the authorities as their special responsibility and sending rebels to dance the Tyburn jig an essential deterrent.

Harvey was a glutton for London history and his mother a firm proponent of capital punishment. 'Too many liberties are taken these days, Harve,' she would often say. 'Examples need to be made.'

As he hurried towards the slender Blue Bridge, which crossed the lake, where he expected to meet Peter Betsworth, he imagined a clutch of union leaders hanging, like Abel Meeropol's strange fruit, from a Tyburn tree.

The park was largely deserted as he stepped onto the overpass. Just a few, like him, going from A to B, hurried to their business. The summer melee of prams, picnickers, joggers, strollers and duck feeders ignoring signs urging them not to, were absent. Parks were healthy things, he thought, in all respects. They brought high-born and low, young and old, eccentric and coy, lovers and lonely, the under-dressed and over-dressed together in a space that belonged to no one and everyone. Even the police, who passed through from time to time on horseback, looked on their best behaviour, far removed from the game of cops and robbers that frequently corrupted their weaker brethren. Parks reflected society as it wished to be: temperate moments before and after the struggle to survive.

Harvey checked his watch. It was not yet ten. He had some

minutes to spare, although it was not a day on which to be early or late. He clasped the handrail, as if to take in the view. It would be another twenty years before the London Eye would turn slowly in the distance and he could envy any who had made it into one of the pods: a mobile cave with an ever-changing view – mankind's advance.

"Mr Mudd?"

The man addressing him was nondescript, as he imagined his father had appeared to most people. Only to Sylvia was her husband a knight in shining armour, a description her son felt strengthened with each year of widowhood.

"Yes," Harvey acknowledged. "Mr Betsworth?"

The man ignored the question.

"Now I want you to understand something," he said. "This meeting is not taking place."

Harvey was used to 'off the record' briefings, when someone wanted to raise an issue and not be identified as having done so. But the assertion that a meeting which was taking place was simultaneously not taking place stretched even his journalistic imagination.

"So you shouldn't be speaking to me?" Harvey replied.

But again, his interlocutor disregarded the question.

"Let us walk a ways," Mr Betsworth said instead. "It is far too cold to be standing around."

With that Harvey heartily agreed and started walking beside the stranger in the direction from which he must have come.

"What do you know about communism?"

The inquiry surprised Harvey and he half-wondered if he had slipped into a version of Alice's Wonderland, where Peter Betsworth was part unsmiling Cheshire Cat, able to appear and disappear at will, and part Mad Hatter, intent on asking unfathomable questions, such as why was a raven like a writing desk, to which he himself had no answer.

"A certain amount," was his guarded reply and as he offered it up, he realized how little he knew.

"Well, all you need to know," his walking companion instructed, "is that communism is an ideology used by those who badly want it, to steal power from those who already have it, by persuading those without it that they will be better off in consequence."

"Power to the people," mouthed Harvey and as quickly wished he hadn't.

"Quite," snorted Peter Betsworth acidly.

"Like early Christianity before it was co-opted by the Roman Empire," Harvey added in an attempt to advance his intellectual game.

"Hardly!" exclaimed the unsmiling Cheshire Cat. "We are a Christian nation and it is our values they are trying to undermine."

"They?"

"Communist infiltrators," came the reply, which was the first straight answer to a question Harvey had so far received. "And believe me," the nondescript man added with unexpected passion, "they exist."

"You have evidence?" Harvey asked.

As George Gilder had beaten into him from the start, to be presented as a probable fact, an assertion had to have support from at least two unrelated and credible sources. Naturally this was not always easy to come by and an attributable quote could often be used to smoke out the truth, as well as – unfortunately – to muddy the waters. Journalism was no exact science and to imagine it ran without an agenda was wishful thinking. But if his editor thought Peter Betsworth was sitting on a story that affected the nation then he probably was.

"The present Chancellor of the Exchequer and the recently retired leaders of the Transport and General Workers' and Amalgamated Engineering Unions were all members of the Communist Party," Peter Betsworth continued in a tone so dry, he might have been listing soiled items for the laundry. "Did you know that?"

"I had heard that the Chancellor fought the nationalists in Spain as a young man," Harvey conceded, but the raw announcement shocked him. Three of the most powerful men in the land, ex-communists! The standing joke in recent years was that the unions ran the country and with some 2 million members, the TGWU was the largest.

"And the problem goes far deeper than young men's fancies, I am afraid," his companion continued. "Communism and its variations are rife within the union movement."

"To what end?" Harvey asked. "I can't see the point."

"You do have a lot to learn," Peter Betsworth snorted, clearly startled at *The Sentinel* journalist's obvious lack of grasp. "Did you not study communism at university?"

"Not in any depth, I am afraid. I do recall something about the inevitability of capitalism destroying itself and the workers' paradise that would follow. But to be honest, I never did grasp the inevitability argument or, for that matter, understand what an earthly paradise might consist of. Free beer seemed like a good place to start back then, and free opera tickets."

"Opera tickets!"

Peter Betsworth's tone indicated disbelief that the highbrow and lowbrow – opera and journalism – could possibly mix. The man next to him was clearly suspect. Had he not had satisfactory dealings with George Gilder in the past, he would have terminated the conversation then and there.

"I like opera," proffered Harvey, undeterred. "It explores the full range of human emotion."

"But communism is not about individuals, Mr Mudd. It is about movements."

"An individual wrote the textbook though, didn't he?" Harvey countered, dredging Karl Marx from the recesses of his mind where, until then, he had been content to leave him.

"Well it's true that Marx constructed a formidable argument about why change occurs and why the monetization of everything in capital-based economies is merely a phase through which societies pass, but it is those who seek to hasten the demise of capitalism that we are talking about and they are a movement."

"Like the Christian movement," interjected Harvey, returning to an earlier theme, "underpinned by the inevitability of the Second Coming and God's judgment of all men."

"Hardly," harrumphed the intelligence officer, which Harvey had concluded Peter Betsworth obviously was. "The Communist Movement is not content to wait until capitalism fades, but is attempting to grab power by claiming to promote Marx's vision."

"Just as religious movements do when they promote the vision of their founders," murmured Harvey, adding, "before getting hijacked by the merely power hungry."

"I suppose there are similarities," conceded his companion. "The Communist Movement is being orchestrated from the Soviet Union. But it's the shop stewards who are doing the damage and the union top brass is unwilling or unable to rein them in. They stop production at every opportunity. It is chaos, frankly. If the public knew what was really going on they wouldn't stand for it. Our government might then have the guts to cut the unions down to size. That's where you come in."

Harvey could hear his mother saying, 'and amen to that.'

"You say orchestrated by the Soviet Union. What do you mean exactly?"

"Oh, just little payments here and some encouragement there; the ambition of men does the rest. Surely your opera has taught you that?"

"But can a handful of power-hungry shop stewards really do that much damage?" Harvey questioned.

"In the right atmosphere, yes they can."

"Right atmosphere?"

"Well what you've got to understand, Mudd, is that in the last war we fought against fascism and if that German madman hadn't turned against the Soviet Union, the continent might have been dominated by two totalitarian states, one communist, the other fascist and frankly, in terms of ghastliness, there would have been little to choose between them. But the Soviet Union ended up as our ally and there were a good few on the left of British politics who considered that evil empire one step away from paradise. Easy to do, I suppose, when you are sitting on an armchair in St John's Wood.

"Anyway, the thing is, there was a good deal of sympathy towards the working man after the war. The Labour Party was tied to the unions and even the Conservatives, under Harold Macmillan – a Tory patrician if ever there was one – did not want to interfere with the collective bargaining process. This permissiveness emboldened the unions and weakened management. By the time Wilson realized things were getting out of hand he and his Labour Party were hopelessly compromised. There was little they could do and now Callaghan is in the same pickle."

"The Conservatives, under Heath, had a go," proffered Mudd.

"Yes," the secret agent acknowledged wistfully, "but the public was not yet ready to bite the bullet. And besides, Heath tried to appeal to the union leaders' good sense and there was just no way individuals like Jack Jones and Hugh Scanlon were going to do business with a Conservative. These men were not cocktail party socialists, like so many in the Labour movement. They were the real deal. For them, the shop floor and its stewards came first."

"Before the country?" queried Mudd.

"Yes, before the country. At least until the country had been torn down and rebuilt in their image."

"So what do you want me to do?"

"George Gilder tells me you are a tenacious reporter and have a nose for corruption."

Harvey shrugged. "I've unearthed some bad practices here and there."

"You should go to Longbridge," Peter Betsworth insisted. "There's a fifty-one-year-old communist shop steward there who has been causing no end of bother."

"That's a British Leyland plant?"

"Right. And their Cowley plant is even worse – riddled with Trots."

"Trots?" Harvey queried.

"Trotskyists. Followers of the Russian, Leon Trotsky, who argued that the proletariat working in large factories could be radicalized and made aware of their predicament in a way a dispersed peasantry could not."

"Predicament?"

"That they were forced to accept the subsistence wages the owners of capital, in place of the landowners, elected to pay them. It was these toilers' ongoing task to overthrow the capitalist system and bring about proletarian government. The bourgeoisie, or capitalist placemen of the ruling autocracy, as he thought of them, had to be swept away so the ongoing revolution could bear fruit. He believed the engine of change would be a network of workers' councils in capitalist factories around the globe."

"Didn't he come to a poor end?" Harvey asked, remembering something he had once read.

"Yes. He was expelled from his country and eventually murdered on Stalin's orders. That was in 1940 I think. He was living in Mexico at the time. A poor end indeed for a man who had once commanded the Red Army."

Harvey thought his companion almost sounded sorry for the deceased revolutionary.

"Now here is some background material on Longbridge and Cowley," he said, handing Harvey a folder. "You'll also see something on a miner we are keeping an eye on, Arthur Scargill. He joined the Young Communist League in 1955 and attended the World Youth Festival in Moscow a couple of years later. Festival!" Peter Betsworth repeated. "As innocent-sounding as an English country fête. He was pretty active in the strike that brought down Heath."

Harvey accepted the folder, which seemed slim, considering the magnitude of what the agent was telling him. His companion had to be from MI5, he thought, the branch of government concerned with internal security.

"Just background material," Peter Betsworth advanced, as if reading his mind, doubtless one of his skills.

"And my role?" Harvey asked.

"Just get in there and start reporting. Tell stories. Explain to the public what is really going on. Our country is on the brink of imploding – step two in the communist handbook," he laughed drily, "after infiltration."

"People must be persuaded that a new style of leadership is needed," he continued. "Our democracy depends on it. Now should you need to, call me on the number you were given. Good luck."

With that, the man who called himself Peter Betsworth peeled off in the direction of Whitehall. Clutching the slim folder, Harvey continued north towards Piccadilly. He thought he might as well take the tube at Green Park and connect with the Central Line east at Holborn.

He hadn't noticed the chill while they'd been talking. But now the frozen landscape seemed anxious to suck the warmth right out of him. Fear and excitement mingled with the outside cold and inside warmth from his over-pumping heart in a sensual congress that stirred him. He walked quicker. A tramp shuffled past from the other direction and mumbled a half-hearted solicitation, which Harvey ignored. On his right, beyond a high hedge, he passed the home of Lord Rothermere. George Gilder had taken him to a reception there once.

The press baron's father, Harold Harmsworth, the first Viscount, had been a hugely successful pioneer of popular journalism and a one-time supporter of the German Nazi Party, until its foul nature became apparent. Harvey wondered if crisis fostered extremes, or if extremes fostered crisis.

'Someone needs to crack the whip, Harve,' his mother would often say. 'Too much freedom just leads to trouble.'

Harvey smiled to himself. Harold Harmsworth and Sylvia would have got on. They sang from the same hymn sheet, which was why the tycoon had been so successful. The forces of radical conservatism were stirring from a long slumber. Suddenly it became clear. His job was to help force them wide awake.

*C*HAPTER

4

"THAT were great, Mabel."

Stanley Preston leaned back in his chair and looked across the table towards his wife with obvious pleasure. They'd been married for forty years and he'd never been tempted to stray. The evening meal was a cherished ritual and his home a contented space. The same, however, could not be said for his place of work.

The fields around Longbridge, on the southern outskirts of Birmingham, had been turned over to industry at the end of the nineteenth century. The copper plate printers who had made the move failed and the site was acquired by a Yorkshire man, Herbert Austin, to build cars. Within a few years he was employing over a thousand people. During the First and Second World Wars, his greatly expanded factories were used for the production of munitions. Austin and Morris Motors amalgamated in 1958, becoming the British Motor Corporation, and ten years later, when Harold Wilson's Labour Government arranged for BMC and British Leyland to merge, Longbridge became the largest car plant in the world, employing over 250,000 workers. Rather than leading to efficiencies, as had been intended, this industrial hubris led instead to an augmentation of government meddling, management weakness and union intransigence.

By 1975, the unwieldy behemoth had run out of money and the government was forced to rescue it, becoming its major shareholder. Two years later, a South African was hired to clear up the mess and Michael Edwards set about his task with gusto. Partnerships with overseas manufacturers were sought, unprofitable parts of the business were earmarked for sale or closure, the senior management structure was streamlined and Edwards began disaggregating the monster into more commercially coherent divisions. With inflation rampant, the government's policy of pay restraint was failing, utterly, and even the union hierarchy had lost control to militant committees on the shop floor. The steady improvement in living standards, which unions had secured for their members at each pay round since the war, was under threat as never before.

It was back in 1934, at the age of sixteen, when Stanley had joined Austin as an apprentice. Four years later, he and Mabel were married and when he went off to war, she entered the factory to help the war effort by making armour-piercing shells. Their three sons, Billy, John and Joseph, named after the Soviet leader, were minded by her mother for the duration. Stanley had become a member of the Communist Party soon after joining Austin, not on account of any strong ideological convictions, but because that was what most of the lads did. At the start of the war, the Soviet-Nazi non-aggression pact caused him and several of his friends to question their allegiance, but by the end, what he came to think of as little more than a misstep could be forgotten. An alliance that was good enough for Mr Churchill was good enough for him.

Billy, their oldest, had left home at sixteen 'to see the world' and now worked for an oil company in Texas. John still worked at Longbridge, although he did not share his father's deep faith in the union and they had grown apart. Joseph had surprised everyone, becoming a chef in London and Stanley looked forward to his youngest son's visits with unexpected hunger. The factory, the union, the *Daily Worker*, or *Morning Star* as it became, were his world. Incidental news from the centre of capitalist power proved to be a guilty pleasure for both him and Mabel, especially as Joseph, unlike John, displayed little interest in politics.

"Will you be going to the institute?" Mabel asked, the name given to the canteen where shop stewards and workers congregated to socialize, hold meetings and generally put the world to rights, a world which had become excessively wrong of late, in all their eyes.

"Yes. Derek wants us out."

"That'll be the second time this month," she said. "What's it this time?"

"Management's trying to cut overtime again," he told her.

"Well, if cars aren't selling," she proffered hesitantly but thought better of continuing along that line and changed tack. "These stoppages are costing us, Stan. Just think what it's doing to families with children."

"Aye. It's hard. But if we lose this one, Mabel, we'll lose everything."

Mabel Preston knew better than to argue. She'd said her piece. Now it was down to her to manage the household finances as best she could. She just wished she had some of the magic on show in the parable of the five loaves and two fish. Especially as she was buying a little extra each week to share with the young family next door who were being hit hard by the frequent disruption in earnings. When all was said and done, they had to stick together. She knew that. Solidarity was their only strength.

* * *

The institute was full, as it tended to be before a vote. Peter Farris was in the chair with Derek Robinson on his left. The shop steward had laid out the position. A minimum level of overtime had been negotiated three years earlier when production was in high gear and now that sales had stalled, management wanted to break the agreement.

'If agreements can be entered into when convenient and dropped when not, they are not agreements,' the steward had declared to the general satisfaction of everyone in the room. 'This is our factory,' he claimed, 'and we must be consulted.'

The room, with windows bolted shut against the outside cold, possessed the moist warmth of a womb. Secure, they felt comforted by each other, packed inside. Like the prisoners of Plato's cave, their assertions seemed real, even though they were merely shadows of reality projected through the lens of Marxist-Leninist theory poorly understood.

"Delegates," Peter Farris announced from the chair after the minutes of the previous meeting had been read. "I have asked Jack Pugh from our sister plant in Cowley to say a few words. As you know, Cowley has been in the vanguard of our struggle and Jack one of its leading lights. Jack."

A wiry, dark-haired man in his mid-thirties, with a clipped goatee beard and piercing green eyes, rose from one of the plastic chairs in the front row which were normally stacked against the back wall to make way for the snooker table now pushed tight into one corner. Even in this simple act of rising to address the crowd, the Cowley delegate radiated a pulse of electric energy that caused the room to fall silent and its occupants, many pressed standing against the walls, to fix on him in anticipation.

"Brothers!" Jack Pugh's greeting was delivered loudly in his shrill voice as a consecration of the faithful. "It is our task," he urged. "No, it is our sacred *duty*," he qualified, in a tone worthy of the most forceful proselytizer, firing the word 'duty' into the hearts of his listeners like a trained marksman, "to tear down a capitalist structure that can upset our lives as easily as a ledger entry. It is our sacred duty, brothers, to reclaim that power which is rightly ours, and which resides here, inside these factories, not in some distant counting house operated for the benefit of people who neither know about us, nor care.

"In light of the hardships you are being asked to bear, it is important that you understand the heroic process you are part of. Many here will already know what this is, but some of you will not, so let me explain." Jack Pugh looked pensive, drawing his hands up to his lips, as if in prayer.

"When the French Revolution brought an end to feudal society in that country," he continued, "which Oliver Cromwell had already achieved here, the working man ceased to be a chattel, the property of another. However, these revolutions were not revolutions of the workers, or proletariat, but of the middle class, or bourgeoisie, who attained the freedom to compete for positions of authority. This was possible because money came to determine the flow of relationships within society, rather than birth or blood lines.

"But this put ultimate power in the hands of the owners of capital, who were happy to employ the bourgeoisie as their placemen, leaving the proletariat to fight between themselves for the crumbs. And crumbs, brothers, are exactly what we would have got had we not organized. And it is crumbs, good people of Longbridge, we will get again, if management gets its way now."

It was already dark outside. The windows were steamed and one or two inside the institute were getting restless. Two late arrivals let a welcome blast of cold air into the room, and the distraction allowed everyone to alter their positions. Delegate Pugh tried not to appear irritated as the arriving men searched for somewhere to stand and polite suggestions were made from various quarters, but to no avail, leaving them squeezed just inside the door.

Picking up more or less where he had left off, Jack Pugh gave them a warning. "Do not imagine," he said, "that the Labour Party is your friend. Members of the Labour Party will make comforting noises, certainly, but in the end, they are bourgeois, jealous of their advantages and will never fundamentally change a system that benefits them. That is why, brothers, we must continue the struggle until property and privilege, however bestowed, are eradicated."

The applause he received was solid and might have been more so had his flow not been punctured. In any event, the membership had never fully embraced the hard left ideology which permeated Cowley, although there was a vocal minority of Longbridge workers who wished it had. This included Harry Blodget, an unmarried, middle-aged fitter, who rose to his feet and clapped keenly but failed to stimulate a standing ovation.

Peter Farris thanked the delegate from Cowley for his insights and opened the floor for questions to either their own steward or their guest, with the proviso that as it was getting late and they still needed to vote, "Could members keep it short and not go over old ground."

He must have known, from chairing past meetings, that this was a forlorn hope and the room immediately exploded into a starburst of questions, statements and accusations. Members did not come to institute meetings to remain silent.

"Some order, please. One at a time and through the chair." His repeated pleas were quickly lost in the raucous noise from the room which only died down when the pressure vessel had released its steam and the membership grew tired of hearing its own conflated sound.

"Ray, yes, you have a question?" The chairman repeated his invitation several times before the room fell quiet and Ray Gosling, a twenty-nine-year-old machinist with a wife and three small children, felt able to speak.

"Yes, this is for Derek, I guess," the young man said nervously.

Derek Robinson, a large man with an open, kind face, but

combustible temper, looked benignly at his questioner from the end of the hall, eager to put him at ease. These last months had been a trial for him. His members were hurting. Inflation was eroding every pay increase they secured. Militancy was growing. The national union had effectively told the plants and every department in every plant that they were on their own. It was up to the shop stewards to strike whatever deal they could. Anarchy was the only word for it. With rumours of cuts and closures swirling through the ranks, the mood was fissile. Stewards were being driven into taking action and making demands by a competitive frenzy. Over the last twelve months there had been over two hundred stoppages in his plant alone. He wasn't sleeping well.

"Don't hold back, son," urged Mark Grass, a spray painter of thirty years whose function would soon be taken over by a robot. "We are all family here."

"Well, it's about family really," the young man advanced. "These stoppages are making it hard to keep up with the payments. The young 'uns need feeding and clothing. The wife's struggling. She keeps asking me what all these stoppages are for."

"Sacrifices must be made," proffered Harry Blodget. "The women need to know that."

"That's grand coming from you, Harry," his neighbour chided. "You haven't got one!"

A ripple of laughter spread around the room. There couldn't have been a married man amongst them who hadn't been on the wrong end of his wife's tongue at one time or another.

"You surely have a hardship fund?" Jack Pugh asked, looking sternly across at the shop steward. Everyone was supposed to put a small amount each week into a kitty, which was matched from central union funds, for the use of members in serious trouble.

"Of course we do," the steward retorted. "But it doesn't amount ter much and besides, I've only had one request for assistance in twelve month and that from a widow needing help to cover her man's funeral expenses."

"That's the sum of it," exclaimed the young man, anxious to get back into his own conversation. "Apart from the rent, the food and the clothing, I have furniture to pay off and there's the car. But how can I claim hardship? All that's just life, isn't it? Oh, and there's the gas and the electricity," he added. It was his wife who kept the accounts.

The murmur of sympathy which the machinist's comments attracted was only too audible, especially from the younger members.

"Bourgeois trinkets," muttered Jack Pugh. But luckily for him, his aside was drowned out by a rising chatter inside the room as people compared notes about their overstretched finances.

Derek Robinson rose to his feet, anxious to reassert his authority.

"Friends!" he called out and the room gradually fell silent. "Of course this is hard – for all of us, and for you with young families most of all. But it is them or us. They would pay us nothing if they thought they could get away with it. Only by fighting them every step of the way will we preserve our standard of living."

"Only by fighting them every step of the way will we smash this unjust system," interjected their guest.

"Quite," asserted the chairman. "Now I think we should call a vote. The motion is that we stop work on Monday" – Monday being a popular day as it extended the weekend – "until management reinstates minimum overtime. Those for?"

Peter Farris cast his eye around the room and noted the sea of raised hands.

"Now those against?"

He could see none. Whatever the merits of a motion, his members were still holding firm. But he wondered how long this would last. The practical concerns of the young machinist seemed more real than the theoretical exposition advanced by the delegate from Cowley.

"Motion carried!" he thundered. "This meeting is now closed."

* * *

Men tumbled into the night. A few stayed behind to drink, in no hurry to re-enter desolate homes from which wives had long since left or had never arrived. Harry Blodget was one and attempted to collar Jack Pugh. But Jack, known behind his back as the Cowley Trot, was too wily an operator to get sucked into a late-night discussion that went nowhere and achieved nothing. He had a world to destroy and a world to build. Besides, there was a young undergraduate, Miranda, at Brasenose College, who found Marxist-Leninist theory profoundly erotic, waiting for him. He understood the need for flattery nonetheless.

Before excusing himself – 'Meetings to go to; the word to spread.' – he assured Harry that he was one of the best, a praetorian of the revolution.

"A great man, that," the Longbridge fitter repeated intermittently as he got stuck in for what he hoped would be a journey into oblivion that shut out his empty life.

Stanley was pleased to be going home. It was too cold a night for carousing. He hadn't noticed his son John slipping out of the institute ahead of him; there had been such a crowd. Mabel would be waiting to brew up a hot mug of cocoa for them both. They would talk awhile before retiring. The heartfelt plea from the young machinist was sticking to him though. Perhaps the world he knew was coming to an end. Things were a right jumble, for sure. All the talk about breaking everything down so it could be built up again, well that might have come out of the Communist Party textbook, but it seemed a crippling waste. Why not just change things for the better? He shook his head, which hurt from the cold or the thinking, he wasn't sure which. He'd leave the question to cleverer men.

Harvey also slipped out of the institute, surprised at how easily he'd gained entry. Back home he typed up his first report and faxed it into the office.

CHAPTER 5

THE NEXT MORNING he woke late and found a copy of The Sentinel on the kitchen table. The headline blazoned across its front page was *Red Robbo to Smash Society!* Underneath, his article had survived more or less intact save for some subtle changes and a harder edge. The delegate from Cowley hardly got a mention, which he was sure would infuriate the young man immensely. George Gilder had been working late.

Sylvia came in with his cup of coffee, beaming. He had told her where he was going the day before and she had recognized his handiwork straight off, although she was inclined to think that every good page in *The Sentinel* had been written by her son.

"That's more like it, Harve," she said, tapping the headline with her finger. "People don't like to be smashed up." He didn't have the heart to tell her the headline wasn't his.

* * *

On Sunday, it snowed off and on all day, but by teatime had more or less stopped. Harvey sat huddled on a bench in Aske Gardens, in front of their home, a plastic bag placed beneath himself and Sylvia to protect them from the fallen snow she had insisted on coming outside to see.

'Crumpets when we go back in, Harve,' she'd offered up with relish. 'A proper weekend treat!' – which she was now leaving him in order to prepare.

Local children were making the most of it. A snowball flew past his head, followed by a 'sorry mister!' barely meant. The gardens were small, yet treasured, the gift of a seventeenth century merchant.

He'd read about the Askes, a Yorkshire family of high ideals. Robert worked for the East India Company, trading in raw silk, and had left a fortune of some £50 million in modern money to the Haberdashers, his trade guild or livery company. An almshouse for the poor was built and a school, all according to his instructions, and while the school still thrived, the gardens were all that remained of the almshouse. Care of the elderly and destitute was now the preserve of the state, not private charity, an advance even his mother endorsed, except when she was fretting about bureaucrats playing Lords Bountiful and feathering their own nests at her expense.

Harvey's visit to Longbridge had stirred unexpected emotions. That his work had been given such prominence, even if the headline was not his, pleased him greatly. When not in Buttesland Street, his home was *The Sentinel.* That was where his loyalty lay; to it and to its political attitude as George Gilder defined it. But the people he had been amongst did not strike him as evil, with the possible exception of the delegate from Cowley whose obvious intelligence he thought was being played like an instrument for his own gratification. Even the shop steward seemed more a prisoner of events than their conductor. What he had witnessed were men in the eye of a storm, seeking comfort in each other's company and clinging to the only secure structure they knew.

Robert Aske's forebear – another Aske named Robert – had

faced a similar dilemma. As a devout Catholic, he had been strongly opposed to the reforms of Henry VIII. Although a lawyer in London, he travelled north to join the many from Yorkshire, Northumberland, Durham, Cumberland and Westmorland in their protest against Henry's pillaging of the monastic orders. He secured safe passage from the king's representative to remonstrate with the monarch directly, but following their meeting, the revolt flared again and he was arrested. Rather than execute him at Tyburn, as befell other leaders of the protest, Henry had him hung in York, bound by chains to preserve his rotting body as a public example to his kinsmen.

Harvey's interest in history was one of uninvolved curiosity and mirrored his work. As a journalist, he reported. That was his job. He knew he was more concerned about his employer's approval than with what he reported on. Only opera engaged his emotions, but that was within the safety of a story that could be picked up and put down, like a book. While he sat looking at the snow and the children playing in it, part of the scenery and observer both, Robert Frost's poem, 'The Road Not Taken,' came to mind, about the often illusory choices people face.

When the world breaks apart, must you not attach yourself to one part or the other, and short of limbo, will you not choose that closest to your familiarity, which makes it not a choice at all? Frost's traveller has the luxury of two paths to take, innocent of outcome. Only in hindsight can such a choice carry any resonance, save that being one traveller you cannot travel both. Harvey knew he was born working class. But there had been schools and universities to go to, free of charge. He had possessed some aptitude and a mother with ambition on his behalf. So had he chosen the path he was on? He hardly thought so. Brought up differently might he not have been Ray Gosling, the machinist worried how to pay his young family's bills?

Robert Aske the elder had been forced to choose between his brand of religion, with its emblematic structures, and a new, more secular order, dominated by a king determined to utilize Church power and wealth for his own advantage. Some choice! And yet Aske the merchant, in whose winter-gripped garden Harvey now sat, had been a Protestant beneficiary of the kingdom Henry Tudor founded. From nowhere, the image of Frances Graham drifted into his head. Her laugh, like Bow Bells peeling across a meadow urging Dick Whittington on towards London where a great fortune lay waiting to be claimed, stirred in his memory. Sod it, he thought. He was his mother's son. If that was a choice, he'd made it.

CHAPTER

THE CANDLELIGHT danced off the silverware and glass, casting an indulgent glow across the animated faces making merry around the long table, before darting with their shadows into the castle walls like furtive lovers. The jazz singer Toots Malone was there and the Gambler John Beacher, along with assorted earls, duchesses and self-made men. All, like their host, had one thing in common: a belief that life was to be lived at full tilt, or not at all. From one end of the banqueting hall, Frances Graham, chatelaine of Graham Castle, oversaw the seamless performance of her staff as dishes were brought and empty plates cleared, always watching her husband's powerful face for any hint of dissatisfaction, while still managing to charm the man on her left and the man on her right with words and laughter and coquettish smiles that stroked and teased and pleased, an amorous potion, convincing them they were in love.

The conversation moved like quicksilver from guest to guest.

"It's a bloody mess!"

"It's the bloody government denying the workers what's rightfully theirs."

"How can you say that? If it isn't there it hardly matters whether it's theirs or not."

"If what isn't there?"

"Money. If there's no selling, there's no earning and so no pay – simple!"

Articulated thoughts jumped and sputtered and sped.

"Christ, this winter's bad!"

"Not so bad if you like snow. The skiing's been exceptional."

"I hate snow."

"So where are you going?"

"South Africa. Or Australia. Ginnie's got a cousin there. One hundred thousand acres and a thousand head of cattle. We haven't decided."

"Jesus. That's a hundred acres a cow!"

"So you can count. And they're not called cows. You milk cows. These are beef."

"A technicality!"

"I'd like to see you milk a steer."

"Fran does it all the time."

"I expect she's into Mickys, not steers. Isn't that right, Fran?" Micky being the name Australians give to a free-roaming bull.

"Well I married one, didn't I?"

"Perhaps we should all emigrate."

"Or take a leaf out of Richard's book."

The conversation stalled for a moment at the mention of Richard Bingham, as if a dark spirit had entered the room. The public knew him as Lord Lucan, but to most of them he was a friend – a high roller, a charmer, a life-liver who had taken a wrong turn.

"Bad business that."

"Enough said," commanded their host. "For god's sake, cheer us up Toots!"

The jazz singer's expressive features rippled into a mischievous grin, the prelude to a short performance.

"There was a young girl from Cape Cod, who thought babies came only from God. But it wasn't the Almighty who lifted her nightie, but Roger the lodger, the sod!"

Richard Bingham's cloud dispersed as quickly as it had appeared and the gathering was merry again.

"Perhaps now would be a good time for the ladies to withdraw!" laughed Frances, rising to her feet.

"Why do we always get to miss the good stuff?" a female guest complained.

"Because it is not actually that good," a sympathetic male diner reassured her. "It is the male equivalent of the seven veils. We like to keep you guessing."

"Guessing about what?" she asked. "By the time you join us your dance is over."

"Come along, Madge," Frances encouraged. "Men only control half the world."

"The half that most often goes wrong," she hissed.

"Touché!" conceded her host, shutting the door firmly after her.

David Graham was a Scot of the old order, a chieftain at a time when chieftains were no more, at least in the eyes of the chattering classes in London. Tall and physically strong with dark hair and dark eyes that took few prisoners, his was a nature that demanded loyalty and expected to be obeyed. As soon as he had decided his wife would be Frances Gaspard, as she then was (her family had dropped the 'i' from Gaspardi shortly after arriving in England in the eighteenth century), his pursuit of her had been relentless. On one occasion, a thousand red roses had been delivered to the small flat she shared with a girlfriend, filling the basin, the bath, the sink and every container able to hold water. Frances had been a prize he expected to win, one of the loveliest girls in her set.

What makes a woman accept a man is a mystery, even to herself, whereas men chase attraction until more powerful men push them aside. The men interested in Frances Gaspard were many, but not one was inclined to hold his ground against David Graham. Flattered, intrigued, excited and with nothing at the time offering greater prospects of adventure than going off with a highland chieftain, as comfortable in London's Clermont Club as he was on the face of a mountain, she had capitulated. Since then she had learned to run his castle and to entertain the flow of high-achieving risk-takers from all walks of life her husband seemed to attract. But even after six years of marriage, she could not say she knew him fully. There appeared to be a part of himself he did not want her to know, and she was too intelligent a woman to pry.

With the men now clustered around David's end of the table, conversation quickly returned to the state of the country. Seeing the way talk was heading, the jazz singer excused himself. With the breezy aside that he intended to become an honorary lady for the evening, he left the dining room. A chorus of quips followed him: 'best keep your bedroom door locked then, Toots;' 'leave some for us, dear boy;' and from one wag, a bow to the old Slim Gaillard song Toots had often sung, 'A puddle o'vooty, old Tooty's a gooty!' No one was offended. The jazz singer was liked.

"What was all that about, Harry?"

"Cement Mixer, Put-ti, Put-ti. You don't know it?"

"Oh yes," the questioner claimed, but clearly didn't.

"To mix a mess o'mortar," Harry continued, warming to his theme, "you add cement and water, and see the mellow roony, come out slurp slurp."

"Pithy!" intoned Frank, a regular at Graham Castle.

"Where do you get such nonsense from?" Peter asked.

"Well while you were at Oxford learning about Plato, I was in Soho listening to the tunes of Buddy Bolden and Jelly Roll Morton."

"And I bet that's not all you were doing there," challenged Malcolm with the undisguised envy of one who had never properly sown his wild oats and was now under the thumb of a wealthy wife.

"Ah, the New Orleans sporting house," rhapsodized Andrew, memories of ladies past flooding into his head, along with the sweet spirit from a Taylor's 1928 their host had had decanted.

Old Archibald sat coiled in his seat, still lean at 6 foot 4 inches, an old soldier whose awkward relationship with authority had led him to special operations and a tailored unit he had moulded in his own image: fast, inventive, clandestine and invariably deadly. David Graham's kinsman had become a legend in his lifetime.

"It can't be allowed to happen." His rasping voice, weakened by age, still had the power to arrest.

Jazz and pleasure were abandoned and the eyes of the small group fixed on him.

"What can't, Archie?" Malcolm asked.

"We fought against the Nazis and we would have fought against the Soviets if we'd had any strength left. Now the commies are stirring up trouble right inside our own unions and this spineless government, utterly compromised by its socialist mumbo-jumbo, is watching the country fall apart around it."

Archibald did not expect any dissent, or interruption. He painstakingly prepared his cigar with the same care he had once applied to explosive charges, oblivious to everything but what he was doing. Satisfied, he drew it alight, savouring its rich incense.

"You see, the tactic is simple. First, you sow the seeds of confusion. In pre-revolutionary France and later, Russia, weak government was made to look even weaker by the covert actions of the revolutionaries. And as you know, I understand something about covert activities."

That was his cue to allow everyone some gentle comradely laughter and all willingly obliged as he filled his glass and passed the decanter on.

"The government of the Weimar Republic that took power in Germany after the First World War was, in many ways, highly competent. Even though the country was divided between a left pushing for full communism and a right wanting strong authoritarian leadership, the government managed to hold the ring. Between 1924 and 1929 things were even looking up. The brutal WWI peace terms had been renegotiated and with the help of American loans, the economy was growing again and extremism began to fade."

Reading their minds he then said with a twinkle, "You probably wonder how a soldier has come to know these things."

Indulgent nods and head shakes accompanied supportive mutterings as the decanter moved slowly from hand to hand.

"Well you see covert activities are most effective when the circumstances are right. Who said that one flap of a butterfly's wings could change history?" He paused briefly, not really expecting an answer. "I forget, but no matter. The point is that when conditions become unstable the impact of covert activities is magnified."

David Graham rose and collected the box of Romeo y Julietas from the sideboard and placed it on the table for anyone interested. Malcolm reached over and helped himself, having declined the butler's offer initially, uncertain as to whether he really liked cigars or not.

"But back to the Weimar Republic," Archibald continued. "As I said, after 1924 things started to go pretty well. Popular culture replaced street violence and the American-born singer, Josephine Baker, who I am pleased to report wore little more than some bananas for one memorable act, was declared an erotic goddess."

Too much history after dinner could be a burden and relieved approval greeted the image of the banana dancer. But the old soldier had lured them into an ambush. He brought the flat of his hand down on the table-top with a thump and a thunderous 'Wham!' that startled even the acerbic Frank, who was not prone to shows of emotion.

"But then came the stock market crash in America, the withdrawal of loans to Germany and the onset of the Great Depression. You all know the rest. Hitler's hoodlums stirred it up something rotten, blaming the poor bloody Jews for everything and by 1933 he had been made Chancellor and his shell-shocked people had given him more or less absolute power."

Allowing all this to sink in, he took a little port and then drew on his cigar.

"We mustn't let it happen here." His stipulation seemed the more powerful for the gentle way in which it was announced. The editor of *The Sentinel*, who had recently become a regular guest at the castle, did not need persuading.

When Frances and the ladies re-entered the grand dining room, along with Toots Malone, who'd been keeping them in irreverent hysterics for the best part of an hour, the sombre mood lifted.

"It's almost midnight, darling," she announced.

"By heavens, so it is," muttered old Archibald. "We've been in conclave too long."

David rose, looked at his watch and started counting. "Ten, nine, eight, seven, six, five, four, three, two, one…"

"Happy New Year!" everyone shouted.

Ignoring his scowling wife for once, Malcolm made a grab for Frances, which she easily dodged.

1979 had begun.

CHAPTER 7

"CALLAGHAN SHOULD HAVE gone for it in September, when he had a chance."

It was the first Monday morning of the new year and *The Sentinel's* editor was firing up his team for the week ahead.

"Serves him right for opposing In Place of Strife," Georgina gloated.

"Wilson could see the problem," Pete interjected. "Labour law needed reform, but the union diehards in the government just couldn't stomach it. His white paper was DOA."

"DOA?"

Porter, the social correspondent, disliked letters.

"Dead on arrival," Pete informed him.

"You've been watching too much American television," Porter carped.

"There is a world outwith Her Majesty's diary you know!"

"Children!"

George Gilder quite liked it when his reporters had a go at each other. It showed they were not asleep. But there were limits.

"Now, Mudd," he said, "what's on the horizon?"

"Blizzards!" Harvey answered. "At least that's what the Met Office is forecasting."

He'd come to think of his editor's preference for his surname as a sign of special favour. In part this was the case. But it was also because George Gilder liked saying 'Mudd', especially in a loud voice.

"So not great for the economy," Georgina concluded, seeing the point immediately.

"Not great for the pickets either," observed Pete who'd followed the Grunwick dispute in which a film-processing company in North London had been used as a stalking horse to test how far unions, sympathetic to a worker's plight, could legally obstruct a company's business, whether the company's workers were members of a union or not.

"Her Majesty has not missed a day yet," announced Porter.

"I can't see her sitting next to a coal-fired brazier in front of Buck House on a cold winter's day, just to stop Prince Philip attending an engagement," chortled Pete.

"No, she'd probably just send all his trousers to the laundry," quipped Georgina.

"We're wandering," chastened their editor. And then fixing on Harvey asked, "What mischief have the unions in store for us?"

"The big one is the tanker drivers' dispute. It's been rumbling for months. But with the Ford settlement it looks as though they are going for it. All members of the Transport and General Workers' Union are out, although at the moment it's unofficial. With fuel supplies drying up, the effects will spread everywhere–"

"Eighty percent of the nation's goods goes by road," interjected Georgina.

"Hospitals, schools, factories, farms, not to mention Joe Public and his blessed automobile."

A broad grin spread across George Gilder's face. "Now let's watch Callaghan's opinion poll lead get flushed down the toilet," he all but rhapsodized. "I want you to get out there and tell the story – no, the stories, as many as you can lay your hands on, about how this is affecting ordinary men and women – and who is doing this to them."

"Is it true that the ports are being picketed?" Pete asked.

"That's what I've heard," Harvey told him.

"The unions are just not in control any more, and neither is the government," concluded Pete. "It's all with the shop stewards now."

"And a fair few of them are taking their orders from the KGB, I wouldn't wonder," growled their editor.

"Quite possibly," agreed Harvey. "Although it seems to me more like a highly contagious virus affecting everyone it touches with madness."

"Ah, but it is only out of chaos that a new phoenix can arise," opined George. "That madness may embody more method than any of us realize."

"I suppose I might be able to find something that has inconvenienced Her Majesty," conceded Porter, torn between being left out and not wishing to dip his hands into such unseemly goings on.

However the meeting was over and Porter's indulgence fell on largely deaf ears. Harvey, for one, knew well enough what kind of phoenix his editor wanted to see rise from the ashes.

*C*HAPTER

THE MAN WHOSE WIFE imagined her husband was a well-paid analyst in a merchant bank became Peter Betsworth and slipped into Hyde Park. He'd had a call from 'Marx', one of his agents. Not the most original alias, but it appealed to him.

* * *

Marx enjoyed his trips to London. Partly this was because it meant he was earning his keep. He only visited the capital when he had something useful to give his handler. But mostly it was because he was given an overnight allowance for such trips and could meet up with Stacy in the Edgware Road boarding house where he stayed and she worked.

There was also something about the city that liberated him. Factory life, even a factory life punctuated by union meetings at which plans to bring about a new order were discussed with surreal intensity, could become downright claustrophobic, especially as the brotherly love that bound them was shot through with hatred, insecurity and suspicion. No sooner had he stepped off the train at

Paddington Station and melted into the crowd with its strangers of different shapes, sizes and nationalities, than the straitjacket of his other life fell away and he could wear a fresh skin.

There were times when he felt like waving two fingers at it all. He and Stacy often fantasized about a new life. But even though he'd never met the lady, he sensed that when it came to it, his friend wouldn't leave the mother she appeared to live with down in Barnes. He, on the other hand, had no ties. He supposed his own mother would miss him but he and his old man had long since ceased to talk, and his parents were close. He had avoided marriage like a poison. The prospect of being locked into a world he wanted to escape was not for him. Part of him admired his father's dogged attachment to the union movement. There was a certain nobility to it, for sure. But the man's blindness to the motives of the young firebrands who had hijacked the shop floor seemed pitifully romantic.

The approach from the security services had been so bloody brazen: an advertisement in the *Morning Star* seeking recruits 'to protect the nation'. 'To protect the effing capitalist class' more like, had been the dismissive reaction from the members of his cell. They'd even suggested he put himself forward as a double agent.

He'd replied anonymously to the box number provided, suggesting a meeting two weeks hence in the Dog and Whistle, a boozer on the outskirts of Birmingham he knew none of his mates frequented. On the appointed day and time he had gone there with little expectation, wearing the leather jacket he had described, hopeful that his demonstration of what he imagined were the black arts of the trade he hoped to join would impress.

There had been no other leather-jacket wearers in the Dog and Whistle that day and the meeting had passed without a hitch and even been an anti-climax. He was invited to attend some evening classes and assessments in Crawley, which had continued for several weeks. Only at the end, when he had presumably cleared some threshold of acceptability, had it been put to him that he inform on his colleagues at Longbridge.

For a year now, he had been coming up to London, seeing Stacy and handing over his reports. And if it hadn't been for her, whom he had met the first time he stayed in Edgware Road, he might have stopped. His reports seemed mundane, often embodying little more than tittle-tattle and a description of his workmates' daft notions. His clandestine work's connection to his nation's security seemed far from obvious. Also he'd been hoping for more excitement and so far, trying to imagine what knickers Stacy would be wearing next time he met her had been about the sum of it. At least his handler said money was being paid into an account he could access when his 'mission' was complete. But what was his mission and when would it be?

* * *

The man from MI5 walked with a light step. At last, he felt, things were shifting into a higher gear. Even though the brutal winter weather belied it, change was in the air. After over a decade in power, with only one brief interruption, the Labour party was losing its grip on the reins of government. He could sense it. The civil service, of which he supposed he was a part, was beginning to reposition itself for the possibility of new masters, or a new mistress as now seemed likely.

He and a number of his colleagues and friends outside the service had been watching the disintegration of the United Kingdom with growing alarm. There had even been talk amongst some of an interim authority taking over if democracy failed to deliver a stable government capable of taking firm action. This was uncharted territory. Like him, a majority of those concerned still wanted a democratic solution if at all possible, and he intended to move heaven and earth to bring this about. The alternative hardly bore thinking about.

Peter Betsworth had been keeping a close watch on his recruit. The handler was now as confident as he could be that the young man was not a plant and was ready for a more active role. Agents were a particular breed. Loners by nature, they appeared to be more detached from their roots than most people. If they had an ideology it was a passion for their own freedom to act, often for a cause but a cause defined in terms of the destruction of a world they had come to hate. As a child of the unions, Marx was now a twenty-five-year-old in revolt, exactly the profile he needed.

* * *

"Sugar?"

"Naa."

Marx stirred his coffee anyway. He always felt nervous in the presence of his handler. The man's nondescript manner could as easily have concealed a killer, he thought, as a favourite uncle. The Serpentine café was congenial and he was relieved not to be outside on a bench, Peter Betsworth's preferred venue.

"Everything all right at the boarding house?"

Marx said it was. The place Peter Betsworth had told him to use on his visits to London – 'We get a good rate' – had become a home from home. That said, his home in Longbridge, which he shared with flatmate Mad Max, a professional agitator whose convictions stretched no further than his love for a good 'whack-around', was a pit compared to the neat room on the Edgware Road, lovingly prepared by Stacy, so it was really the other way around.

"Seeing anyone?"

Peter Betsworth's question caught him off guard. But he tried to sound casual. He'd been warned against entanglements.

"Naa, not really."

To his relief, his handler didn't press the point.

"Now we want you to start playing a more active role," he said instead.

"In what woy?"

"Following the Ford settlement our sense is the unions want to let rip and blow the government's pay policy to kingdom come. We'd like you to push this in any way you can."

"You mean you want mower strikes, not less?"

"Exactly."

He knew that after a champion good year, the Ford Motor Corporation had settled with its unions on an inflation-busting pay rise which other workers were now drooling for. This had skewered the government, whose public sector wage bill was already daft. And now here was one branch of government actively siding with the workers against the official government policy of pay restraint.

"What bleeden side am we on then?" Marx asked.

"Right now, the union's," Peter Betsworth answered, without a hint of irony.

"Well that's 'un rowad I'll not be guin down. I thought it was the unions that 'ad got us into this codge and it was the unions we were tryen ter break."

"And how do you propose the unions be made more accountable?" the MI5 man asked.

"Change the bloody law," Marx snapped back, "so that these shop-floor crazoys can't bottle production whenever they fancy an' spread their scabby notions ter every other industry in the country whenever they ployz."

For the first time since Marx had known him, his handler just laughed. Not a mocking laugh, but an indulgent one.

"So?" Marx pressed, feeling embarrassed, certain that he must be missing something obvious.

Peter Betsworth felt hugely encouraged. If a young man from a working-class background could see the problem and its solution so clearly, then surely a majority of the electorate could too.

"Every time this government has sidled up to a change in the law," he explained, "it has been forced back on account of the Labour Party's deep roots within the labour movement. Even Heath's ill-fated conservative government of '70 to '74 wasn't willing to go for the jugular, at least without a mandate, which it didn't get."

Marx paused to organize his thoughts. "You're sayen we need a government that *'as* a mandate an' *wull* goo fer the jugular, roight?"

"Exactly."

Suddenly the laughter was gone and Peter Betsworth's crisp answer seemed cold and calculating.

For what seemed like a long time the two didn't speak, but just sat there, surrounded by the noisy comings and goings inside the café. A young mother struggled to get her pushchair and baby between the chairs and was helped by an elderly Jamaican man who rose from his seat to assist her. A boy, in too much of a hurry, dropped his ice cream, just missing a lady's handbag. He stared at the white mess on the floor in disbelief. Outside the glass walls, a row of ducks huddled in the cold, overlooking the water, waiting for any scraps that might come their way. Inside was not for them. Inside was for humans, upwards of fifty, happy to be warm, to be together, to be unaware – for a time at least – of the forces shaping their lives.

"So we're aimen ter topple this government an' put another in its place, that it?"

Peter Betsworth simply shrugged. Such treasonable thoughts were never to be expressed. He knew the history of Tyburn, even if his agent did not.

"Democracy only works," he said eventually, "if people know what is really going on. And as importantly, or perhaps even more so, understand the consequences of what is going on. Strikes they can see. The consequences of strikes they can feel."

"If there is a change," Marx asked, "what makes you fink a noo lot would do anny be'ah?"

"That depends on how steely they are, how angry the electorate has become and how big a majority they get."

"Three 'depends'!"

"Life is a succession of 'depends'."

Marx looked concerned.

Seeing that his companion was unimpressed by the odds, Peter Betsworth added, "I'm told that the lady who now heads up the Conservative Party is nothing if not steely, so that is one down."

"Fatcher?"

"Yes, Margaret Thatcher."

"I'm worken fer a skirt then?"

"Indirectly, I suppose you are – a skirt with an idea."

One of the few things Marx had remembered from school was the story of Joan of Arc. He even remembered having a fancy for her, so the idea of helping a woman fight for her nation's honour against weak, self-interested countrymen rubbed him the right way.

"Fair enough," he acknowledged, to his handler's evident relief, and reaching inside the slim satchel he had brought along, extracted five handwritten pages.

"Here's me report. The brothers believe they yav capitalism on the run."

"One can but hope!"

"That they does or that they fink they does?"

Once again Peter Betsworth allowed himself to laugh. He was definitely warming to this agent.

"Now turning from theory to practice," he said, "there is someone we are interested in. You've mentioned him in your intelligence, Jack Pugh. Get close to him. Encourage him. Be his friend. I want to know every little thing about him."

* * *

Marx left the Serpentine café energized. Matters had at last become clear. His mighty mission was to bring down a government – how about that? – and pave the way for a new style of management: everything the Trots, Commies and their assorted agitators were working for. He was on their side. The thought of it! He might even be able to talk to his dad again. As he boarded the train, he could hardly wait to file another report – and to fuck Stacy.

CHAPTER 9

J ACK PUGH had never been more excited. He'd joined Militant Tendency in his last year at university and helped to deselect the moderate Labour MP, Reg Prentice, from his Newham North-East constituency: a coveted first scalp. Jack took the Tendency's mission seriously: to infiltrate the Labour movement in order to promote the Marxist-Leninist agenda from within. While Militant's control over the Labour Party Young Socialists was not as firm as it had been in 1972, its influence over the shop stewards inside the nation's leading industries was at an all-time high.

Finally it was happening. He was sure of it. The tanker drivers had been operating a go-slow since December and now lorry drivers as a whole were on strike and their union, the Transport and General Workers' Union, had not even authorized it. The Labour Government and its partners in moderation, the union bosses, were in disarray. The potential to bring the nation to its knees had never been greater. There wasn't a sector that didn't depend on road transport for some of its supplies. This was the revolution he had dreamed about, the revolution that would bring him power.

They arrived at the Kingsbury Oil Terminal at first light. Most of the fuel used in the Midlands was distributed from the depot, one of the largest in the country. As he approached the first group of pickets he rolled down his window and called across.

"Brothers!"

His greeting was met with a mixture of suspicious stares and grunts. It had been a cold night.

"Is it tight?" he asked.

"As a tick's arse," came the reply.

He and his two colleagues drove on to the small office the organizing committee were using and only found Ralf Drydon. The two knew one another and Ralf was pleased to have some company.

"You know Max, don't you?" Jack asked.

"Won't be much for him here, I don't think," Ralf proffered, eyeing up the pugilist Jack had brought. "Running like clockwork. Some tea?"

"Yes please, while supplies last!" Jack answered, enjoying his own joke. "And this is John, Max's flatmate."

"John," Ralf acknowledged. "Haven't seen you here before."

"John's a Longbridge man," Jack explained. "Max has hauled him along for support."

"Well, as I say," Ralph Drydon continued, as he moved a single tea bag from one mug to the next, "there won't be much for you boys here."

While the mugs were being distributed – the strongest brew to Jack, the weakest to the new face: there is a hierarchy in all things – the door opened and a young woman came in holding a piece of paper.

"Been up all night, lass?"

"Best time for faxes," she answered, "when company business is light. This one looks important. It's from the union."

Ralf took it from her.

"Thanks, love. You'd best go home and get some sleep. I'll make sure you're covered."

"We're going to win, aren't we?" she questioned. "My man's on the picket line and we could sure use the extra money."

"Aye, lass, we're going to win."

Ralf Drydon's certainty reassured her and she left looking fulfilled. For her, and most of the wives whose husbands were 'out', it was about keeping ahead of inflation, not changing the world.

"A communication from the top," he announced as he read the faxed message. "From our executive officer, Alex Kitson, telling us to let essential supplies through or have the government declare a state of emergency and bring in the army."

Mention of the army pumped Max up like a shot of steroids. In his eyes, any week without a confrontation was a wasted one.

"You're not going to agree to that, surely," Jack demanded.

"We'll see," he answered. He knew his members were more interested in getting a good part of their 40% pay claim than in adhering to the fine print of the Marxist-Leninist rulebook.

"Solidarity, brother," Jack reminded him, but Ralf had his mind on other things and the telephone rang. Answering, he listened, looked pensive and then cupped the speaker.

"There's trouble up at Hunters, an independent distributor near Tamworth. You boys interested?"

"Right bloody right we are," answered Max before Jack had time to assess the full, strategic implications of the situation.

Taking that as a collective 'yes' he told the caller: "I'll have some lads up with you within the half hour." And then, turning to Jack, explained: "Hunters are trying to get their lorries out. They're only a small outfit with five tankers, I think it is, but letting them get away with it wouldn't sit well with my boys here. You up for it?"

The strike at the Kingsbury depot was a big story and Jack had hoped to get himself onto the evening news. But with Max already flexing his muscles and Ralf Drydon's men exhibiting all the discipline of a well-trained army, making his presence redundant, he had to agree.

"I'm not sure the three of us will achieve much," he prevaricated.

"I'll send five of our lads along in the van," Ralf countered, adding with a grin, "five of our more motivated brethren."

It only took him a few minutes to pull his posse from the picket line because the night shift was over and a fresh batch of men, for want of anything else to do, had already started to drift in. Jack could see that those selected were not unexercised tanker drivers, but some of the shock troops Ralf Drydon used to crack the whip and ensure that any driver foolish enough to cross the picket line remembered his mistake.

As he and his travelling companions left Kingsbury, having expressed their fraternal solidarity, the Trot from Cowley feared he was about to be part of little more than a barroom brawl. But events are rarely predictable, even in a Marxist world, and before the day was out he would have garnered more publicity than he could possibly have imagined.

* * *

Harvey had received a message from George Gilder the day before that he and his photographer should get up to Tamworth right away. An independent distributor, incensed by the union's grip on his business, had agreed to take a stand and there was sure to be a confrontation. Harvey suspected his editor had been alerted by a contact in MI5, probably the fabled Peter Betsworth, whose real name George Gilder undoubtedly knew. Sylvia had taken the call from *The Sentinel* and was in a state of high excitement when her son returned for the evening, barely allowing him over the threshold before sending him off to the station with a packed sandwich and thermos of tea.

The bed and breakfast his taxi driver had taken them to was

walking distance from Hunters' yard and their hosts, Doug and Marjory Faversham, seemed to have as little time for the unions as did the taxi driver who brought them to the door. 'They shouldn't be allowed to hold the country to ransom,' was Mrs Faversham's opinion, candidly delivered along with that morning's bacon, sausage, fried bread and two eggs, a sentiment his mother certainly shared.

He probably shouldn't have been surprised to discover a handful of other journalists already outside Hunters, being handed cups of coffee and tea by Doreen and Anthony Hunter, assisted by their two sons, Amos and Virgil, and daughter, Abigail. The Hunters had even typed up a page of history about the firm. It was started by Tony's father, Tom, shortly before the Second World War, which it had survived thanks to Tom's wife, Constance, driving their one truck in support of the war effort. The aftermath had been harder on account of the depressed conditions, but they were up to three trucks when the first Arab oil embargo hit in 1967. This they overcame, but were almost brought down by the second oil embargo in 1973 and rapid inflation it caused, followed by the three-day week introduced by Edward Heath at the end of that year as part of his battle against the National Union of Mineworkers.

Somehow they pulled through and had since even managed to increase their fleet to five trucks, with the help of a sizeable bank loan secured against the business and their homes. Now, however, they were boxed in. Although all five trucks were full of diesel oil, they knew they would be barred from entering the Kingsbury depot to replenish their supplies. Hunters' loyal customers, built up over many years, depended on them and there was simply nothing they could do. So the family had decided to go out, if that was to be their fate, in a blaze of adverse publicity for the unions. They had even had one of their drivers pretend to be a member of the TGWU and alert the Kingsbury shop steward that his firm planned to make deliveries.

It was not a good morning for any kind of outside confrontation;

so bitingly cold, even the scattered snowflakes were half-hearted. Harvey felt sure that opposing sides in a mediaeval battle around Tamworth Castle would have agreed to postpone hostilities, at least until the frost had left the soil and made the ground safe for horses. But such considerations were not part of modern man's lexicon. So much now took place inside that the outside and its character was unfamiliar territory, leading urban children to think that cornflakes were grown at supermarkets inside pretty coloured boxes.

The journalists had quickly turned their backs on winter but the arrival at Hunters' gates of Jack Pugh's battered Ford Cortina and the van from Kingsbury caused them to consider leaving the warmth of Doreen Hunter's kitchen. But Tony told them to 'sit awhile,' saying 'that lot can freeze their buns off until we're good and ready'.

The plan was simple. On his nod, the trucks would drive from the yard, single file, at slow speed, so that the photographers, who would already have taken up positions beyond the gate, could get some action shots of the gauntlet his two sons and three other drivers would have to run. The rest would be down to the stories accompanying the images which he was confident, following his and Doreen's hospitality, would be well weighted in their favour.

* * *

They'd arrived around 9.00 a.m. and it was now approaching midday. The van had kept its engine running, but Jack was trying to conserve fuel and the three inside the Cortina were numb with cold. Max's 'for Christ's sake, Jack. You're a bleeding shop steward. You can get as much fucking fuel as you want!' had yielded nothing. Jack had not wanted to get into the subtle difference between a shop steward and an organizer, which he was, and expose the limitations of his power. Real power would come later. For now his priority was to conserve sufficient fuel to get himself back to Oxford where he expected an enthusiastic Miranda would be waiting to welcome him from the revolutionary front.

"Here we go," Max said as people started to emerge from the house adjacent to the yard.

"Are those reporters?" Jack asked, seeing cameras slung over the shoulders of some of those exiting the building.

Things were at last looking up: action and limelight, his twin passions. Stiffly the three eased themselves from the car. But like reptiles emerging from the night's cool air, it was taking time for their metabolisms to become fully charged.

Next to them bodies tumbled from the warm van and it was clear these had not been idle. A playing card fell to the ground and Jack noticed what looked like an empty bottle tucked under one of the back seats. The heavies stamped the ground like bulls and watched their breath vaporize into steam.

"Had a good morning boys?" one of the cameramen mocked, as he passed through the open gate.

"Fair to middling," a heavy replied, eyeing the cameramen up with obvious distaste. Their kind of work was best practised away from public gaze.

As the photographers and journalists clustered on one side of the road, the Kingsbury boys stood ready on the other, the side the tanker drivers would be on when they finally made a run for it. Max drifted over to join them, but Jack and John Preston stayed with the press.

The confrontation started in surreal slow motion. At a crawl, the five tankers, headlights blazing, moved out of the yard towards the gate, one after another. The throbbing sound of their engines swallowed up the space around them, obliterating the outside world. Three of the pickets moved to the centre of the road. The photographers moved behind them to get shots of the first vehicle approaching the human barrier. Its driver appeared heavily dressed, with a grey woollen hat, but his youthful features were evident.

As the cameras clicked like castanets and the first truck pulled level with the van, the driver was dragged from the cab, becoming invisible to the onlookers. A rain of blows fell onto him from boots with metal caps as the truck lurched to one side, scattering journalists and cameramen, and only just missing the Cortina, before sliding drunkenly into a ditch.

Barely audible, the cry came up from Max: "Jesus, it's a bloody wench!"

Against her father's orders, Abigail had persuaded her brothers to let her drive the first truck. 'It'll show them at their worst,' she'd said.

And now she lay by the side of the road, bloodied and beaten, her long hair clearly visible beside her grey hat.

Incensed, the Kingsbury men reached inside the van for clubs just as the cameramen grasped what had happened and descended on the prostrate girl like vultures. As fast as they snapped, their cameras were grabbed from them and smashed to pieces on the frozen ground.

By now Abigail's two brothers and the two other drivers, each with clubs of their own, had waded in and a group of men, led by Tony Hunter was approaching from the house. As he and one of his lads pulled Abigail clear, the fight became brutal until it was obvious to Ralf Drydon's men that they were outnumbered.

Thrashing and hacking, with the Hunters side increasingly gaining the advantage, the Kingsbury lads backed themselves towards the van. They wouldn't have got away unless Tony had reined in his men. With the five surrounded, he could have had them reduced to pulp. Instead he told the interlopers to bugger off and that it was about time they did an honest day's work. As the van was manoeuvred away, a cascade of blows fell on it, converting the carrier's outside into scrap metal.

Following his gruesome discovery, and seeing that the odds were against him, Max had panicked. Screaming at Jack to 'get the fucking Cortina away', the two had slipped on the ice while racing towards it. The club Max had used flew up, catching Jack on the side of the head, knocking him unconscious. Max and John bundled the organizer into the car and succeeded in driving off while the action was focused on the van.

* * *

The drive back down to Longbridge was fraught, with John at the wheel of an unfamiliar car and a sobbing Max, repeating ceaselessly, 'I didn't know she was a girl. She shouldn't have been there. How was I to know?'

"Do you fink you killed 'er?" John quickly regretted his dumb question as it unlocked another torrent of self-recrimination from Max. Meanwhile, Jack Pugh had come round and was burbling about a great victory while clutching his throbbing head and speculating that he might have broken the leg he'd twisted in the fall. His nose must have taken a knock as well because it was bleeding like an open tap, further adding to the bedlam inside the car.

"For Christ's sake, block it man," pleaded Max who was showing an unexpected aversion to blood. "It's fucking well getting everywhere."

At Longbridge John dropped Max at their flat. The man was falling apart, now concerned less with the girl and more with the possibility that the Kingsbury boys would fit him up for a murder he might have committed.

"You'll back me up, John, won't you? I wasn't there."

John couldn't be bothered to remind him that Jack had introduced them both to Ralf Drydon. What was the point? The poor bastard was screwed whatever way round you cut it.

"I'll be back inside the hour," he reassured him. "Must drop Jack back at Cowley. He's in naa fit state."

As he closed their flat door, Max was still baying like a bereft she-wolf. "I wasn't there. I just wasn't there."

* * *

A few miles out of Longbridge, with Jack now nursing himself in the front seat, John asked, "Where exactly d'ya liv' in Cowley?"

"On the south side," Jack told him. "But you can drop me at Oxford University. It's closer."

"Goen ter drop a bomb then?"

"I've an engagement."

"Whereabouts?" John asked, resisting the temptation to press what a Trot from Cowley planned to do inside the establishment's advanced seat of learning. "Yoi'r in naa fit state ter walk."

"Brasenose College. I'll give you directions when we get there."

Jack's conversation was monosyllabic, as if he were giving painful birth to every word. After establishing their altered destination, he just fell asleep.

* * *

With the help of a college porter, John Preston managed to get the Cortina round to the back of the building, along Brasenose Lane. As luck would have it, the porter had seen Jack before and after they had deciphered his repeated 'Miranda, must see Miranda', helped him haul the wounded revolutionary up to the lady's room.

Out for the count on her small bed, Jack Pugh looked like the girl had looked, curled up defenceless on the ground, arms wrapped around her head protecting it from the blows. Max might have been distraught to discover the sex of his victim, but John had been disgusted by the whole fucking thing. If this was Jack's revolution, he could stuff it.

As he started to check over the room's contents, he wondered if he should have asked the porter to call a doctor. Then something caught his eye – a letter addressed to Miranda de Coursey. He'd read about a financier called Sebastian de Coursey who was interested in parts of British Leyland. His Longbridge brothers had pinned the article with a picture of the man to their dartboard and there hadn't been much of it left last time he looked. But what a sweet effing possibility! This surely warranted a report and would justify a visit to Stacy. Then a troubling notion occurred to him. Supposing the Trot from Cowley was working to save the nation too?

* * *

The aftermath at Hunters' yard reminded Harvey of Wellington's comment in a letter to a friend after his battle at Waterloo, that nothing except a battle lost can be half so melancholy as a battle won. The ambulance had collected Abigail and she was now on life support at the local hospital. Tony had ranted at his sons for letting her drive and then cursed himself for delaying their exit.

"Those men had been drinking. If we'd gone out first thing, maybe it wouldn't have happened."

Amos and Virgil, caked in their own blood and that of their adversaries, had tried to comfort their mother. Now the family was standing vigil beside Abigail's hospital bed.

The photographers had combed the ground for their camera parts like scavengers searching for anything that could still be used. Hunters' other drivers quickly extracted the first truck from the ditch and had already left to deliver what was likely to be their last load. A couple of policemen were taking statements and measuring distances and a colleague was photographing the blood on the ground where Abigail fell.

Harvey took one last look at the scene before he and his neutered accomplice climbed into one of the taxis summoned to take the journalists to the station. On the train he wrote, crossed out and wrote again. By the time they'd reached London he felt he had it, but still managed to make some changes on the way to St Paul's.

George Gilder was grim-faced.

"I need pictures. I must have pictures."

While Harvey's almost indecipherable freehand piece was being coaxed into life by an imaginative typist, George Gilder was on the telephone to the other editors whose journalists had also been at Hunters – had anyone retrieved a useable image? A photographer with *The Tamworth Herald* had managed to secure a picture of Abigail in hospital and was now negotiating his price, while the local police were being persuaded to release a picture of the blood-stained snow to a courier standing by.

By 6.00 p.m., things were looking up. The police, anxious to catch Abigail's assailant, had agreed to release a picture and it was now in *The Sentinel* office. One of the photographers, although not Harvey's, had had the presence of mind to gather up all the unfurled film spread around the site like tagliatelle, and one grainy image had been retrieved. It hurt George Gilder to have to negotiate with a counterpart, but his determination to get a photograph of the blockade overcame his natural frugality. Only then did he grab Harvey's piece from the typist's desk and retreat to his office.

The day had been something of an epiphany for Harvey. For the first time in his life he had come face-to-face with thuggery, the muscles of the authoritarian mind. He had also witnessed the courage needed to resist it.

In her primitive, intelligent way, his mother had often talked not so much about as around *freedom*, a concept she instinctively understood but would have been hard-pressed to define, just as countless academics had been. For her, it didn't need defining. It was obvious. If there was no law which applied to all, and if people were unable to associate with one another for their mutual benefit as they chose, there was no freedom.

'Lawlessness in one direction and beliefs in the other, Harve, are freedom's arch enemies,' she'd once told him, 'and both are masters of disguise.'

"Mudd!"

Harvey smiled to himself. He'd miss that cry. Even if others hearing it for the first time would have been shocked, he knew the heart it came from and they didn't. Inside he found George Gilder at his desk with tears streaming down both cheeks.

"You've nailed it, Mudd. You bloody well have. Now let's get this into print and pray our great British electorate is woken from its sleep!"

* * *

Miranda returned to her room to find her revolutionary hero sitting on her bed with caked blood around his nostrils and a bump the size of a cricket ball on the side of his head. Overwhelmed by feelings of motherhood and desire she had attended to his wounds and then to her need with such passion that the girl in the room next door, who had grown used to the sounds of rapture, was driven to come and ask if all was well. Jack had been far from sure that it was. Every part of him ached as Miranda extracted from him the highlights of his battle along with his last drops of energy.

'It was an epic,' he assured her, 'a battle like no other. You should have been there.' And he fell asleep with the words 'a triumph' and Miranda on his lips.

Early next morning, she slipped out to get a newspaper, half expecting to read that her lover had been made Commissar of the People's Committee, Midlands District. She opened the enemy publication first, hoping that self-interest would have forced it to reverse its normally hostile coverage, but her hopes were quickly dashed. The headline across the front of *The Sentinel* read: *Flying Pickets Blockade Family Business – Owner's Daughter Near Death.*

Beneath a grainy picture of a lorry approaching a row of pickets, she read that a forty-year-old family business had been brought to its knees by thugs intent on preventing it from making fuel deliveries to its customers. The owner's daughter had been pulled from her cab and savagely beaten. A picture of the woman's blood in the snow ran alongside another of her lying on a hospital bed, heavily bandaged and attached to tubes.

Convinced it was largely propaganda, she scanned the other papers, but all reported essentially the same facts. Returning to *The Sentinel*, she forced herself to read it in full until she came to the words '…Mr Jack Pugh, a member of Militant Tendency based in Cowley, and a witness to the outrage, fled the scene with two accomplices, although "fled" might be generous, as Mr Pugh was seen colliding with a club-wielding colleague in his rush to the car with such force that his two companions had to throw him into the vehicle before driving off.'

The words 'a witness to the outrage' made her feel physically sick. Had her lover only been a witness? Had he not been directing events? And if he had been directing events, would he not have been responsible for the woman's condition. Feelings of hot and cold, fear and anger, swept over her. And to think his 'war wounds' might have been self-inflicted! This was not what she had imagined. This was not what she wanted to read. The police would now be involved and the only name mentioned in the entire article belonging to a likely perpetrator was that of Jack Pugh. He had to go – and now.

* * *

Jack hobbled out of Brasenose College like a smitten dog and stood in the archway wondering what to do.

"Looking for the car?" the porter asked solicitously.

"Yes," answered Jack hopefully.

"Your friend took it."

C*HAPTER* 10

F*AKE SNOW DAPPLES* the stage. Marcello's painting has become a sign above the tavern door. The friends – poet, painter, philosopher and musician, have fooled their landlord out of another week's rent for the garret they share in the Latin Quarter. Rodolfo the poet and Mimi, the embroiderer who lives downstairs, have already met and are in love. Now it is winter and Rodolfo's feigned jealousy is driving Mimi away. He hopes she will find a wealthy lover who will pay for the medicines she needs. Harvey is moved. Puccini's score opens an ache in his own heart for a kind of love he has not known. The custom-house officers, asleep around a brazier, make him think of the pickets doing the same back in Britain. Did Abigail have a lover? Does life change, or just repeat, again and again, in a cycle of domination and resistance, love gained and love lost? He knows Mimi will die of consumption and that Rodolfo will be bereft. He has seen La Bohème before.

Mimi's illness had a deeper meaning for Harvey. His mother's mortality had started to weigh on him. She had complained of tiredness, which she had never done before, and he had paid for her to see a doctor.

'Right as rain, Harve,' she said afterwards. So, in celebration, he had taken her to Milan. His star was rising. George Gilder even mentioned the editorship one day, but that had been after a heavy session at the bar, so he thought little of it. His pay was good though, which was a reality he could bank on – or spend.

His mother had never been on an aeroplane. So he had booked them first class to Malpensa International Airport, which delighted her, although the expense of it would have upset him greatly in any other circumstances. But that was nothing compared to the Grand Hotel and car he'd hired for the evening.

"Look, Harvey, it's all lit up like a fairy castle," she said as their limousine glided to the front of the Teatro alla Scala and they were ushered inside. As they settled into their box, Sylvia's diminutive body swathed in a flowing chiffon gown smothered with costume jewellery, she leant over, revelling in the imagined intrigue of it all, and whispered, "They'll think we're a duchess and her lover, Harve!"

Mimi appears on stage and finds Marcello. She tells him of her problems with Rodolfo. He goes into the inn to find him but when they come out together, Mimi is hiding. Rodolfo confesses to Marcello that his jealousy was a ruse to drive Mimi away so that she might find a rich lover. Mimi's consumptive cough gives her away and the two agree to stay together until the spring – 'Ah!' she sighs. 'That our winter might last forever.'

In the last act, Mimi is dying. He sings, 'How cold your hand.' She sings back, 'They call me Mimi,' to the music that accompanied their first meeting. As she draws her last breath, Rodolfo's friends gather round in disbelief and he throws himself onto her now lifeless body sobbing, 'Mimi! Mimi!'

For seconds that feel like hours, the audience is silent, undone by the tragedy it has witnessed. Then eyes are dabbed, handkerchiefs put away, and everyone jumps up and claps frantically, as if trying to attract a passing ship that will pull them back on board to a safer reality. Ileana Cotrubaş and Luciano Pavarotti come forward with the players and then again with their conductor, Carlos Kleiber, to acknowledge the applause. A moment in time has come and gone, never to be repeated.

"That was sad, Harvey," she said as they were making their way down the stairs to the door. "I don't want you to miss out on love because of me."

"Don't be silly. Now let's hope that car is waiting."

It was probably only a five minute walk to the hotel, but Harvey was determined to do this in style. The lobby was a crush and not much better outside and he was anxious not to lose his mother. As he looked around he found himself staring at a familiar face just as the face was staring at him.

"Lady Graham!"

"Mr Mudd!"

He was surprised she had remembered his name.

"Waiting for your driver?"

"No, a taxi."

"How many are you? I have a car here somewhere I hope."

"I am on my own."

"Well you must certainly let us give you a lift. This car of mine, if I can find it, is costing me a fortune!"

Frances Graham threw her head back and laughed. She was not used to being amongst people who were concerned about the cost of things, especially hired cars.

As Harvey stared through the crowd at the traffic jostling for position in front of the opera house, their limousine came into view. The large tip he had already handed over was working its magic. Quite unperturbed by the cussing and honking, the driver got out and held the door open for his customers.

"In you go, dear," Sylvia instructed and followed Frances, leaving Harvey to take one of the seats facing them. "This is fun!" she said.

THE STORYTELLERS • 71

"Al Grand, signore?" the driver asked. "Hotel, yes?"

"If you don't mind, dear. It's been a long day for me."

"Of course not," Frances told her.

"So where are you staying?" asked Harvey. "I am sure the driver would be happy to take you anywhere you wanted."

"A flat near the Piazza dei Volontari. I don't think it is too far."

"*Non lontano* – not far," confirmed the driver. "*Ed ecco il Grand Hotel*. We arrive!"

"Mother, this is Lady Graham."

"Frances, please!"

"Well it's very nice to meet you, dear. Now, Harvey, you must see this lady home. I'll be quite all right."

Harvey excused himself and took his mother inside. But she was unusually firm and told him to get right back out as she wanted to sit in the lobby for a bit and watch the people, and yes, she was quite capable of getting the key to her room without him.

Harvey slipped into the back seat beside Frances and the driver moved off. He could smell her scent and felt intoxicated.

"That was a wonderful production," she said. "I am told Carlos Kleiber is a hard man to work for, but what a perfectionist!"

"I read that his family left Austria for South America in 1940, at the start of the Second World War. He was called Karl then."

"Yes," she answered. "Such disruption. None of us really knows what lies around the corner, do we?"

"I suppose not," he agreed.

"Pretty," she said looking out of the window, "but not half as lovely as Rome!"

"Ah, but the Milanese make the money. The Romans only know how to spend it!"

"A characteristic of the cultured class!" she laughed.

"Do you often go to the opera on your own?" he questioned.

"Quite often. David, my husband, does not really like it. So rather than have him next to me fidgeting, I prefer to go alone or with a girlfriend."

"And to Milan?"

"This is only my second visit. David had a meeting here, so I thought I would make the most of it."

"What does your husband do, if you don't mind me asking?"

"He's a soldier, mostly. But he and his friends always have some scheme on the go. I tend to stay clear of all that."

"Sounds interesting!"

She just shrugged.

"You're a journalist, aren't you, Mr Mudd?"

"Harvey, please. Yes, with *The Sentinel*."

"That's George Gilder, isn't it?"

"You know him?" Harvey asked, somewhat surprised.

"Yes, he's stayed with us two or three times at Graham Castle. My husband likes gatherings of the great and the good – and the not so good!"

Suddenly Harvey felt tongue-tied. Was he sitting next to his editor's friend or to a woman he had now met twice, and to whom he felt strangely drawn?

"Oh look!" she exclaimed, "the Arco della Pace. We must be close."

"Yes, the Peace Arch," he echoed, relieved to be talking about something else. "I read that it has a fractured history, like Italy itself. There was a Roman arch here once. But that arch was moved in mediaeval times and became part of the Sforza Castle. Napoleon commissioned this arch as the entrance to the city on a road that ran all the way from Paris. But when the Austrians took over Milan, following Napoleon's defeat, it was completed and given its present name. This was in honour of the 1815 Congress of Vienna which laid the ground for a peace in Europe that lasted for the next one hundred years."

"You like history," she observed, amused that the mention of George Gilder had made him turn serious.

"Yes, I suppose I do. I think the past helps you understand the present."

"*Piazza dei Volontari*," the driver announced. "*Volete che guidi intorno al Parco Sempione di nuovo?*"

"What did he say?" Harvey asked, annoyed that his Italian was less good than he thought.

"He wonders if we would like to drive around the park again," she told him with a smile.

Harvey looked at her, embarrassed and uncertain what to say.

She looked at her watch.

"My husband will not be back until the early hours, I don't suppose, but perhaps we should leave the park for another day, Harvey."

"Yes, perhaps we should," he accepted, savouring her use of his Christian name.

Looking back, it was then that both recognized the attraction each had for the other. Had their circumstances been different they would happily have driven all round Milan, not just one of its parks. But their circumstances were not different and Harvey realized he could not see Frances Graham again. During the flight home, when his mother said, with her customary certainty, 'One day you will marry that girl, Harvey,' he experienced a sharp stab of anger at what felt like her cruelty.

*C*HAPTER 11

A NDREW CHAMPION felt relieved. At last the company he had started eight years earlier was gaining some traction. It looked as though all those sleepless nights, long hours and nail-biting risk-taking were about to pay off. His wife certainly hoped so. He was not an engineer by training but the engineering industry was where he had ended up. A chance call from an accountant had brought him into contact with a small sheet-metal-working company in Henley which needed a £6,000 loan – 'Just to tide us over,' the company's new owners had said.

Andrew had become that fabled creature, an entrepreneur. The label at least assured others even if its coverage was wide. After business school and a short spell as a banker he'd started his own venture-capital business from a windowless basement office in London's Mayfair. Although the air became stale and headache-inducing if ingested for too long, the address was good.

Looking back, he still found it hard to understand why he had been attracted to the Henley venture. When its retiring founder sold his creation to two local men, the business was already on life support. Its workforce and machines were over-ripe for retirement themselves and with only one steady customer, its weakness was clear. On paper, there had been little to recommend it, other than its obvious need – the same thing that attracts people to a runt in the dog pound.

Shortly after making the loan, secured against every conceivable part of the business, Andrew took up residence, partly to escape asphyxiation and partly to escape the Mayfair rent which even for a subterranean room had been eating into his savings. The directors had been surprised at first, but doubtless thought it best to humour the person who had saved their commercial bacon.

Due diligence, the process of trying to work out what one was about to get involved in before there was no turning back, was rarely perfect. One hoped that after the event, one would unearth a previously hidden asset and he had discovered one of sorts. When a locked cupboard at the back of the ex-owner's office was opened, shelf upon shelf of boxes, labelled *USAF Supplies,* were revealed. It seemed that the company had done work at a United States airbase and been paid in kind – fifty cartons of rubber condoms. But as no one had known how to move such sensitive merchandise, the products had languished and to Andrew's disappointment, were no longer serviceable. After closing a deal, the fear was that one would be confronted by an unexpected liability. And what appeared on this side of the balance sheet was altogether more alarming.

The directors informed him, in hushed tones, that the buyer at their only serious customer was in receipt of a regular envelope. Keep up the tradition or lose the business, was their candid advice. But Andrew was buggered if he was going to get involved in such whoopee. Besides, short of handing over the envelope himself, he had no means of knowing where the money inside actually went. For several weeks he fully expected sales to slump, but they never did. In fact, they increased. However, this only laid bare the factory's woeful shortcomings: quality and productivity were abysmal.

A smart man would have walked away, but the smell of machine oil and the physical making of things were getting to him. Even the bloody hand he incurred operating a fly-press – a weighted screw you swung to drive a metal punch through a sheet of steel into a matching metal die to generate a particular shape of hole – failed to deter him. There was romance in engineering. However mundane your product, you were creating. So instead of retreat, he advanced, converting his loan into a controlling interest in the company as its terms allowed. The previous owners needed little persuading to move on and were lucky to escape with their skin.

Thinking about it now, the adage that fools rush in where wise men fear to tread surely applied. But as he considered the journey he had taken, he wondered how much would ever be achieved without such folly. Or at least how much would ever be attempted if the obstacles ahead were known in advance. Faced with a moribund factory – workshop would have been a more apt description – located in a part of the country where the skills he needed no longer existed, he decided on a radical step. He would relocate the business to an area where light engineering was still practised, and fill it with machines that were not decrepit.

It was while researching what machines to buy that he met Freddie Stern. Another free spirit on the lookout for opportunity, Freddie had gained control over a company that made a range of machines to replace the fly-press, under licence from a company based in Canada. But the Rolls Royce he drove belied the tenuous hold he had over this creature. A flirtation had ensued between them with Freddie looking for finance and Andrew looking for a way to increase the sophistication of his product range.

Eventually he had acquired this company simply because he understood the financial system better and was able to offer Freddie's edgy backers stronger credit. Not long afterwards, the Rolls Royce crashed with Freddie at the wheel, killing him. The harsh purity of the capitalist system was not lost on Andrew. He knew that any misstep on his part and it would spit him out just as quickly.

Not long after relocating to their new factory, they were battered by the three-day week (an embargo on industrial activity introduced by the Heath government to conserve energy, in its battle with the National Union of Mineworkers, whose coal supplied much of the country's power). For over two months, in mid-winter, he and his men had spent two days a week in a factory without electricity. All they could do was move things around by hand, so that when production proper was allowed, it was as efficient as possible. That had been in 1974, a year in which Britain's engineers haemorrhaged cash.

The industry's ills went back to the Second World War, or even, some thought, to the First. Once dominant in the world, the sector had lost its way. Japan and Germany, whose manufacturing capacity had all but been destroyed by 1945, were making better-engineered products in almost all sectors and the Americans continued to dominate in their home market, although this was beginning to change. He had read of many reasons for this decline. Winning the First World War had drained Britain of financial and human resources. After that, the emphasis had been on living well, not on driving productive efficiency. Workers and managers had gone through hell together and owners, by and large, did not have the stomach to face up to their country's declining position in the world.

The Second World War put America in the driving seat and although Britain's manufacturing industry was intact, it was worn out. Had it been destroyed, government, owners and workers would have had no option but to rebuild and refocus from top to bottom. Instead, a sprawling mass of disjointed inefficiencies was laid out like a threadbare carpet over a genteel but impoverished land.

Not long after his encounter with Freddie Stern, Andrew had visited a once-proud company near Southampton which was adrift. The frustrated managing director had been on the lookout for anyone willing to invest. Andrew remembered thinking that the place smelt of death: a hospital with corridors of tired linoleum whose patients could check in but not out save via the mortuary – an industrial Hotel California. However, in amongst the rancid pessimism, he had found treasure: an optimist working away on the design of a new machine his company would never build.

Harold Loxley was one of those life-enhancing people one comes across all too rarely and he and Andrew hit it off. Andrew knew that the machine designs he had purchased from Freddie were out of date, even though far in advance of a fly-press, which could only punch out one type of hole at a time, manually. The latest Canadian-designed machines could hold a number of different punches and dies in their thick circular discs, and the sheet of steel could be moved between them by an operator guiding a stylus around a template in the way those old double-writing machines forced a second pen across the paper to match the pen being used. But the Japanese, Germans and Americans were moving to machines operated by a computer rather than an operator following a template and to survive, he knew he had to follow suit.

Harold needed little persuasion to abandon his sinking ship, and Andrew made him managing director of the machine tool business. Within a year, he had come up with a revolutionary new computer-controlled punching machine that could be sold cheaper than its competitors. In spite of teething troubles, a result of its rapid development, the product was a success. At last the groaning debts Andrew had built up accumulating the bits he had now fashioned into a working whole could start being repaid. But it was then that fate chose to reveal the dark side of her nature.

It was one of those clear, cold mornings in which pockets of mist dot the landscape like floating cobwebs. Harold was hurrying to a customer. He always drove fast, especially on motorways. Inside the bank of fog he entered at full speed was an invisible row of stationary vehicles, brought to a halt by an accident further ahead. Harold's car hit the tail end of a lorry and he was killed instantly, his life insurance policy still unsigned within a breast pocket. He left behind a lovely young wife, two dear children and a gaping hole in the lives of all who knew him. Andrew did his best for them, which even now he felt had not been much, and turned to steadying his shell-shocked company.

Within a year, a new managing director was hired along with a cocky ex-army engineer who set about designing a new model. Andrew's empire now consisted of three parts: the original revitalized subcontract engineering business in its new factory, the machine tool business and a new unit tasked with utilizing the rapidly-evolving micro-computing technology to help with production scheduling – the task of optimizing the flow of work through a factory.

So long as sales were increasing, the machine tool business was a cash generator. A deposit was taken with each order and machine components were purchased from outside, leaving only the assembly, design, maintenance and marketing in-house. So while suppliers could be paid after two months, most of every machine ordered had been paid for prior to delivery. This positive dynamic was dented slightly by the fact that some of the components in the punching machine were made by their own sub-contract unit, but at least that was cash neutral.

The micro-systems business was decidedly cash negative as it consisted of a small team writing production-programming software suitable for use in a micro-computer. Andrew knew he would have to attract outside investors to augment his company's meagre £100 in share capital and mountain of debt courtesy of the bank. A subcontract engineering business would attract no interest and although a machine tool business might attract some, it would be the micro-computer products outsiders would want to back.

In spite of the bedlam in the country generally, with over 1.5 million unemployed and much of private industry ignoring the government's restrictive pay policy, 1978 had been a reasonable year for the Champion Group, the name Andrew had given his commercial activities, and 1979 looked as if it would be better still. He'd even been interviewed by a journalist from *The Sentinel* doing a piece on what the nation can achieve without the unions. They had all been a bit chuffed by that. He knew his company's balance sheet was severely stretched, with a preponderance of creditors, but cash was finally beginning to flow in rather than out.

The nation's predicament was simple enough. Unlike the private sector, which had been forced to come to terms with inflation and marry what it produced to what it could sell, government-controlled industries were being run to maximize employment and the government simply couldn't meet its escalating wages bill. Neither taxes nor prices could be raised and public sector employees could not be reduced quickly enough without triggering waves of strikes. From autos, to coal, to steel, industries taken into public ownership by past socialist governments were becoming progressively uneconomic. Although few on the left cared to admit it, capitalism was proving smarter than Karl Marx. Even the centre ground was shifting. Under a barrage of bad publicity about public sector strikes, the 5% lead Prime Minister Callaghan had enjoyed in the polls before Christmas was gone.

Andrew wasn't much interested in politics. He had backed Edward Heath against the miners. He'd even gathered all his workers together at the time and told them that if Heath lost, which, in the end, Heath had, the country would go to hell in a hand cart. Now the Conservative Party had a female leader who seemed to believe that a nation's economy was little different from a household budget. Perhaps such simplicity was all an electorate could understand. In any event, this time he planned to keep his views to himself, although he had spilled his heart out to Harvey Mudd, the journalist from *The Sentinel*. He'd liked that man and people needed to know what it took to build a business.

CHAPTER

THE CAR CARRYING George Gilder and his wife left their five bedroom house overlooking Primrose Hill at 8.20 p.m. As the editor travelled down Albany Street, the sun was setting across Regent's Park. It had long been his paper's tradition to host an election-night party and he expected that tonight's would bear witness to two great events: the rise of Britain's first female prime minister and the start of a radical new direction for his country. But had *The Sentinel* done enough? Were a majority of the British people persuaded of the need for change?

His paper had shown corpses piling up in Liverpool when gravediggers had gone on unofficial strike, rubbish bags stacked high in London's Leicester Square, motorists queuing at petrol stations for scarce supplies and dead piglets dumped in front of union offices in Hull by furious farmers unable to get deliveries of animal feed. The general sense of chaos had been augmented when a group of Protestants bombed several pubs in Glasgow frequented by Catholics; although in Scotland, discontent with a Labour government tended to migrate to the Nationalists rather than 'they Tory toffs' as Conservatives were disparagingly called north of the border.

Nonetheless, the Scottish National Party had done its bit for the cause by withdrawing support from Callaghan's coalition when it didn't get its way on devolution, bringing down the government and forcing the election that was approaching its conclusion. One thing did still rankle though. In January, when the Prime Minister returned to his cold, unhappy nation from a conference in the sunny Caribbean and said that things didn't look so bad from overseas, it was a rival newspaper that had come up with the headline '*Crisis? What Crisis?*', nailing the public's growing frustration with its government.

Turning into Woburn Place, he passed a large billboard with a seemingly endless line of people snaking across it under the words *Labour Isn't Working*. Over a million were unemployed, the highest number since the war. And only three years earlier the government had been forced to secure a loan from the International Monetary Fund to stabilize its finances. As he turned these things over in his mind, he marvelled at the stoic nature of the British people. Surely enough was enough?

The new leader of the Conservative Party had promised to lower taxes, cut government expenditure, curb the power of the unions, bear down on inflation and outlaw the kind of secondary picketing that had done for Hunters. All the opinion polls indicated that her message was finding an increasingly receptive audience. Looking back, years later, he considered it a blessing no one had known how ruthless she would be in pursuing those objectives and how much worse things would get before they were attained.

* * *

When the small group who'd had dinner in *The Sentinel* dining room entered the main office it was approaching 11.00 p.m. The polls had been closed for an hour, but no results had yet been declared. From a large screen, David Dimbleby was welcoming viewers who had just joined the BBC's election coverage – *Decision 79*. The room was full, with staff and guests making the most of the open bar and buffet set out at one end.

"Now she needs a swing of 4.5% to get a working majority," the Canadian political analyst, Bob McKenzie, was explaining. "If we aggregate all the opinion polls we get a swing to Mrs Thatcher of 4.7%. But if we look at the constituency polls they are showing a swing to Labour of .7%, enough to put Mr Callaghan back in Number Ten. But remember, both polls have been wrong in the past."

"Who is that young woman in a wheelchair?" Frances Graham asked her host.

"That's Abigail Hunter. I'll get Harvey Mudd to introduce you. He broke the Hunters' story and has got to know the family quite well."

There had been only twelve in the dining room, but she and Harvey had been at opposite ends of the table and neither had attempted to build on their unexpected encounter in March.

"The indications are," the forty-one-year-old broadcaster was explaining, "that there has been a high turnout, in spite of the bad weather, and our first result may come from the smallest constituency, Glasgow Central. Do you expect a fairly even swing across the country, David Butler?"

"Yes, I think there will be a more even swing than many have been expecting," the Oxford researcher answered, "except in Scotland, where our first result could come from, so it probably won't tell us much."

"I see Mudd is tied up, so let me introduce you myself."

George Gilder guided Frances through the crush and cigarette smoke to a petite woman whose chair was parked by a side wall with a clear view of the screen.

"Miss Hunter, I am George Gilder, editor of *The Sentinel*. This is my guest, Lady Graham, who has asked to meet you."

"Frances, please," Frances Graham implored as she bent down.

"Yes, that's the trouble with these chairs," Abigail Hunter acknowledged. "You are always at one level, usually the wrong one."

"I read *The Sentinel* piece. It must have been horrific."

"To be honest, all I know about it has come from what I have been told and from reading that journalist's quite brilliant article."

"Mr Mudd?"

"Yes, Harvey Mudd. He really captured it I'm told."

"They arrested the man who did this to you, didn't they?"

"They did. Max something or other. He's in prison now, thank God. And, do you know, he wasn't even a member of a union?"

"There was another young man arrested as well, wasn't there?" Frances asked.

"Yes, a Trotskyite organizer from Cowley. He was acquitted unfortunately. The pickets proper were from the Transport and General Workers' Union. They weren't even prosecuted," Abigail recounted, the first note of bitterness sounding in her voice.

"And what is going on at Flood Street, Michael?" the broadcaster asked, trying to maintain a momentum that could not be allowed to flag until 4.00 a.m.

"Well, I think we are all watching you, David."

"So no sign of Mrs Thatcher then?"

"No. No sign. We believe she is inside with her family."

"With all her family?"

"Yes, all her family is here. We expect her to travel to her Finchley constituency later."

"Will you get out of this?" Frances asked.

"No, they don't think so. But we are hoping to modify a truck so that I can drive again. I would really like that."

"So your family still has trucks?"

"Not at the moment, I'm afraid. We're starting again. And to think, my grandparents survived the war!"

They both looked across at the big screen where Robin Day, sporting his trademark bow tie and brandishing a large cigar, was talking so unconvincingly about his humble opinion that David Dimbleby could barely keep a straight face.

"I really hope she wins," Abigail said, as one of her brothers came over with a glass of wine and Frances left in search of her husband.

* * *

"These are the forty-one marginal seats Mrs Thatcher must win if she is going to get a working majority," Bob McKenzie was explaining standing next to one of his boards. "A rosette will mean a Conservative win, a tick a Labour hold."

"Now let's go to one of those constituencies, Derby North," the broadcaster picks up, "to see what the floating voters we have been following finally decided. Bernard, what have you got?"

With two on either side of him, one woman and three men, Bernard Falk asks the question. The lady says she decided on the way to the polling station that a change was needed and she'd voted Conservative. Mr Callaghan, she thought, was too old; Mr Steel, the Liberal leader, too young; and Mrs Thatcher was just right! The man next to her says he voted Labour last time and had again. He wanted continued moderation. On the other side of Bernard Falk, the first man admits that he had voted Conservative because he thought a vote for the Liberals would be wasted and he did not want Labour. The remaining man had also voted Conservative, which, he explains, was a change from last time.

"That's Mrs Thatcher leaving Flood Street, dressed in the most brilliant blue. So thank you, Bernard, and now over to Flood Street."

The sound of boos and cheers are audible as reporters press towards her.

"Mrs Thatcher, Mrs Thatcher, the returns are moving in your

direction…"

"We are just reserving judgment," she says in that buttery-crisp accent Britain's voters will come to love or hate.

"Are you cautiously optimistic?" they call out.

With a dazzling smile, she turns briefly and answers, "Yes," before a car whisks her and Denis Thatcher away to Finchley for the count.

* * *

By 12.45 a.m., it was still not clear. Only seventeen results were in. There appeared to be a small swing to the Conservatives in the north, but a much larger one in the south.

"That's a 9% swing to the Conservatives in Walthamstow," David Butler calculated. "If the country behaved like the East End of London there would be a Conservative landslide, but if it behaved like Lancashire, we would have a hung parliament."

"The interesting thing," David Dimbleby observed, "is that the National Front vote dropped."

"All the fringe candidates have been doing very badly," his colleague elaborated.

Frances Graham, together with Mrs Gilder and several other ladies, were sitting together and clearly getting bored, all praying for a clear enough pattern to emerge so that they could justify going home. David Graham, by contrast, was well stuck in. He and three of *The Sentinel* journalists, used to killing time, were playing a game of poker in which money was changing hands and the circle of onlookers around them was growing in number.

"Men just like risk," observed Andrew Champion looking across. He had been surprised to receive an invitation from the newspaper, but it had come via Harvey and everyone in his company had liked the *Sentinel* piece.

"Either taking it or watching it," Harvey modified. "I guess I'm a watcher."

"Well someone has to tell the tale of us lunatics on the frontline," the entrepreneur urged.

"And it's not just men who like risk," elaborated Harvey. "Many an upper-class lady over the centuries has had to turn to her husband to pay off her gambling debts."

"And to assume paternity of her lover's child," chuckled George Gilder who had been passing them and picked up the tail end of their conversation.

"It is probably the desire to avoid boredom that drives most of us on in the end," the entrepreneur confessed as they glanced towards the screen where the broadcaster was attempting to introduce some clarity as the top of the hour approached.

"Well after twenty-two results our computer is saying that Mrs Thatcher will form the next government with three hundred and thirty-seven seats in the new parliament, and that Labour will have two hundred and seventy-one, the Liberals nine and the SNP three, way down from where they were, and the other parties fifteen."

"The assassin's curse," muttered the editor, recalling that it was the Scottish National Party which had brought down the Labour coalition. "He who pushes in the blade rarely rides off with the prize!"

Andrew Champion thought about Freddie Stern and wondered.

"So what do you make of the results so far, Perry?" Robin Day asked of his guest, the veteran high-Tory journalist, Peregrine Worsthorne, who considered Margaret Thatcher too bourgeoise to make much difference, and prophesy to be the most unnecessary of all human error. "Do you see a north-south split?"

"These results leave me baffled," he said. "But we are paid to appear wise before the event. So while I don't know if I'd categorize it as north-south, I do think the problem for Mrs Thatcher will be that while there is a large body of opinion moving right, there is also a substantial element who won't want to be pushed around by the kind of things she wants to do. So even if Mrs Thatcher wins a clear majority, there will be a substantial minority that does not want to go along with her."

"A true romantic," eulogized the editor. "He is one of the few writers who still manage to be anti-capitalist and anti-communist in the same sentence!"

"The Conservatives hold Chingford," the broadcaster continued. "That's Norman Tebbit's seat, one of Mrs Thatcher's gang of four, who make raids – intellectual raids – on the Labour Party from the Tory backbenches. That's an 8.5% swing to the Conservatives."

* * *

It wasn't until after 3.00 in the afternoon that speculation gave way to a new reality. Harvey had hung around until 5.00 a.m., but most of the ladies had left shortly after 1.00. He had even joined David Graham's poker game for an hour. Having done no more than exchange nods with Frances, he was curious to find out what her husband was like. But all he learned about the Scot was that he was a better poker player and utterly ruthless when applying the bluff.

There had been one surreal experience around midnight. A man looking like Peter Betsworth had joined the *Sentinel* party for a short period and when Harvey addressed him by name, he'd been told, quite sternly, that he must be mistaken. Nonetheless, the look the man had given him suggested otherwise. George Gilder, who had been witness to this brief exchange, simply said, 'Wheels within wheels, Mudd, nothing more,' as they stood at the bar collecting drinks.

He rose late. His mother was ecstatic. Mrs Thatcher had been called to the palace and invited by the Queen to form a government.

"Now things will get done, Harve, you'll see!"

With 608 results in, Labour had lost 42 seats and was on 264, the Conservatives had gained 56 seats and now had 323, which gave them a working majority. The Scottish National Party had all but been eviscerated, retaining only 2 seats and losing 9. Their vote, it seemed, had largely migrated to Labour, blunting the Conservatives' advance north of the border. Other parties, such as the Ulster Unionists and Plaid Cymru, would end up sharing 14.

As he glanced at the constituency results he noticed that the swing to the Conservatives in Dagenham, where the Ford factory was located, had been a massive 14%, against the national average of 8%. Even in Longbridge the swing had been 10%. The working man's blind attachment to the union was over. Sylvia's ferocious independence was more widespread than he had imagined. Hers and the voices of those like her had found an echo in a hard-working lady, with forceful political opinions and a science degree from Somerville College, Oxford, who had pulled herself up by her own bootstraps and saw no good reason why others shouldn't do the same. Something really had happened during the night. The age of the principled patrician and all-seeing union boss was over. The individual as consumer now sat on the throne. For good or ill, their country had been reborn.

Part Two

CHAPTER 13

THE NEXT TIME Harvey and Peter Betsworth met, the ambience was markedly different from what it had been during their first encounter. For a start, it was June and the weather had finally turned warm. Although St James's Park remained the MI5 man's venue of choice, he also appeared more relaxed.

"Forgive my manner at *The Sentinel*," he said. "These little subterfuges serve their purpose."

Harvey said nothing, as there seemed nothing he could usefully say. Subterfuge was subterfuge.

The two men sat on a bench overlooking the water enjoying the sun in the way men released from incarceration savour their first mouthful of decent food.

"What a winter it's been!" Peter Betsworth exclaimed, relieving some of the tension which had been building up over the last few months.

"You will have been pleased with the result," Harvey said.

"Yes, we needed a change and we needed clarity and remarkably, considering the opacity of the democratic process, we seem to have got both."

"But I take it there is still more to be done," speculated Harvey, doubting he had been summoned for a chat.

"The hard part starts now," stated his companion with a finality Harvey found alarming.

"Surely she can just do what she wanted to: curb inflation, reduce union power, lower taxes and cut government expenditure?"

"All things the previous government would like to have done," the intelligence officer said laughing. "The body politic is better at defining objectives than attaining them. The problem, you see, is that the systems we are part of make many of our decisions for us and have vested interests. When the Shah of Iran was deposed in January, my profession – I regret to say – was caught on the hop. The monarch might not have been perfect, but he believed in a secular state, the education of women and the modernization of his country's economy – all objectives we in the West considered laudable.

"What we failed to notice was that many ordinary Iranians preferred Shia Islam to Western culture and when the beneficiaries of his push for greater education failed to find jobs because the economy was insufficiently developed, a combustible mix was created that the Shah's increasingly heavy-handed suppression of opposition only served to ignite. It was, I think, Otto von Bismarck who said, *Die Politik ist die Lehre vom Möglichen* – Politics is the art of the possible – so simply wishing for good things, Mr Mudd, is not enough."

"Harvey, please. I would feel more comfortable."

"Certainly. And on that basis you had better call me Peter," his contact invited, adding with a dry laugh: "A sort of familiarity, I suppose."

"So where do you think the problems lie?" Harvey asked, thinking that if this was going to be a tutorial he might as well make the most of it.

"The central problem of government, Harvey, contrary to what most people imagine, lies in the limitations of power, not in its surfeit.

Now don't get me wrong, governments can do a lot of unpleasant things to large numbers of people and that is real, especially to those affected. But a polity is a complex entity which must feed, clothe, house, entertain and protect those who make it up. This entails thousands of individual decisions, taken daily, that no rule book could prescribe.

"While a governing elite can always use force to impose its will, even picking on this or that minority to satisfy the worst instincts of its majority, terror tends to freeze decision-making, causing people to do what they imagine is expected of them, rather than what is best for either themselves or their polity. The great beauty of free-market capitalism is that it is a process which depends more on countless individual decisions than it does upon government edict."

"So capitalism is without fault," Harvey suggested wryly, slipping easily into the role of sceptical student.

"Certainly not!" exclaimed Peter Betsworth, rising nicely to Harvey's fly. "The redoubtable Karl Marx drew out most of its faults, but was blind to the fact that what he was talking about was the distribution of power and the self-interest of those who possess it, rather than about free-market capitalism per se. Winston Churchill said that democracy was the worst form of government except for all the others, and as political economies go, you could say the same about free-market capitalism. The two are joined at the hip, which is not to say that both can't be improved.

"The difficulty our new government faces is that it only has a limited number of tools it can use to make things better. The last government and indeed the Conservative one before it, both tried logical persuasion and even legal sanction. But how do you persuade unions to persuade their members to take pay cuts, which is what below-inflation pay rises are? Unions exist to protect their members and if union bosses agree to do otherwise – to see the big picture, whatever that is – it serves only to empower their shop stewards who live daily with the concerns of their members.

"And why should a profitable corporation make its workers take a pay cut? It wants smooth labour relations. Inflation is something it must contend with, not something it is responsible for.

"So the government's policy of attempting to keep wage increases below inflation was unacceptable to the unions as well as to the private sector. But unlike the private sector, the government could not afford to pay inflation-matching wages without borrowing more money from increasingly reluctant lenders and the public sector unions simply went on strike whenever the government threatened to pay less. Logical persuasion, therefore, was not a runner. The Trots say the system is bust and to some extent, they are right. But their solution that all payments should be mandated by the state, in accordance with 'communist principles', walks us straight into totalitarian hell."

"But didn't something like that work during the war?" the sceptical student asked.

"It did, and for short periods, when a polity has a single objective, more or less shared by everyone, such as to defeat an enemy, it can. Perhaps it even enabled the Soviet Union to launch mankind's first satellite into space. But state-mandated objectives eventually undermine the creative energy of an economy which relies on individuals interacting freely in their search for new and often unexpected ways to improve one another's lives."

"So what options do our new masters have?" Harvey asked, beginning to think that the task sounded impossible.

"Well, what I am hearing is that they intend to pull government out of the economy. Not entirely obviously, but out of such things as trying to operate car companies, steel mills and coal mines."

"Privatization?"

"This is turning into a lecture," Peter Betsworth admitted, "and I am sorry. But you asked, and it is important, so let me do my best. To cover the cost of public sector wages, a government has three sources: taxation, borrowing or a combination of the two. Generally, governments use a combination, but by and large government expenditure and tax receipts should balance over time, with borrowing used to smooth things out. But because people don't like paying taxes and politicians like being popular – whether elected or not, I have to say – the temptation to borrow is great. Now when you borrow, you are adding to the supply of money in an economy, just as any loan you get boosts your personal liquidity.

"If the extra money is spent on existing things that do not help you to repay the loan it simply pushes up the price of these things, causing inflation. Or, to put it another way, borrowing to pay ever-higher wages without any increase in the output these wages buy is inflationary: more money is simply chasing the same number of things."

"So the government should tax more or borrow less," suggested Harvey.

"Quite logical," agreed Peter Betsworth, "but there is another factor to consider. Let's start with the 'tax more' option. All the money raised in tax is money the state spends and individuals do not. Now if the creative energy of an economy depends upon individuals making decisions, the more their individual decision-making capacity is taken over by the state, the less effective that state's economy is likely to be. So there is a limit to how high taxes can go.

"As far as the 'borrow less' option goes, the question here is how to manage the transition, because borrowing less means paying less and paying less means people getting hurt. The best analogy I can think of is that it is like trying to ease a person off a heroin addiction. Each injection of the drug produces a smaller high, so the taker increases his use until his body is overwhelmed by the drug and he dies. That is the position we were approaching last year. But to start reducing the amount of drug being taken causes the body great pain because it has become dependent. This is what we have ahead of us. I don't believe anyone in the new administration has any idea how long our rehabilitation will take or how painful it will be."

"And how is this going to curb the power of the unions?" Harvey wondered.

"Ah, now that is slightly different. That will be done through legislation: no more secondary picketing, no strike without a secret ballot, no forced enrolment – that sort of thing. But the real test will come when the government privatizes all those industries taken over by the state since the war and that won't be possible until they have shed all the men and women they can no longer afford.

"There will be a lot of anger and some fierce battles. There are signs the motor industry is starting to face reality. There is more debate going on within its unions than you might think. The worst confrontation will almost certainly be with the National Union of Mineworkers. The government will have to pick its moment. It must not get knocked off course this time.

"Here is a file on some of the key players in both industries. You might care to pay particular attention to Mr Derek Robinson, a Communist shop steward in British Leyland's Longbridge plant. He can take credit for causing more stoppages than anyone: approaching five hundred, I believe."

"I've come across him," said Harvey. "He seemed like a nice enough fellow. He thinks management has screwed up his industry and that the workers can do better."

"Yes," mused Peter Betsworth acidly. "I wouldn't wholly disagree with part of his analysis."

"You seem to be preparing me for Armageddon," Harvey said, smiling weakly.

"Well, let's say this government is likely to be a lot less popular in three years' time than it is today. We must just hope its members have the balls for it – although that is perhaps not the most appropriate expression in the circumstances."

CHAPTER 14

STANLEY PRESTON edged the car cautiously out of Longbridge. He was not a frequent driver but considered himself steady, although his 15 miles per hour in built-up areas and 45 more or less everywhere else did not always endear him to fellow motorists. He and Mabel had decided to visit Mabel's sister, Rita, who had married a Welshman from Merthyr, Davyn Pritchard, and perhaps take in the Brecon Beacons.

"He developed Cardiff docks," recounted Mabel, reading from her guidebook. "Fair shovelled money in, it would seem, the money he hoped to make from his coal."

"Who's that dear?"

"The Marquess of Bute. Poor man lost his wife. He did marry again though and had a child."

"I don't suppose it was his coal," muttered Stanley, forever puzzled by his wife's fascination with the aristocracy.

"Well it says here it was his coal," complained Mabel.

"Yes, but who pulled it from the ground?"

Safely on the road south, Stanley locked into 45mph and held his ground.

"I still can't believe it Mabel. A 10% swing to the Tories – in Longbridge! A fair few of our brothers must have voted for her. It's not the world I knew, I can tell you."

"Well things do change, dear," soothed Mabel who had been on the end of her husband's discomfort since the election and would never confess that she had voted for Mrs Thatcher.

"It says here," she went on, "that the population of Glamorganshire almost tripled in the first forty years of the nineteenth century, all on account of pig iron and coal. Imagine: farming one minute, factories the next! The Marquess helped make that happen. He built a railway to get coal from the valleys and the docks to ship it out."

"Exploited on the land, exploited in the factories. Marx got that right," Stanley growled, unsettled by the steady stream of cars that passed him whenever opportunity allowed and sometimes, even when it didn't. "Idiot!" he cussed under his breath as another frustrated driver squeezed passed just ahead of an oncoming truck.

"Who is, dear?"

"Didn't you see that?"

"Well if you went a little faster, dearest, they might be less inclined."

It was a pleasant enough day and the miles were ticking by, with Stanley occasionally nuzzling 50 mph, while Mabel watched the passing fields, dipping back into her book whenever the view offered nothing new. She hadn't seen Rita for too long. It had caused a stir when her sister ran off with a Welshman, and a miner at that. Engineers saw themselves as a cut above, even when their task was on the assembly line. No black faces and a life underground for them.

"Here's an interesting fact," she announced. "In 1913, over ten million tons of coal were exported from Cardiff docks and more than one hundred shipping companies were based there."

"It's nothing like that now, I wouldn't think," said Stanley.

"No, ships started using oil instead of coal, it says here. Sad that, really," Mabel mused. "Just to think: if we had stuck with coal we wouldn't be having to kowtow to those sheiks now."

"Yes, we could have carried on kowtowing to your Marquess instead," chortled Stanley, feeling that he had hoisted his wife on her own petard.

"Well at least he was a Scot," snapped Mabel defensively. She rather liked the picture of the man by Henry Raeburn in her guidebook.

"Yes, and they now have the oil, too," grumbled Stanley.

Mabel decided to keep her research to herself from then on. It was a long way to South Wales.

* * *

Mabel, Rita, Stanley and Davyn entered the town hall, next to the Carnegie Library, around 6.00 p.m. to be sure of a good seat. The Quar Ladies were meeting in another room and it had been a toss-up for Mabel and Rita whether or not to join them. But when Stanley told them their John would be there and that Jack Pugh was an energetic speaker, they had decided to stick with their men.

At 6.30 p.m., the local union officials entered with their guest and following the usual flattering introduction, which Jack considered no more than his due, the now national organizer began his talk.

"The election was a disappointment," he admitted. Capitalist propaganda had bamboozled the electors, he claimed.

Mabel shifted in her seat. She had not felt in the least bamboozled. But then he started to say something that caught her attention.

"Coal made this country," he asserted. "The industrial revolution was driven by coal. In 1700, less than three million tons was mined but this had more than doubled by the end of the century reaching sixteen million in 1815 and some thirty million by 1830. Those numbers speak for themselves. And when the easy money had been made by the iron masters and colliery owners, they went inland after the deeper seams. The population in the Rhondda Valley went from some five hundred in 1800 to over one hundred and sixty-two thousand in 1921 after the Bute Merthyr Colliery was sunk and the Taff Vale Railway was extended to carry the coal to Cardiff docks. Coal, people, progress – it is as simple as that!"

'And what about the Bute family's great borrowings and mighty investments?' Mabel wanted to call out. 'Didn't vision and money fit in there somewhere?' But Jack Pugh had moved on.

"And what more can we learn from the people of the Rhondda Valley?" he pounded out, his reedy voice rising to its theme. "We learn about communitarianism; about the precious gifts of community, of sharing, of equality.

"Now I hardly need tell you, good people of Merthyr, about these things. It was the Rhondda Socialist Society that helped form the Communist Party of Great Britain; it was the people from these valleys who stood up against Tommy Moran and the British Union of Fascists; it was men from here who joined the International Brigade in Spain to fight General Francisco Franco; and it was to Tonypandy, just eighteen miles from here, the government sent troops to stop miners securing a fair wage from greedy mine owners intent on getting more for less.

"These are things you know," he said, lowering his voice. "I am here to call upon that spirit again. Our new fascist government – and yes, that is what I believe we now have – is intent upon destroying the coal mining industry. Why? Because oil and foreign coal can be purchased more cheaply, enabling business to make even greater profits, profits which flow to the few, not to the many."

A rumble of approval spread through the room and Mabel felt herself being carried along.

"Yours is an industry under great threat. Between 1920 and 1945, the number of men working in the mines fell from 1.2 million to eight hundred thousand, and in 1947 the mines were nationalized. But did that help? You be the judge. In 1920, there were two thousand eight hundred and fifty-one working collieries producing two hundred and twenty-nine million tons of coal. Last year, one hundred and thirty million tons were produced from just one hundred and seventy. Brothers, nationalization was a boon to the owners not the workers."

An even stronger murmur of approval ran through the audience. The now national organizer, albeit one of several, had them eating from his hand.

"We can expect no favours from this government..."

The sound of 'No!' rose from the gathering.

"We must take a stand..."

The 'Yes!' was half-sigh, half-release of pent-up worry and emotion, like a spontaneous response in one of the Baptist churches many in the room still attended. Even Harvey, sitting at the back, was ready to shout 'Alleluia!' had anyone else been inclined.

"Now there is a man in Yorkshire, Arthur Scargill, who will take this fight to the government if you will give him your support.

"When the miners went on strike in 1972, thirty thousand engineers in Birmingham came out in solidarity. The mass picket of the Saltley Coke Depot, which Arthur helped organize, was a success. Solidarity with the miners closed power stations and docks and after seven weeks the government was defeated. Again in 1973, Arthur was a key figure in organizing the strike that brought down Edward Heath's Conservative government. Next year he will be putting himself forward for the presidency of the National Union of Mineworkers. I urge you to vote for him. If anyone can take on this heinous government and save the coal mining industry, it is Arthur Scargill."

For a moment, there was silence. The message had been brought down to them from the mountain. Now what?

"Thank you," Jack Pugh prompted, his arms outstretched, and they rose to give him the standing ovation he craved.

* * *

Harvey had come with Alun Davies, a seasoned reporter from the *Merthyr Express*. Although this was now the third occasion at which he'd seen Jack Pugh in action, he thought it time he met the man in person and Alun had been lined up by the national organizer for an interview after the meeting.

The venue was Y Dic Penderyn, a pub opposite the town hall.

"An insufferable little prick, I expect," confided Alun as they walked from the hall. "They come here from nowhere, promising to refashion the earth in less time than it took God in the book of Genesis and after getting the people all wound up, they float off leaving us somewhere in the Book of Revelations to be crushed in the winepress of God's wrath."

Inside they found a squash around the organizer, of people anxious to draw out some last drop of wisdom they might have missed and to be associated with the expression of their dreams. On seeing the reporter, Jack Pugh excused himself from his admirers – 'Work to do, I am afraid' – and joined the journalists at a table with John, John's parents and their hosts, Rita and Davyn Pritchard. After introductions were made and drinks ordered, Alun Davies quickly got to work.

"Now tell me, Mr Pugh, how is this Arthur Scargill going to save our mines?"

"Jack, please."

"Jack, Mr Pugh, certainly. Now what is the answer to the question?"

Stanley was bristling at the reporter's tone, but Davyn knew the reporter took no prisoners in his search for truth, a characteristic that endeared him to his readers, and so settled back with his beer to enjoy the joust.

"You are asking our communities to make a big commitment and probably, down the road, an even bigger sacrifice," Alun elaborated, "so they need to know."

Jack didn't like any encounter with an intellectual equal, especially one who appeared hostile to his views and launched into a diatribe about the government being captured by the capitalist class.

"The government must be forced to keep the mines open," Jack said, "and our power stations should be obliged to use our coal, rather than gas and cheap imports. Arthur has forced the government's hand twice before. He's a winner."

"I could offer up the tale of King Canute," Alun began, "but let me tell you instead about Dic Penderyn, who this fine establishment is named after. Davyn, you'll know this narrative well, but our visitors might not."

Davyn Pritchard nodded a comfortable, worldly nod. Such stories had been the lifeblood of his youth.

"The great influx of people into the valleys happened because the ironmasters and colliers needed workers. The ironmasters and colliers came to the valleys because there were deposits of coal and iron ore. These industries expanded as fast as they did in the late eighteenth and early nineteenth centuries because Britain was industrializing. The population was growing. Cities were growing. The nation's wealth was growing. The place was abuzz with opportunity. Change abounded. Everyone wanted a piece of the action.

"After Boney was finally defeated in 1815, the continent was no longer off limits and industry had to adjust to new markets, new competition and to ever-improving ways of doing things. There were now more workers in the valleys than the factories needed. So factory owners laid off men and cut wages. But people were less quick to leave than they had been to come. They had built communities.

"In early 1831, frustrations boiled over, and the men working for the ironmaster William Crawshay, who had built Cyfarthfa Castle a few years earlier for a cost of some five million pounds in today's money, downed tools and took to the streets of Merthyr. Soon their protest spread and in June the government sent in a Scottish regiment to restore order.

"A battle between soldiers and workers ensued. Many were injured, some were killed and the soldiers were forced to withdraw. Around eight thousand workers, waving red flags, effectively took control of Merthyr."

"And it can be that way again," interjected Jack Pugh, glowing with vicarious pride.

"It must have been frightening," said Mabel, oblivious to Jack Pugh's withering stare.

"And so it was," continued Alun. "The protest ran out of control and many of the families felt things had gone far enough. The rioters' council was split and by 7th June, the authorities had regained control using force. Twenty-six were arrested and two of them sentenced to death by hanging. One of these was Lewis Lewis, convicted of robbery, and the other was Richard Lewis convicted of stabbing a soldier in the leg with a seized bayonet.

"The sentence passed on Lewis Lewis was eventually downgraded to a life of penal servitude in Australia because a soldier testified that he had protected him from the rioters. However, the sentence on Richard Lewis, better known by his local name Dic Penderyn, was upheld even though the people of Merthyr were convinced of his innocence and eleven thousand signed a petition calling for his release."

"So was he innocent?" asked Mabel.

"It seems he was," answered Alun. "In 1874, it was discovered that a man called Ianto Parker had stabbed the soldier and then fled to America. It also came to light that James Abbott, who had testified under oath against Penderyn, had been put under pressure by the Home Secretary, Lord Melbourne, who was adamant that there should be at least one hanging."

"That's your aristocracy for you, Mabel," chipped in Stanley.

"Capitalist pig!" hissed Jack.

"So are you saying we should or shouldn't support this Arthur Scargill?" asked Mabel, quite shaken by what she had just heard.

"I am not saying one or the other," answered Alun. "But what I am suggesting is that confrontation for the sake of confrontation usually ends badly."

"But if it brings down a rotten system, that's good," asserted Jack.

"Unless the system that replaces it is even worse," replied Alun.

"How could it be?" snapped Jack, now regretting he had asked the journalist from the *Merthyr Express* to meet him.

"Very easily," explained Alun. "You have to see Lord Melbourne's decision in the context of the time. The French Revolution had descended into the murder of an entire class—"

"And a good thing, too," interrupted Jack.

"Which included, Mr National Organizer, Maximilien de Robespierre, the brilliant young lawyer and passionate advocate of the revolution, who argued that the king must die so that France could live."

For once Jack Pugh was silent.

"And after that bloodbath," Alun continued, "France resorted to a military dictatorship. This led to a continental war which took the combined strength of the British and Prussian armies to bring to an end. And that was after Napoleon's ill-fated attack on Russia which resulted in the death of over five hundred thousand men."

"How interesting!" exclaimed Mabel.

"Haven't we lost sight of Dic Penderyn in all of this, Alun?" asked Davyn, who was more comfortable with the folklore without Alun's extraneous embellishments.

"Perhaps we have," admitted Alun. "But from the Home Secretary's point of view, restoring order and preventing a repeat of the riots was more important than justice. People had seen what took place in France and did not want to see the same happen here."

"Of course they didn't," smirked Jack.

"Oh yes, they kept their heads all right," chortled Alun. "But we should not see Dic Penderyn as a champion of revolt, but rather as the innocent victim of a clash between the hot-headed and the thick-headed. By all means, follow this Arthur Scargill, but first make sure you understand where he's leading you. King Canute was a wise enough king to know that there were tides he could not turn, however much his enthusiastic followers wished otherwise."

"Well I'll be!" enthused Mabel, although it was not until some days later, in the public library, that she read how the tenth-century King of Denmark, England, Norway and parts of Sweden had made his courtiers place his throne on the beach at low tide to illustrate that there were forces even a great king could not command.

Seeing the fallow ground on which his wisdom would be broadcast, Jack excused himself – 'Meetings to go to' – taking John Preston with him, but not before Mabel and Stanley had embraced their prodigal. The young man might have been associated with someone Alun Davies considered a hothead, but at least, from Stanley's point of view, his son was now on the right side of the argument. Mabel was just happy to have reclaimed him.

"An insufferable little prick he was," concluded Alun when the two men were out of earshot. "Where do they find them?"

* * *

During the drive back to the Midlands, Jack Pugh was glum, but Alun Davies's report in the *Merthyr Express* the following day, while not enthusiastic, was factual. The reporter concluded his article by saying that communities were easier to build than dismantle and that if this Arthur Scargill could bring the miners' plight to the attention of the government, that would be no bad thing. But to lose the goodwill of the public, he cautioned, would be folly.

With Max housed at Her Majesty's pleasure, Jack had moved in with John. Ever since Miranda had shown 'her true capitalist colours,' his interest in Oxford had waned. Besides, with his new national responsibilities, Longbridge was even better placed than Cowley had been. But as they drove through the darkness and away from the South Wales valleys, a thought that had been festering in his head, ever since the debacle at Hunters, finally broke cover.

"Why were you not arrested along with Max and me?" he asked.

"Max was a crazy: had it coming," John answered, "and you're a big man. I'm nowt."

That satisfied Jack Pugh entirely.

What John Preston did not say was that he had told Peter Betsworth about his erstwhile flatmate and when the police were informed, his handler made sure John faced no charges.

* * *

Harvey and Alun Davies talked long after the Prestons and Pritchards had left. Y Dic Penderyn was convivial and he found the old Welshman the best of company. Full of the seasoned wisdom that comes from a half-century observing the rich and the poor, the lazy and the diligent, the decent and the dishonest, he considered it essential that the present be set in the context of the past.

"The Spanish-American writer, George Santayana, said it best Harvey: 'Those who cannot remember the past are condemned to repeat it.' Our own Robert Owen had true wisdom, but somehow what he said was lost in translation." He explained how the great Welsh industrialist concluded that men and machines should not compete and that capital and labour should work together for the prosperity of all. For a time, Alun recounted, the model factory Owen built up in Lanark, Scotland, where workers and their families were fairly paid, well housed and properly educated, was much admired.

"The trouble, Harvey," he bemoaned, "is that his socialistic principles were turned into coercion by ambitious men, hungry for power. Who really wants to live in a world where everything is controlled by some higher authority, however benign? And imagine what they feel when that authority ceases to be benign! A slave is a slave no matter how honourable his master. That left libertarians with Adam Smith's invisible hand. He argued that when each of us pursues his own self-interest within a properly regulated, free-market economy, the well-being of everyone will steadily improve. I suppose we are about to give that a try," he said. "But I feel for the communities in these valleys. What brought them here is leaching away. If the people of the Nile delta awoke one morning to find that their river no longer flowed, what would they do? They would lavish tribute on their priesthood from their dwindling resources and pray for a miracle."

* * *

The following day, Harvey struggled with his piece for *The Sentinel*. He wanted to write about the rich culture he had found and how the economic winds that had enabled it to form were now blowing that culture away. Instead he wrote about a looming battle. He predicted that a man called Arthur Scargill would soon lead the miners in a make or break confrontation with the country's democratically elected government. As George Gilder had often told him, newspapers sell on the basis of black and white, not subtlety.

C*HAPTER*

15

L IKE MOST OF his friends, Ray Gosling was a member of the Amalgamated Union of Engineering Workers. But he and his wife, Mary, had grown sick and tired of the stoppages and the damage these were doing to their lives. Mary never did tell her husband about the help she was getting from Mabel Preston, but even with this she was struggling. Both had voted for Mrs Thatcher, although it would be several years before they would admit it, even to each other.

John Preston, Mabel's son, had suggested he vote for Terry Duffy when Hugh Scanlon had retired as union president the previous year, because Duffy was no friend of the communists. Ray would never have thought of doing so otherwise. The favoured candidate was the left-winger, Bob Right, but Duffy had won. Like Ray, many of the younger Leyland workers were growing restless and John Preston was finding ready recruits willing to break the left wing's grip on their union.

No one expected things to change overnight. In fact, the communist shop stewards inside the Transport and General Workers' Union and AUEW had been gearing up for a fight since before the election. Mass action was being planned to keep volume car production going, even as the Leyland CEO was eliminating loss-making units and laying off workers as fast as the stewards could cry 'all out!'

The rumour was that Michael Edwards had threatened to wind up the whole company unless the government underwrote redundancy payments for as many as 50,000 of its 165,000 workers. By all accounts, the new Secretary of State for Industry, Keith Joseph, needed little persuading. A passionate believer in the need for productive industries operating in a free market, he had been the intellectual driving force behind the Conservative Party's new hard-edged approach to economic management.

The way Ray Gosling saw it, an industry unable to sell its products for a profit was unlikely to see him out. He could always find some other work if he had to and a little redundancy money would not go amiss. What he liked about the AUEW's new president was that the man seemed to see things the same way: get the best that was on offer and move on. What the dictatorship of the proletariat actually meant he never rightly knew, and hadn't much liked the sound of it anyway.

* * *

A proposal by the government to fund postal ballots in union elections was at first bitterly opposed by the Trades Union Congress: left-wingers saw it as taking the devil's shilling. However, Duffy's more pragmatic view prevailed. The showdown between the AUEW and its shop stewards came towards the end of the year.

Throughout 1979, the popular press wasted no opportunity to mock the communist stewards and 'Red Robbo', the name given to Derek Robinson, himself a member of the AUEW, had been the focus of their bile. As the Longbridge convener, Robinson had coordinated a succession of strikes in the forty-two plants over which he had influence and Edwards was determined to get rid of him.

* * *

It was shortly after the election when Jack Pugh found himself bundled into a car and taken to a meeting with a nameless man who had talked to him from behind a wall of reflective glass. How had this voice known about his liaison with Miranda de Coursey? He suspected it had come from Miranda herself. Following the Hunters debacle, she had thrown him out of her room and although they had taken up again, her passion had dulled.

No longer could he rely on a quotation from the great Vladimir Ilyich Lenin – 'People always have been the foolish victims of deception and they always will be. We can't expect to get anywhere unless we resort to terrorism: speculators must be shot on the spot. Hang no fewer than one hundred known kulaks, rich men, bloodsuckers.' – to cause her ecstasy.

There was even the copy of a passionate letter he'd written to this daughter of a capitalist laid out on the table in front of him. How would it look to his communist brothers should it fall into their hands, the voice had asked? His assured 'They'd think it a fabrication' convinced neither him nor his interrogator. He knew how jumpy the brothers were.

He'd been given a simple choice. Leave here and become a marked man who might have his kneecaps shot out at any time, by goodness knows who, or continue with his revolutionary life and the admiration it brought him in return for a little information. The voice knew the brothers intended to close down the entire automobile industry and that a meeting was planned to coordinate the action. A copy of the minutes of this meeting would be appreciated.

When the brothers met to finalize strategy, the meeting had been electric. As a trusted organizer, Jack had, of course, been present. He made a passionate speech about this being the moment when the capitalist edifice would crumble and a new breed of leader would take over, which had gone down well. The contents of a pamphlet were agreed and he'd even managed to have it hardened by quoting from Lenin, his intellectual mentor – 'You cannot do anything without rousing the masses to action.'

The minutes of the meeting were thorough. The brothers regarded themselves as nothing if not professional. As he walked to the post box he felt strangely elated. He, Jack Pugh, was at the centre of great events, exactly where he had always wanted to be.

* * *

When the stewards' pamphlet was circulated with Robinson's name on it, criticizing management and calling for mass action, Edwards saw his chance. The convener was called in and asked to withdraw his name. He refused and was fired. Another name on the pamphlet, belonging to a member of the TGWU, was ignored.

The Longbridge plant stopped work immediately in defence of its convener. The Birmingham East District Committee called upon the AUEW executive to declare an official strike. The TGWU executive met and agreed to call an official strike if the AUEW would do so also. Five days after the sacking, the unofficial walkout was still holding and several thousand assembled in the Town Hall, but the AUEW executive did not show up. Its representatives were meeting with Edwards in a nearby hotel.

There the AUEW offered to set up a Committee of Enquiry into the sacking, a proposal the Leyland management were happy to accept as long as Robinson was only in receipt of an ex-gratia payment, in lieu of his salary, while the committee deliberated – and if the committee's deliberations were 'thorough', so much the better. With this deal done, the men had little option but to return to work. Edwards didn't even have to make public the minutes of the mass-action planning meeting which had come into his hands.

When the AUEW finally did consult its members about whether to strike on behalf of Derek Robinson, some 14,000 votes were cast against strike action with only 600 in favour. Ray Gosling was relieved to find himself in the majority.

CHAPTER 16

W HILE WAITING TO SEE his dentist, Harvey picked up one of the more serious news magazines lying on the waiting room table. It was a May issue of *Business Perspectives* and the leader article caught his eye:

In August last year, President Carter appointed Paul Volker chairman of the US Federal Reserve. An economist by training, whose grandparents were German immigrants, the new chairman found himself confronted by an inflation rate that was already over 11% and rising rapidly. Like James Callaghan in Great Britain, the US president had inherited an economy that was barely growing and prices that were rising. When the cost of oil quadrupled in 1973 following OPEC's embargo, a reaction to the Arab Israeli war started and then lost by the Arabs on the Israeli holy day of Yom Kippur, Western central bankers lowered interest rates to protect their economies, believing that a little inflation was better than no growth. What they got was not much growth and a lot of inflation which we wordsmiths have called stagflation.

At the start of the Carter presidency in 1977, Western economies had been showing signs of recovery, but the Iranian revolution two years later, which deposed the American-backed Shah and elevated the Ayatollah Khomeini to the position of supreme leader, disrupted oil supplies once more. If the economy isn't a dark enough cloud, the President's fight for re-election is also being overshadowed by the Iran hostage crisis. It was in November when Iranian revolutionary guards seized the US embassy taking 52 hostages, and despite April's courageous attempt to free them, they remain captive. President Carter's challenger for the presidency is expected to be the former governor of California, Ronald Reagan.

"Mr Mudd. The dentist will see you now." The receptionist's unwelcome words brought him back to his own reality. Visits to the tooth doctor were always at Sylvia's instigation. 'You've got the money now, Harvey. So spend it looking after yourself.'

As he lay there and the inside of his mouth became a Lilliputian version of one of Andrew Champion's factories, the similarities between Britain's and America's situation struck him. As far as he knew, the United States had got rid of its communists and their fellow travellers in the 1950s, so could union militancy in the United Kingdom be as much a symptom as a cause of his country's malaise? And how could the same illness have struck two nations three and a half thousand miles apart? Like the cavities being discovered by his torturer's sickle probe, there were gaps in his understanding that needed to be filled.

* * *

While familiarizing himself with the team Mrs Thatcher had assembled to take up the reins of government, Harvey discovered that one man had started his life in Port Talbot, an industrial town in South Wales where his father was a solicitor. The port itself had been built by the Talbot family and at its peak in 1923, over 3 million tons of coal were being exported from its docks. As demand for Welsh coal declined, the town had reoriented itself and by 1952 was home to one of the largest integrated steel mills in Europe, employing 18,000 people. However, the eyes of the solicitor's son were set elsewhere. He worked hard at school and secured a place at Cambridge University. There he studied law and became chairman of the university's Conservative Association. But he hadn't quite finished with South Wales.

Twice he'd stood for the Conservative Party in Aberavon, but Labour's grip on the seat was unassailable. Later, as a London solicitor, with a continuing interest in conservative ideas, he had been rewarded with safer seats, eventually becoming a minister in Edward Heath's government until it was brought down by the National Union of Mineworkers. After her election victory, Mrs Thatcher had made him her Chancellor and her brief to him was clear: wring inflation from the system and free the British economy from the dead weight of government and the trades unions.

The Federal Reserve Chairman, Paul Volker, was a Democrat appointed by a Democratic President and the new Chancellor, Geoffrey Howe, was a Conservative appointed by a Conservative Prime Minister, and yet both seemed intent on cutting the level of inflation in their countries. Price controls had been tried and failed. It now seemed to be the turn of monetarism. But where had the idea come from and how was it supposed to work? As a journalist reporting from the frontline, he felt he should have some grasp of these things.

George Gilder was sceptical when they'd discussed it. 'Just get in there and report, Mudd,' he'd said. 'The eggheads will come up with the theories to explain why what happened happened afterwards. If you really are interested, though, Dr Ferman Chase is giving a lecture on the subject at the Fishmongers' Hall in a couple of days. I'm told he's good.'

* * *

Harvey arrived in good time. The Fishmongers' Company was

one of London's oldest guilds with 700 years of history. Their hall overlooked the River Thames and the meeting had been readied in the building's magnificent banqueting room. He found a seat near the back and quickly felt the reassuring peace which comes from being enveloped in history.

He knew that the company's first building on the site had succumbed to the Great Fire in 1666 and been rebuilt by Sir Christopher Wren, the genius behind St Paul's Cathedral. The hall was again rebuilt in 1832 to make way for an improved London Bridge, and yet again after sustaining bomb damage in the Second World War. Whatever one might sometimes think, physical structures were important to men. As he sat there waiting, he contemplated on how they were often the only trace of a people's existence.

Dr Chase walked to the podium without fanfare. He tapped the microphone twice with his finger to assure himself that it was working and to alert his audience of around 200, perhaps two thirds students and the rest curious professionals, to the fact that he was in position and about to start.

"Ideas are strange things," he began. "They can sit around in books, on bookshelves and in cupboards, sometimes for centuries, without anyone giving them a second thought. At other times they can spread as a fire does through dry grass, igniting an eruption of energetic action that bursts forth, Roman candle-like, before quickly dissipating, leaving only a charred landscape in their wake.

"The domain of ideas is consciousness, but like a seed of wheat an idea needs the right conditions before it can germinate. To exist at all, however, it must possess structure. The essential form of this structure is simple," he maintained. "It should comprise a subject, a verb and an object. 'I eat you' is such a structure, but this is merely a statement, not an idea. To become an idea it also has to possess causality. 'Eating you will make me sick' introduces such causality. In effect what we have are two statements – 'I eat you' and 'I vomit'

('I' being both subject and object) – joined by the assertion that one causes the other.

"Consciousness," he asserted, "is really all about causality. It entails an ability to create a set of ideas about how the world around us works. The process of being conscious is the process of interposing this map of causality between us and that world so that we may act upon it and achieve specific results.

"Now the alert amongst you," he said with a wry smile, "will note that our map and what it purports to describe are unlikely to fit that well. So let's give managers and forecasters some slack and," he added, pausing for effect, "ask the Almighty to endow them with a little humility."

Realizing that they had been treated to a joke, a ripple of laughter spread through the audience and Ferman Chase sipped from the glass of water provided.

"The medium of ideas is language," he continued. "Language has evolved to incorporate many subtleties, which are simply conditionalities. 'I will eat you tomorrow' introduces a temporal condition. 'I will vomit violently' introduces a quantitative one. The combination of causality and conditionality is, in many ways, contradictory. If A only causes B when there is C, A does not really cause B, at least unaided. But this is where the power of ideas lies. Ideas are intrinsically creative.

"When a wheat seed finally germinates in response to the right amount of warmth and the right amount of moisture, it expresses its structure. And although this structure is largely predetermined, variations in soil content, moisture and warmth influence its exact shape and character such that, over time, it may evolve differently from wheat growing under different circumstances, even into a new species and perhaps a new genus. That is creativity.

"Although an idea, like a grain of wheat, is self-contained – and has to be if it is to be coherent and understood at all – it must exist in a dynamic environment. Indeed, we construct ideas so as to impose some understandable order on the world around us. This has two implications. The first is that what we regard as reality is, to some degree (perhaps even to a large degree) a construct of our own making. The second implication is that individual ideas, like soldiers in an army, are often only relevant in the context of the whole that sustains them. This gives rise to a third implication. Ideas and context interact.

"Think of shared consciousness as a complex network of interlocking ideas that more or less rub along together in a more or less sensible fashion. These sit within a framework we sometimes call our culture or story and are reflected in our structures which can be both hard, like this splendid building, and soft, like laws and customs. It is not difficult to see why new ideas are often rejected. If an idea supports the existing edifice, fine. If it undermines the existing edifice, no thank you. But change does happen.

"This, of course, leads into political structures and the nature of their hierarchies and the stories that support them. The impulse for change comes from individual dissatisfaction which may start amongst a few people, but then spreads. Martyrdom, for example, challenges the status quo. Can such and such an idea really be right if this man or this woman is willing to die opposing it? The social consciousness inherent in Marxist thinking, where one part of a society perceives that it is being subjugated by another part and rebels, is also a method by which change can occur.

"The embedded nature of ideas was described well by John Maynard Keynes who said, 'The ideas of economists and political philosophers, both when they are right and when they are wrong, are more powerful than is commonly understood. Indeed the world is ruled by little else. Practical men, who believe themselves to be quite exempt from any intellectual influence, are usually the slaves of some defunct economist.' Had he been alive in the 1970s, he would have appreciated the irony of his remark."

Once again the audience felt able to laugh. On the half-page programme describing the good doctor's background and accomplishments, Harvey had written the word 'genus' followed by a question mark. He hoped there would not be too many more things he would need to look up when he got home.

With the mention of Lord Keynes, however, members of the audience were reminded of what they had come to hear Ferman Chase talk about and started to regain their footing.

"Until the depression of the 1930s," he said, returning his listeners to more comfortable territory, "the prevailing economic 'idea' was that markets would self-correct. Upswings and downswings would take place around a trend of steadily improving economic activity. Governments, it was felt, should leave well alone. However, the stubborn nature of what became known as the Great Depression challenged this view.

"Keynes's great insight was that economic activity was ultimately a function of aggregate demand. If an economic shock undermined people's ability to purchase things, companies would stop producing them and economic activity would get stuck at a permanently lower level, which was exactly what seemed to have happened in the 1930s.

"His solution was elegant and simple. To offset a collapse in personal consumption, governments should step in and purchase things on their behalf. This would increase aggregate demand and lift economic activity up to a level that brought employment back to where it had been, at which point governments could reduce their own expenditure.

"It is probably true to say," he expounded, "that rearmament ended the depression, first in Germany and then elsewhere, although that was hardly the kind of government expenditure Keynes had in mind. Following the Second World War, however, demand management by governments, using both fiscal levers (taxation and government expenditure) and monetary levers (interest rates), was an idea that had firmly taken root. Importantly, it also dovetailed nicely with the more general idea that management was a scientific discipline that could be learned and applied.

"But by the 1970s it was becoming clear that in mitigating the discipline of economic contraction, this demand management, which increasingly followed the political calendar, was causing inflation in the general economy and overmanning in many companies, especially those possessing political influence.

"As is frequently the case with old ideas, the notion that government was as often the cause of economic problems as their solution was not dead but had merely slipped from general consciousness. This illustrates another characteristic of ideas: they are subject to fashion. We do not know exactly why this is, but it almost certainly has something to do with the fact that ideas have to resonate emotionally if they are to stimulate action.

"Emotions and identity are close allies," he claimed, "and it is far easier to march behind a single flag, be it that of communism or fascism, Islam or Christianity, this nation or that, than behind some opaque notion of multifaceted complexity. The priesthood of ideas," he almost chuckled, "spends an inordinate amount of time fashioning its raw material in such a way as to support whatever the prevailing emotional identity happens to be.

"This is why pluralistic societies are generally more effective and better able to adapt than those with singular orientations. Pockets of differing identity nurture competing ideas, any one of which might appear useful when it comes to dealing with changed circumstances. In competition with what became known as the Keynesian School of Economics, which grew in ways its namesake would almost certainly have disavowed – might not the same be said of Christianity?" he quipped. "The old idea was still being nurtured and developed by the monetarist school whose centre had moved from Austria to the

United States."

Ferman Chase was now in overdrive and his listeners were set for the ride.

"In 1963, at the University of Chicago, Milton Friedman argued that inflation, and by implication deflation, 'is always and everywhere a monetary phenomenon'. He and his colleagues carried out extensive research which they believed suggested that the severe recession of 1929 was turned into a depression because the Federal Reserve inappropriately maintained a tight money policy, by raising real interest rates. Additionally, the Smoot-Hawley Tariff Act of 1930, which sought to protect American manufacturers from foreign competition, set in train a chain reaction of retaliation that devastated world trade. Far from being the world's saviour, governments had been its curse.

"Never, ever, underestimate the capacity for human folly," he almost thundered, reaching once more for the glass of water before continuing.

"While output might be stimulated by easy money in the short run, Friedman's research indicated that over the longer term the output benefit tailed off but the inflationary impact remained. Fiscal stimulus was no less problematic. Not only might it distort an economy by directing resources towards goals government planners wanted rather than those individual consumers wanted, it was likely to divert scarce capital – human and financial – away from more productive endeavours.

"Given a choice between having to compete for customers and accepting a taxpayer-funded subsidy, most rational beings and organizations, they maintained, would opt for the subsidy. Those looking for a set of ideas that were different from those which had prevailed since the war found them inside the University of Chicago.

"I guess," he shrugged, bringing his lecture to a close, "that on both sides of the Atlantic, we are about to find out just how useful these ideas are."

Against his normal instincts, Harvey found himself in the crush of individuals which gathered at the front, all eager to interact with the star and touch his garment for one last charge of the truth drug he had brought. It was a young woman ahead of him who pre-empted his own question.

"Dr Chase, Dr Chase," she almost shouted, "I loved your lecture, but which is the best: free markets or demand management?"

As this was the question in everyone's head, the jostling subsided and the expectant cluster held its breath for the answer.

Ferman Chase looked pensive and almost pained at having to shatter their quest for certainty.

"Neither and both," he said crisply, before leaving his acolytes to their confusion and slipping quickly away.

CHAPTER 17

HARVEY FOUND Andrew Champion in a sombre mood.
"Can I offer you some coffee, or tea?" the businessman asked.
"We also do a nice line in biscuits."

Harvey opted for the coffee. No one's tea was a patch on Sylvia's.

His editor thought it time for another 'good news' story. 'What about that machine tool chap?' he'd said and Harvey had agreed. Besides, *The Sentinel*'s new deputy features editor – one of three – was in need of an antidote to Dr Ferman Chase. His beloved opera seemed closer to reality than some of the things the good doctor had been talking about. But perhaps it was just a question of mental preparedness. He could get his head around the Champion Group. It purchased things, it made things and it tried to please its customers. In contrast, even the great nationalized industries – steel, coal, automobiles, public services – which were generating most of the headlines, had become politicized monsters, for which customers were an afterthought – if thought of at all.

"Who was that good-looking woman at your election-night party?" Andrew asked. "I tried to sidle up to her a couple of times, but never made it through the crush. Just as well, probably. I don't suppose she'd have been interested in my line of work. It seems to have a deadening effect on the opposite sex. Even my wife's eyes glaze over!"

"If you just said you owned a factory…" Harvey suggested. "That might reel them in."

"Possibly. But they'd want to know what it made and I'd be back to square one."

"You could always dress it up a little. Something hush-hush. People aren't really interested in answers. They just want to be entertained."

"So speaks the journalist!" chuckled Andrew.

"You got me there," Harvey acknowledged. "But even serious stuff has to be engaging these days otherwise people won't bother with it."

He considered mentioning the lecture, but thought better of it as he'd have to say what it had been about and still wasn't sure he knew.

"We did make a component which went into the Hunterston B nuclear power station," Andrew offered up after some thought.

"Well that sounds intriguing," Harvey encouraged.

"It was only a small part!"

"No matter," Harvey assured him. "In the social world, attitude wins over substance every time. Show enough brio and your besotted audience will be convinced you built the whole thing."

"I'll bear that in mind."

"It was an enjoyable evening, though, wasn't it?"

"I'm not sure her husband thought so," Andrew said. "He never left the card table all evening."

"You *were* paying attention! That would have been Frances Graham's husband. A low threshold for boredom, I'm told."

"So you know her?"

Harvey thought he detected just a hint of envy and was tempted to display some brio of his own. "No, not really," he confessed. "We have met a couple of times. She likes opera and so do I."

The word 'opera' had the same numbing effect on Andrew as Andrew imagined his own customary subject matter had on others.

"So what do you make of our new leader then?" he asked.

"*The Sentinel*'s behind her one hundred percent. In fact, in our more delusional moments we imagine her victory was engineered by us."

"That sounds like your version of Hunterston B," ribbed Andrew.

"Where is Hunterston B, by the way?"

"North Ayrshire, in Scotland. It came on line in 1976 and can supply electricity for a million homes."

Small part it might have been, but Harvey detected a hint of pride.

"What do *you* make of our new leader?" he asked.

"I don't know," admitted Andrew. "We had our best year ever, last year. Made over half a million clear profit. Ploughed it straight back in, of course. Things might be a mess in the public sector, but a lot of us outside it are coping pretty well. I just hope they don't try to sort out a problem in three years that's been building for a quarter of a century. This monetarism they keep talking about seems like a very blunt tool."

"I'm still trying to work out what exactly monetarism is," declared Harvey. "I even went to a lecture about it and am not sure I came away any wiser."

"Imagine a world in which everyone has become dependent on an increasing amount of a substance called oxygen that can cause inflation," Andrew explained. "Now take away the substance. That's monetarism."

"But without oxygen, people will die!"

"That's my point," said Andrew.

"You ever thought of going into the lecturing business?"

"I might have to if all this blows up," Andrew laughed, casting his eyes around the room. "But if I am to be Alfred P. Doolittle I'll need you to be Henry Higgins and put in a good word."

The businessman might not have been keen on opera, but he did like a good musical and *My Fair Lady* was one of his favourites. Luckily it was also one of Sylvia's and so Harvey knew exactly what he was talking about.

"I'd be happy to," he said, doubting if there would ever be such a need.

* * *

He wrote another up-beat article on the Champion Group. The company was selling its products across Britain and throughout Europe, he reported. Its new Pulsar computer-controlled sheet-metal punching machine looked extraordinarily sexy, even to his un-mechanical eye, and he assumed it did what it was supposed to. Andrew had let him roam through all three of his factories and everyone seemed motivated and keen to make a success of what they were doing. He detected a little frisson between the parts business and the machine tool business, but that was to be expected: sibling rivalry.

The unit developing the production-scheduling system had been like a closed order with its own language and mysterious habits. On the door into the room where the computer code was being written, Andrew had affixed a notice – *DO NOT ENTER unless absolutely necessary* – to deter casual visits. It was essential, he was told, for the work to continue uninterrupted.

One of the salesmen had told him a story which he incorporated into his piece. The Champion Group had naturally been represented at the machine tool trade fair in the spanking new National Exhibition Centre which the Queen had opened in 1976 next to the M42 motorway, adjacent to Birmingham Airport. It was the showcase for British engineering and Champion's customers and agents from across Europe had been invited to see its latest products.

One agent, Martti Fastbjörn, was always a sharp dresser. On the day of his visit he had chosen to wear a crisp white linen suit. What makes a punching machine punch, Harvey explained to his readers, was hydraulics, a system that utilizes a fluid, often oil, under considerable pressure. The point of impact, as the punch is driven down though the metal sheet into the die, is the moment of maximum pressure.

Martti had been given a good lunch and everyone was buoyed up for the demonstration. As the agent stood there, eager to be wowed because the machines he sold paid for his lifestyle, the oil line became detached in the middle of the punching routine, spraying him and only him with a jet of brown oil. The storyteller did not enumerate exactly how much grovelling and stroking had taken place that evening, although the Playboy Club on Park Lane did come into it, but it must have been enough. The following day, Martti Fastbjörn placed his full complement of orders.

Under the headline *Accidents Will Happen!*, Harvey's piece was effusive, but that hadn't stopped Andrew calling the following day to complain – 'All they'll remember is that effing oil line!' This was true, of course, but Harvey knew that few, if any, of his readers would be in the market for a punching machine any more than they would have known where the Hunterston B nuclear power station was located.

* * *

Andrew Champion was not overly cross with Harvey. He'd grown to like *The Sentinel* reporter and besides, there were more important things to worry about. In Geoffrey Howe's first budget, shortly after coming into office in 1979, the Chancellor had raised indirect taxes, lowered direct taxes and increased interest rates. In May, he raised indirect taxes further and continued to cut public expenditure. His upward pressure on interest rates was relentless. At the beginning of 1980, the base rate for bank loans, onto which the banks added their margin of several percentage points, depending on who the borrower was, stood at 17%. This meant that the government's monetary policy was at last catching up with inflation which was hovering around 20%.

The problem for the Champion Group was not the rate of interest, but the effect of the government's medicine on the economy. By June, this had been forced into recession. Perhaps the election message, that Labour had not been working, with unemployment at 1.5 million, had been misunderstood because unemployment was now rising rapidly towards 2 million.

Andrew found himself heading into a perfect storm. Since the start of the new government's squeeze, sterling had risen by between 13% and 18% against the currencies of the group's main overseas customers. And thanks to North Sea oil, the pound was already over-valued on account of its perceived status as a petro-currency. When it came to the purchase of a machine that might cost as much as £100,000, customers could wait until sterling fell back, as they were sure it would. They were not fools. And now home orders, too, were drying up. His clientele were worried and so was he.

*C*HAPTER

18

BILLY strode into the Blue Moon off Belmont Street. He'd finished a three-week shift on Transworld 58, the rig sucking oil from the Argyll Field, 200 miles east of Montrose. The skills he had come by in Texas had brought him back to Britain. Who'd have thought it? Certainly not him. With more money in his pocket than most of the locals and a Texan lilt, Billy had little difficulty attracting companions. Life was exceptionally good. He knew he should call his mother. He *would* call his mother – later. Although it was only October, she was sure to ask, as she always did whenever he called, which was not often, if he would be home for Christmas, a home he had not seen in twenty-four years.

"What'll it be, Billy?" Mark the bartender asked. Since coming to Aberdeen from Houston, Billy had become a regular. "A boilermaker?"

"Yeah, let's start with a boilermaker. I intend to get properly fried tonight."

"Why's that Billy?"

"Fog. Two weeks became three weeks. They couldn't get the eagles down, so we just kept hauling ass. I don't think there was one of us not floating by the close. Where does all that shit come from?"

"Do you know Paul?" Mark asked, fulfilling his other function as social facilitator.

Billy looked at the young man on the barstool next to him. He was small but neat, with a narrow face and pretty hands.

"How you doing, Paul? Can I get you something?"

"A screwdriver, thank you," answered Paul.

"A *screw driver*," repeated Billy, trying to copy the young man's rather genteel accent. "Naht a screwdriver? I like it. Where you from, Paul?"

"Edinburgh," the young man answered, although his answer was almost swallowed by the other voices filling the Blue Moon.

"Come to check out the oil crowd then?" Billy shouted. "I've been wanting to go to E-din-burg," he confessed, having absorbed his adopted countrymen's difficulty with the word. "Ah hear it's a fine city."

Gathering the drinks from Mark and asking him to open a tab, Billy assumed command over his new friend. "Now let's go 'n get a table, Paul, 'afore they're all roped."

Billy led the way and found a vacant stall in one of the rooms off the main bar. The two men sat down and Billy took down a third of his glass in one swallow.

"My, that was good!" he exalted. "There's no booze and no sex on the rigs, just work."

Paul sipped at his screwdriver and tried not to show the discomfort he felt with the word 'sex'. That was his father's doing. The subject was not one for polite conversation – or any conversation.

"So what do you do, Paul?"

"Student. I'm a student."

"Well that's just great. I never got to do that myself. Left home at sixteen. Made my way to Liverpool. Got a job on a boat and after fourteen days, found myself in the Port of Houston. I wasn't supposed to go ashore without papers, but some of the older boys had a way and I tagged along. There was a bust-up in a hen house we'd gone to with police and everything. It got pretty nasty. One of the ladies hid me – Shelly was her name – a real nice person. When everything had quieted down, she said I should get back to my boat, but that spelled trouble to me. So I stayed a while in the hen house, doing odd jobs. One day, Shelly asked if I'd like to work on a farm. I told her I never had, but would be happy to learn. So she wrote a note and I took it to this farm north of Houston. It belonged to her ma and pa and she knew they needed help. I never did let on what Shelly really did. I just said she worked in a hotel, as she'd told me to.

"I worked on that farm for five years and loved every doggone moment of it. But then Old Man Peterson had a heart attack and died and Ma Peterson had to sell up and move into town. She and Shelly opened a boarding house together. That was when I got work in the oilfields. I became pretty good at it. It was hard, but I liked what I did and the money was good. When the company I was with had to send men here because there weren't the skills locally, they picked me. I don't know how they sorted my papers, but they did. And here I am."

"You never went back home then?" Paul asked. He had barely touched his drink while Billy told his tale; he was so engrossed.

"Nope."

"Did you mind? I mean, did you miss home?"

"Sometimes I guess I did. But I must be one of those curious types. I was always too interested in what tomorrow would bring to get that wound up about what I had left. And you can take that both ways."

Paul seemed to be hanging on Billy's every word. He sat there, staring, just sipping from his glass as his new friend talked and consumed a succession of boilermakers brought by serving girls familiar with his appetite and generous tips.

"Oil sure will be a shot in the arm for the UK economy," he was saying. "But you do things different here. What with the royalty payments, the special tax levies, not to mention the cost of the drilling licences, your government's the main beneficiary. I'm not saying that this town hasn't done well, Paul, but you should see Houston. Now that's a city! When the oil here's gone, what will be left? A mighty metropolis with new industries, or the bitterness I left behind in South Wales when the coal stopped selling?

"My pa, now he was for the union and for coal, in that order and still is as far as I know. What does your father do, Paul?"

"He's a doctor," Paul answered.

"A good profession, but ah'm thinking you're looking for something different. Now ah'm not a union man like my pa and ah'm none too set on government running my life either. Which is not to say that the boys with money are saints – that they ain't, but you kinda know where they're coming from. They want to make more money and for that they have to keep doing more things right than wrong.

"If it's not oil it has to be summat else and that keeps Houston growing – unlike Detroit which is pure union these days and in bed with Washington for any favours it can get." Billy's intake was slowing. He'd lost count and his eyes started to wander around the room in search of activity, before alighting once more on the youth in front of him. "So what *are* you looking for, Paul?"

"I don't know," Paul admitted. "The courage to find out I suppose," he added disarmingly.

"Well, the first thing's to become free. Now to be free you must be able to pay your way, and to pay your way you must find work you can do. That'll be your passport, see. What are you studying at college?"

"Political science," answered Paul.

"Doggone it, Paul! What's that going to do for you, if you don't mind me asking?"

That had been a question Paul had been asking himself, so he just shrugged.

"Take my brother, Joseph," Billy continued, "I'm told he is a chef and if his mother is to be believed, he's become a pretty good one. That's his passport, see. People will always want feeding."

"My father wanted me to study medicine," said Paul, "but it didn't work out, so I switched to politics – the university had places."

"Fathers! Can't see beyond their own dicks, if you'll excuse my French. And did you ever wonder why your university had places, as you put it?"

"Not really," admitted Paul.

Just then, two girls passed by, dressed up and on the pull.

"Hi there, Billy. Who's your friend?" Jackie Shannon called out. She and her friend Wendy Arbuthnot often came to the Blue Moon to see what was cooking. "Youse wanting some company?"

"Jackie, my darling. I've been thinking of you and only you. This is Paul," he said, getting up. "We were just going our separate ways."

Wendy looked disappointed, but Billy put an arm around both of them.

"How about I take you fine ladies to the Howard Hughes for a steak dinner? I'm famished. A man can't live on boilermakers alone."

The girls giggled enthusiastically.

"Well it was mighty nice meeting you, Paul," Billy said, feeling just a twinge of guilt at leaving such a lost soul on his own. "Get a passport and be your own man. The rest of it, frankly, is crap."

As he left with the two girls, regaling them with how it was Howard Hughes Senior who had invented the oil drilling bit, a piece of information they would instantly forget, Wendy cast a backwards look at the lonely figure in the booth.

Passing the bar, Billy saw a familiar face. "Jeremy, you old queen," he called out. "What are you doing here?"

The two embraced.

"I owed Mark money," Jeremy said, casting his eye over Jackie and Wendy. "I guess I can't entice you over to my side of the aisle just yet!"

"No you can't! Though there is a lonely young man called Paul in a booth at the back struggling to make sense of his life. You might see if you can straighten him out – or un-straighten him, I guess it would be. But for heaven's sake take the lad somewhere else. The two of you are likely to get flattened in here when things heat up."

Billy Preston paid off his tab and left with the two girls. He would call his mother in the morning, for sure.

* * *

In October, a housing act gave Britain's council house tenants of three years' standing the right to purchase their homes. Shortly afterwards, long distance bus routes were deregulated and what would become a multi-million-pound business was started by a sister and her brother in Perth where they lived. They called their first route between Dundee and London, The Stagecoach. The government might have had its hands thrust firmly into the North Sea oil trough, but elsewhere the state's tentacles were being cut.

It wasn't until December that Billy finally called his mother and it took a news item to prompt him. On Monday 8th December John Lennon was shot outside his apartment building in New York. Fame had attracted the infamous. An uncompromising character had been compromised by little more than a plain man's urge to kill a butterfly and revel in the notoriety of his act.

Along with most men on the rig the following day, Billy felt a keen sense of loss. Part of his emotional landscape had been removed, but how? Were the songs gone? No. Had he ever met the man? No. Was he ever likely to? Not now. Had he any sense of songs to come that now would not? He didn't believe so. Was he a sentimental fellow? His life hardly suggested it. Had the past, in some subtle way, been altered by the present? To be so would be the realm of science fiction.

In the end he decided that the singer-songwriter's death had brought him face-to-face with his own mortality and the random nature of existence. It got him thinking about what he had achieved and the mark he would leave on life. The self-sufficiency he took such pride in was something, certainly, but would his passing be noticed by any more than the last crew he had worked with, the last barman he had bought a drink from or the last lady whose bed he had shared? And then it dawned on him – his mother would miss him.

* * *

"Mother, it's me, Billy."

"Billy, is that really you? Where are you?"

"Aberdeen, Scotland."

"How long have you been there?"

"Recently arrived, Mother," he lied.

"So are we going to see you this Christmas?" she asked, as he knew she would.

"I was thinking so."

"Are you married?" she asked. "Or will it just be you?"

"No, I'm not married, Mother."

"Well you should be married Billy," she counselled. "A man without a family is a man without a life."

"How are John and Joseph?"

"John's a union man now. He's still working and Joseph is a chef, I think I told you."

"Yes, you did. And Pa? How is Pa?"

There was a pause.

"Your father was laid off a month ago. There was a redundancy payment, a nice one on account of the years he's worked for the company, but he hasn't taken it well."

"I'm sorry. But he must have been close to retirement anyway?"

"Everything's changed Billy. Thousands and thousands of jobs have gone. Whole communities have gone, although I don't suppose it's as bad here as it is in the valleys. We visited Auntie Rita this summer."

Billy could just remember his one trip to South Wales, on the train, to the beach at Swansea. Many years later, the town had been declared a city at the investiture of the Prince of Wales, an event his mother had cherished and which had even made its way into the Houston Chronicle. She'd posted him cuttings. He remembered thinking what an awful job a king-in-waiting must be.

"I'll call you when I know my shifts."

"Now you will come to see us, Billy, won't you?"

"Yes, Mother. I'll come."

His parents seemed so rooted. In part, it was that rootedness he'd wanted to leave behind. But now, aged forty and with the money he'd not spent on booze and broads safely in the bank, perhaps it was time to root himself, otherwise, what was the point? And perhaps, too, the destruction of communities already built was as wanton as the murder of an iconic man.

CHAPTER 19

A S 1981 STARTED to show its hand, the new Republican President of the United States was cutting taxes and increasing defence spending at the same time as the Democratically-appointed Chairman of the Federal Reserve, Paul Volker, was bearing down on inflation with interest rates approaching 20%. In contrast, the United Kingdom Chancellor was raising taxes and cutting public expenditure as well as using high interest rates to quell inflation. This cocktail was sustaining an uncompetitive currency, crippling Britain's exports, and pulverizing domestic demand. With unemployment approaching 2.5 million and rising, the British Government was deliberately pushing its economy into a recession that would be its worst since the 1930s.

So concerned were they about this policy that 364 economists wrote a joint letter to *The Times* newspaper saying that there was no basis in economic theory or supporting evidence for the government's belief that by deflating demand they would bring inflation permanently under control and thereby induce an automatic recovery in output and employment. They went on to suggest that the government's policies would deepen the depression, erode the industrial base of the economy and threaten its social and political stability.

"They'd have been given short shrift if they'd approached us for publication," George Gilder scoffed, adding with impish relish, "Besides, when have two economists, let alone three hundred and sixty-four, ever come up with an accurate forecast? They are the shamans of our age."

"Why is it we need shamans?" Harvey wondered.

"Because the world is an uncertain place, Mudd, and we hate uncertainty," his editor asserted.

"I guess that makes the government's strategy a shot in the dark as well?" Harvey posited.

George Gilder harrumphed and asked Harvey to do a piece on the miners' latest ultimatum.

* * *

On 10th February, the Coal Board announced its intention to close twenty-three pits. Some of the more militant miners went on unofficial strike right away and there were widespread calls for the National Union of Mineworkers' executive to declare an indefinite strike covering the nation's 240,000 miners.

The government quickly agreed to meet with the union and the NUM President, Joe Gormley, indicated his confidence that an understanding could be reached.

The Scottish Area president, Mick McGahey, a hard-drinking, poetry-loving, lifelong member of the Communist Party who had been outvoted for the NUM presidency by Joe Gormley, was known to be wary of any agreement.

The Scottish area president had become a miner at fourteen, following in his father's footsteps, as well as a member of the Communist Party of Great Britain, which his father had helped found. Jack Pugh greatly admired him, especially when he read that McGahey had supported the Soviet Union's suppression of the

Hungarian uprising in 1956: the mark of a true communist, he felt, who understood that ends justified means. Since being hauled in by his country's security service, however, his view of the state had altered. Added to which, he found the area president's thick accent so incomprehensible that fraternal fellowship seemed unlikely. And now he was travelling north to Lanarkshire to address a meeting in support of the NUM President, not his communist hero.

* * *

"Last year's Coal Industry Act called for the cessation of operating grants to the industry," the local NUM officer explained.

Jack sat on the podium waiting for his turn to speak. The room was full, with men standing at the back. This was their livelihoods, the future of their communities being discussed, not some political abstraction.

"As you know, comrades," their leader explained, "the National Coal Board was established in 1946 as a public corporation to run all the mines brought into public ownership by the post-war Labour government."

"And how much were the mine owners paid?" a voice called out from the audience.

"A deal too much, but that's a different matter," the leader asserted, clearly of the view that no amount was justified. "I believe around two hundred companies were taken over at a cost to the taxpayer of over three hundred million pounds."

"That's one and a half million each," a mathematical type called out. "I'd be happy with that!"

The area president's withering glare from the podium faced down the ripple of excitement that trickled around the room at the prospect of such winnings.

"The NCB found itself responsible for over seven hundred

thousand men back then," the local leader said, adding so as to prove his own mathematical competence, "which would have been about five hundred pounds a man if I'm not mistaken."

"Or around ten thousand in today's money," the mathematician called out, not to be outdone. But the mood was no longer on his side and besides, while all of the men knew that prices had risen in recent years, few could think in terms of £1 being anything other than £1.

"Ten years later, that number had dropped to just over six hundred thousand," their leader continued," and today stands at two hundred and forty thousand. The NCB has run our industry down even though we have enough coal to serve the energy needs of the country for a century or more: and its justification? Our coal is too expensive.

"Well that's hardly surprising," he almost shouted. "West German coal receives four times our subsidy and French coal three times. Added to that, our mines here in Scotland, like those in South Wales, have been starved of investment. Now of course we can purchase cheap coal scraped from the surface in South Africa or Australia, but when the cheap coal's been scooped up and taken from people who need it a deal more than us, what are we going to do?

"We need investment, not pit closures. We need a continuation of subsidies to keep our mining communities intact, not cuts. This government wants to accelerate the contraction the NCB has managed over the last thirty-five years – if you can call what they have done management. Comrades, this government, through the NCB, intends to destroy our industry and we must fight them both."

The room was infused with a comforting murmur of approval.

As representative of the NUM executive, Jack Pugh's comments were awaited with a degree of suspicion. Their own man had been defeated for the presidency by the present incumbent. Added to that, the NUM President had helped negotiate a wage settlement in 1977 that linked pay to productivity. This favoured the Nottinghamshire miners, whose mines were amongst the most efficient, reducing the industry's sense of solidarity. The dictum of Karl Marx that true communism would march under a banner inscribed with the words *From each according to his ability to each according to his needs* was an ideal easier to pay lip service to than support with one's own money. Besides, needs were infinite and capacity constrained.

Harvey watched Jack Pugh rise to his feet. The national organizer seemed nervous. Gone was the brash certainty born of an ideology whose legendary promises had not yet been put to the test. It might have been too soon to say, as the communist Zhou Enlai once said about the beneficial consequences of French revolutionary protest, but Jack Pugh's time horizon had clearly shortened.

He greeted his fraternal colleagues and was asked to 'speak up' which threw him. He fumbled his expression of gratitude to the others on the podium, thanking them for their hostelry instead of hospitality. After that his customary enumeration of Marxist imperatives became confused and rambling. When he got to the centrepiece of his delivery – the announcement that the NUM President had secured agreement from the government that no pits would be closed, that the grants would be continued and that the miners' claim for a 9.3% wage increase had been agreed – his peroration that the Thatcher Government had been 'utterly defeated' received only muted applause rather than the loud cheers he expected.

The mood of the meeting was captured better by the Scottish area president who growled, 'She's no ready te tak us on yet, that's a'.'

Within eighteen months, the NUM President would be replaced by the left-winger, Arthur Scargill, and Joe Gormley would become a Labour peer in the House of Lords.

* * *

When Harvey sat down to write his piece he found himself

unusually stuck. *The Sentinel* could not run a headline like *Thatcher Government Forced to Back Down by Miners,* as that would smack of weakness at a time when the rest of the economy was spiralling into recession and ministers needed to hold their nerve. Neither could it responsibly proclaim, *Government Makes Tactical Retreat,* as this was a supposition which would serve only to blow the government's cover, even if it was clear to many people that that was exactly what had happened.

By the time his train pulled into London's Euston Station he had still not cracked it, even though his notepad was full of jottings and drafts. Back home, he confessed to his mother that he was starting to see the neighbourhoods which had grown up around coal, steel and the manufacture of automobiles in a fresh light.

"These are families who have built communities," he told her, "with men who want to work and pay their way."

"Well of course they are, Harve," she accepted. "And didn't these come about quite naturally? Enterprising individuals found ways to produce things people wanted, and ways to pay for the work that made it come about."

"Yes," he agreed. "That seems to have been what happened. But now we have these communities without the activities to support them."

"And whose fault's that, dear?" she challenged.

Harvey was often silenced by his mother's directness and as he pondered her simple question, he struggled to formulate a simple answer. He could take a leaf out of the Marxist handbook and blame it on capitalist exploitation, but without capital and enterprise the communities would not have come about in the first place. He could go to the other extreme and blame it on union militancy, but men had every right to organize themselves to improve their pay and conditions of work.

"I don't know," he conceded. "Tell me."

"Everyone who promised those poor people they could go on living off the same patch of grass is to blame's how I see it, Harvey. And too many people believed them."

"Our need for shamans," murmured Harvey, thinking of his conversation with George Gilder.

"What's that, dear?"

"Oh, just something we were talking about in the office."

"There's a basketful to go around."

"Of blame?"

"Of course blame, dear," she answered tetchily, irritated by her son's apparent slow-wittedness. "When the grazing's exhausted animals move on. They don't form a union and insist the grass grow."

"But mother, we stopped being nomadic millennia ago!"

It was now Harvey's turn to sound exasperated. But Sylvia wasn't about to be deflected.

"Yes, Harve," she said, "and when we settled we built cities in which people doing their own thing could create fresh grass all the time so that no one had to move. That's what individual freedom makes possible. It's those people set on controlling others, even for the best of intentions, who cause the problems. They are the ones to blame, Harvey – always."

The finality of this summary indicated that her exposition of the nation's ills was over, so he retired to his room intent on finally pulling his troublesome piece together. Unorthodox his mother certainly was, but her largely uneducated views invariably hit the mark in unexpected ways.

It was not long before her influence bore fruit.

Under the headline *Let Down By Government, Let Down By Big Business and Let Down By The Unions!*, he described the hardships being faced by families whose communities had been built around single industries. At the end he reported that the government and NUM had come to an agreement and trailed the government's new policy of creating enterprise zones. These were areas stripped of red tape, in which individuals were being encouraged to build anew so as to counter the long-term decline of their old industries. *It may be too little too late,* he wrote, *but if it puts men and women back in charge of their own lives that, at least, is something to cheer.*

For once, George Gilder did not change even a comma.

C*HAPTER*

ANDREW CHAMPION was struggling to keep up with the news. A small group of Conservatives were rumoured to be planning a leadership challenge, so bad was the economic situation in their constituencies. The Labour Party hadn't had the stomach to elect its strongest candidate as leader the previous year, opting instead for a left-wing intellectual, and a new political party – the Social Democrats – had been formed by several of its disaffected members. And as if to confirm the confusion of the times, Bobby Sands, a member of the Irish Republican Army on hunger strike in Northern Ireland's Maze Prison, had been elected Member of Parliament for Fermanagh and South Tyrone.

Andrew had taken to having a Monday morning meeting with the heads of his three companies to try and get ahead of the crisis unfolding around them. Since the start of the year, each week's sales forecast for the year had had to be revised down. Overseas customers were delaying orders, some of their domestic customers were cancelling orders and several suppliers had already gone out of business. Rumours were rife about banks calling in their loan facilities as a sense of raw panic spread though the nation's manufacturing heartland.

Driving home at the end of each day, he felt like a general confronting an escalating body count with no prospect of relief. He supposed that he should be proud of his country for having won the Eurovision Song Contest, but if he had to listen to Buck's Fizz sing 'Making Your Mind Up' one more time he would be ready to seek sanctuary in a Trappist monastery. But the unaffected were always able to laugh and sip exotic cocktails no matter how many bombs were falling nearby.

* * *

The Industrial Revolution, which powered Britain's rise to world dominance, is often thought to have started around 1750. Its roots, however, ran far deeper, at least to the ascendancy of the Protestant Parliament of Oliver Cromwell over the monarchy during the first half of the seventeenth century. And one could reach back further still. The knowledge of Ancient Greece, which sparked what would be called Europe's Enlightenment, or interest in applied knowledge rather than religious knowledge, found its way into Europe from the Muslim world, which only came to an end on the Spanish peninsula in 1500, eight years after Isabella of Castile sent Columbus off on an adventure which would bring the New World into Europe's view.

The second half of the eighteenth century saw revolutions of every hue, not just of the industrial kind. The Seven Years War (1754–1763) pitted Britain against the Bourbon Dynasties of France and Spain, adding French North America and Spain's Florida to Britain's existing American colonies. Only twelve years later, the American Revolutionary War began which would end in 1783 with Britain's defeat and France's near bankruptcy supporting the nascent republic against its old enemy.

So potent was the mix of economic strain and combustible ideas that the absolutism engineered by Cardinals Richelieu and Mazarin and exemplified by France's Sun King, Louis XIV, broke asunder with the storming of the Bastille in 1789 amid calls for *liberté, égalité, fraternité*, democracy and republicanism. But after ten years of blood-letting and class genocide, the French again opted for absolutism, this time in the guise of a military dictatorship under Napoleon Bonaparte.

For fifteen years, Napoleon's armies spread republicanism across Europe before being undone by the Russian winter and finally defeated in 1815 by British and Prussian forces. At the end of these Napoleonic wars, the Holy Roman Empire, that coalition of countries in Central Europe left over from Ancient Rome's western empire, had been untied, German and Italian nationalism had found their voice, Spain's hold over its Latin American colonies had been weakened and Britain elevated to the status of predominant world power.

The war's end also filled London with demobilized soldiers without work and often without homes. Added to these was an influx of economic migrants from Ireland and also from Scotland whose rebellion against English rule had been defeated at Culloden in 1746. So concerned were the authorities by the criminality that accompanied such a large number of rootless people, that a Vagrancy Act was pushed through Parliament in 1824, giving the police power to detain individuals they suspected of being vagrant and so prone to criminality.

As the government-induced recession of 1980 accelerated into depression, large numbers in Britain's most populous cities, especially amongst the ethnic minorities whose parents had been economic migrants from Britain's West Indian and African colonies, found themselves without work or the prospect of any. Inevitably, criminality rose and the police dusted off the 1824 Vagrancy Act to stop and search individuals they suspected of potential wrongdoing. This SUS law, as it came to be called, set predominantly white police forces against predominantly non-white communities in the most economically distressed parts of England's inner cities.

In March 1981, a protest walk to Hyde Park had been organized by the inhabitants of Lambeth, a London borough, to highlight what they considered an inadequate police response to a house fire in January which had killed several black youths. Although the bulk of the protest passed off peaceably, an altercation at Blackfriars between the police and a small number of the several thousand demonstrators was played up by the national press in racist terms. One paper even ran a headline quoting a march organizer that it had been 'a good day', which it had, next to the photograph of a police officer with a bloody nose, which the organizer almost certainly knew nothing about.

Lambeth's depressed Brixton community had developed its own Afro-Caribbean counterculture. Drug-taking, gambling, reggae and street life were its hallmarks along with a high incidence of robbery, vehicle crime, burglary and prostitution. At the beginning of April, the Metropolitan Police decided to crack down on what they saw as its growing lawlessness. Codenamed Operation Swamp, plain clothes officers moved in, stopping and searching around a thousand individuals and arresting eighty-two.

* * *

It was Friday morning. Sheldon MacDonald and his friend Chris Tigo were walking down Railton Road to fetch some groceries for Olga Tigo's wedding. The atmosphere was poisonous. Short-haired white men in plain clothes were standing at every intersection. They would not have looked more conspicuous in full battle dress.

"Something's going down, bro," Chris said. "I'd better call Olga and tell her to keep away."

"That's a smart thing," Sheldon agreed. "See if the phone in that box is working."

Chris dove into the box and Sheldon waited outside, staring into a men's clothes shop. A blue tie with light grey polka-dots caught his eye. He was a snappy dresser and wondered if what he had picked out for Olga's wedding couldn't be bettered. While imagining himself in his white shirt and dark suit with the polka-dot tie, he became aware of a van, full of men, reflected in the glass. The van stopped and he turned in time to see ten or twelve rushing towards him. He started to run.

"Not so fast, sunshine," one of the men said, grabbing his collar, while a second caught the side of his jacket, ripping a pocket.

"My jacket!" Sheldon shouted. "Look what you've just done to my jacket!"

"Easy, black boy. It didn't suit you anyway. Now let's have a name."

He saw Chris emerging from the phone box and heard him shout "What's up, bro?"

Four of the men broke off and grabbed Chris.

"You jungle-bunnies working as a team then?" one of the men mocked as Chris was being pinned to the ground.

"Sheldon McDonald," Sheldon answered, ignoring the provocation, as his friend disappeared behind a wall of attacking bodies.

"What kind of name's that? You got a kilt back home?"

"They wear skirts, these primitives," one of the men jeered.

"A wee jock must have got up his mother's," another sneered.

Sheldon turned furiously towards the insult.

"Steady, my little lovely. Now what were you doing in front of that shop? Planning to improve your wardrobe free of charge were you?"

Sheldon heard Chris shout, "You all right, Sheldon?" and then "Man, that hurt. What the fuck did you do that for?"

Sheldon tried to free himself to get closer to his friend, but couldn't.

"Now, Mr McDonald, it's time to see what a black Scottie dog wears under his fur – strip!"

"What the fuck for?" Sheldon shouted, his anger overcoming his fear.

One of the men rammed his baton into Sheldon's stomach, winding him.

"There's no need for that, Percy," the one who seemed to be in charge said. "Mr McDonald here is going to show us what the good Lord gave him; isn't that right, Mr McDonald?"

As Sheldon undressed, a crowd started to form and the policemen began to look nervous.

"What you stop him for?" someone shouted. "I saw him. He was waiting for his friend. He was doing nothing."

"No, he was doing nothing," someone else shouted. "Why don't you do your job and find some real criminals?"

The crowd, over twenty now, was closing around Sheldon standing naked next to the pile of his own clothes. The men began to pull away. The one called Percy was heard to sneer, "and I thought these coons were supposed to be big," as another gratuitously kicked at Sheldon's clothes. "Just lay off, both of you, and get into the bloody vehicle," the one in charge ordered.

Only then did the crowd notice that Chris was being dragged into the van. "Tell Olga," they heard him shout. "That's Olga Tigo…"

As the men and their captive sped away, the crowd closed around Sheldon.

"You a'right, man?"

"Was that Chris Tigo? His sister's getting married Saturday, right?"

"They's complete pigs."

"They's fucking filth."

The comments came thick and fast, turning from concern about Sheldon and his friend into utter hatred of the authorities.

* * *

"Send an ambulance to Railton Road."

It was now 6.00 p.m. and a black youth with a knife wound in his back was being questioned by police. After five hours, Chris Tigo had been released from the station without charge. Still seething with anger, he was helping his mother prepare for Olga's wedding. On the street below, black youths, with a peppering of white, were congregating. The pack's dendrites were setting off synaptic rumours in every direction:

"They're roughing him."

"He's being left to bleed."

"He was pushed down."

"They couldn't give a fuck."

It was looking ugly.

"Send reinforcements."

The call went out as police, some in their twenties and a few fresh from the academy, milled around anxiously looking down at the bleeding youth and across at the gathering human storm in front of them.

When wailing, flashing squad cars burst into Railton Road and black uniforms spilled out, the invisible thread restraining the youths snapped. Two hundred or so surged forward, raw with anger. Scared policemen lashed out at any black who came near as they fell back with officers screaming at them to hold a line. After an ambulance made its way through the mêlée and carried the stabbed boy away, an uneasy stand-off was established. In police headquarters the decision was made to send in more uniforms and continue with 'stop and search'.

* * *

It was drizzling on Saturday morning. Around midday, Olga leaves the hairdresser to go down Railton Road. By the time she reaches Burton's she realizes people are not chatting and exchanging gossip as normal. Instead there is an eerie silence. The vibrancy of the community is gone. Later, in a nearby street, Sheldon sees traffic jamming up and notices a helicopter circling overhead as he makes his way to the church.

Olga is carried to her wedding in a white, open top, antique Rolls Royce, garlanded with cream-coloured ribbons.

By 4.00 p.m., rumours are spreading that the stabbed youth, carried off by ambulance on Friday, has died as a result of police brutality.

When two officers stop and search a minicab driver in full view of the enraged crowd, anger erupts. As if trained for this moment, youths become a fighting force, hurling bricks and stones at police vehicles as they speed down Railton Road.

Every time a brick hits its mark there is a cheer.

"Hey man, dat babylon he gat it! De beats is running scared."

Two hundred yards away, Olga is married.

After the service, she and her new husband drive towards Brixton Road for the reception but are stopped by a line of police. The driver insists and they are allowed to continue at their own risk. As the Rolls approaches the people filling the road like ants, it edges slowly forward. The crowd parts, echoing the biblical Red Sea, and the bridal couple pass through.

Shortly afterwards, widespread looting breaks out across Brixton, with white gangs from other neighbourhoods joining in.

Driving to the station in his own car, a young police officer gets stuck in traffic on Brixton road. A large group of youths appear in front of him from Ackers Lane and start gutting an electrical goods outlet. He crouches down, removing his uniform and prays for the traffic to move.

When looters approach Temples, a white-owned store where

blacks buy their fancy clothes, the cry goes out: "No, man, don't hit dis shop cause dat's where we get our clothes, right." So Temples is spared.

* * *

Harvey gets a call from George Gilder around 5.30 p.m., telling him to go to Brixton pronto: riots are in progress. He wonders if 364 economists had been right after all, at least in one respect, or is it just that forces, pent-up over decades, have been goaded into life?

At 6.15 p.m., a police van is set alight. A young fireman, newly qualified, drives his truck to the scene with no idea what to expect. He is waved through the police cordon without a word of warning. As he approaches the hostile crowd he hears a loud thump on the side of his vehicle. Worried that he might have hit someone, he draws to a halt. His station officer yells at him to drive on and not to stop under any circumstances. A hail of missiles hits them. A concrete slab flies through the windshield rupturing his spleen. The ambulance carrying him to hospital is pelted with bricks.

Harvey arrives to find the place ablaze. There is now open warfare between the police and several hundred youths.

Brixton police call on other forces across London for assistance. Men assemble in the station yard and are issued with heavy plastic shields. Their helmets are wholly inappropriate and the shields not fireproof. Even the vehicles they must use have no protection and the radios frequently fail.

At 6.30 p.m., from the back of a squad car, Harvey sees that some members of the community are trying to intercede between the rioters and the police.

"The only way to defuse the situation is to decrease the presence of the police in this area at the present time," one black man urges. "The police are the target."

"I hear what you say," the senior officer in charge answers, "and I appreciate what you are trying to do. But there is no question of me withdrawing police from here."

By 8.00 p.m., all attempts at mediation have failed and the rioters go on a burning rampage. Harvey sees Molotov cocktails being thrown for the first time. Later, he discovers that this is also the first time these homemade firebombs have been used on mainland Britain.

Two pubs and twenty-six businesses are set alight while scores of residents are blocked in, either by rioters or police. A white family in Mayall Road is robbed at knifepoint and a young woman raped by an intruder nearby.

By 9.00 p.m., over a thousand police have been assembled and start to squeeze the rioters out of Railton Road. By 11.00 p.m., they have regained control of the streets. With his clothes now reeking of acrid smoke, Harvey returns home, in no doubt that he has been witness to a war.

* * *

Olga's wedding reception had been abandoned. When she returned on Sunday the food was still there, but had started to smell, and all the drink was gone. Over 2,500 police officers had now been brought into the area and by Monday the last of the rioting had fizzled out.

Both Chris and Sheldon joined the rioters on Saturday night. Years later, Sheldon would admit that doing so 'had felt really good'.

On Sunday night, Harvey wrote his least inspired piece, in spite of Sylvia saying that the whole thing was disgusting.

The national papers were full of Brixton, of course. As one of a great many, Harvey's report on the riots seemed irrelevant. Even George Gilder couldn't be bothered to pass comment on his conclusion that violence was just an extreme form of communication and that if we wanted less of it, we should communicate better.

CHAPTER 21

"RAISE YOU TEN."

Charlie studied his cards for a long time. He already had a pound on the table which he was loathe to give up, especially to Martin, but his hand was looking less good than it had at the start.

"Fold," he said, as if choking on the word.

"Sorry, Chuck, I didn't catch that."

"Give him a break, Marti," pleaded Dave who had dropped out at the start. "That's the fifth time this evening you've walked him up to the trough and not let him drink."

Martin overcame his hearing problem and scooped the winnings into his corner.

"You're sure to get me soon," he said.

"Here, have a splash of this to cheer you up," comforted Pete, pouring some of what he called his little pick-me-up from a flask into Charlie's mug of tea.

"One day you'll get caught with that," warned Charlie, while not refusing the offer.

Martin and Dave both declined and Pete tucked the flask back into the inside pocket of the blazer hanging over the back of his chair.

"I swear it's the only reason you wear that thing," taunted Martin, handing the pack to Dave who started to deal.

"You going anywhere this summer, Chuck?" Dave asked as he handed out the cards and everyone added their ante to the pot.

"Ballycastle."

"Isn't that where you went last year?" Martin noted, with as straight a face as he could muster.

"And the year before that," Charlie confirmed, as Martin already knew, "and as many 'before thats' as I can recall."

"Not time for a change then?" goaded Dave.

"I suppose it's somewhere exotic for you?" Charlie grumbled, looking at Martin and adding to the pot.

"We thought we'd try the Algarve this year. I've heard there are some good golf courses."

"Fold," said Pete discarding his cards. "That won't please Margaret, surely?"

"Actually she's becoming quite keen," Martin told him as he peered at his hand. "I'm folding too."

"That's you and me, Charles," Dave noted, adding to his stake, "and I'll raise you."

"You should all try Ballycastle," Charlie told them. "It has a fine little beach and the most lovely view across to Rathlin Island and the Mull of Kintyre. Come in August and you might catch the Lammas Fair."

"Now what are you going to do?" Dave asked.

"You know it was Fergus of the Scotti people who sailed from Ballycastle in the sixth century, conquering the Picts and taking control of Argyll and Bute," Charlie expounded, increasing his bet by the fixed limit their rules allowed, "and I'll call you. That's why Scotland is Scotland."

"You're a fount of information, Chuck," mocked Martin. "Now

let's see what you've got."

Dave had already laid his three fives and two eights face up on the table, but quickly saw that he'd been topped by Charlie's four sixes and a random ace.

"Well I suppose you've got to win sometime," conceded Martin, with as much bad grace as he could muster as Charlie shovelled the meagre pot to his side.

Just then the door opened and Rolland put his head round the door.

"It won't be long now," he said.

"Why don't you join us?" invited Pete, patting the jacket on the back of his chair. "It's not as if there's much you can do."

"You don't think we should be doing something?" wondered Dave, as he had wondered many times before.

"Strictly hands off," intoned Martin. "Those are our orders from on high."

"And a damn good thing too, if you ask me," said Charlie as he took his turn to deal out the cards, "especially after what happened at Bundoran."

"Well, I'll see you boys later," said Rolland, adding as he closed the door behind him, "The press Johnnies will be all over this I dare say."

"Decided yet where you're going, Pete?" Martin asked, anxious to keep everyone's mind off what was going on only a few yards away. "And I didn't see your ante."

"Oh, sorry," said Pete, pushing his stake forward. "I think I'll visit my sister in Norwich."

Pete's marriage had crumbled many years previously and holidays were always a testing time for him.

"Fold," he said after giving his cards a cursory glance.

Martin increased his bet, as did Dave.

"Do you see much of Megan and Ryan these days?" Martin asked.

"Or are they off limits?"

"Shona remarried, as you know," answered Pete – which they all did, "and Michael, her husband now, seems to get on well with the kids so there doesn't seem much point."

Martin added to his bet and so did Dave.

"Well you should try to see them," prompted Charlie. "They are your flesh and blood, after all. I'll raise you."

"The wind's in his spinnaker now," observed Martin sardonically.

"Match and raise again," said Dave.

Suddenly the puff blew clean out of Charlie's sail. "Fold," he said, looking crestfallen.

"Ah ha, a contest at last!" crowed Martin. "Raise again."

"OK, Marti, I'm calling you," announced Dave as he pushed the appropriate sum into the pot. "What have you got?"

The eyes of the other two were fixed on Martin, hoping for a bluff to be exposed, but Martin laid down five spades.

"Got you!" he crowed, reaching towards the pot as Dave pulled a sorry face. But the face was a bluff.

"Not so fast," Dave chortled, laying out three fours and two sevens.

Martin's ever-eager hand hovered over the little pile, appearing reluctant to withdraw.

"I think he's got *you*," Charlie corrected with undisguised relish.

"I wish that had been my play," said Pete.

"Nicely done, Dave," Martin conceded, pulling himself together and making out that the little people deserved a round occasionally. Besides, it was on Charlie and Pete that he relied to supplement his income. Young Dave was becoming a threat.

The four men played on for a while until Charlie had reached his limit, which he regarded as the price of friendship, and Pete had become so morose at the state of his life that Martin worried another losing hand might have consequences. A cow was to be milked, not butchered, after all.

To enliven the mood, Charlie pulled a folk song from his compendium of local knowledge about a man who brings a lobster home which he plans to give his wife the following morning. As a holding operation, he parks the crustacean in their chamber pot. Naturally a call of nature intervenes during the night and the poor woman is grabbed by her private parts. During his frenzied attempt at rescue, the man is then grabbed by his. The fate of the lobster goes unrecorded.

When Rolland reappeared, all four men were splitting their sides with laughter. Pete had tears streaming down his cheeks, tears which he had been longing to shed anyway, but manliness forbade. Even Martin could not resist, although doing so was tantamount to acknowledging that Charlie had attributes besides an unfailing ability to lose at poker.

"What's so funny?" Rolland asked, angry at them for having such a good time while he had been confronting a different reality.

The seated men turned towards him like schoolboys caught in the middle of an illicit prank.

"You'd better pull yourselves together," Rolland chastised. "He's gone. I've told the governor."

One by one, their laughter dried up. Like professional undertakers anticipating the imminent arrival of the bereaved, they adopted a suitably sombre air, with Martin, the least affected, the most sombre, and Dave the most affected, hardly sombre at all. While Pete slipped back into his personal darkness, Dave's manner was one of almost childlike bewilderment.

"Why do we do these things to each other?" he asked, addressing no one in particular.

"Because we are sodding human beings who haven't learnt to do anything better," growled Charlie with a passion that surprised them all.

* * *

The Member of Parliament for Fermanagh and South Tyrone had starved himself to death aged just 27. Few in the English establishment were sorry. Airey Neave, a close associate of Margaret Thatcher and one of the few to have escaped from Colditz, had been blown up in his car outside the Houses of Parliament by Irish republicans two years earlier. The murder of Earl Mountbatten and two boys, one his grandson, while out fishing in the Bay of Donegal five months later, was still seared into the English public's imagination: a republican double.

Oh, *the troubles* as they were called! Even Britain's great liberal Prime Minister, William Gladstone, had been unable to push through Irish Home Rule in 1893 against the wishes of Irish landowners (most of whom had come to consider themselves Anglo-Irish or British), and the descendants of those Protestant families who had populated the north during England's cultural domination of its Irish colony. In the end, all but these northern counties secured their freedom from London's political control, but it left Catholics living in those counties at the mercy of a Protestantism made rabid by its fear of abandonment.

One such had been Bobby Sands, the MP for Fermanagh and South Tyrone. All his life he had endured second-class status, being forced from jobs and homes by Protestant bigotry. Frustration led to violent protest, and this, over time, led to his arrest. Inside Northern Ireland's Maze prison, he and those like him pushed for political rather than criminal status, and went on hunger strike until it was granted. It never was.

As Harvey left the Maze prison with as depressed a group of journalists as he had ever encountered, all of them were wondering how the cycle of violence could ever be ended. The British government's policy had created a martyr and world opinion was divided. Some regarded the Prime Minister's intransigence over such a small issue as status barbaric. Others felt the rule of law had to be protected at all costs. But one thing was certain: a very ordinary young man from an insignificant part of the world had called the authorities' bluff. In doing so he had attracted worldwide attention, leaving them with a pot full of still more anger and still more questions. Even Martin might have turned up his nose at that.

When Harvey wrote his piece for *The Sentinel* he concluded with a question: Hadn't the British Government a responsibility to every one of its citizens in Northern Ireland to enforce integration and stamp out bigotry in all its flag-waving forms, just as Lee Kuan Yew had done in Singapore between ethnic Malays and ethnic Chinese? He was rather pleased with this insight, but George Gilder cut it out.

"It is often better to be part of the problem, Mudd," he said "than part of the solution."

CHAPTER

PETER BETSWORTH had cut Stacy some slack. It was obvious she and Marx were growing close. That had been the point, after all. Expecting a woman to ingratiate herself with a man and not feel anything, especially if the target was personable, was not realistic. It could hardly be otherwise. And now that he had satisfied himself that Marx was committed, he felt he could let nature take its course. But he had cautioned her.

"Love and duplicity make uneasy companions, especially at the outset. I know."

Whatever the MI5 man's wife suspected she now knew better than to pursue. Young love lacked the same maturity.

* * *

Marx confessed his double life to Stacy early on, which she had promptly reported to her employer. The intelligence officer had expressed no surprise, simply telling her to maintain the fiction for John Preston's safety.

"A shared secret," he said, "will tie him closer to you. It will also make it more bearable for him. But in any communication between you and me about him, he is Marx. That is essential."

Part of her resented her puppeteer. But a far larger part enjoyed the work and took pleasure in the knowledge that she was helping protect a person she increasingly liked.

* * *

It was a Saturday in June. He'd met his handler the previous afternoon and decided to stay the night in London at the government's expense. To her surprise, he suggested they drive in her car almost two hours west to a country house. She knew events were getting to him. In May, he had 'Marched for Jobs' to Trafalgar Square with over 100,000 others. More than eighty had just been arrested during clashes between white power skinheads and blacks in Coventry. A man had fired six blank shots at the Queen in Horse Guards Parade. The total of IRA protesters starving themselves to death in the Maze Prison had reached four. Over 2.6 million were unemployed and that number was rising. Manufacturing companies, unable to keep going for want of work, were closing their doors for the last time across the country. And the Liberals and Social Democrats had formed an alliance to defeat one of the most unpopular governments in living memory – a government he had helped to get elected. Enough was enough.

"Let's goo an' see summat beaotiful, fer Christ's sek," he said, "an' forget all this rubbish, at leus fer a doy."

A photograph in a local tourist office had caught his eye. It was of an Eden, so colourful and lovely and peaceful, and so utterly different from his day-to-day experience. *Visit Bowood's spectacular rhododendrons…* it urged, and that had been enough for him. He had not come across the word rhododendron before and was far from sure how to pronounce it, but that hardly seemed to matter. The photograph offered a way into a different world, away from the single-minded bloody-mindedness that was destroying every fucking thing around him.

* * *

They sat on a bench, their picnic laid out between them. Late bluebells fell away in front, one after another, in rows, in lines, a stationary hoard of cobalt conquerors carpeting the forest floor with colour, an electric counterpoint to nature's green. High above, across a matching sky, white clouds scudded, capturing and releasing in playful dance the oak-tree-dappled light. And then there were the rhododendron blooms – reds, creams, yellows, mauves: how they shouted. We are here! We have endured! This is our moment! Enjoy!

John and Stacy just sat and stared. This was even better than he had expected, but it was also real and he didn't know what to make of it. How could it exist in the same world that he knew? Had the M4 west out of London become a wormhole to a different universe? A cuckoo sounded, its melodious notes belying the trumpeter's dirty little habit of laying eggs in another's nest. A robin tossed at fallen leaves in its search for grubs. Intercepting insects by the score, swifts screeched through the air like fighter jets. Nearby a badger slumbered. Come nightfall, it would set out to kill. All around nature was feeding on itself, but all they saw was its beauty.

* * *

"What's this?" he asked.

"Cheese," she told him. "Don't you like cheese?"

"Yes, I loik cheese well enough."

They picked at the meal Stacy had prepared. A bee flew past, startling her and she flapped ineffectively moments after the insect had determined her red tank top held no nectar. The garment's tight-lined roundness, however, had not gone unnoticed by her companion.

"Muggin girl!" he mocked. "It's juss a tiny th'n."

"I'd like to see you get stung," she scowled.

"Charm'n!" he protested, extracting a sausage from the pack.

"I don't suppose we're allowed to drink here," she speculated, pouring beer into a plastic cup and handing it him.

"Oo's ter stop us? The place seems 'alf empty."

"Yes, I thought it would be teeming, a lovely place like this. Still, good for us, right?"

But John Preston couldn't keep his eyes from her tight shorts.

"Hoo d'ya get into those things?" he asked.

"The same way I get out of them," she teased.

"I'd loik ter see that!"

"In your dreams!" she challenged. "Now do you want some fruit?"

"I'll yav 'un of those undersoized oranges."

"Mandarins, you chump. They are supposed to be that size."

"Hell, I knoo that. You fink I don't knoo that?" And then a small black object crashed into him. "What the fock!" He shot up from the bench sending the remains of his sandwich flying and spilling his beer. "What the fock was that?" he protested turning around himself like a dog chasing its tail. "It was a bloody zeppelin!"

"It was a tiny little flying beetle," she taunted with undisguised pleasure. "Now sit down and stop saying 'fuck' so much."

"I'll say 'fock' as often as oi want,' he retorted sulkily only just regaining his composure. "Now is there a Kit-Kat or summat?"

Stacy fished in her bag and found a Mars bar which seemed to be acceptable.

"Do you fink it just happened loik this, Stace?' he asked, taking in their surroundings once more.

"It says it was laid out in 1854, by the third Marquis of Lansdowne," she said, reading the brochure they had been given with their entry ticket, and enunciating the name with care. "That sounds like the right sort of name for a gardener."

"Some gardener!" he exclaimed. "I don't suppose 'ee did much wi' a sped 'imself, moind."

"No, I don't suppose he did," she agreed. And they sat in silence looking, as they had when they first arrived.

Snatches of conversation reached them from time to time but the 60 acres crisscrossed with paths and shrubs, many 20-or-so-feet high, could have hidden a small army. No other soul had passed by all the time they'd been anchored to their bench. Admittedly they had walked to the top and perhaps others hadn't bothered. Slowly their ears became attuned to woodland sounds, so different from the grinding, screeching, thumping noise of the metropolis that city people had programmed themselves not to hear.

A flock of jackdaws squawked overhead, alighting in a large beech tree nearby for a noisy get-together before moving on. Sleek pigeons floated by from time to time with effortless purpose. Two grey squirrels chased each other through the trees, leaping from branch to branch like Evel Knievels. The sweet smell from a giant Loderi, 25-feet high and as many wide, brushed past in the breeze. Nature was hard at work reproducing itself.

"What a pretty butterfly!" Stacy exclaimed suddenly as a Holly Blue zigzagged down from the canopy and alighted briefly on her knee before fluttering away.

John stared at where the lepidoptera had been and reached across to touch the spot.

"Too late!" she taunted, "and just as well. All men want to do is squash things."

But John did not remove his hand. Instead he moved it inward.

"Oh for goodness sake," she protested lightly, looking around. "Come on."

She led him towards a large rhododendron bush with dark red flowers and thick green leaves which touched the ground like an old-fashioned skirt. Beside himself with want, he blindly followed as she found an opening and squeezed inside. As she lay down on the fibrous earth and started to wriggle out of her shorts while he, hopping like a pogo stick, freed himself from his pants, they heard the sound of an engine. Staring through the foliage, they saw a miniature tractor, pulling a trailer, coming up the path. It stopped near their bench and its driver looked around. Seeing no one, he gathered up the remains of their picnic and threw it in the cart. They listened to the putter, putter of the engine retreating into the distance and burst out laughing.

"Bloody 'ell, Stace. That were close!"

"Just look at you now," she smirked, staring at her beau. "You'd better bring it here."

John's desire had folded like an ice lolly in the sun.

* * *

He was shrouded in gloom during the train ride back to Birmingham that night. Stacy had wanted him to stay on and he'd been greatly tempted, but on Sunday morning he and Jack Pugh were due to meet a group from the NUM who were working to have Arthur Scargill elected their next president. Besides, he'd already stung Peter Betsworth for an extra night in London as it was.

Bunched in a corner seat, he stared at himself reflected against the darkness. Clackety-clack, clackety-clack: the sound and the motion had a way of making one feel introspective and in the mood to take stock. Looking through his own disembodied face at the stationary lights rushing by, the reality of things foxed him. What was and wasn't real? Was anything real? Little did he know that such questions had occupied some of the greatest minds in human history and that none of them had reached a satisfactory conclusion.

What he did know was that his time in that woodland garden with Stacy had been the most magical in his life. Next to his encounter with Joan of Arc in a school book, nothing had made a greater impression on him. But the world was topsy-turvy for sure, without rhyme or reason. That he, a union mole, still had a job at British Leyland and his father, who had given the company his life, did not was, he supposed, just one of those things. And when he wasn't moleing, he was preparing for the launch of the Triumph Acclaim in conjunction with the Japanese company Honda, once one of his country's fiercest competitors. Perhaps Britain had won the war, with a little help from its friends, and lost the peace but never realized it.

He didn't like Jack Pugh one bit. The man's Marxist passion reeked of self-interest. His own code name could hardly have been an accident, although he didn't place humour high on the list of Peter Betsworth's characteristics. And what did he make of his Prime Minister now? She seemed more like a vengeful Old Testament God laying waste to a sinful populace than a modern-day Joan of Arc defending her people's honour. Clackety-clack, clackety-clack; the image of Stacy seeped back into his head, lying there, warm, welcoming, soft, in that garden, on that earth, in that time.

C*HAPTER*

A NDREW CHAMPION now faced each day with the grim determination of a man walking across an ice field no longer caring that he mightn't reach the other side. The journey was to be endured, the circling wolves kept at bay, the numbing cold ignored, each step treated as an achievement in itself. The distant possibilities he could see on the horizon hardly seemed relevant. His team had been pushing everything it could into generating overseas orders but people were hesitating. Their agents said sterling was still too high. What they asked themselves privately was would the Champion Group survive Britain's collapse?

In the last fortnight alone, riots had broken out in twenty-five cities across the country. Violence had also erupted again in Brixton after police searched houses for petrol bombs that were never found. In the Maze Prison, six of the IRA hunger strikers had now starved themselves to death and the Prime Minister blamed the IRA, which Harvey thought must have been an unintended compliment as martyrs were not that easy to come by. Amid this gloom, the British people were trying to convince themselves that the imminent marriage between the heir to their throne and the lovely Diana

Spencer foretold a happy ending just around the corner.

* * *

Andrew parked his car. It was still only eight and there were not many people around. Monday often seemed to get off to a slow start. He had deliberately taken offices away from his three factories so as to give them autonomy and not be swayed by any one. They also had a sales and service unit near Charles de Gaulle Airport as France was one of their best markets. On pushing open the office door he noticed a white envelope that someone must have slid under it over the weekend. He put it with his things and went to make a cup of coffee.

Back at his desk he liked to skim the newspaper and gather his thoughts for the day ahead. His priority that morning was a hard drive from the French company, Honeywell Bull, which they were having difficulty integrating into their micro-computer. He didn't want his developers wasting time on it. If Bull couldn't sort out the problem, he suspected he'd have to try the American Seagate Technologies again, a highly innovative new company specializing in data storage which he'd already visited once. As he toyed with how best to fit in a trip to Les Clayes-sous-Bois and California sometime over the next few days, he casually opened the letter.

The Royal Bank's letterhead surprised him and then as he read the quite crudely typed note asking that the Champion Group's £1.2 million overdraft be repaid forthwith, he suspected a prank. Hell, the bank had increased the Group's facility by £300,000 three months earlier. This had to be a joke. He looked at his watch. It was still only 8.30 a.m. His bank manager would not be in his office until 9.30 at the earliest and more likely 10.00.

Clocks always seemed to move slowly when one wanted them to move fast and too fast when time was scarce. To fill the minutes he pulled out his 'survival strategy' folder whose contents he already knew inside out. The mathematics were simple. Without money the company had to stop trading and there were only two ways to get it: from customers and from lenders. They had tried raising fresh capital some months earlier but the atmosphere was already becoming poisonous and manufacturing a pariah. He'd negotiated a loan increase from the bank at the start of the crisis and still thought there was a reasonable chance that this would carry them through. But there was absolutely no way that they could pay off their bank overdraft 'forthwith'.

Andrew's doomsday scenario was to cut overheads to the bone and hope that there was still enough of the company left when they finally poked their noses out of the long tunnel they were in. The most cost-effective overheads to cut were his top management. He had already stopped drawing a salary himself and although it had taken him ten years to build up his team, his senior appointments had always been ahead of growth. With no growth he knew he could run his operations through middle management alone – for a while. He'd done it when Harold Loxley had been snatched from them, after all. But he also knew, from what he had observed and read, that more companies failed at the tail end of a recession than when the demon was at its peak. Utterly exhausted by the struggle, they simply had nothing left to give. This, presumably, was what the Prime Minister meant by survival of the fittest, although he doubted she understood that the survivors of her 'cure' for what she considered the 'British disease' would be based in America, Germany and Japan.

As he played with the numbers, he heard his secretary coming in. The sound was a comfort until he remembered that unless he found a way to keep his ship afloat she would be out on her ear.

"A refill, Andrew?" she asked, poking her head round his door.

"Yes, June, thank you. And could you get Nobby Bruce on the phone just as soon as he gets in. I found a damn silly letter that claims to come from the bank stuffed under our door. I'm hoping it's a joke – a thoroughly bad joke."

June knew better than to ask what the letter said, but she was well aware from the dismal reports that graced every newspaper and broadcast what was going on across the country. Three of their own suppliers had already called it a day. The signs of economic and social disintegration were everywhere.

He heard the phone ring and June answer, but it was still only 9.15 and he didn't think it could be the bank. His light came on and he lifted the receiver.

"That's Harvey Mudd, Andrew," June announced. "Shall I say you'll call him back?"

Andrew thought for a moment and said, "No, June, put him through. I could do with a distraction. But if you get Nobby, interrupt."

"Andrew, is it a bad time?"

"Yes, Harvey, these days it is always a bad time! Are you after something from the frontlines?"

"As a matter of fact, Andrew, I am. George Gilder, my editor, wants me to work up a piece on how this recession is impacting Britain's manufacturing capacity."

"In three words Harvey, its buggering it!"

"Another perfect summation! Have you ever thought of writing copy for a living?"

"No, but I might have to!"

"It's that bad?"

"Yes, Harvey, it's that bad. Companies are falling like autumn leaves and it's not even August."

"What about the Champion Group?"

"Well, we're still on the branch, Harvey, still on the branch."

They talked for a while and agreed to meet, but neither was able to pin down a time or a place. It was now 9.30 and June rang through to say that no one at the bank could say when Nobby Bruce would be in.

Andrew left it for fifteen minutes and then called the bank himself.

"Mr Bruce, please."

"Who's speaking?"

"Andrew Champion."

There was a pause and an unfamiliar voice came on the line.

"Mr Champion, I have a number for you to call. It's our head office. You are to ask for Mr Murray."

"Can I speak to Mr Bruce, please?"

"I am sorry Mr Champion, but that is what I have been instructed to tell you. Your account is no longer with this branch. It has been taken over by our head office."

"Fucking hell it has!" Andrew exploded and the line went dead.

So now he knew. The letter was no hoax. This was war. It was time to reach for the lawyer.

"June, get me Donald Fraser at Brightman and Meadows will you. Say it's urgent."

He only had to wait a minute before June called back.

"I have Mr Fraser on the line."

"Thank you, June."

"Andrew, I'm in a meeting. What's up?"

"The bank's called in our entire overdraft."

There was a pause.

"Can you get to my office by midday?"

"You bet."

"Well, I'll see you then and bring every scrap of paper you have relating to the bank's facility. Remind me, Andrew, which bank is it?"

"The Royal Bank."

"Oh yes," he drawled. "Not known for their rigour, which may be a blessing. Until midday then."

Thank God for the law and lawyers, he thought to himself, a

civilized alternative to the Colt 45. No sooner was he through with Donald than June came back on the line.

"Andrew, I've got Mr Bruce. He's been holding. I think he's in a payphone."

"Nobby, it's Andrew. What the hell's going on? That noise; are you calling from a box?"

"Andrew, I'm most awfully sorry. We're under lockdown." Nobby Bruce sounded as distraught as he.

"What's lockdown?"

"Head office has taken over our loan book. They're calling in loans wherever they can. It's a major panic."

"Christ, Nobby, that's like telling the boys on the frontline that their ammunition is being withdrawn!"

"I know, Andrew, I know. But the bank's just looking after itself right now."

"A bloody funny way of doing it, if you ask me. And you; are you all right? Have you still got a job?"

"I don't know, Andrew, I honestly don't know."

"Well thank you for everything you've done for us up to now Nobby and good luck. You'd better get back to your desk before it's carried off to head office as well."

There was a weak laugh.

"And good luck to you, too," Nobby just got in, before the pips cut him off.

* * *

Andrew sat in Donald Fraser's office with its view of St Paul's, only a stone's throw from *The Sentinel* building, while his lawyer sifted through the bank's papers. An owlish man with a sharp mind, Donald liked batting for the small against the large, although it was from the large that he earned most of his money. He punctuated his progression through the Royal Bank's pages with an occasional 'uh-huh' as his client sat on the edge of his seat like an accused man waiting for a judge to overturn or confirm his death sentence.

Peering over his spectacles he asked, "I take it you are over the facility at this point?"

"No," Andrew told him. "We are still under by about a hundred thousand."

He nodded and went back over the papers again.

"Not very professional this," he said after what felt to Andrew like a spell in purgatory. "Do you want the good news or the bad?"

"Some good news would be nice for a change," Andrew answered, clearing his throat, alert to the sudden weakness of his voice. "We've had nothing but the other kind lately."

"Well the bank can't call in its loan to you. Their people have completely screwed up."

"Are you sure?" Andrew asked incredulously. He'd already had a session with his finance director before coming up to meet Donald in London and neither of them had seen any way out.

"Yes, I'm quite sure, but here's the bad news. The fact that they have put you on notice means that if your group goes one penny over the agreed facility they *will* be entitled to call in the loan."

Andrew felt like kissing Donald Fraser on all four cheeks, but Donald wasn't really the kissable kind.

"So what do I do about their damn letter?"

"Let me make a call. I have already had some dealings with their legal department. They don't know whether they are coming or going, frankly."

"Please. Go right ahead."

Donald had his secretary make the call and they talked for a short while about trout fishing on the River Test which was Donald's passion. It was not Andrew's, but at that point the head of the Champion Group would have happily scrubbed his lawyer's office carpet if asked.

"Anthony, how are you?" Donald oozed when the call came through. "Busy are you...? Yes, I expect so. You'll have to come and work with Brightman and Meadows." His look at Andrew conveyed the certainty that whoever this Anthony was, he would never be allowed within a million miles of Brightman and Meadows. "Quite so. Now, Anthony, about your bank's letter to the Champion Group ... The Champion Group ... Yes I expect you have sent out a great many letters recently ... Yes, these are very difficult times, but it's good to know that the banking industry is doing its bit for the economy ... Yes, that's right. The Champion Group, with your Mayfair branch, I believe." Donald looked across and Andrew nodded. He had never changed banks from his time in the airless basement on South Audley Street. "Right, well I've been going over the papers and I think you boys have jumped the gun a bit ... A clerical error? ... Easily done ... So shall I tell them to shred it? ... Very good, Anthony. I'll tell them ... No, Anthony, I don't think we have grounds for a suit at the moment ... Nice talking to you. Let's have a drink sometime."

Andrew moved from a feeling of complete elation to one of extreme anger in the space of a moment.

"Do you want to sue?" Donald asked. "You'd have to prove damage."

"Wouldn't I just," Andrew fumed. "But unfortunately we couldn't afford to and I have a company to run."

"Well I hope you have the money to pay my bill," Donald drawled.

"Unless it is more than one hundred thousand, we do."

"No. More like ten."

"Jesus!" Andrew exclaimed. "I'm in the wrong bloody business."

Donald just shrugged. He wasn't joking.

Before he left Brightman and Meadows he called his finance director to give him the news and then he called Harvey Mudd. As luck would have it, Harvey was in with George Gilder and they agreed to meet for a drink, and in Andrew's case, for several. He half expected to see his flow of indiscretions about Britain's non-existent industrial policy plastered across the next morning's edition of *The Sentinel*. That they were not owed as much to George Gilder not yet being ready to break with the government as it did to Harvey's scruples.

Looking back on that extraordinary day there was one thing he wished he could have reversed. The rumour that the bank had called in its loan had spread quicker and further than the later rumour that it had not. Such secrets were always hard to contain and the bad secrets inevitably had the most traction. Had a telephone conversation been overheard? Had a wife spoken to another wife and the bush telegraph been primed? He never knew. What he did know was that his company never fully recovered from the effect of that 'clerical error'. Business has a nose for vulnerability. It has to have.

C HAPTER

A S HARVEY toured the country over the last five months of 1981, firing back stories that appeared under the by-line *From The Front*, Andrew Champion's experience became depressingly familiar, but with one key difference: few of the companies he encountered had access to Brightman and Meadows. But to judge by what he saw, his friend had only purchased a stay of execution. British manufacturing was grinding to a halt. Thousands of companies were failing. Only the corporate liquidators were thriving and even they, like good undertakers, displayed a sombre demeanour.

It was the most vicious of vicious circles. Every death was a debt not paid, a product no longer supplied, capacity permanently removed and money destroyed. The government's industrial strategy looked more like a ten ball sending every skittle flying than anything approaching a surgical strike. In an attempt to improve his understanding of economics, he read an essay by Joseph Schumpeter, a famous economist who had died in 1950. The professor had coined the phrase 'creative destruction' to describe the way capitalist economies reinvigorate themselves.

His idea seemed to be this: businessmen invest in sets of ideas for making money and then overinvest in those that work best. When it becomes clear to them that chasing the same rabbit generates diminishing returns, they stop investing and instead of growing, the economy contracts. During these contractions many companies go out of business. This creates space for new sets of ideas to be pursued. As people invest in them, the cycle turns up once more, and the economy is renewed and reinvigorated. Naturally, being an intelligent man who had started life in Austria and ended up a Harvard professor, his argument appeared quite logical. But Harvey was left with a question. He wondered what Schumpeter thought was created by the destruction that had engulfed his homeland immediately after he left it in 1939?

In other words, just because an economy, like nature, is often able to recover from disasters, surely it didn't mean that one should court disasters. And even if it could be demonstrated that the state of things after disasters was in some clear and consistent way always better than the state of things that precede them, relying on disasters to get from A to B did not strike him as a mark of great intelligence. But then what did he know? He was just a journalist.

Harvey had not seen Frances Graham since the election night party at *The Sentinel*, although he had read about her from time to time in the society pages of his own paper. 'Best not dwell on the unobtainable' had become his mantra, as often repeated as undermined by his own hope and Sylvia's 'That's not over yet, Harve; you mark my words.' His mother concerned him. She was slowing. He could see that. At her age it was to be expected. But it still came as a shock to realize that her seemingly indestructible nature might be fallible to the ravages of time.

And time was weighing on him too. He and Suzie, a publicist whose career was on the up, had reached an understanding. Their well-organized, weekly encounters were leaving him empty and hungry for something more, although he couldn't honestly say what that something was. The publicist was excellent company; however her career, even more than his, was always the elephant under the blanket. Sylvia knew about her, but expressed no desire to meet and took his weekly absences from Buttesland Street in her stride.

'I might ask Trevelyan round to watch some television,' she would say of her charming gay neighbour from two doors down whenever Harvey appeared to hesitate on her account.

His encounters with Peter Betsworth had almost stopped. During the last, it was clear the intelligence officer had started to wonder whether the cure was turning out to be worse than the original disease. In fact, this was a growing concern amongst many of the government's supporters. Britain's first female Prime Minister was turning out to be more single-minded than most had expected. Those in her own party keen to offset her tough love with full-blooded investment into those areas worst affected were branded 'wets'. Even George Gilder wondered if being a woman inside a male preserve was causing 'Saint Margaret' to adopt more extreme positions than was wise.

On one thing, though, Peter Betsworth remained adamant: the NUM, he believed, was still deeply infected with communist ideology and this had to be exorcised at all costs. On that, he and the Prime Minister were at one. What his agents were telling him was that the miners themselves were split, with a sizeable minority in the most profitable mines determined not to be dragged down by the rest. A confrontation would come, but not while the government was so unpopular. Even the new Liberal-SDP alliance was ahead of all other parties in the polls and at its annual gathering in September, the Liberal leader had roused his delegates with the ringing war cry that they should go home and prepare for government.

In October, the final six IRA hunger strikers gave up. By then ten were dead and the British public had lost interest. *The Sentinel* hailed the capitulation as a victory for the Prime Minster and a vindication of her steadfastness. George Gilder penned that one. Like most journalists, Harvey hadn't bothered to go to the Maze Prison when the tenth man died, but suspected none felt comfortable about it. The ease with which people became inured to a cycle of death which didn't directly affect them seemed to be a characteristic of human nature.

Now and again he liked to have a drink with Desmond O'Connor of the *New Irish Times*, just to get a feel for the other side. In the Irish Republic, Desmond told him, perceptions were quite different.

"Did you know that over a hundred thousand attended the funeral of Bobby Sands?"

Harvey said he knew it had been quite a number.

"His election to parliament fair boosted Sinn Féin," Desmond explained. "It'll be Armalite and ballot box from now on."

Margaret Thatcher had become as big a hate figure as Republican England's self-styled Lord Protector, Oliver Cromwell, he said, reminding Harvey that Cromwell's Protestant forces had brutally subjugated Irish Catholicism in 1652–53. "Cromwell even paid his soldiers wid stolen Irish land," the *Irish Times* reporter exclaimed in mock horror. "T' cheek of it!"

"Our publicity's on t' up t'ough," he went on with his countrymen's customary black humour. "Back t'en you had to kill several t'ousand of us to be hated: now ten will do!"

CHAPTER

SITTING IN FRONT of him, Stacy looked nervous. Peter Betsworth had been expecting this moment. She was an attractive, intelligent woman and he was loath to lose her.

"I expect you know what I am here to say," she said.

"Yes, I think so. You've grown close to John Preston, right?"

"Have I been under surveillance, too?"

The intelligence officer allowed himself one of his dry laughs.

"We don't have unlimited resources, unfortunately."

"I want to be relieved from this operation."

"I understand," he responded, pleased that she had not simply handed in her resignation. "Do you intend to go on seeing Mr Preston?"

"I think so," she answered.

"And how is my Marx?" he asked. "Will he continue working for us?"

"He has not told me he wants to stop, but he does wonder sometimes if anything good is coming out of what he does."

"I think we all wonder that from time to time," her handler admitted, "and working in the field does put a particular strain on a person."

"Can I ask something more general?" she said.

"Of course, Stacy. What?"

"Who decides what is right or wrong, who to encourage and who to stop?"

"We work for the government, Stacy, as you were taught during your training."

"But that wasn't the case before the last election, was it?"

"Sooner or later, every intelligence officer finds himself staring into the grey area," Peter Betsworth started to explain. "If there were always rules to follow, we would be machines, and we are not. The general rule, of course, is that we are here to protect the state."

"But when the state is the problem," Stacy interrupted, "or at least when some people in it are, what then?"

"Well there you have the grey area. There was a famous German called Max Weber who helped draft the Weimar Constitution. It was hoped this fine document would lay the foundations of democracy in Germany after the First World War. Sadly he died in 1920 aged only fifty-six after contracting the so-called Spanish Flu that killed millions of people around the world."

"Nothing the security services could do about that then," remarked Stacy.

"Quite so," conceded Peter Betsworth, mildly irritated by her interruption. "Now one of the things Weber argued – and by the way, he is considered a co-founder of sociology, along with Émile Durkheim and Karl Marx – was that authority could be categorized into three broad types: charismatic – you submit to someone's authority because you are attracted by his persona; traditional – you submit to someone's authority because he embodies the familiar order of the past as in divinely-ordained kingship; or rational-legal – you submit to someone's authority because rational laws oblige you to."

"I don't know about Mr Durkheim," Stacy interrupted again,

"but I hope he was less wrong than Karl Marx proved to be!"

"I am coming to that," pleaded her boss, unable to suppress a laugh. "Now Max Weber suggested that to run efficiently the state needed a bureaucracy which would operate purely on the basis of rational-legal authority: no cronyism, no corruption, no personal empire building."

"I'd like to see an organization without any of that!" Stacy protested.

"Which is exactly the point I am trying to make. Take marriage for example: its authority is traditional, but the persona of the male and the female determines its particular character, even as each party abides by certain rational and legal rules which appear to make sense to both. But you tell me what marriage does not have grey areas!"

"Or what relationship," conceded Stacy.

"OK. Now we are on the same page," Peter Betsworth noted with evident relief. "The security service is bound by rational-legal rules and these you were taught during training. But contrary to what Weber hoped, it is absolutely impossible for any organ of the state to be politically neutral. In its purest Weberian form, a bureaucracy is simply an instrument of politics, as the bureaucratic path to the gas chambers in his then-blighted country proved to be."

"But you can't have everyone acting for themselves," asserted Stacy. "That would produce chaos."

"Exactly," Peter Betsworth agreed. "That is the other extreme. Now as a general rule, companies, armies, bureaucracies – any organization in fact – can only function if those individuals who populate it follow its rules. The 'grey area' enters the picture because every organization is held together by a vision of its purpose which those both inside it and outside it hold in their heads. And unless it is purely mechanical, like a car, there exists no set of rules which can ensure, absolutely, that its 'purpose' will be fulfilled.

"Our vision of hospitals, for example, is that they exist to cure ills and save lives. That is what people inside and outside expect them to do. However, if they are put to some other political purpose, are poorly led and badly structured, or are populated by individuals without the requisite skills and equipment, they will start to lose internal cohesion and external credibility. In short, they will fail."

"I think I might know a hospital like that," said Stacy.

"Sadly, so might I," agreed Peter Betsworth. "Now, Stacy, if you cast your mind back to the 1970s you will recall that the country was functioning very poorly. Large swathes of industry were nominally under government control. This meant that steel mills, mining operations and automobile plants were no longer in existence because someone wanted to purchase their products. They were part of government with a claim against the public purse which their unions and to some extent even their managers, were more than happy to exploit. This led to rampant inflation, because governments virtually printed money to pay the bills, and horrendous inefficiencies because the link between what these organizations did and their customers had been utterly corrupted.

"You might be surprised if I told you, Stacy, how many individuals in the then-Labour government, in the nationalized industries and even in the unions concluded, privately, that the structures they found themselves with had become wholly dysfunctional. We saw our job, in the security services, as trying to facilitate a major change, ideally through the democratic process, even though that same process got us into the mess in the first place.

"So how about that, for a grey area?" he laughed. "A rational-legal bureaucracy that had become irrational and possibly even illegal, but certainly conflicted, requiring a personality strong enough to put it right and traditional enough, in the democratic sense, to be accepted."

"So we really were trying to protect the country?" Stacy said, with noticeable satisfaction.

"Yes we were, and still are."

"But things seem to be in a terrible mess all over again," she protested. "Just a different sort of mess."

Peter Betsworth simply shrugged. He disliked what was going on as much as everyone.

"Are you going to tell your John?" he asked after a while.

"I think I must if we're going to get anywhere," she answered.

He clasped his hands in front of his face. For close on a minute he sat there in deep concentration while Stacy turned over in her head everything he had said.

"I have been thinking of making him permanent, not just a paid informer. Do you imagine he would be interested?"

"Yes, he might. He knows he would be a marked man inside any union if his cover was ever blown."

"Quite," he acknowledged. And then after a further pause he said, "It's probably best that you tell him now that you've taken yourself off his case. At least that's natural. He should be flattered you've fallen for him."

"Grey areas," mused Stacy.

"Life is full of them," he said, "which is why each of us needs that still, small voice of calm some call God."

"Dear Lord and Father of Mankind," she quoted. "It was one of my mother's favourites."

As they parted company, Peter Betsworth felt a glow of satisfaction. Stacy was his recruit. He liked her.

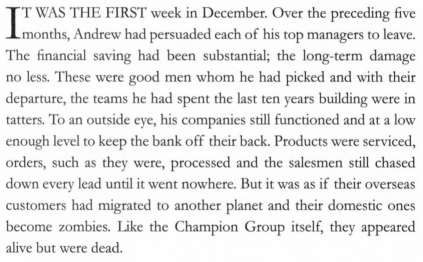

*C*HAPTER 26

I T WAS THE FIRST week in December. Over the preceding five months, Andrew had persuaded each of his top managers to leave. The financial saving had been substantial; the long-term damage no less. These were good men whom he had picked and with their departure, the teams he had spent the last ten years building were in tatters. To an outside eye, his companies still functioned and at a low enough level to keep the bank off their back. Products were serviced, orders, such as they were, processed and the salesmen still chased down every lead until it went nowhere. But it was as if their overseas customers had migrated to another planet and their domestic ones become zombies. Like the Champion Group itself, they appeared alive but were dead.

As for himself, he was exhausted. For two years he had been fighting the steepest downturn in living memory and what made it worse, the severity of the downturn was his own government's doing. Inflation *was* coming down and union monopolies *were* being smashed, but as strategies went, this one seemed no more intelligent than solving an urban overcrowding problem by lining up half the population and having it shot. Still, he knew it was a conceit to imagine that the men and women his companies employed wouldn't be able to survive without him. They would. It was time to call a halt.

The appointment of a liquidator was distressingly straightforward, like summoning the undertakers when Great-Aunt Molly has finally passed. Andrew then visited each of his companies to tell his people the game was up. Fighting back tears, he was barely able to look them in the eye. Some had been with him from the start. A few days later came the creditors meeting. Like the reading of a will, guaranteed to disappoint one and all, those owed money were asked to register their claim in the certain knowledge it would not be fully met. Liquidators must sell things for what they can get, not for what they might be worth tomorrow. The biggest loser, as it turned out, would be The Royal Bank whose half-hearted paperwork left it exposed as an unsecured creditor. Feeling full of shame, Andrew sat alongside the liquidator and marvelled at the politeness of those small traders owed money. Doubtless each one worried that he could be next.

When the company car was driven away from his home, a feeling of utter failure engulfed him. It was over, all over. He smiled at the thought of Freddie Stern looking down at him from wherever Freddie had ended up, not cruelly but wistfully, as if to say, 'Well, it wasn't so easy chum, was it?'

Sitting alone in his front room, he was aware of his heart thumping like a jackhammer. Christ, was this it? Thump, thump, thump! – deafening, like a rain of shells except that the explosions were coming from within, like pistons. He might have sat that way for five minutes, or twenty or even for an hour: he had no sense of time. Then suddenly his head cleared. This was not his moment to die. He still had a wife and children to think of. They would have to sell the house and find somewhere smaller, and he would have to find some other way to make a living. OK. So the world was full of mantraps. Well next time, he'd try not to be so dumb as to get caught up in one.

* * *

To check on the economic pulse of the nation as 1982 got under way, Harvey started his fact-finding odyssey in Aberdeen. What he encountered lifted his spirits considerably. The place was humming with energy and activity, much as he imagined the South Wales valleys had been in the 1750s. The town had almost seamlessly turned from supporting the North Sea fishing industry to doing the same for its new industry built upon the discovery of oil.

Still on the east coast, but an hour or so further south, he found Dundee in a less ebullient mood. In the early part of the previous century there had been as many as sixty-two jute mills and at its height, two hundred ships were built at its docks in a single year. Things were not nearly as bad as they became following the collapse of the jute industry at the start of the twentieth century, but several of the light-engineering companies, lured in from America to soak up the town's then chronic unemployment, had been laying off workers, and people were anxious.

From Dundee he crossed over towards the west coast and stopped in Cumbernauld, a town built from scratch in 1956 as an overspill from Glasgow. There he learned that the Burroughs Corporation, one of America's eight major computer companies, had cut its workforce from 3,000 to 1,600 and planned to cut it by half again.

In complaining that the ideology of the Prime Minister prevented her from intervening when an international company 'was destroying Scottish jobs', the Labour Member of Parliament for West Stirlingshire, Dennis Canavan, deployed a kind of self-serving logic that Harvey frequently encountered. Having been created by the company in the first place, the jobs were hardly the Prime Minister's to give.

If criticism was levelled at where he thought it should be – at the political class as a whole for failing to create an environment in which new jobs were created at the same time as old jobs died – the

MP for West Stirlingshire would find himself as much in the firing line as the Prime Minister. Bearing witness to the Herculean struggle taking place between left and right of the political divide, Harvey increasingly found himself wishing for a plague on both their houses.

From its halcyon days as the Empire's second city, Glasgow itself had fallen far. Britain's decline after the First World War and the Great Depression which followed it brought immense hardship to the city's people, augmented in number by immigrants from its earlier, glory days. In self-defence, many of them had turned to radical socialism. Rearmament in the Second World War brought some respite, but there was no peace dividend. Attempts to revive the city in the 1950s had stalled and a surly mood prevailed, now made worse by high unemployment generally and high youth unemployment in particular.

Wishing to report on manufacturing, he had decided to avoid the coal mines on this trip, and drove straight from Glasgow to Newcastle. Like many of Britain's great conurbations, the city on the Tyne had flowered during the Industrial Revolution, feeding off – and feeding – Britain's imperial reach. Shipbuilding and heavy industry lay behind its now faded prosperity. The adjustment to decline had been no easier for it than for Glasgow. Rising public-sector employment empowered politicians and provided much-needed work, but on the trading estates he visited, the high death rate amongst private companies, many low-margin subcontractors to larger concerns, themselves struggling, was plain to see. Newcastle had also experienced its share of riots when young men without work had lashed out against each other and any buildings that came to hand.

Harvey's trajectory was like the sign of Zorro reflected in a mirror: from right to left, to right and back to left again. If Glasgow was the British Empire's second city outside the capital, Liverpool was its second city, period. The wealth of this metropolis, briefly and depending on how measured, even exceeded that of London itself. The foundation of that wealth was slaves. From its start in the early

1700s to the trade's abolition in 1807, some 1.5 million Africans were transported across the Atlantic in Liverpool vessels. On their outward journey to collect this human cargo, the ships were not empty but carried textiles and other manufactured goods from Manchester and elsewhere in England's industrial heartland.

As a foretaste of what awaited a city that once saw 40% of the world's trade pass through its docks, Liverpool was the Titanic's port of registry. The great Belfast-built ship went down with 1,517 of its passengers and crew on 15th April 1912. Another telling detail was that many of those drowned were seeking a new life in America, just as their forebears had sought out a better life in Liverpool.

Harvey had never visited Merseyside before, but even more than the metal-masters and merchants of Glasgow, where Protestant and Catholic had achieved an uneasy truce, Liverpool held a special fascination for him. The popular music of his generation was forged within the city's crucible. The sorry soulfulness that had flowed across the Atlantic from Africa in Liverpool's ships was picked up, reworked and thrown back by Bill Haley, Fats Domino and Elvis Presley, to mutate again through the prisms of LSD and preludin, into the complex, lyrical beauty of Strawberry Fields Forever. The music's high priest was unquestionably that tormentor of perceived wisdom, John Lennon, whose simple song 'Imagine' so offended America's religious right.

But all that had been in the 1960s. In early 1982 the people of the city could only immortalize the Cavern Club, where their home-grown heroes had cut their teeth, and mourn the loss of their greatest son who had been shot outside his apartment in New York just over a year before. Containerization had finished off their docks in the 1970s and now they had to contend with a brutal recession which was pushing unemployment in the city towards 17%. Riots in Liverpool's inner city district of Toxteth had equalled those in London's Brixton, even prompting the Prime Minister to visit the area in her black Jaguar.

She was pelted with tomatoes and toilet rolls and never returned.

As this visceral hatred permeated Liverpool's politics, Harvey found that moderation's demise was creating space for the Trotskyist faction Militant, and its figurehead, Derek Hatton, to establish themselves. In time, by taking on unfunded debt while living high on the hog, this man and his movement would wreak as much damage on the city as their nemesis. It seemed to the journalist that extremes bred extremes: that when consensus failed, raw energy searched for new concepts, new ideas, around which to coalesce. The battle for power between ideas was emotional. Its rationality came later when one idea prevailed and a fresh consensus formed.

The misfortune, it seemed to him, lay in what America's war planners euphemistically called the collateral damage of the process. He had read that the German philosopher Friedrich Nietzsche saw life as a tragic struggle between chaos and order, where order was the imposition of a great will that would always be overtaken by events. If Britain came though the hardship he was witnessing, would the consensus then be Thatcherite? He supposed so. But as Nietzsche also suggested, consensus without curiosity for truth would engender a shallow land.

From Liverpool he drove south to Birmingham before his return to London. In November, British Leyland's now 58,000 strong workforce (down from 250,000 at its peak) had gone on strike over pay. The company seemed to symbolize everything that had gone wrong with British industry since the Second World War. When Clement Atlee's great reforming government took the coal industry into public ownership and created the National Health Service, succeeding socialist administrations seemed uncertain whether industry was a business to be run for profit or a branch of the social services to be kept on a tight leash by the UK Treasury.

Thirteen years after Morris and Austin merged in 1952 to form the British Motor Corporation, BMC purchased Pressed Steel. This company made the bodies for Britain's remaining car manufacturers. From thirty-four British-owned registered car-makers in 1950, most had been absorbed into British Leyland, a colossus created after BMC, now called British Motor Holdings, was merged with Leyland Motors in 1968 to create the second largest motor manufacturing company outside North America. The creator of this monstrous enterprise (taken into full public ownership in 1975) was the socialist, Tony Benn, a man more interested in the exercise of workforce democracy, under his indulgent authority, than in either business or engineering efficiency.

The upshot was an enterprise, shot through with inter-brand rivalries, whose management was shared by shop-floor unions, a government minister, the UK Treasury and professional administrators (one could hardly call them managers) who reported to the government like civil service officials. It seemed to Harvey that a structure less likely to succeed would have been hard to conceive. To use the German philosopher's parlance, this was disorder onto which a powerful vision needed to be imposed.

Short of running the show herself, Harvey could understand why Margaret Thatcher had not stopped Michael Edwards, the South African chief executive appointed by her desperate predecessors to thrust a stake through the heart of the Frankenstein monster they had created, from chopping up the cobbled-together body and selling off its parts to whoever would buy them. But it was a poor advertisement for his nation's collective intelligence. Collateral damage was everywhere. The road to hell *was* paved with good intentions.

In a state of despondency, he thought he would look in on Andrew Champion before heading home. Surely his favourite entrepreneur would have some good news to report not linked to North Sea oil?

* * *

"Excuse me. I'm looking for the Champion Group?"

Harvey's question was met with a blank stare from the woman coming out of the next door office.

"I think they've moved," she said. "There's been no one for several weeks now."

"Do you know where they've moved to?" he asked.

"No, I am afraid not," she replied, hurrying away. "I think they had a factory on the trading estate."

"Yes, I know it," he called after her.

"Good luck!" she called back.

Only when the woman was gone and he had given up searching for signs of life did her 'had' rather than 'have' come back at him like indigestion. The stack of unopened mail outside the door concerned him. He was growing accustomed to the signs.

Round at the factory, everything seemed normal as he lifted up the telephone in reception and said to the voice on the other end that he was looking for Andrew Champion. He could hear sounds of busyness coming from inside and felt relieved. But his relief was short-lived.

"Can I help you?" The young man asking the question looked disoriented and nervous.

"Yes, I am looking for Andrew Champion," Harvey said again.

"He's not with us anymore."

"How do you mean? Has he died?"

"You could say that," the man answered, passing the side of his hand across his throat in a slicing motion.

"But this is his company," Harvey asserted.

"Not any more it isn't," he said. "It's the liquidator's."

"Oh hell," gasped Harvey. "When did this happen?"

"Before Christmas. It really shook us. We thought he had this thing licked and then there he was telling us it was all over."

"Do you know where I can find him?"

"No."

"So what's happening to all of you?" Harvey asked.

"We're being wound down. There's just a handful of us left."

"But the business, what's happened to the business?"

"I don't rightly know," he said, "but the service side was bought for a song, I heard, and our designs too."

"Do you know by who?"

"Some foreign outfit I believe," the young man said with obvious disgust. "Now if you'll excuse me…"

"Of course," acknowledged Harvey as he watched the young man disappear back through the door to the factory floor, leaving him alone in reception. So that was it.

On the way home, he couldn't get Queen's song 'Another one bites the dust' out of his head. How many thousand was that now? Was anyone even counting? '...... *another one gone, and another one gone, another one bites the dust.*'

And because he had got to know Andrew Champion, this one felt personal.

* * *

Back home, he ignored Aberdeen and punched out his piece about the trail of devastation he had encountered under the headline *There Has To Be a Better Way!*

Change, he wrote, *was a constant but to leave things entirely to Schumpeter's creative destruction was surely no better than allowing vested interests to resist change until the artificial dam they constructed to hold back the inevitable burst, as it now had, flooding innocent and guilty alike.*

He marvelled at the hubris of men who imagined that whole industries could be run by politicians, bureaucrats and union organizers, none of whom were accountable to the one party that mattered – the customer.

He wrote, too, about the communities which had grown up around single activities left largely in the lurch like jilted husbands when the industries that created them bolted for pastures new. Were these transitions not inevitable? Could they not have been foreseen? Rather than attempting to prop up what was failing, should these industries not have been taxed in the good times to fund alternative activities when the bad times came round?

Within the government, only Michael Heseltine, the Environment Secretary, seemed to be attempting this with his enterprise zones, Harvey reported, but it was – as always – too little too late. *And in any event,* he wrote, *according to unnamed sources, the Secretary was regarded by the Prime Minister as a competitor and a* wet, *even though he had been a remarkably successful businessman before becoming a politician, so his efforts were tolerated rather than cheered.*

* * *

George Gilder let his piece stand without alteration. It was clear the great editor was starting to question his own judgment, so alarmed had he become at the state of the nation and plummeting support for the government. Opinion polls indicated that the new SDP-Liberal Alliance was now supported by 50% of the electorate. As a further indication of editorial discomfort, George Gilder even referred to him by his Christian name: 'It's all a bloody mess, Harvey, it truly is!'

The Sentinel's political editor supposed that when two men were walking together along the road to perdition, a little extra intimacy was appropriate. After the accounting was finally complete, a year or two later, it would reveal that around 2 million manufacturing jobs had been lost, most never to return.

C HAPTER 27

HARVEY hurried into *The Sentinel* building as he was running late for one of George Gilder's power lunches, as the great editor liked to call his regular get-togethers with the good and not-so-good. He needn't have worried. The only other guest was just moments ahead of him. Peter Betsworth had come to check on the heartbeat of the Fourth Estate.

"Good article," he said looking across at Harvey as they started on the soup. 'There has to be a better way, although I'm damned if I know what it is.'

Momentarily pleased, Harvey then suspected the compliment might have come from the intelligence officer's left hand.

"Things really are pretty bad, Peter," George insisted. "We'll soon be a nation of shopkeepers again."

"Wasn't that how Napoleon saw us?" Harvey proffered.

"Yes, although I think it was more to contrast us with the land-based economies of Central Europe that he had so easily conquered than to cause offense," George explained.

"Adam Smith certainly didn't think shopkeepers could build an empire," Peter added, "but he did think an empire-building government should be informed by their views. After all, what's the point of an empire but to provide a flow of raw materials in one direction and customers in the other?"

"Glasgow made a fortune importing tobacco from American planters and selling them manufactured luxuries, often on credit," said Harvey: "a triple profit! And Liverpool grew rich shipping Africans to the Americas and textiles to Africa."

"Those were the days," mused Peter. "All I read in your paper now is about how much of our manufacturing capacity has been closed or sold off to foreigners."

"You read it because that's what's happening," countered George testily. "It's looking like the aftermath of a war out there; isn't that right, Harvey?"

"In most places away from the capital, that is exactly how it looks," agreed Harvey, pleased that his surname seemed at last to have been abandoned. He missed 'Mudd!' though, and suspected it was in hibernation until George Gilder had regained his confidence. "You can always go to Aberdeen for a burst of optimism," he informed them. "It's all green lights up there. The place is humming."

"Thank heavens for North Sea oil," rhapsodized Peter. "Without it, sterling would be in the can, interest rates through the roof and the government would have had to go cap in hand to the IMF."

"I'm not sure our exporters see it that way," said Harvey, "at least about sterling. Its ludicrously high level crippled them. The government should have lowered interest rates, not lifted them."

"But then we wouldn't have had such a deep recession," declared Peter. "Inflation would still be rising and the unions would still be in the driving seat."

"I see the miners have just accepted a 9.3% pay rise from the Coal Board,' interjected George. "That doesn't sound like union capitulation to me."

"King Arthur's first victory as president of the NUM," mused

Harvey.

"And his last," snapped Peter. "Margaret, I mean the Prime Minister, just couldn't afford another battle at the moment."

With the soup bowls cleared, plates of sliced venison were brought in, served with potatoes dauphinoise and Brussels sprouts, no doubt a hold-out from the festive season.

"Rather good this," prompted George, holding up his glass of wine. "Gruaud Larose '59. If our nation is going to implode, I thought we should at least go out in style."

"Yes, very good, George," agreed Peter, savouring the dark red delight in his glass. "But don't give up on our lady yet. She is trying to unwind decades of poor governance."

"But if unions, management, banks and government can work together in Germany to build up that country's manufacturing capability, why on earth can't we?" asked Harvey.

"Yes, that's a good question," agreed George. "So what's the answer, Peter?"

The intelligence officer pursed his lips. To be bested by anyone, especially the Germans, was not where he liked to be.

"It's not the Anglo-Saxon way," he said eventually.

"What on earth do you mean by that, Peter?" George asked.

"I mean we like our freedoms. We don't like being organized. We're just not corporatist and neither are the Americans."

"But at least the Americans seem to get through these things quicker," posited Harvey.

"Not in the 1930s they didn't," said George.

"And that was because their central bank cut the money supply at just the wrong time," asserted Peter. "Our problem is that since the war we have been neither fish nor fowl – part-socialist, part-market-driven, the absolute worst of all worlds."

"Leave it to the market then, Adam Smith's invisible hand?" elicited George.

"Well," answered Peter, "if you are going to be corporatist you had better know where you are going and how to get there, and you absolutely must have everyone on board. But if you think life is exploratory and creative then market mechanisms are a far more powerful tool than grey suits and cloth caps trying to decide the future."

"Governments must still plan and think strategically, surely?" urged Harvey.

"Of course they should," agreed Peter, "but they must recognize their limitations too. Are politicians scientists, or engineers, or business managers? Only if they couldn't make it in those fields. And can a civil service populated by intelligent men and women with liberal arts degrees run entire industries? I think not. The socialist impulse to make everything better – and let's give it the benefit of the doubt here – is laudable. But a great deal of complexity lies between a wish and its fulfilment. This government is attempting to roll back decades of muddled thinking and reinstate the disciplines of the marketplace. It took us thirty years to get into this hole. This government has a lot less time than that to get us out of it."

"The opinion polls are looking awful," George pointed out. "If there was an election today she'd be out on her ear."

"That's where you boys come in," stressed Peter. "You must talk things up, not down."

"There's precious little to talk up at the moment," complained George. "That's the trouble."

"I think it was Joseph Goebbels who said that propaganda should be popular not intellectually pleasing," Harvey remarked.

"Ah!" extolled George. "Another fine German example!"

Peter shifted uneasily in his chair.

"Well you know what I mean," he said.

"No, I'm not sure that I do," George challenged, much to Harvey's delight. "We are not an organ of the state. We are fallible searchers for the truth."

"With a very particular political bent," countered the intelligence officer. "Don't tell me that you haven't shaded a story to flatter your point of view."

"So we are back to that old question – what is truth?" George laughed. "What do you think truth is, Mudd?"

The editor was clearly feeling better. Whether induced by the wine or the conversation, who could know.

"Well all I can say, in answer to that," said Harvey, "is that I have seen an awful lot of people around the country who are suffering. That is a simple truth. A more complex truth is how it came to this. But if we could agree on ends and not be ideologically fixated with particular means, we might do better. It's like watching a Catholic priest and a Protestant minister debating the value of last rites while a man lies dying at their feet."

"Your man's becoming too sophisticated for this line of work, George," Peter chortled. "It sounds to me as though he is also developing a conscience!"

"Which is why he is becoming a first-rate journalist," responded George with the fierce protectiveness of a mother hen. "Now, Peter, can we offer you some coffee?"

The Sentinel had closed ranks.

* * *

Harvey left the meeting buoyed up by the gastronomic ambience he had enjoyed and yet forlorn at the state of things. He felt like a man who had savoured one last banquet before an advancing army overwhelmed his city. He called Suzie. As luck would have it she had no pressing engagements that day either and felt the same need as he to blot out everything inside one wholly absorbing moment.

They arrived at her apartment simultaneously. She struggled with her key as he pulled at the zip of her tight-fitting black skirt with one hand and pulled out the white silk blouse she was wearing under her black jacket with the other.

"Stop it!"

"No!"

They tumbled inside, just managing to close the door before a neighbour crossed the landing from an adjoining flat.

"Just a minute," she said as the skirt and jacket fell to the floor.

He followed her, hopping out of his trousers with the grace of a one-legged kangaroo.

Suzie sat, her tights and pants around her ankles, and ran her tongue over his offering. Harvey listened to the hiss and shuddered at the sensation. He pulled her head back, freeing himself and pushed his hand between her thighs, catching the last drops while kissing the mouth that had just pleasured him like an eager wildcatter drilling for oil.

There was a certain violence between them. It was as if they wished to reduce their encounter to one that was utterly primal, without affection, without emotion of any kind save for the desire to express an overwhelming urge to conjoin and be done with it. They were like animals whose normal solitary nature has been interrupted by the need to procreate, except that procreation was the last thing on these human minds.

Her face, reflected in the mirror above the washstand, looked almost pained as he drove into her again and again, staring, with a ferocity indistinguishable from anger, searching for a sign of submission only his instincts would recognize while his hands bore down on her shoulders to prevent any escape. But she had no wish to. She was where she needed to be, lost in the moment.

Suddenly he pulled away and she fell limp across the counter, sobbing. Both knew their marriage of convenience was at an end.

Later, as he was about to leave, having dressed with what he hoped had not been unseemly haste, she followed him to the door.

"That was a side of you I have not seen before," she said, her tone hinting at something inside herself newly discovered which she would revisit. "We'll see each other again?"

"Why not?" he answered and left, knowing they would not.

CHAPTER

IN THE THIRD week of March, Argentine soldiers landed on the British island of South Georgia, a remote and largely uninhabited territory in the South Atlantic, once used for whaling. A fortnight later, and taken completely by surprise, the British Falkland Islands Government surrendered to Argentinean troops. Located some 300 miles from the South American coast, and almost 1,000 miles northwest of South Georgia, the Falkland Islands had long been claimed by Argentina even though it was the British who had colonized them in the 1840s. A day after the surrender, a Royal Navy task force set sail from Portsmouth to the Falklands, a journey of 7,876 miles. The hastily drawn-up plan called for the ships to be provisioned en route. The British were at war.

From the first moment of hostilities, Sylvia was on the edge of her seat following every twist and turn of the unfolding drama on her little monochrome screen.

"Now you'll see what a woman can do," she almost sang as the Prime Minister declared a 200-mile exclusion zone around the islands.

When a party of Royal Marines recaptured South Georgia at the end of April, and a week later a Vulcan bomber from Ascension

Island made the 8,000-mile round trip to bomb Port Stanley Airport so that it couldn't be used by the Argentine Air Force, being refuelled in mid-air on the way out and on the way back, she was ecstatic.

"The Argies don't stand a chance against Maggie," she whooped when it was announced that the nuclear submarine *HMS Conqueror* had sunk the Argentine battle cruiser the *General Belgrano*.

When *HMS Sheffield* was hit by an Exocet missile and sank a few days later, she was crestfallen.

"Those poor boys," she said, almost weeping when it was reported that the frigate *HMS Antelope* had been torn apart following an unsuccessful attempt to defuse two Argentine bombs which pierced the ship but had initially failed to explode.

Harvey was in and out of *The Sentinel* offices getting updates from their embedded reporter on the scene. The British amphibious landings at San Carlos Water were being relentlessly harried by Argentine fighters. Initially it was hoped to bypass the Argentines' well-defended but largely static encampment at Goose Green, some 13 miles south of San Carlos, and advance directly on Port Stanley, 50 miles to the east. But, with the landings at the beachhead appearing to stall, the government was anxious to demonstrate momentum and a decision was taken to attack Goose Green.

It was late evening on 29th May when Harvey was called into *The Sentinel* office. George Gilder was looking anxious. The first land offensive of the war had been underway for almost 48 hours.

"We're getting reports of casualties, Harvey," George told him as soon as he entered the conference room the great editor had established as his command centre. The use of his Christian name suggested to the journalist that all was not well.

"Have we lost?" Harvey asked.

"No," George replied. "The reports coming in suggest we have won. But it looks as though David Graham might have been killed."

"Frances Graham's husband?" Harvey asked incredulously. "I

didn't know he was involved."

"An SAS unit took part in a softening-up exercise apparently," he explained. "The usual stuff: ludicrous bravery and horribly effective. You knew he was a Special didn't you?"

"I suppose I did," Harvey answered. "But I hadn't really got much beyond him being a Highland chieftain with a great eye for beauty and a low threshold for boredom."

"A typical SAS officer!" George mused. "It seems the battle that followed was a lot tougher than expected. The final count's not in yet," he added, as if recounting a cricket score, "but it looks as though seventeen of our lot were killed and some sixty or so wounded. The Argentines almost certainly lost many more and we have ended up with a thousand of them as prisoners."

"A thousand!" Harvey exclaimed. "It must have been a big encampment."

"Mostly conscripts, we're hearing, who weren't that thrilled to be stuck on a barren island, but they were well dug in and we were outnumbered. Downing Street is cock-a-hoop. There'll be medals for sure, quite a few posthumous, sadly."

"A great comfort to their families," Harvey remarked drily, the image of a distraught Frances Graham welling up inside his head.

"Fighting's what soldiers do, Mudd, and with fighting comes dying."

His editor's gentle rebuke was clear. And of course he was right. But it was politicians who moved the chess pieces taking much of the glory from success and escaping most of the blame when there was failure. Several months later, he learned that Lieutenant-Colonel Piaggi, the Argentine officer who had surrendered after fourteen hours of fierce fighting, when continuing would have been pointless, had been discharged from the army in disgrace. The man he had surrendered to, Major Chris Keeble, who had taken over command after his own officer, Lieutenant-Colonel H. Jones, had been killed in the action, was awarded membership of the Distinguished Service

Order. Sara Jones later accepted her husband's Victoria Cross, awarded for his conspicuous bravery in the face of the enemy, proud that he had helped prevent a small country from being overrun. These were the fortunes of war and perhaps, Harvey thought, of life itself.

* * *

It was after 5.00 a.m. when he eventually left *The Sentinel* offices. The news from the front was in and the blatantly jingoistic front page crafted: *Argentines Trounced – Goose Green and Darwin Liberated!* Inside were pictures of sorry-looking prisoners and residents happy to be free and out of harm's way, along with stories of derring-do which would have sat easily inside any *Boys Own* magazine.

As he walked the largely empty streets, he smiled to himself at the thought of a hard-nosed conservative doing more to discredit a Latin American junta than all the liberal handwringing that had accompanied South America's uneasy path towards democracy. Even Margaret Thatcher's warm relationship with General Pinochet of Chile was pragmatic. She simply admired people who got things done and did them properly. Democracy could be as messy and unproductive as dictatorship could be cruel and fallible. Democracy may have been a terrible system of government although better than all the rest, but he did think too many excuses were made for its failings. It could surely be improved. Even dictators knew how to hide behind a plebiscite, and as the troubles of the 1970s amply illustrated, vested interests within a democracy were no less artful.

He passed two young men staggering back from a late-night party. The girl they were propping up grinned at him and then bent over to be sick. He couldn't get Frances Graham out of his head and tried to persuade himself that he was concerned for her welfare, which he was, but what about his mother's conviction that their inauspicious friendship had a future? In a witch-believing world it would have been said that she had ridden on a broomstick to Goose Bay, transformed herself into an Argentinean soldier and done away with the obstacle to her son's happiness. What rubbish!

As he approached Buttesland Street, tiredness, which the excitement of the night had kept at bay, began to catch up with him. And yet he felt content. His work was going well. He was seeing the world more clearly, although that could have been an illusion. His relationship with Suzie had been going nowhere and was over. Now there seemed reason for hope.

Frances Graham! Would a note of condolence be appropriate? Or was that a little formal and working class? He could hardly say nothing. A short note might be better, expressing his concern without assuming too much about their relationship. Something casual, not forced, warm and yet respectful, and then he laughed out loud. How hard was casual? Only when he was outside the door did he notice the light shining through the curtains of the front room. Leaving lights on was not something his mother did.

'Don't forget the lights, Harve,' she would say. 'The electricity company makes enough money without us giving them extra.'

Entering the room, he could see the top of her head above the back of the chair and the cold grey light of the television staring back at him, showing only the test card. His heart muscles became tense and felt fear.

"Mum?" he said as he moved in front of her, only to find her head bent back, her mouth open and her eyes staring up at the ceiling like a loon. He reached down for the spot on her neck where one was supposed to feel a pulse, but felt only a clammy cold. He quickly went back to the hall and started to dial for an ambulance – but stopped halfway, replacing the receiver.

Back in the living room, he closed her eyes and sat down in a chair opposite. The familiar sounds of the house were strangely reassuring. He could pretend that nothing had changed. The wheels of death would start turning soon enough: ambulance, hospital, death certificate, funeral arrangements, the funeral itself, replying to letters of condolence, sorting through her things, the will – he knew what that contained; they'd written it together, probate, wondering what to do with the house, adjusting to life without her. For what remained of the night he simply wanted to be alone with the person who had been the mainstay of his life for thirty-five years.

And who was this person, or who had this person been? She was the child who had sat on her father's knee listening to tales of The Great War. She was the twenty-two-year-old who had sat by her parents' radio listening to the Prime Minister's gravelly voice urging his countrymen 'to fight on until the curse of Hitler is lifted from the brows of men'. She was the young woman in the audience with her fiancé to hear Carmen performed at the Royal Opera House in Covent Garden, the company's first operatic production since the war. She was the mother holding a Union Jack who had been waiting in the Mall, undeterred by terrible weather, to cheer the Queen on as she passed by towards her coronation. She had become a widow; she had worked to sustain herself; she had brought up her son, never once complaining about life's injuries, because for her, life's blessings had always seemed greater.

Harvey tried to remember his father, but beyond the photograph lovingly placed above the mantel, he couldn't. He remembered the funeral. He knew that his father had been a hard-working, decent man, because that is what Sylvia told him.

'Your father was a good man, Harvey, a good provider.' How many times had he heard those words? Looking back he realized they had been offered up as an incantation against his own moments of idleness. But the man himself? Whenever he attempted to look back, it was his mother's presence he encountered. He smiled, recollecting the ceremony in Oxford's Bodleian Library where he had received his degree with his mother standing so proud telling anyone within earshot, 'That's Harvey Mudd, my son!'

He had come to realize that those of his university acquaintances of a socialist persuasion would have regarded his mother's ideas as unsophisticated and simple. And perhaps they *were* simple. Her two core beliefs were that deeds counted for more than words and that to give up responsibility for oneself was to accept a form of slavery. While left-wing radicals talked loudly about saving mankind, she would be round at a neighbour's house helping out. It was not that she thought men shouldn't organize to protect themselves – that was what a nation was for, after all – but to sell one's soul to the devil, to union bosses, or to national politicians in return for promises of succour, well that, for Sylvia, was a blank cheque too far. She admired the sentiments behind the welfare state, created after the Second World War, but remained acutely suspicious of its implementation.

'You mark my words, Harvey,' she told him, more than once, 'if it is left to politicians, they'll just try to bribe us with our own money. It will end badly.'

Had she studied economics, Harvey thought, she would have added 'and better still, try to bribe us with our children's children's money', until that great Ponzi scheme was exposed for the fraud it was. Her sophistication lay in an implicit belief that life was about what individuals did to and for each other. Institutions were essential means to specific ends, but never a substitute for that. Had his mother lived long enough she would have understood exactly what Margaret Thatcher meant when she said there was no such thing as society, only individual men and women and their families, even if more sophisticated commentators would feign otherwise.

He must have dozed off because suddenly he became aware of sunlight streaming though the curtains and the smell of death permeating the room. He got up, kissed his mother on the forehead and went to the hall to call an ambulance, dabbing tears from his eyes. Life was for the living, not the dead.

Part Three

C*HAPTER*

IT WAS 1983. Since his compact with the security service and break-up with Miranda de Coursey, Jack Pugh had become an increasingly bitter man. He had seen the financier's daughter once since Oxford. She had taken him on holiday with her to the French Riviera where he had wallowed in the luxury that surrounded her, only to be humiliated in front of her friends and dismissed at the end with the crushing rebuff: 'when it comes right down to it, Master Trotsky, you are nothing, not even a good fuck. I don't really want to see you again.' MI5 appeared to have dropped him, too. More than ever, he was convinced that the system was rotten to the core and had thrown himself behind Arthur Scargill, elected president of the National Union of Mineworkers by a landslide in 1981.

To make matters worse, Margaret Thatcher, buoyed up by her victory over the Argentines, had been returned to power in June, winning a majority of one hundred and forty-four seats in the House of Commons with only 42% of the popular vote, against a hopelessly divided opposition. From demon to demigod in the space of a few months! If that didn't illustrate the false consciousness that underpinned democracy, he didn't know what did. Voting was little more than a sham in support of the status quo and financiers like Sebastian de Coursey. The right had shown all the daring. That had to change.

He strode into the room, accompanied by John Preston. This was the fourth meeting he had addressed that day. In spite of their working relationship, he wasn't close to his colleague. The man toiled hard enough for the cause, but rarely stayed for the late night 'put the world to rights' sessions he so much enjoyed. Jack reasoned that not everyone could have his intellect and besides, armies needed their foot soldiers.

"Brothers!" he called out. His customary greeting was met with nods and grunts, and sometimes silence, depending on the mood of those being addressed. On this occasion, the sounds were warm and supportive. The NUM had secured a substantial pay rise and a promise of no immediate pit closures from the first Thatcher Government. Now, with their champion, Arthur Scargill, in charge, the men were starting to feel invincible.

"As you know, in March of this year, Margaret Thatcher" – he had learned to fairly spit out the words *Margaret* and *Thatcher*, eliciting the desired murmur of disapproval – "appointed Ian MacGregor to head up the National Coal Board. I have been finding out about this man and, brothers, we have Thatcher in trousers, or possibly a kilt – he is a Scot.

"He was born in 1912, in Kinlochleven, some two hours north of Glasgow. His father was an accountant at the nearby aluminium plant and his mother a teacher – so the MacGregors were a bourgeois family to the tips of their fingers."

Not much imbued with Marxist theory, the bourgeois reference was largely lost on his audience, but Jack had become used to that. His job was to lead the proletariat, not educate it.

"Young MacGregor studied metallurgy at Glasgow University," he continued, "and then joined his father at the plant. But Ian had ambition and was soon recruited as a junior manager by William Beardmore and Company at their Parkhead forge making vehicle armour. It was there he had his first run-in with organized labour, seeing off a strike by crane drivers when he actually drove the cranes himself. A super-scab from the word go! Naturally the chairman of the company was impressed, and Ian's career has been on an upward trajectory ever since. The ruling class supports its own."

By now his audience was quite impressed with the Coal Board's new chairman and a few even wished that their sons could do as well. One thing Jack Pugh did not mention, doubtless because he didn't know it, was that, from its foundation in 1894, British Aluminium, where MacGregor had cut his teeth, was increasingly run as an arm of the state, supported by highland landowners. As the importance of its product to aircraft manufacture in the First and Second World Wars increased, its relationship with government grew closer. The statist model, implicitly endorsed by Jack Pugh, had served the country well in wartime, but had produced nothing but rigid inefficiencies afterwards and it was these that Mrs Thatcher was attempting to unwind. So, youthful communist agitator though he might have been, Jack was actually an arch conservative. What drove him, however, was not a love of the past, but his ill-disciplined frustration at not being central to the present.

"At the start of the Second World War, MacGregor went to work for the Ministry of Supply," Jack elaborated, "travelling to the United States and Canada on procurement missions. So, as you can see, his relationship with government goes back a long way."

The irony that the career moves he was describing could as easily have been applied to a communist apparatchik was quite lost on Jack and hadn't even occurred to his audience who were more concerned with such bourgeois issues as the size of their pay packet and the security of their employment.

"Our man remained in America after the war and became known, brothers, for his aggressive tactics against organized labour."

Recognizing that the word 'brother' was their cue to participate, a rumble of disgust spread around the room and Jack looked fulfilled.

"In 1977, it was Prime Minister James Callaghan, a union man himself who should have known better, who brought MacGregor back to this country as the number two to that South African snake Michael Edwards, at British Leyland. But after helping to get rid of our esteemed brother, Derek Robinson, he left."

There were a few gasps. Red Robbo had become an icon.

"As Secretary of State for Industry, it was our Prime Minister's intellectual guru, Keith Joseph, who appointed MacGregor chairman of British Steel. Well you all know what happened there!"

This evoked widespread murmurs, as to some degree or other, everyone did.

"When he arrived in 1980, British Steel employed one hundred and sixty-six thousand people and was producing fourteen million tons of steel a year. When he left early this year to become chairman of our Coal Board, there were seventy-one thousand people employed and less than twelve million tons being produced."

There were gasps across the room. The parallels with their own industry were clear. Few were sufficiently good at mathematics to see that if employment had fallen by 57% and output by 14%, productivity had improved dramatically and Jack was not about to point this out. Neither did he intend to mention that when MacGregor arrived, British Steel was losing £1.8 billion annually and that when he left the loss had been cut to £265 million.

"Can you imagine what this did to the steel communities?" he shouted instead. "Yes, it has utterly devastated them. That, brothers, is what capitalism does to you. That is what we must resist!"

John Preston watched from the side as the men in the room fell squarely behind their organizer, clapping enthusiastically as much to counter their fear of the future as to congratulate Jack Pugh. Who was fooling whom? Hadn't Joseph Stalin's forced collectivization of farms in the Soviet Union resulted in the death of millions? It sure as hell wasn't just capitalism that could make people's lives a bloody misery.

* * *

The girl at the bar didn't seem to be attached to anyone and Jack felt like company. He had agreed to have a drink with John Preston and his girlfriend, after their last meeting of the day in Barnsley. The crowd had been enthusiastic. This was Scargill country.

"My friends and I wondered if you'd care to join us?" he asked as he stood at the bar waiting for their drinks.

The girl looked at him and then towards the table he had come from.

"Yes, why not," she said.

"What are you drinking?"

"Shandy," she answered.

"And could you add a shandy?" Jack called across to the barman who had already earned his respect by recognizing him as the speaker earlier at the Cortonwood Institute.

"Great talk, by the way," the barman said as he handed Jack the tray of beverages.

"Thank you," Jack acknowledged, gathering up the tray with aplomb and guiding his catch back to their table, although it was unclear who had caught whom.

"Mona Dexter," the young woman announced, leaning over and shaking hands with John and Stacy.

As Mona slid into the booth next to Stacy, her already short black dress crunched up like a compressed accordion before she managed to pull it back down again. Jack felt immediately aroused in the way of a bee attracted to pollen inside a flower. There was just something about white knickers next to brown skin.

"So what was your talk about?" Mona asked after everyone had been introduced.

"You are in the presence of *the* union organizer," Stacy eulogized, knowing that any such introduction would have stuck in John's throat. "Jack travels round the country motivating the members and explaining the big picture."

Instantly John's girlfriend went up in the organizer's estimation and for a moment he imagined a threesome. But then there was John to consider and he certainly didn't fancy making it four.

"Explaining how the mining life is under threat, mostly," he told Mona, with uncharacteristic modesty, "and that miners had to stand firm against this evil government."

"So are you a miner then?" she asked.

Luckily Jack did not spot John Preston's smirk as the organizer told his new disciple that only someone like him, with a true Marxist understanding, could explain to the miners how they were being manipulated and describe to them the nature of the forces they were up against.

"We must engage in permanent revolution," he told her, "and not allow the social democratic charade, so beloved of the bourgeoisie, to distract us from our objective. I am at the coalface of ideas each and every day," he explained, adding with a theatrical flourish: "I am, indeed, a miner!"

"How wonderful," expostulated Mona as John Preston almost choked on his beer and Stacy had to lift a napkin to hide her mirth.

"Well, just this 'un an' we'd best be off," said John. "It's a two hour drive ter Longbridge. You comen' wi' us, Jack, or are you stayin' here tonight?"

"The union's booked me a room in the Bull, so I guess I'll stay here."

"That's a shame," complained Mona, "I've hardly got to know

you people before you're off."

"Oh, I'm sure Jack will make up for us," said Stacy.

"Yer can be sure o' that!" added John.

"At least I might be able to enjoy a sensible discussion tonight with this intelligent lady," Jack protested, which John and Stacy both knew meant treating Mona to one of his political monologues and then attempting to bamboozle her into bed with fancy words.

The four talked on until their glasses were empty and the travellers left. Jack wasted no time in suggesting he and Mona continue their drinking at The Bull, which was more intimate and conducive to discussion, he said, and only a short walk away. Mona did not need persuading as she had already decided how the evening was going to end.

"They just don't understand," the organizer protested as they huddled together in a corner of The Bull bar with a fresh round of drinks.

"What don't they understand, Jack?" Mona asked.

"How capitalism works," he said. "If you've got the money, you call the shots, you see. And what do the people with money want? They want more money. So what do they do? They pay their workers as little as possible to maximize their profits."

"Who'd be a worker, then?" quipped Mona.

"Just about everyone without capital," Jack told her, his irritation that she did not appear to be taking his revelation seriously tempered by his desire.

"That's what you're here for, Jack, to explain things to the workers."

"Yes, that's true. But it's really the whole system we want to tear down. And all these bloody workers want is higher wages and jobs for life. They are so damn bourgeois!"

"Well I wouldn't mind more money," said Mona, "although I'm not sure I'd want a job for life. How boring would that be!"

"Unless power is taken from the owners of capital and transferred to the people, they will always be slaves."

"So if everyone has a little and no one has a lot," questioned Mona, "who gets to make the decisions?"

"The party does, for the people."

"So we become slaves to the party rather than to capital?" she asked.

"But the party works for the people. Capital just works for itself."

"Well, you've clearly thought it all out, Jack. I wish I had your brains."

That was just what Jack needed to hear. There were not enough people like Mona able to grasp the essentials.

"How close are you to Arthur Scargill?" she asked.

Jack pressed two fingers together. "That close," he said, exaggerating, but how was she to know?

"Will there be strikes ahead?" Mona asked.

"When Arthur thinks the time is right."

"When will that be?" she asked.

"When he's got the membership behind him. People are not riled up enough yet. As soon as the government starts closing pits. That'll do it."

"Then what?"

"Then we bring down this fascist government."

"That sounds exciting," she purred, moving closer.

"Another drink?" he asked, "or shall we go upstairs?"

It was always a tense moment in a man's life when he revealed his intentions. That was when courtship was over and rejection hovered overhead like an ugly bird, ready to pounce. But Mona had no intention of rejecting him. She had a job to do.

"I thought you'd never ask," she said.

Upstairs Mona slipped into the bathroom only to come out and find the organizer perched on the side of the bed in his underwear with tears streaming down his cheeks.

"Heavens, what's the matter?"

"Sorry," he said, his earlier bravado having melted like an early dusting of autumn snow. "I just don't know what I'm doing."

"I rather hoped you were doing me," she said sitting next to him and reaching down to find some life, but he pushed her hand away.

"You're just tired," she told him while stroking the back of his head. "You're doing great things. You know you are."

"Am I?" he protested and she marvelled at how easily grown men could become little boys.

"How many of your talks have you given lately?" she asked.

"Twenty-eight in the last seven days," he told her. "It's as if I'm running for office."

"Well there you are," she comforted. "That would be enough to tire any man."

"I was so certain once," he rambled on. "Provided I spoke eloquently enough, the workers would see sense. They had to. They would withhold their labour, the government would collapse and a new order would rise from the ashes. But instead of that it's all being broken up, shrunk and sold off. Workers strike, here and there, but it's all random and usually for money. And then that woman goes and fights a pointless war thousands of miles away and the country loves her again. It wasn't supposed to be that way."

"It never is," whispered Mona into his ear as she massaged the back of his neck. "Now, let's get under the covers and forget all that."

"I've done things. I don't think I can," he responded mournfully, at which she sunk her teeth into his earlobe.

"Ow! That hurt. Why did you do that?"

She studied his angry face, dug her fingernails hard into his flesh and grinned.

"Damn!" he protested again and nature offered up her answer. Looking down Mona could see that it was still somewhat tentative, but it would do.

Later the following day, after Jack Pugh had returned to Longbridge a reinvigorated man, Mona called Stacy and told her that she didn't think strike action was imminent.

"It will probably take a pit closure before King Arthur feels he can risk it."

CHAPTER

A S THE TRUCK approached Longannet Power Station on the north bank of the River Forth, the early morning sun lit up its tall chimney and bathed its four cooling chambers with a soft orange light. The largest coal-fired station in Europe, it devoured 4.5 million tons of the stuff every year. The crushed coal was conveyed into its four boilers which heated water into a steam that drove four turbines linked to two powerful electricity generators. The charged particles these emitted were fed into a network of conducting wires that carried their energy to every household, factory and appliance bound to them. The steam was then passed across pipes carrying cool water from the Forth to make it condense so that it could be used again and again and again.

Harry greeted the gateman and entered the yard to empty his load. Something of an armchair physicist, he could see a poetry in the place others couldn't. He imagined energy from the sun, that incandescent hydrogen bomb at the centre of our lives, once worshipped, without which we would not exist, being absorbed by plants eventually compressed into coal dug out by men and burned so that the sun's energy could be converted into steam and then into the electricity his wife needed to boil her kettle. The wonder of it!

"The yard's filling up, Bert," he said to the gateman as he headed out.

"The government's no wanting te get cot oot this time, I wouldna' think."

"How much can you hold in here?" Harry asked.

"Twa million ton, gi or tak," Bert informed him. "Guid fi four month or so, depending on the time o' year."

"So you think there will be trouble?"

"Aye, I de. That woman's no' forgiven the miners. She's jest biding her time. McGahey had her number back in eighty-one."

"You're not a Scargill fan then?"

"He talks wiel, he does that. But does he ken what he'll be taking on? I rither doot it." As he said that he nodded towards the deep piles of coal now filling the giant yard like veiled monsters from the dark side.

"I'll see you in the new year then," Harry called out as he pulled away.

"Aye, nay doot," Bert called after him.

From West Thurrock in the South to Willington in the Midlands and Wakefield in the North of England, the yards beside Britain's coal-fired power stations were filling up. Those that could be converted were being adapted to burn oil as well as coal and here and there, extra land was being purchased to provide additional space for deliveries.

* * *

Inside Whitehall, a secret committee had been established to plan for the inevitable confrontation with the miners and had begun its work in the run-up to the general election in June. By the start of 1984, its plans were largely in place, but as the battle approached, there was an air of heightened tension in the government about what lay ahead.

"So you think it should begin in March, Ian?"

"I do. We know the pits we want to close. In fact, the board knew that in eighty-one but the government was not ready for a confrontation. March gives us the full summer to see this through, while power demand is light."

"What's your intelligence, Peter?"

"The NUM President will call a strike as soon as the first closures are announced. Yorkshire will be solid and Scotland too, we think. But the Nottinghamshire miners are paid well and know they have modern pits, so they won't be so keen. But the miners' sense of solidarity is strong. They know they have whole communities behind them."

"Nigel, can we withstand a strike economically?"

"The worst of the recession seems to be behind us, but as you know, unemployment is still close to twelve percent. That's some three million people and if we have a long strike those numbers are not going to get any better."

"But what's it going to do to our GDP?"

"If the strike is contained, perhaps knock it back by anything from half a percent to one percent. But if it spills over to other parts of the economy, that could hurt us badly and affect sterling. At that point, we might be forced to negotiate."

"That is not going to happen. Norman, what pressure could we bring to bear on the strikers?"

"You mean withholding benefits?"

"Yes. The longer this goes on the worse it will be for everyone. We need to bring it to a swift conclusion."

"I'll look into that."

"Is there anything we could do in respect of union assets, Quintin?"

"I rather doubt it. Although, should the NUM not follow its own rules or even act illegally then perhaps their assets could be frozen for a time."

"We should look into that too. And the position in Scotland?"

"That would be a question for the Scottish courts to decide."

"I take it the Secretary of State for Energy is satisfied we have done all we can to maintain power supplies?"

"I believe we now have enough coal stored to cover a six-month strike. But if it goes on for longer that will be difficult, especially if the NUM pickets the power stations. The drivers are unlikely to cross the picket lines."

"Robert, what scale of deliveries might we be talking about?"

"We estimate that moving half a million tons of coal a week from the pitheads to the power stations will involve between four and five thousand lorry journeys a day."

"Can the police stop the drivers being intimidated, Leon? Can we contain the strikers?"

"Our strategy is to use the Metropolitan police where needed. They will not have ties to the local communities and can be relied on to take a firm stand. But we have only around twenty-seven thousand police officers in the Met and the Yorkshire NUM alone has a membership of over sixty thousand, so we need to target our resources carefully."

"Could we use troops to make deliveries, Michael?"

"It is possible and we have made contingency plans, but soldiers are not paid to be strike-breakers or delivery drivers. It is certainly not an optimum solution. And heaven forbid if it should coincide with something they are paid to do."

"Quite."

Everyone round the table had been made aware that this was a confrontation that could not be lost. The Prime Minister had won a war and was not about to be defeated by a strike.

"If I can emphasize one thing?"

"Yes, Home Secretary."

"It seems to me essential that the miners do not win public support. This has to be a battle fought as effectively in the media as it is on the ground."

The chairman of the meeting nodded and fixed on the editor of *The Sentinel* with an unforgiving stare.

"That's you, George."

"Not entirely me, Prime Minister," the editor responded, "but I think we know what is expected of us."

"Good, gentlemen. Then to battle."

* * *

On 5th March, the Coal Board announced the closure of five pits, including those at Cortonwood in Yorkshire and Polmaise in Scotland. The battle had begun.

C*HAPTER* 31

I T WAS ONLY a small article tucked inside *The Sentinel,* but it caught his eye immediately. *Ancient Family Estate Sold,* ran the headline above a piece informing the reader that Graham Castle in the Highlands, together with its land, had been sold to a Scottish transport magnate who had made a fortune buying up deregulated bus companies and welding them together into a successful business. The article explained that the estate's former owner, David Graham, had a number of financial interests which had not yet come to fruition at the time of his death, forcing his executors to crystallize debts that might otherwise have been cleared over time. Harvey looked for mention of Frances Graham but other than recording that she had been David Graham's wife, the report did not elaborate.

He collared the author of the piece who admitted he had lifted most of it from a local newspaper in Inverness and so knew little himself of the background. But with his help, Harvey tracked down Robbie McEwen, the reporter with the *Inverness News* who had broken the story. However, Robbie knew little more than what he had written. He did tell Harvey that it had been a big shock to the local community and that Frances Graham had been well liked, but where she had moved to he 'couldnae rightly say'. Someone had mentioned that she owned a house in London, he thought, but that was hearsay.

* * *

Following the Coal Board's announcement of pit closures, the NUM President had called the miners out on strike. As a result, the jungle telegraph that fed the pressrooms was in overload and Harvey had to put Frances Graham out of his head. George Gilder was firing off instructions to his reporters like a machine gun:

"Find out if the NUM has followed procedures. Get a handle on how popular this strike will be amongst mineworkers and amongst the wider public. I want human interest. I want to know who this strike will hurt. I want you to dig deep and find out how much of the mineworkers' pay is being subsidized by the taxpayer."

Harvey discovered that Arthur Scargill had called the miners out without a national ballot, leaving it to the members in each area 'to defend their jobs as they saw fit'. A precedent had been set, it seemed, by his predecessor, Joe Gormley, in 1982 when the then president allowed the area committees to decide on a scheme to tie wages to area productivity, with or without a regional, let alone a national, vote – a move Scargill considered divisive and opposed, but which the High Court had upheld. And divisive it certainly seemed to be. Harvey's sources told him that the Nottinghamshire miners, who were amongst the best paid in the industry, were the least enthusiastic about a national strike, particularly as none of their highly productive mines were slated for closure.

* * *

On 6th March, the NUM President and his delegation went to the Coal Board's London headquarters for a consultative meeting. There the union was informed by the Coal Board Chairman that not just five, but twenty mines were scheduled for closure over the course of the year, with the probable loss of 20,000 jobs.

The union delegates departed empty-handed and angry, especially as the Coal Board Chairman had taunted them with the observation that 'even some American pits employing females were more productive than several of the pits in Britain. Capacity had to be cut,' he told them. 'Supply must match demand.'

Scargill and his vice-president, Mick McGahey, escaped this bruising encounter certain that they were in a fight to the finish. If the Coal Board Chairman won, there would be no United Kingdom coal mining industry left. The stakes were that high.

* * *

Stacy had admitted to John Preston that when the two had first met, she had been employed to keep an eye on him but had quit the job as soon as the two had become close. She shaved the truth in not telling him that she had been working for the Service as a fully-trained operative. Now that John was one himself and Stacy had been re-engaged with an oversight role 'on his recommendation', the past – at least as it impinged upon their relationship – seemed to have been laid to rest.

As a general rule, Peter Betsworth did not like running couples. The risk of emotional cross-currents getting in the way of the job at hand was just too great. But in this instance, he judged the benefits to be greater than the risks. For a start, Stacy was very good at what she did. Better educated than John Preston, it seemed likely that she would continue to keep part of herself outside the relationship. It was also clear that John Preston admired her, quite apart from finding her physically attractive. And he was becoming increasingly pleased with 'Marx'. While some might have branded the young man a traitor to his class, what Peter Betsworth saw was an individual with a deep dislike of the collectivist mentality and a growing sense that a lot of good men were being led astray by a warped brand of self-serving, political mumbo-jumbo. He looked at his watch. They were late.

* * *

The café near Waterloo Bridge seemed a strange place to meet, but in light of the cold sodden day, both thought it preferable to one of the parks. They had not met with Peter Betsworth together before and felt nervous. Both wondered if this aspect of their clandestine lives would be compatible when brought face-to-face.

The coffee shop was busy. Peter Betsworth was seated in a corner and looked down at his watch as soon as he saw them. OK, so they were a little overdue, but this was London on a rainy day when every taxi seemed to be occupied and the underground choked with damp bodies.

"Sorry we're late, Peter," Stacy said, sensibly offering no explanation.

"Coffee for you?" he invited, and both said yes, pleased to be out of the rain and about to get something warm inside them.

"Well, the start'n pistol's been foired now," John advanced as he emptied several packets of sugar into his brew.

"You've a sweet tooth," remarked Peter.

"Just trained frum birth not ter pass up anythen' free."

"What a shocking day," the intelligence officer then announced, confirming the English obsession with the weather and fondness for stating the obvious about it. "Is there anything new from your end Stacy?"

"It's all a bit chaotic, frankly. Without a national vote, each area has to decide, but they do seem to be coming out."

"Did King Arthur think he'd lose a national vote?"

"I'm not sure. At least my source is not sure. There is a lot of confidence, apparently, but I'm being told that the NUM executive didn't want to broadcast any divisions. Going area by area, with those most in favour, like Yorkshire, South Wales and Scotland coming out in support of a national stoppage right away, puts pressure on the less convinced to fall into line. The Nottinghamshire miners are their big worry."

"We need to keep working on that," Peter Betsworth said, looking pensive. "I think we'll have something there for you, John."

"Marx" had been retired for the moment.

"So what's the strategy?" John asked, keen to get to the meat of the matter.

"I'll come to that, but first, Stacy, I need to know how tight we are with the organizer."

She smiled to herself. It wasn't 'we' who had to sleep with him but Mona Dexter.

"Very tight is my estimation. I think we caught him at just the right moment."

"Probably what you were sayen' abart me a while back," John muttered, but the other two ignored him.

"The key thing now is how close is he to the decision-makers?"

"He thinks highly of himself without a doubt, and I don't imagine he's much liked. But he's useful, works hard and is good at what he does, even if he's the only one who knows what he's talking about half the time."

"John, you know this man as well as anyone. What do you make of him? Is he trusted?"

Peter had told neither of them about Jack Pugh's brief fall from ideological grace.

"Well I sure as hell wouldn' trus' him," John declared. "But I fink he's trus'ed. He definitely seems ter be a believer. I'm not se sure he trus' me that much."

"OK, strategy," Peter announced, like a drill sergeant calling his troops to order. "It's not complicated: attrition, division, intelligence, force, propaganda and no outcome save unconditional surrender."

"Sounds loike a farmer's address ter his turkeys in the run-up ter Christmas," John observed drily.

"If it were that easy, Peter, we'd never have got into the mess we're in now," Stacy declared.

"No, of course not," agreed Peter, backtracking from his overly robust statement. "Those are the things we *must* do and not one of them is straightforward. Attrition: we think we have prepared for a six-month strike. If it goes beyond that, we could be in trouble. Division: traditionally, the miners have been a cohesive group. If we can, we must try to prise the Nottinghamshire pits away from the others. But it doesn't stop there. Secondary picketing can do great damage to the economy. There are our ports, our power stations and our steel mills. If any of these is prevented from functioning, the effect on the economy could be substantial.

"Also, there is a little-known group we must win over, or at least neutralize: they go by the grand name of the National Association of Colliery Overmen, Deputies and Shortfirers. Essentially, they oversee mine safety. By law, no pit can function without their say-so. If they come out, even the Nottinghamshire mines will be halted. This brings us to intelligence: the more we know about the intentions and state of mind of the NUM leadership, the better able we will be to defeat them. Force: we will have to use force to prevent the worst effects of secondary picketing. And finally, propaganda: the miners must be made to feel utterly alone in their struggle, so we don't want to go around stirring up sympathy for them. It might surprise you to know that even a good few at the top in the Trades Union Congress would like to see King Arthur get his comeuppance.

"This is a battle about how our country is run. The choice is between an open economy able to compete because businesses vie for customers on the basis of excellence and a closed economy in which everyone's current position is protected, even as the rest of the world moves on. The first thrives on change, the second abhors it. And don't forget, every one of these mining communities evolved spontaneously because there was a need for coal. Since the nationalization of the industry in 1947, the tendency has been to resist change at every turn. Instead of helping the coal-mining communities to adapt over these last thirty-five years, governments of all stripes have pandered to them because coal had a lock on the country's energy, and without energy our economy could not function.

"If the miners are allowed to win this battle it means they are running the country not the government. And if our communist friends in the unions imagine that the statist regime, or *people's party* they talk about endlessly, would make their lives lovely, they should talk to some folk inside the Soviet Union who have experienced it for real. That is why the only outcome our prime minister will accept is their unconditional surrender. Many innocent people will be hurt. It will not be pretty. I just hope her cohorts will be as steely as she. This is one battle we must not lose. And for those who like to apportion blame, blame everyone – in government, in the unions, in management, in the electorate – who has refused to face reality since the last war and who chose instead the seemingly easy option of the status quo."

John and Stacy were both struck dumb. Neither had heard Peter Betsworth speak with such passion before.

It was John who eventually broke the silence.

"What a roit roar'n fuck-up!"

CHAPTER  32

FRANCES GRAHAM sat in reception. Over the twenty-one months since her husband's death she had been in and out of Butterfield de Souza, her late husband's solicitors, more times than she cared to count. Even now there seemed to be a hushed frisson about the place. People came to discover their fate. In ancient times, they would have entered a holy place with an offering in the hope of guiding providence. Now they approached gatekeepers like Butterfield de Souza.

On one side of the gate, an often anxious individual; on the other a cold cosmos which owed them nothing more than they could prove was their due. In the middle were the temple priests, men and women who toiled to interpret laws they had helped draft to regulate the universe but which possessed sufficient ambiguity to make intercession highly profitable.

"Frances, I hope you have not been waiting long. Come on in."

Robert Cohen was in his late fifties and now the senior partner in Butterfield de Souza. He looked like a baggy-skinned bloodhound with an avuncular manner, but between his oversized ears, sharp eyes expressed a fierce intelligence and a determination never to be bested. For reasons she could not quite explain, Frances found him strangely attractive, just as she had Henry Kissinger.

Richard Nixon's foreign policy maestro had once taken a shine to her at a party in Winfield House, the American Ambassador's London residence in Regent's Park. Purchased and rebuilt by Barbara Hutton, the Woolworth heiress, in 1936 and sold by her to the US government for $1 in 1950, the neo-Georgian mansion was surrounded by the largest private gardens in the capital after Buckingham Palace. This said a good deal about Britain's 'special relationship' with its former colony, David Graham had grumbled on the way home that night, faintly irritated by his wife's success. Frances remembered feeling quite proud of herself. In her mind she had chalked up her conquest as a small victory for the old world, although Kissinger was hardly a stranger to it, being born as he was in the Weimar Republic to a family of German Jews.

But these last months had been the most painful of her life. First there had been her husband's death. She had not even known he was in the Falkland Islands. He would often go away for weeks at a time. Back on such and such a day, Fran, was all he would say. That was the man she had married. Then to be told by Robert Cohen that David's finances had been 'a little tangled' – so tangled, in fact, that she had been forced to sell her home to pay his debts – had piled night-destroying anxiety and then anger onto grief. It seemed he had borrowed money which was unlikely to be repaid without him, and his creditors had called in their loans.

"Well, I think we are nearly there, Frances," her lawyer said as he poured tea into Meissen cups from a matching pot – a ritual Frances found reassuring as she was doubtless meant to. As long as there was tea, the world could not be wholly bad. 'David's creditors have been reasonable. You won't be destitute."

"That's something," she answered. "There were days when I feared I might end up with nothing."

"Oh no, we couldn't have allowed that!"

Frances looked at him as if to say, "Then why did you allow any of it?"

"Your husband was a forceful man," he explained, fully aware what her look had implied. "This room bore witness to many battles between us. Whenever I asked him what would happen to you and the children if he was killed he would just shrug and say, 'If you live fearing death, you are dead already.' But I did persuade him to put some things into yours and your children's names, so he wasn't entirely blind to the possibility. How are the children taking it?"

"They've been marvellous. I'm not sure I could have coped without them, frankly. Now they just want to get on with their lives."

"And you?"

"I think I must get on with mine."

"You must. I feel for your son, though," he said: "the name, the history, a feeling of shame even, however unjustified."

"The curse of expectations!"

"Yes, we are slaves to our past. As a Jew, that is something I know only too well! Perhaps we shouldn't be, at least not so much."

"They are all strong teenagers. They can cope."

"That *is* a blessing."

"So what more needs to be done, Robert?"

"Nothing I can't handle. You are free, Frances, so go and live your life. It may not be Graham Castle, but you have a house to live in and enough money to get by on and most of all, you have yourself."

Robert Cohen looked at her with genuine affection. He hardly dare admit it, even to himself, but he was a little in love.

"I couldn't have done it without you."

"Of course you could, dear lady. You'd have just found some other overweight, overpriced lawyer!"

Frances Graham laughed that bell-like laugh that drew men to her like congregants.

* * *

Back in her small London house, she collapsed onto a sofa, exhausted. The tears of anger, frustration, shock and anguish she had bottled up at last poured free, along with great sobs and gulps for air squeezed out by the contractions which were giving birth to a new life.

Much later, while she was busying herself around the house, moving things from here to there and back again, she came upon the advertisement for a performance of Gaetano Donizetti's *L'Elisir D'Amore*. She knew the story. A peasant girl, Adina, aware of her beauty and frustrated by the timidity of her long-term suitor, Nemorino, agrees to marry Belcore, a visiting soldier on the lookout for recruits. Distraught, Nemorino turns to the quack Dr Dulcamara who sells him some cheap Bordeaux wine as a love potion. Emboldened by the alcohol, he struts around the village attracting the attention of the other girls. To pay for a second bottle of the magical elixir, he takes the fee offered by Belcore for joining the army. Now with visions of himself as a great soldier, he spurns Adina's attempts at reconciliation. Distraught, she confesses to Belcore that she can't marry him and buys back Nemorino's contract. Meanwhile the villagers learn, before Nemorino does, that his uncle has died and left him money and so pay even more attention to him. Convinced all this is a consequence of the elixir, he brags to Adina that he intends to die in battle as a soldier in any event, at which she faints into his arms and the villagers queue up to purchase Dr Dulcamara's cheap wine.

If her life were an opera, it would have become a tragedy. That had to change. Her mind turned to Milan, to a chance encounter, to the limousine, to Sylvia and to Harvey Mudd.

"But why," she wondered in a crippling loss of confidence, "would he be interested in me?"

CHAPTER

THE STRATEGY was clear enough: the government would not be defeated by the National Union of Mineworkers this time. Preparations had been extensive and long in the making. The Prime Minister had been expecting a strike towards the end of 1984 when the nation would be heading into winter and required the most energy, but the NUM President, Arthur Scargill, had been forced by the National Coal Board's announcement of pit closures to respond. The NCB Chairman, Ian MacGregor's, deliberate provocation had seen to that. But the government's pollsters were finding that the Scottish-American's gruff manner was not proving popular.

* * *

"I know, Peter, it is essential we get public opinion behind us. You are going to have to rein Ian in."

"I think he's aware of the problem, Prime Minister. I suggest Tim handles all his public statements. Tim's agency still seems to have a sure touch."

"Yes, they did a splendid job in the run-up to the seventy-nine election; just splendid. How widespread is the strike?"

"From what I understand, it's quite solid, Prime Minister. The South Wales pits were grudging at first. They felt they had received less backing than they should have when they came out in support of the steel workers in 1980. The Nottinghamshire pits are lukewarm by all accounts. But elsewhere, miners seem to be falling into line. There is a long history of solidarity, as you know."

"That man's use of Rule 41, without calling a national strike, was utterly ruthless, Peter. Sending his militant shock troops to lock in support across the industry has proved most effective."

"Yes and I think we all know that defeating this strike will need more resources than the Coal Board can muster."

The Prime Minister's countenance was explosive.

"People should be free to work. They cannot be denied that right by Scargill's pickets."

She could hardly bring herself to mention the NUM President by name.

"Ian is threatening to take out an injunction against the NUM, Prime Minister, because the police are simply not upholding the law."

"I will not have it, Peter. We cannot surrender to the mob. The right to work has to be upheld. The Home Secretary must make that clear. I'll speak to Leon."

* * *

In March, Walter Marshall, chairman of the Central Electricity Generating Board, ordered all stations able to do so to switch to oil. The switch-over from coal to oil took time but his prompt action meant that, by September, half of the nation's electricity generation would no longer be powered by coal.

* * *

At ACPO, the Association of Chief Police Officers, the Public Order Tactical Operations Manual had been revised to take account of the 1980 and 1982 laws on picketing. Strictly speaking, only six pickets could legally remonstrate in a peaceful manner with individuals wishing to work. The long and short shields were almost ready for deployment. The first would afford officers substantial protection, especially in battle formation when held overhead by back rows and vertically in front. The second could be used as a weapon for making arrests and for crowd dispersal.

Truncheons were only to be used in self-defence and never applied to the head and although mounted police were permitted to charge at a crowd for the purpose of intimidation, they were not permitted to ride into it or through it. There had been much discussion about when to use local police or those drawn from outside an area. Some officers felt that local police would have a deeper understanding of their communities and so be better able to head off trouble. Others felt that local police might be inhibited from applying the full force of the law against people they knew.

There was a heightened sense of tension and some excitement across the police service, together with the hope that the coming weeks would lead to generous overtime earnings. The Met, London's Metropolitan Police Force, fully expected to be deployed around the country to counter the NUM President's army of flying pickets and most of its members were looking forward to this change in routine.

There were some who remembered what became known as the Battle of Saltley Gate. To combat the ravages of inflation in 1972, the miners went on strike for a 43% pay increase. Concerned that his flying pickets (never used before in such large numbers) had failed to shut the Saltley Gate Coke Depot, Arthur Scargill, then a young union activist, called upon local engineering unions for support. When 10,000 engineers from around Birmingham joined around 2,000 miners picketing Saltley Gate, the 700 police, who had kept the facility open, became overwhelmed and were forced to close it. This deprived the depository's dependent power station of fuel forcing Edward Heath's Conservative Government to capitulate. The police, as well as the government, had a score to settle.

C*HAPTER*

J ACK was happier than he had ever been. At last he was working for men with real vision, even if the union vice-president, Mick McGahey's, accent frequently confounded his comprehension. This did put the boot on the other foot, as many of his own more esoteric pronouncements confounded everyone else's. Arthur Scargill had been his hero ever since the Battle of Saltley Gate. And he knew that Peter Heathfield, who had become general secretary of the NUM in March, had stood aside to give Arthur a clear run at the presidency. He also knew that Peter's wife, Betty, had been a member of the Communist Party for over thirty years. Bob Dylan's 1960s prediction was finally coming true: *the times they* were *a-changin'*.

He visited every pit, every dock, every branch of the Transport and General Workers' Union, calling upon the brotherhood to support the miners and bring the government to its knees. Only in Nottinghamshire was he not welcomed as enthusiastically as he considered his due and so had handed that area over to John Preston whose ideological reticence was riling his nerves.

The humiliations inflicted on him by Miranda de Coursey were becoming a faded memory, although he did occasionally fantasize about impaling her on a stake as the Russian Tsar Ivan the Terrible had done to his enemies – but *he* would do so for the pleasure of the people. The French revolutionaries certainly understood how cathartic an execution could be, especially when guilt was decided by hatred rather than due process: such a bourgeois concept in any event and so wasteful of resources.

His personal life had taken a 180 degree turn for the better. In Mona Dexter he felt sure he had found a soulmate. She soaked up his wisdom, had eradicated his self-doubt and would have won a gold medal for her sexual inventiveness if the Olympic committee had been sensible enough to offer one. It was true that she did not seem as stimulated as Miranda had been by ideas such as the need for permanent revolution or for the dictatorship of the proletariat, but everyone might be allowed a few failings.

* * *

Peter Betsworth hurried to his meeting. Stacy had indicated its urgency. The June weather was starting well, warm and dry, ideal for one of his park encounters. His diary informed him that he was in a leap year with 366 days, the extra one needed to keep the human calendar and astronomical seasons synchronized. He couldn't help reflecting that 1984 was also the year chosen by the novelist, Eric Blair, for a book in which Winston Smith has to disavow his love for Julia in order to prove he is worthy of a greater love, that of the state.

Written nearly forty years before, under his *nom de plume*, George Orwell, the author conjured up a super-state called Oceana of which Airstrip One, formerly Great Britain, is a province. Winston toils within the Ministry of Truth concocting lies, next to the Ministry of Peace which deals in war and the Ministry of Plenty which deals with rationing and starvation.

When Julia, who repairs Minitrue novel-writing machines and is a member of the Junior Anti-Sex League, falls for him, the Thought Police are summoned to detain the deviants as love is not permitted. Charged with Thought Crime they are captured and taken to the Ministry of Love for torture and interrogation. Told that the only reality is that proclaimed by the state and that only acceptance will set them free, they are ushered separately into Room 101 to be confronted by their greatest fear. Rather than submit to this, each disavows the other and Winston emerges broken but eager to use what remains of his body and soul in the service of state tyranny, epitomized by Big Brother.

In Orwell's novel, there were three classes of people after Big Brother: the Inner Party comprising less than 2% of the population, the Outer Party which included middle-class functionaries like Winston and the Proles who made up some 85% of the state. The intelligence officer smiled to himself. Was it ever thus and would it always be so? Perhaps the proportions had changed with fewer Proles and more in the Outer Party. Democracy, he thought, had seen to that. But the dynamic was essentially the same.

The state was held together by a story about itself – the pronouncements of Big Brother – that most people went along with and which justified membership of the Inner Party. The battle he was engaged in was against those who wished to propagate a different story and elevate themselves to the Inner Party. But to assert one story over another required that the besieged story appear threadbare by comparison. The dislocations in people's everyday lives, culminating in the Winter of Discontent, had created the space for this to be possible.

Eric Blair's bleak forecast of life in 1984 had not altogether turned out as he expected. Post-war governments in general and socialist ones with their Labour Party and trades union constituents in particular, had found themselves in a bind: how to reconcile their support of organized labour (tacit or overt) with what were often harsh economic realities. Had Britain been isolated from the rest of the world this consensus story could have remained unchallenged, at least until the oversized state-run industries, created out of a naïve faith in the efficacy of large scale, politically-controlled bureaucracy, had crumbled under their own weight. But given the power of their purse, their vote and that derived from their largely free access to information, individuals came increasingly to demand better.

Governments of most political hues had attempted to buy their way out of trouble – the trouble caused by a mismatch between those expectations Big Brother's propaganda had stimulated and economic reality – by taking on debt to pay for their promises. Although successful at first in electoral terms, it led ultimately to inflation and insolvency which only currency devaluation, or the kind of deep recession they were now in, could wash away. Faced with the rapid erosion of their living standards, it was hardly surprising that working men in state-run industries turned from their official trade unions to shop stewards that they knew personally who offered them a better-sounding story. He had concluded that, in times of crisis, whoever was able to tie force to the most popular account of how the world worked would inherit Big Brother's mantel.

Faced with the prospect of losing power, most members of Oceana's Inner Party realized that they needed to embrace a new narrative, but without appearing to do so. Monetarism, a set of ideas which held that the problem was invariably too much government rather than too little, and that free markets served people's interests better than state bureaucracies, seemed to offer a way out. So when Margaret Thatcher and her cohort appeared on the scene espousing such a story, she faced an already defeated political enemy at the top, most of whose members secretly wanted her to confront a far more dangerous one struggling to emerge from the bottom.

What Peter Betsworth knew but the Proles and most of the Outer Party did not, was that even members of the socialist Inner Party had been running scared for years. It had been a Labour Government in 1975 that broadened the definition of subversion to include 'organizations and individuals whose intention was to overthrow or undermine parliamentary democracy by political, industrial or violent means' and it was this which underpinned his activities now.

He saw Stacy waiting for him on the bench and glanced at his watch.

"I'm late," he said sitting next to her, thinking that they must look like a father and his daughter or an older man with a substantially younger lover. "It's a nice day at least."

"Yes. I've been watching the geese beside the lake. They waddle and honk with great busyness."

Peter glanced across at a group of five cutting a swathe through children on scooters, anxious adults and wary dogs, their black heads bobbing back and forth like rabbis in earnest discussion, oblivious to the world they were dissecting.

"I take it we have some movement?" he said.

"Mona tells me they are going to go after the Orgreave coking plant which serves British Steel."

"South Yorkshire?"

"I believe so."

"I thought the NUM had given the steelworkers dispensation for limited deliveries, just to keep their furnaces ticking over and hopefully to get them on side."

"Apparently they have been outmanoeuvred by British Steel and its union with far more being shipped out than the NUM realized. King Arthur was furious when he found out, Mona tells me. They plan to send in pickets from around the country to close the depot down."

"Do we have a date?"

"The eighteenth."

"Of this month?" Peter sounded alarmed.

"That's the date Mona has given me."

"Can she be sure?"

"I think she is quite sure."

"What's her source?"

Stacy was surprised by the question.

"Jack Pugh, naturally. He's been helping to organize it."

"Yes, of course," he responded, but she could see that his mind was racing ahead.

"Anything else?" he asked. "What's their mood at the moment?"

"Very determined, very confident, Mona says."

"We'll have to change that," he grumped, his brow now furrowed in concentration. "And my Marx, what's my Marx up to these days?" he asked. "I think I must see him again soon."

"He and Jack Pugh have had something of a falling out, although, to be honest, they never really had a falling in. Jack's sent him off to cover the Nottinghamshire pits because Jack doesn't feel welcome there."

"Perfect, absolutely perfect!" Peter seemed ecstatic. "Tell him to come and see me soon. And you? How are things with you?"

"All right, I suppose."

"Romance cooling?"

Stacy shrugged. "I think you know me by now," she said. "I like a mission but right now I'm little more than a part-time girlfriend and a post box between you and Mona Dexter."

"So you want to keep working for the service?"

"Of course!"

Peter Betsworth nodded. Agents like her were hard to come by. When all of this was over he was sure he'd have little difficulty thinking of something. With her charm and sophistication, she'd be perfect for the embassy circuit.

"Well, Stacy, I think that's it for now," he said. "Keep close to your source. I need to know how the mood of the NUM leadership is evolving over these next months. With luck, it should all be over by Christmas."

"I certainly hope so," she said with a resigned smile and he left her on the bench looking at the Canada geese, the lake and the people ribboned around it, half-wishing he was twenty years younger.

C*HAPTER*

THERE WAS a holiday atmosphere inside the bus bringing the men out of Durham. Buses from as far away as South Wales and Scotland converged on Orgreave. For once these were not stopped on the motorway, as was normal police practice, but allowed to disgorge their occupants near the village. Amidst much good-natured banter, the police then escorted the travellers to a field just short of the plant. Within the British Steel facility, lorries were being filled with coke, ready for their drivers to take out: drivers King Arthur intended his army of pickets to stop.

Harvey had been alerted by George Gilder the day before. He had not been the only one. The entire national press corps seemed to be milling around in heightened expectation.

"This is the big one, Mudd," his editor had said. "The government intends to put a stop to the use of mass picketing – or mass intimidation as the Prime Minister regards it – once and for all."

Yorkshire's rolling countryside was spread out around them like a patchwork. Corn fields were ripening under a summer sun blotted only intermittently that day by a quick succession of flighty clouds. In hedgerows the county's emblem bloomed, a white rose, symbol in the struggle for England's crown between Yorkists and Lancastrians, whose own rose was red. After much strife between them, one family emerged with roots in both camps and almost by accident the Tudors set the nation on a path to maritime greatness. As a centre of coal and steel production during the Industrial Revolution, the county had flourished, and after the Second World War it became home to Bomber Command. Yorkshire men were Yorkshire men and London a distant place.

Struggling to be heard above the ribald chatter emanating from the wheat field, larks sang their hearts out high in the sky, but few below were in the mood to hear their call. The men, who came from far and wide, had answered a different summons. Although not many had any great notion what they were supposed to do, they did know that they were there to support their side as they did their football team nearly every weekend in the season. Dressed mostly in jeans and T-shirts, which a good few discarded as the morning wore on, they looked like what they were: a high-spirited bunch of lads, some 5,000 strong, let loose from the humdrum of everyday life.

Having taken lodgings the night before, Harvey had toured the site early. The coking plant was as ugly as most such plants and did not employ a large number of men, but its coke was needed to keep the blast furnaces at British Steel's Scunthorpe plant going. If these furnaces were allowed to go out, the production of steel would be halted for some time and the jobs of steel workers adversely affected. Harvey had learned that neither British Steel management nor its union were anxious for this to happen.

The police had set up their command centre next to the facility and had arrayed their men in lines several deep across the entrance to the plant well beyond the road the drivers needed to take if they were to escape with their cargo. On one side of the field, which the pickets had been ushered into, there was a steep bank down to a railway line with dog patrols stationed beyond it. On the other side there were more dog patrols as well as a detachment of mounted police. Harvey estimated the number of officers to be around 6,000, drawn from forces across the country. Their unpreparedness at Brixton was not going to be repeated. A core of specially trained men, wearing helmets Darth Vader would have approved of, had been armed with either the new long shields or the short ones and all carried truncheons. The contrast between the two groups was stark. It was clear the pickets had been led into a trap. Short of breaking through the police lines, their only escape was back across a bridge to the village.

As Harvey took this in, he couldn't help thinking that any general who had allowed his men to be manoeuvred into such an abysmal position should have been shot. Worse still, and what he didn't find out until much later, there had even been some disagreement within the union about the merits of diverting pickets from the Nottinghamshire mines, which were crucial to the strike, up to Orgreave, which was not. But convinced he could repeat his Saltley Gate success, their president's wish that they do so had prevailed.

* * *

A murmur spread through the crowd. The first of the loaded trucks was leaving the depot. Miners coalesced into a loose phalanx and moved to test their opponents in the ritual trial of strength that accompanied meetings between mass pickets and police. Like sumo wrestlers, they pressed against each other for advantage. At one moment the pickets gained ground as men piled in from the back only to lose it again when extra police weighed in to strengthen the weakest point of their own line. Back and forth it went with shouts from the pickets escalating as each side's blood became charged.

Missiles were thrown, although the sky was hardly black with them as the police later claimed. But little provocation was needed for the officers to implement their battle plan. As the pickets pulled back after one unsuccessful push, the long shields parted and horsemen rode through, scattering men in all directions. No sooner had the riders spread confusion than they turned back behind the protective screens. The assistant chief constable then ordered the men in his specially trained short-shield units to draw truncheons and attack. Dressed in their black riot gear, they spread out and fell upon any retreating picket who came their way. Once immobilized, captured individuals were dragged back behind police lines where they were roughed up some more if not adequately subdued and then incarcerated.

As the day wore on, the specials made repeated forays into the increasingly angry crowd like wolves, picking off stragglers or any protestor foolish enough to taunt them. In the manner of anguished wildebeest besieged by a predator, the bulk of the pickets just milled around together booing, throwing stones, shouting insults and attempting to sidestep capture as the police force gradually pushed them back up the hill. Perhaps it was the sight of their opponents in such disarray that enticed them, or perhaps an order was given, it hardly mattered, but hundreds of officers suddenly joined the specials, lashing out at anyone they encountered. This was their chance to teach the miners a lesson and they were not about to hold back.

Over to one side of the action, a shield caught the NUM President on the head, sending him to the ground. A young lad pulled him clear of the battle which was now raging as riot police pushed protestors back up the hill towards the village. Injuries and arrests multiplied. A rowdy teenager cornered against a building was stamped on and ended up in hospital with a fractured leg. Pickets attempting to escape tumbled down the steep embankment onto the railway lines. One miner, who had retired to the village for refreshments, came back carrying a can of shandy and some cream buns. He was caught in the crossfire and felled. Picking himself up, he reached down for the buns and had his hand smashed.

"You can leave those bastard things there!" he was told.

Another picket who had made it back to the village with the riot police on his heels finally gave up only to have his head cracked open with a truncheon. It was a rout. Arthur's army had been out-manoeuvred, out-classed and out-fought. Dazed pickets huddled around everywhere examining each other's injuries with the muted pride of the battle-scarred, uncertain what had happened to them.

* * *

Inside Rotherham's detention centre, ninety-five mostly bloodied picketers were charged with various public order offences, fifty-five of them with riot. The place looked more like a battlefield hospital than a police station. The human rights advocate, Gareth Pierce, who had come to help the arrested men, remarked that for once she wished she had been a doctor not a lawyer. Later she observed magistrates working through the night to process charges with scant regard to evidence and listened to them setting bail conditions which were clearly punitive.

One of the young men remanded in custody that night was only released after six days on bail conditions that required him to attend Rotherham police station, some two hours from his home, by 11.00 a.m. – every day. He was also prohibited from setting foot on British Steel property, National Coal Board property, the Central Electricity Generating Board's property, British Rail property or in any of the country's docks. In the weeks that followed, the Home Secretary was heard to say, on numerous occasions, that the crime of riot carried a life sentence.

It is sometimes said that although the wheels of British justice grind slow, they do, at least, grind fine. By 1987 most of the charges raised that night against individual pickets had been dropped and the few cases that made it to trial collapsed. South Yorkshire Police were eventually forced to pay thirty-nine pickets some £425,000 in damages and another £100,000 in legal costs for unlawful arrest. Michael Mansfield QC later remarked that the judicial system had clearly been used that night for political ends. And, so it had. But the British public had grown tired of being held to ransom by the NUM in particular and the trades unions in general and probably regarded the compensation payments they as taxpayers had to pay out for 'allowing' their government to misuse their justice system as money well spent. However, few sane people could really have been pleased that things had come to that. For the nation to have stopped a few runs short of a communist or fascist state was hardly much to brag about.

* * *

Like the rest of the media hurtling back to London on the train that evening, Harvey was in high spirits. They had been witness to a great event. Mob rule had been crushed. From the vantage of the police command centre, they had watched as the police withstood wave upon wave of attempts to break through their lines. They had observed as the unruly pickets had been pushed slowly away from the British Steel coking plant by a disciplined and well-orchestrated counterattack. Most of them had even cheered when the police broke ranks and pushed home their advantage. One wag was heard to remark that he didn't much like horses at the best of times, but greatly preferred observing their back ends in motion to their front ends, prompting another to jibe that he had obviously never worked in a stable.

On the television that night, the state's victory over the mob was amply displayed. Shots of stone-throwing youths and a sequence which had captured four uniformed officers attempting to restrain a bare-torsoed, tattoo-covered, beer-bellied bruiser shouting obscenities was shown over and over again. Arthur Wellesley's observation about battles won and lost had been taken to heart by the programmers. This was a victory and the public's evening meal was not about to be sullied by any of its grim details.

Before retiring to bed, Harvey prepared to file his copy for the following day's issue. Under the banner *Our Victory at Orgreave*, he trumpeted the fact that thirty-four drivers had been able to deliver their precious cargo not once but twice during the day thanks to *brave and skilful police action*, which had enabled *industry to function, jobs to be protected and the nation to go about its lawful business*. With a whisky and water on the desk beside him, he thumped out his words. *What God-given right did the miners have to expect people to buy their coal when it could be purchased from elsewhere for less or not used at all? Wasn't gas now a cleaner, safer, cheaper alternative?*

He looked up and wished Sylvia had been there to relish the triumph. But as he sat back sipping his drink in the warmth of his home in Buttesland Street, wondering how best to finish his piece, he heard his mother's voice.

'Don't forget, Harve, these were people desperate to save their communities and livelihoods. The union sold them false promises, is how I see it.' So he concluded by urging *The Sentinel's* readers not to forget the men and women whose lives were being turned upside down by a changing world and whose predecessors had fuelled the nation's greatness and prosperity.

Our government certainly won an important battle at Orgreave yesterday, he wrote, *but the war will not be won until mining communities have been put back on their feet – with or without the help of their union.*

* * *

George Gilder's secretary called the following morning to say that the great editor wanted to see him. He'd been hoping for a slow start after Orgreave, but wasn't that sorry to be summoned. The house felt empty these days and he preferred to be out and about. Doubtless it would be a new assignment; perhaps some line fed to him by the paper's contact in MI5 which needed following up. And then an unsettling thought occurred to him: had his article fallen short in some way? If it had, it wouldn't have been the first time George had altered some aspects of what he had written, although that hadn't happened for a while now.

Slightly anxious, he purchased a copy of *The Sentinel* on the way to the Tube. His headline was intact, bold as brass, which was a relief. There was too much of a breeze for him to try reading the rest as he walked and too much of a crush underground to do more than squint at the front page. He couldn't see any changes and as George generally didn't bother with the continuation inside, he relaxed. That is until he entered *The Sentinel* offices.

"Good morning, Mr Mudd."

Mary, the receptionist, looked furtive. And where the hell had 'Harvey' gone?

"Solid piece," remarked Porter who generally thought only something about the Royal Family worth reading. Harvey had long ago concluded that the paper's royal correspondent must have the same compulsion as those who enjoyed listening to the shipping forecast. He conceded that both did offer a kind of comforting reassurance:

Viking, southwesterly 7 to severe gale 9; Dogger, southwesterly severe gale force 9 continuing: The Queen, Honorary Air Commodore, today visited Royal Air Force Marham, Kings Lynn, Norfolk, and was received by the Station Commander. Her Majesty was received at the Weapon Load Trainer Hangar with a Royal Salute and viewed static displays, before meeting Station Officers and Airmen.

"It must have been pretty wild up there, Harvey," Georgina cooed as he passed – Georgina who normally paid attention to no one.

"You fairly aced that one, Harve," Pete called out – Pete who generally could only praise someone else's work with clenched buttocks.

Harvey stopped dead in his tracks. He had learnt to smell an office conspiracy at five paces.

"OK, people, what the hell's going on?"

He had hit the whisky bottle harder than intended the night before, trying to obliterate the fact that his life seemed to be going nowhere, and so sounded more crabby than he wanted to.

Just then George Gilder appeared from his office.

"Harvey, my boy. Come, come."

Jesus, this must be serious, he thought: a 'my boy' and no 'Mudd'.

His unusually smiling editor beckoned impatiently for him to come forward and then standing in front of a mahogany door next to his own, said, "Behold!"

Harvey looked and he looked. There on the door, in discreet gold lettering, were the words: *Harvey Mudd – deputy editor.*

"Now don't get carried away, Mudd," the great editor announced with more like his normal vim. "It doesn't really mean anything!"

A chorus of claps and 'Go Harvey!'s came from the office floor behind him. Blushing slightly, he turned and thanked them.

"Now, back to work, you lousy bloodhounds," George Gilder barked. "And, Harvey, there's a telephone message for you on your desk."

Harvey entered his new room. It was not big but comfortably furnished with a mahogany writing table and dark leather chairs. St Paul's Cathedral loomed large beyond the window, the same St Paul's he had looked at when George Gilder first interviewed him and on the many occasions since when his mentor had attempted to adjust his protégé's trajectory. He imagined it would have to be 'Harvey' from now on. He was going to miss 'Mudd!'

Almost casually, he picked up the folded note. *Please call Frances Graham,* it read, followed by a telephone number.

C*HAPTER*

I
T WAS THE DAY after what the national press had christened the Battle of Orgreave when Peter Betsworth got the call he had been expecting.

"We have a Jack Pugh in custody," the caller said. "What would you like us to do with him?"

The intelligence officer paused for a moment. He had been thinking about this eventuality for some time.

"Release him," he said.

"Without charge or charged?" the caller asked.

"Without charge," he answered.

"Released by the front door or the back door?"

"By the back door."

"Very good, sir," the caller acknowledged and rang off.

The MI5 officer tapped the desk with a pencil. He was feeling particularly pleased with the previous day's events. His main concern now was Mona Dexter, but he thought the risk worth taking. Only Jack Pugh knew about his encounter with the service and the organizer was hardly likely to tie his release to her rather than to his own guilty secret.

The balance Peter Betsworth had to strike was between continuing to use Jack Pugh as a valuable asset, trusted by the NUM leadership, and using him to sow mistrust within its ranks. With careful handling, he hoped he could do both. He knew that it was still chaotic in the Rotherham station and so one more individual being moved around was unlikely to appear suspicious. But at some point in the future, at a time of his choosing, doubt could be sown.

* * *

"All right, brave boy, out!"

Jack sat in the back of the police car wondering what was going to happen to him next. His night in the cells alongside his fallen comrades had been unpleasant, to say the least. All of them had been caked in blood from various injuries. One had been drinking and threw up in the cell. Another must have been badly hurt because he moaned off and on all night. Jack had found one fellow inmate happy to talk about the plight of the working class and the need to smash the capitalist system until another, with a badly cut lip and peach of a swollen eye, told them both to 'shut the fuck up!'

"Here?" Jack asked plaintively, seeing nothing but rolling fields without a house in sight.

The two officers in the front looked at one another.

"So you'd like us to drop you off at miners' headquarters, right?" said one.

Jack shrugged and tried the door, but it was locked.

"Let the lad out then."

There was a click allowing Jack to push it open.

"Friends in high places, you?"

"What?" Jack said as he eased his bruised body from the vehicle.

"'T's a'right. Secret's safe wi' us," one of them smirked. "'Spect Arthur put in a good word wi' duty officer at station. We are all up wi' you miners, we are!"

Jack was tempted to give him the finger, but was sure it was already broken.

"Which way's Rotherham?" he asked instead.

"That way," said the driver.

"Na, 't isn't. 'T's 'at way," said his partner, pointing in the opposite direction.

Both thought that funny and drove off laughing, leaving Jack to contemplate life's uncertainties – and the Yorkshire countryside.

C*HAPTER* 37

T HE EVENING got off to a rocky start. They tiptoed around
one another like teenagers on a first date. Harvey, who had been
suppressing the possibility of this moment since meeting her, felt
tongue-tied and Frances could hear herself talking like a tour guide
about everything save what she wanted to.

The opera, however, helped to pull them from their mutual funk.
She had chosen *L'Elisir d'Amore* because it was on her mind and only
halfway through wondered if it had been too suggestive. It was to be
the great Welsh baritone, Geraint Evans's, last performance as the
quack doctor Dulcamara. Harvey chose Rules to go to afterwards
because he had read that its food was as close to country-house
cooking as one could get in London and imagined she might be
missing it.

They sat at a corner table cocooned within the restaurant's heavy
opulence. Their fellow diners, John Bulls to a man and woman,
were devouring dishes of rabbit, pork belly, pheasant, partridge and
roast loin of roe deer washed down with claret. Those further along
were already chewing on cigars and murdering port, while the more
recently arrived seemed to be favouring oysters. Harvey stared at

the menu and wondered what he was doing in such a place until he spotted steak and kidney pie, one of his mother's favourites.

Frances appeared to be having as much difficulty with the menu as he and eventually opted for the fillet of halibut, which sent Harvey into mental overload about what wine to choose. He went for the potted shrimps to start with and she for the terrine of foie gras, which allowed the wine waiter to suggest two half bottles for them to share, one of white burgundy and the other of claret. Its name meant nothing to the deputy editor but he worried he might never forget its price. There were bottles on the list in the hundreds.

'Buck up, Harvey dear,' he imagined his mother saying. 'This is what I have always wanted for you!'

"Such a wonderful performance," Frances said when their orders had finally been taken. "It is hard to think that will be his last. He has been a fixture in my life since childhood."

"And mine," echoed Harvey. "My mother always liked the way he played the wise buffoon or loveable rogue. You know his father was a coal miner?"

"No, I didn't."

"I think that was partly why my mother liked him. She couldn't abide talk about the working class as if it were a life sentence."

"How is your mother?"

"Sadly, she died two years ago," he told her.

"I am sorry. That would be about the same time as my husband."

"I know," murmured Harvey.

They sat in silence for a while contemplating their loss.

"I think the aristocracy was quite pleased with theirs, if that's what it was," she quipped.

'Their life sentence, you mean?' he asked, guessing she had reverted to the earlier subject.

"Yes, although it was hardly a bed of roses for them either. There's a lot more to life than fixtures and fittings."

Harvey thought about Graham Castle but didn't want to raise the subject himself.

"You heard what happened?" she asked.

"I read about it in my own paper, as a matter of fact. I even contacted a reporter with the *Inverness News*, which broke the story, to find out where you'd gone, but he didn't know. I'm sorry. It must have been a terrible experience."

"So you wanted to find me. How nice!"

Harvey felt blood rise to his cheeks and looked sullen, almost fierce, in his effort to compensate.

"Your mother would have been pleased," she laughed. "There's not much room at the top. For everyone who moves up, someone else has to move down. So I've done my bit!"

"Actually, I don't think she would have been pleased at all. She liked you."

"But she only met me once."

"Well she liked the idea of you."

Harvey was not about to tell her what else his mother had prophesied.

"I heard that you had been made deputy editor. Congratulations."

"Yes, but as my editor told me at the time: it doesn't mean much!"

"George Gilder?"

"Yes. George Gilder."

"He has quite a following."

"I hope you like this sort of food?" Harvey asked. "I imagined it was what you were used to."

She smiled across at him. "Actually it has never been at the top of my list of gastronomic cravings. I'm as happy with a pasta dish as anything. It must be my Italian blood."

Harvey laughed out loud at himself and his assumptions.

"That's a great relief! I saw myself having to cook jugged hare and plucking grouse if I was ever going to get to know you properly."

"So you cook?"

"Yes, I like cooking. And right now if I didn't I'd starve, so there is an incentive. Actually I cooked while my mother was alive from time to time, but could never match her pasta dishes. She said I came close though. I suppose it was because she was a generation nearer to Italy. She gave me my love of opera too, but I don't think that was diluted."

"What part of Italy did your mother's family come from?"

"Genoa. Well, outside it really. They were peasant farmers, although my mother said they always lived well. According to her, the communists were always trying to persuade the family that they were being oppressed, but my great-grandfather kept asking them why he should want to be oppressed by them instead and they eventually gave up. I think she learned a lot from him."

"You knew him?"

"No. I never met any of my Italian family. First it was the war, then the expense I suppose. And your Italian family: where did they come from?"

"Rome. They were merchants. My great-grandfather came to London as a young man and stayed. He was pretty smart, I think, and married well," she said, poking at her halibut. "Your father was English?"

"Yes, a Londoner from the East End. He was a junior bank clerk, which I suppose squeezed us into the middle class. But he died when I was twelve. After that we lived off his small pension and my mother's cleaning jobs, so I always thought of us as working class. My mother said class talk was nonsense anyway. She thought the whole notion had been invented by intellectuals to assert their material superiority over those below them and mental superiority over those above. I'd love to have seen her and Karl Marx in a room together!"

"You went to university?" she asked.

"I did: Oxford. I think my mother was prouder of that than

anything. You could forget about class, she thought, as there were just four types of people: good people and bad people; lazy people and hard-working people; people who wanted to get on and people who didn't; people who were lucky and people who weren't. She brought me up to be good even though I often fell short; never let me be lazy but knew I sometimes longed to be; drummed into my head that I should 'get on' and was convinced I had been born under a lucky star. When she was in the mood to talk about herself, which wasn't often, she would say, 'You know, Harve, I want for nothing. That's the God's honest truth.' One day I'll tell you what she had in mind for you."

"Something nice, I hope," Frances said. "I could do with something nice."

Harvey, who was definitely taking to the claret and worrying less about its price, adopted the appearance of a schoolboy with a secret to trade. "Yes, I think it could be nice," he said, looking at her indulgently.

Frances studied him. She realized she was feeling excited again, but didn't feel ready to play his game.

"So tell me about these miners of yours. Are they going to bring down the country?"

"I think some of their leaders would like to, but most miners I've listened to simply want to save their jobs and their communities. One can't fault them for that."

"No. One can't," Frances agreed. "But change does happen. I'm a good example of that!"

"Are you angry?"

"I was, very angry, although less so now. New money has pushed aside old money since the dawn of time. That's the Prime Minister's meritocracy for you."

"You dislike the Prime Minister?" Harvey asked.

"If some Highland chieftain, like my husband, had mounted an attack on her and her self-righteous middle class meritocracy, I might have been inclined to follow. But that would have been the act of a romantic, wouldn't it?"

She paused and Harvey thought better than to interrupt.

"Strangely," she went on, "my husband – who was both tough and fearless - was also a romantic. I think he considered life too rich and wonderful to calculate, at least with any precision. For him, chance was always the wild card and he loved to flirt with her. But she got him in the end."

"I suspect our Prime Minister is more of a romantic than she realizes, but I'll tell you who I think is the biggest romantic of them all right now – it's the president of the National Union of Mineworkers, Arthur Scargill. I have him as a younger version of Cervantes's Don Quixote, fighting an enemy who is not there in order to recapture a world that no longer exists. At one level, he is hard not to like, but I fear he is leading his faithful followers into oblivion."

"So you think the miners will lose?"

"I think that even if they win, they will lose."

"So they might win?"

"This battle? They might. But I sincerely hope they don't because it will damage the country even more than it has already been damaged and only buy them and their families a little more time – time to do what should have been done for the last fifty years."

"And what is that?" she asked, intrigued by his passion.

"Rebuild their communities around something other than coal. But the NUM couldn't have that, it would have done it out of a job, and successive governments were too supine to make the miners and their leadership see sense. Or perhaps no one knew how – the mining communities were never the product of governments in the first place. Anyway, past failures have now inflicted a scorched earth policy on the rest of us and yielded up to the miners their most implacable opponent yet. If grand opera were still being written, this would be a tragedy of epic proportions!"

"This has affected you, hasn't it?" she said.

Harvey sat back from himself and felt embarrassed.

"I'm sorry. I've been going on, haven't I?"

"Yes, you have. But passion in a man is not necessarily unattractive," she teased. "It is a great deal more interesting than some of what I have had to endure at cocktail parties, I can tell you!"

"Until a few years ago," Harvey confessed, "I was just a rather lazy, rather cynical journalist out to unearth a story, any story really, that my editor would print. But I've seen a lot of suffering over these last several years – people's lives ripped apart, companies and communities gutted – and it's made me want to do more than just report. It's made me want to get at the truth – whatever the hell that is!"

"Which is probably why you are now a deputy editor," Frances suggested, in a tone Harvey hoped was a benediction.

"Finally growing up!" he laughed.

"Don't we all have to do that, one way or the other," she said with what sounded like heartfelt resignation.

* * *

By the time he got to the English cheese plate, accompanied by a glass of port, which Frances insisted he have, Harvey was starting to feel that he might have managed quite well in a country house. She, on the other hand, had picked away at her foie gras and addressed her halibut with more politeness than enthusiasm. Her lemon meringue pie, however, seemed to have gone down well and she even took a glass of port herself.

The bill, when it came, was meaningful, but the wine waiter had not overloaded his selections, which made Harvey sufficiently grateful to part with an equally meaningful tip. He also hoped this made him look generous. In the warm night air, they both felt content and walked for a while before trying to flag down a taxi.

"No limousine then?" she commented.

"No. That was a one-off for my mother. You caught us with our best suits on."

"And very nice they were. I enjoyed that evening."

"Yes, so did I."

"But tell me, what *did* your mother have planned for me?" she asked.

"She said you and I would marry one day," Harvey told her in a fit of alcohol-induced bravery or lunacy; he wasn't sure which.

For several paces, Frances Graham said nothing.

"A perceptive woman, your mother," she responded eventually, "but not tonight."

"No, not tonight," Harvey agreed and she slipped her arm through his. They could stay inside the harbour of hope for a little longer before striking out across the uncertain sea of reality.

*C*HAPTER

FOLLOWING THE hunger strikes three years earlier, the Prime Minister had authorized one of her most senior civil servants to open secret discussions with his opposite number in the Irish Republic. A solution to the stand-off in Northern Ireland had to be found and the cabinet had approved her endeavour. Peter Betsworth was not directly involved, but had long been of the view that an understanding between the Irish and British Governments offered the only escape from the cul-de-sac the IRA and UK Government were in. An endless succession of tit-for-tat killings and the need for a permanent garrison of British soldiers to keep Republicans and Loyalists apart hardly seemed the mark of a civilized society. The sins of England's colonial fathers had certainly been visited on their sons' sons' sons – and some.

He often thought 'intelligence' was too precise a term for the currency he and his kind traded in. His own focus was on the mainland in general and industrial relations in particular. With the miners' strike now in its sixth month, he had a clear objective: to do all in his power to bring it to an end before any concessions were forced on the state. That seemed clear. It was a war of attrition. But like radio static, sounds came in from the field all the time and every night he wondered what he wasn't seeing.

* * *

Roy Walsh checked into The Grand, every inch a travelling salesman out to impress a client. The more customary boarding house just wouldn't do. This was going to be his deal of a lifetime. If it came off, he would be able to dine out on it for the rest of his days.

"We have a room for you on the sixth floor, Mr Walsh, as you requested," the receptionist confirmed. "Do you need a morning call?"

Their guest said he did not and was invited to enjoy his stay.

He felt unusually alive in the elevator. His satchel was full and heavy, more so than the small suitcase the porter insisted on carrying. There followed the customary tour of the room and lesson in how to work the controls of the airflow system, sufficient to warrant the practised pause and collection of whatever small change a guest could locate. Mr Walsh was feeling generous and the porter appeared happy knowing that he had escorted a man of means up to room 629.

"Will you be wanting any company this evening?" he asked before leaving. The girl who paid him a small retainer had been complaining about the return on her investment lately. What he needed was a doctor's convention. Members of the medical profession invariably required his extra services. He put it down to the stresses of the job and to the fact that they had the money.

But Mr Walsh was not playing.

"Well, if you should change your mind, sir…"

Having got rid of the porter, Roy inspected his quarters. They were a good size with a spacious bathroom and after slipping the catch across the door, he emptied the contents of his satchel onto the washstand. Taking the screwdriver, he removed the access panel from the side of the bath. He could see no leaks. It wouldn't do at all if one of the maintenance crew was called upon to fix something.

The gelignite was well wrapped in cellophane to prevent its smell alerting one of the specially-trained dogs the police used to detect drugs and explosives. Only the detonator wires poked through and these had been sealed with resin. How to control detonation was always the problem and where particular skill was needed. In this case, timing was crucial. The device had to come alive on 12th October, four weeks hence, in the early hours of the morning. Parts of a video recorder had been used and he'd been advised by their best technician that it would work.

'Get it into a confined space near a load-bearing wall,' the technician assured him, 'and that hotel will collapse.'

After placing the bomb hard into a corner beyond the bath pipes and checking that the timer was running, Roy screwed back the panel. He then washed his hands, combed his hair and took the elevator down to the lobby. In the adjoining bar, he ordered himself a double whisky. The question kept circulating in his head: 'What if the bloody thing goes off with me still in the hotel?'

Revived, he walked the streets for as long as he could, ate in an Indian restaurant and walked some more before finally retuning to The Grand. Two more double whiskies in the bar followed. He was tempted by a smile from a woman three stools away and thought briefly about being blown to kingdom come while enjoying an act of passion – surely a reasonable down payment for his impending martyrdom? – but resisted in case he blurted out an indiscretion.

Up in his room he tried to sleep. But the thought of what lay just a few feet away, ready to release its fury as soon as an alarmingly simple technology told it to, kept him tossing and turning and wondering if he shouldn't have invited the woman up after all. And why were sex and violent death so often related? That their natural by-product was life seemed perverse. Were we not better than salmon bent on one last burst of egg-laying and fertilizing before exhaustion turned our flesh over to parasites? No, we were worse, he concluded. Not only did we know what we were doing, we had interfered with nature in order to subvert its consequences. The words of his Sunday-school teacher, Miss Lafferty, came flooding back to him along with his desire for Miss Lafferty herself. Who would be a Catholic!

He struggled over to the mini-bar and poured everything he could find – whisky, gin, vodka, the lot – into a plastic cup and gulped it down. Back on the bed, reality started to dissolve and alter and fade and reappear like Marvel Comic shapeshifters, a kaleidoscope of memories: his mother, Miss Lafferty, Belfast. Suddenly he was inside the Maze Prison staring at the youthful face of Bobby Sands. If vengeance was the Lord's, as he'd been taught, then surely he must have become His instrument.

* * *

Not long after 7.00 a.m., Roy Walsh sat bolt upright on the bed. He was still fully clothed. There was no pounding head. There were no distorted memories. There was only complete clarity. He'd come to do a job and now needed to get out of the place. He inspected the room, looked at the bath panel, gathered up his satchel, seized his case and checked out of the hotel. Yes, he'd enjoyed his stay and would be back, he said, knowing full well that he wouldn't.

C*HAPTER*

'O UT OF THE fucking question!' Jack Pugh almost screeched when John Preston informed him that some of the Nottinghamshire miners were thinking of setting up a breakaway union. 'They cannot be allowed to do that. You must stop it.'

"Per'aps you could speak ter 'em," John suggested.

"Nottinghamshire is already letting more coal through than was agreed," Jack fumed. "Enough coal has been delivered to hospitals, care homes and schools under the NUM exemption to feed a bloody power station. Arthur is mad as hell about it."

"So 'd you cum an' address 'em?' John asked again.

"That's your damn job."

"It needs yer authority, Jack. They'll listun ter you," John urged, playing on the organizer's oversized vanity.

"I've got a lot on," Jack grumbled, wary of having to address an unappreciative audience. "Set something up and I'll try to fit it in."

"When?"

Jack looked uncomfortable and John could see him twisting inside like an eel on a hook.

"Make it a week Thursday, say six o'clock," he said eventually.

"I've another meeting at eight. That's the best I can do." He was planning on taking Mona to a hotel for dinner that night and there was sure to be something suitable in Nottingham. It was her birthday.

"Good. I'll see what I can fix up then."

* * *

Stacy and Mona huddled together at the back. Advised about the meeting by Peter Betsworth, the deputy editor of *The Sentinel* sat off to one side. 'Not all miners are created equal,' the intelligence officer had stated. 'You might want to alert your readers to this.'

John and Jack graced the podium on either side of the NUM area representative who looked distinctly ill at ease. His president's fiery intransigence did not go down well in Nottinghamshire. Worse than that, the room was half empty.

Following a less than fulsome introduction, the organizer rose nervously to his feet.

"Brothers!" he began, but his trademark greeting bounced aimlessly around the room like a ping-pong ball hit into an empty cathedral.

"We are winning!" he attempted to enthuse, but his second volley sounded more like air escaping from a tyre and Mona registered a twinge of compassion as she watched Jack deflate in front of their eyes.

"Your brothers and sisters – and I say sisters because this affects the wives as much as their menfolk – have been holding solid for five months now, at considerable hardship to themselves. If we have you with us this government will be forced to negotiate."

"Negotiate what?" someone called out.

Jack was not used to being heckled and momentarily lost his footing.

"Wages, pit closures, for Christ's sake!" he blurted out as if the question had been nonsensical.

"Pay's good here and pits aren't closing, so what's there to negotiate?" someone else in the audience asserted loudly.

Jack pulled himself together and had a run at class solidarity but when he fumbled his way into the concept of false consciousness, the Marxist idea that the proletariat's subservient position could be hidden from it by unrealistic aspirations propagated by the ruling class, a handful of miners decided they'd heard enough. One muttered that 'if pay's right we work, if it's not, we don't – that's reality enough fer uz', while another said that if he had to listen to anything more about false consciousness he'd bloody well lose consciousness.

As laughter at the departing men's wisecracks rippled around his depleted gathering, Jack lost his temper completely.

"You are ignorant, plain ignorant and have no idea of what's good for you," he all but shouted. "Capitalism will crush you, utterly crush you and you know, I actually hope it does. Comrade Lenin was always sceptical about the ability of the working class to see where its best interests lay. It was he who understood that global capital, in its quest to maximize profit, would drive down wages. You tell me why you are not vulnerable to the importation of cheap foreign coal extracted from the ground by men driven deep into the darkness in order to survive; men who are little more than slave labour. In fact, comrades, you too are slaves. You just don't know it."

As Jack accelerated into his rant, men started to leave. Not one amongst them considered himself a slave or anything close. They were men who worked hard for a good wage; men who supported their families and paid their way. But Jack ploughed on, oblivious to the sound of sliding chairs.

"Comrade Lenin did not accept the argument, which Marx advanced, based upon his theory of scientific determinism, that the bourgeoisie had to revolt against the strictures of capitalism, as they inevitably would, before the proletariat could be roused to action. No, that was not how he saw it and he proved his point. By appealing directly to the working masses, over the heads of the timid bourgeoisie, he brought down the Russian state. You," he thundered, "have joined the bourgeoisie. You are traitors to your class, creatures of the rich. And when our great president brings communism to this blighted land, as he surely will, you, brothers, will feel ashamed!"

Mona was starting to enjoy the energy in Jack's words, but she was almost alone. Apart from Stacy and the deputy editor of *The Sentinel*, the room was all but empty. Only one man in a wheelchair remained, and he was waiting for someone, anyone, to help him.

"Don't worry, son," the man said, when Jack finally ground to a halt. "This is the land of Robin Hood. We know well enough how to take from the rich and give to the poor."

Jack stared at him blankly, uncertain how to reconcile his own erudite, twentieth-century knowledge with the man's fifteenth-century English folklore. Instead, he turned to John Preston with undisguised fury. Mona realized she had a tough night ahead.

* * *

After the organizer had stormed from the hall with Mona in pursuit, Harvey walked across to John and Stacy.

"Quite a spectacle!" he said, introducing himself, blind to the fact they had Peter Betsworth in common. "Could I offer you both a drink?"

John and Stacy looked at each other and shrugged.

"Yes, I don't see why not," John said. "But per'aps sumwheres outta t'way. *The Sentinel* i'n't widely read in these parts."

It was hard to know what constituted 'out of the way' and they opted for a café near the station because Harvey needed to catch a train to London later. As a journalist with a working-class background himself, he was curious to know how a scouser machinist-come-union-organizer had hitched up with an educated young lady from the Home Counties.

"It's a long story," proffered John without any further attempt at elaboration.

"John came to a hotel I was working in," Stacy added, "and it just happened."

"Yea, it juss 'appened," confirmed John.

That was the wonder of university, Harvey thought, reflecting on his own situation: it was a leveller. But this couple was running against the odds. Stacy did not strike him as someone determined to make a statement of her love life in order to piss off some pompous parents. The journalist in him smelt a story, but it would have to wait for another day.

"So what happened this evening then?" he asked. "I've listened to Jack Pugh address audiences before, and they usually lap him up. He's one of Arthur's inside men, is he not?"

"Likes to think so," confirmed John. "But King Arthur's none too popular in these parts."

"This talk of a breakaway union then: is it for real?"

"How's you get wind o' that?" John asked.

"So it's true?"

"I've heard talk o' it," John acknowledged, playing down the fact that his handler wished him to do all in his power to bring it about. "There's a good few round 'ere who aren't that stuck on NUM, that's fer sure."

"If the Nottinghamshire mines are not solid behind the strike, the strike will fail, surely? They can't want to be responsible for that?"

"They'll mak' supportive noises from time t' time, but the men 'ere want t' work. Simple as that. It's NACODS you want to worry about. If they come out, the government's finished."

"That's the National Association of Colliery Overmen, Deputies and Shotfirers?" Harvey asked, still finding his way around the often byzantine structure of the country's unions.

"Quite a mouthful, i'n't it? No mine can function without their oversight. That's the law. It's a safety issue. In Yorkshire, NACODS members are refusing t' cross picket lines, but not elsewhere."

"Might that change?" Harvey asked.

"There's pressure fr'm a' sides," John told him. "Ah wouldn't mind be'n be'ind those close' doors when that deal gets done, ah can tell you!"

"Have you heard anything lately, John?" Stacy asked, concerned that she might have missed something.

"Only that 'ere most miners want tha' pits kept open. We'll jess' 'ave t' see."

"Have you always been a union man, John?" Harvey asked.

"Me dad was, an' a communist too. Still is, I dare say. But British Leylan' laid him off a while back an' since then ee an' me mother 'ave been doen what they can fer the miners. I'm wary of collectives meself, 'specially those that tek awoy yous liberty."

Harvey suspected John Preston and his mother would have got on.

"Have you family?" he asked.

"An older bruv, Billy, who med it ter Texas woy back but is on the rigs up in Aberdeen at the moment, an' a younger 'un, Joe, who's a chef in London: an' a pretty sound 'un by all accounts."

"Aberdeen's about the only place in the country that's doing well right now," Harvey told them. "We've moved from coal to oil."

"And that's what most of these miners don't see. You'd yav thought men ood be chuffed ter escape t' pits. Our Billy 'as a roight aud loife if 'is letters am ter goo by."

"It's the mining communities, the families that haven't moved, who are suffering," Harvey said.

"Suppose so," agreed John, "but sticking we' head in t' sand is hardly the smart thing, at leus as I see it. NUM can't see beyond coal."

"What do you make of it all, Stacy?"

"I hate seeing all this energy spent so unproductively," John's partner answered. "The sheer cost of it, too," she added. "I know change isn't always easy, but there has to be a better way than this."

"Roight boys' pissing contest, is what it is."

John Preston's succinct summary said it all. They talked for a while about other things – about how a Berlin court had cleared the Beatle Paul McCartney in a paternity suit and the Prince and Princess of Wales's second son was to be called Henry ('A champion good nem 'arry,' John thought) – until Harvey had to leave for his train.

* * *

The deputy editor discussed his day with George Gilder who advised him to leave NACODS well alone.

"We don't want to go stirring that one up, Harvey, not right now."

He then filed his piece under the heading, *Is the National Union of Miners Losing Its Grip?* He thought it a good article, by and large: measured, not too triumphalist, just pointing out that there were miners largely content with their lot who wanted to work and had little interest in toppling a government. But it ended up deep inside *The Sentinel* because the paper's front page that morning sailed forth under the banner: *High Court Rules Miners' Strike Illegal.*

This judgment exposed NUM funds to sequestration. The screws were being turned.

* * *

Up in Yorkshire, Arthur Scargill was seething, although the judgment had not been entirely unexpected. The NUM President had even managed to place some union funds out of reach, but that put them out of the union's reach as well. He instructed Jack to make contact with 'our friends overseas' and ask for financial support. Transporting pickets around the country cost money and there were union salaries to cover.

CHAPTER

40

THEY ARRIVED at 71 Buttesland Street by taxi, emotionally at sea. Puccini's *Turandot* could do that to people. Not only had the great composer died of a heart attack before completing it, but his sympathies seemed to lie more with Liù, a faithful slave girl willing to die for the man she loved, than with Turandot, a self-centred heroine happy to have unsuccessful suitors put to death. Harvey and Frances were also nervous, but that was not Puccini's fault. Neither had entered the other's home before.

"I hope you're up for something simple?" Harvey asked when they had got inside. "I thought penne run through with ricotta, diced smoked ham and a little spinach in a cream sauce might do it."

"That sounds lovely. Is there anything I can do to help?"

"How about a starter of sliced mozzarella, fresh tomatoes and basil drizzled with olive oil? The mozzarella's in the fridge, basil and tomatoes are there and the olive oil over here. Put on this apron," he instructed, handing her one with Pisa's leaning tower and the words *Viva Italia* printed on it.

"Very classy!" she joked.

"Oh yes, it's all class in here – East-End Italian class!" And he slipped the apron over her head and tied its bow at the back.

Frances rearranged it slightly. She wasn't used to being dressed by a man.

"Now I think I've got a reasonable Sicilian wine somewhere," he said disappearing down a set of steep steps into what had once been the coal hole.

The displaced chatelaine of Graham castle started to busy herself with the first course, while looking around Harvey's kitchen with that sense-making curiosity particular to the female character. She wasn't sure what was going to be hardest: competing with Harvey's dead mother or with Harvey, a man so clearly set in his ways. The kitchen was immaculate.

"I think we'll enjoy this," he said, emerging triumphant from the coal hole. "It's a red from the Bondi vineyards on Mount Etna. A blend of two local grapes, apparently."

"Mount Etna?" she said, sounding surprised. "That can't be very safe?"

"It's not, but the Sicilians have a love-hate relationship with their mountain. She is angry one minute, sublime the next, like a petulant mistress."

"Have you had a girlfriend?" she blurted out. The question came from deep inside her. She had read about the unbreakable bond between some men and their mothers.

Harvey laughed as he poured them both a glass of the wine.

"You are worried I might be a mother's boy – even a dead mother's!"

She shrugged and looked embarrassed.

"Sylvia, my mother," he began, by way of explanation, "and I think of her as Sylvia as often as I do my mother, said I would never get a woman as long as I lived here with her. And in a way, she was right. From the age of twelve she looked after me and never once did I imagine that I wouldn't do the same for her. So I suppose you could say we were as good as married. But did I have a girlfriend? Well, let's say that my mother and I had an understanding. There was someone I saw pretty regularly, but never here and we never talked about it. If she was lonely when I was out, she would have our gay neighbour, Trevelyan, round and they'd watch television together."

Suddenly Frances found herself worrying about the girlfriend rather than the mother. "Are you still seeing that someone?" she asked cagily, "if that isn't too nosey?"

"Yes, it's very nosey, but no, I'm not still seeing her. It was becoming too mechanical, if you know what I mean."

"I'm not sure I want to," Frances answered, sounding more relieved than she intended.

Harvey seemed to be everywhere: finishing off the penne, laying the table, refilling their glasses and looking over her shoulder, rather attentively she felt, which was not altogether unwelcome, to see how she was progressing.

"What did you make of the production?" he asked.

"Turandot?"

"Yes."

"It left me a little dissatisfied, I have to admit," she confessed.

"Yes, it's hard to feel much sympathy for Turandot when she spares her last suitor, especially as one's sympathies still lie with the slave girl, Liù. Apparently Puccini was very fond of his own maid, Doria, and some think he invested his creative energy into her as Liù rather than into the heroine."

"Do we know what happened to Doria?"

"The poor girl committed suicide after the maestro's wife accused her of having sexual relations with her husband. At the autopsy she was found to be a virgin."

"How terribly sad."

"Yes. And it would probably have made a better opera, too," Harvey speculated. "But Madame Puccini would soon have put a stop to that I fear!"

The candlelight flickered and they talked the talk of two people happy to be in each other's company, taking pleasure in the fact that it had come to this, regardless of the path each had taken to be there. Like two creatures who had stumbled out of a forest into the same clearing, they found themselves wrapped in nature's momentary communion, oblivious of past and future, aware only of a seemingly eternal present that reached back and reached forward without any need for justification.

Harvey and Frances could have been in the eye of a storm, or paradise, or one and the same because the intensity of a moment is a function of its transience. But neither cared nor thought about such things. Romeo's love for Juliet and hers for him was enriched by its impossibility. The wine and food elevated pleasure above all other concerns. The voices of Buttesland Street were coming alive and slipping their moorings: from hawkers to harlots, mothers and their children, men and their work, from music hall darlings skirting the edge of respectability to Salvationists decrying the evils of drink and loose living, the conflicted nature of human experience had been corralled within a rainbow and they were inside its bag of gold.

As they gathered up the dishes and fed them distractedly into the sink's open mouth, their proximity – a brush here, a touch there, her smell, his – could no longer be ignored. Harvey placed his hands on her shoulders with the firmness of a writer placing a full stop to end a sentence and turned her towards him. They looked at each other with a mixture of fear and hunger. Tomorrow's words had not yet been written, but the piggybank of hope was about to be broken and its contents spent.

"Perhaps we should go upstairs," Frances whispered, wondering what her body would look like to another man. "I haven't done this in a while."

"Oh God," cried Harvey. "There's only mother's double bed!"

But Sylvia's ghost was no impediment. The joy of physical concert and exploration came readily to them both and the bed bore witness to acts of tender inventiveness that might have surprised its prior occupants. Strange thoughts did float around, though. For a moment Frances came face-to-face with David although he didn't seem angry, just amused. And Harvey could not quite escape the thought of his mother shouting encouragement from the sidelines.

'Go, Harve – now didn't I say!'

C*HAPTER* 41

N ORMALLY George Gilder liked to attend the Conservative Party conference, but this year he could not. He would be over 11,000 miles away visiting his sister in New Zealand. She was fighting a losing battle against cancer and this would likely be his last chance to see her. Harvey would have to go instead. His deputy editor could enjoy the special status accorded to *The Sentinel* for the paper's steadfast support of the Prime Minister and listen to the interminable speeches from party members which passed for consultation with the rank and file.

* * *

It was approaching 1.00 a.m. when Harvey dropped Frances back. Her sister had given a dinner party for her at which he had been the object of interest and he now had to haul himself off to Brighton. He always had a second wind around midnight and whenever he could reach it, enjoyed the night-time. It was a different world, one in which human beings ceased to be mere functionaries governed by clocks and schedules, hierarchies and etiquette, but creatures driven by instinct, the veneer of civilization rubbed off.

The cold lights along the Chelsea Embankment looked much as they had in Victorian times, although now electric, not gas, and the brown water of the River Thames slipped by like a stealthy vagabond carrying away everything in its path as it had been doing for centuries, long before the city was conceived. But top hats, silver-topped sticks, street ladies and dirty urchins out to make a penny, the imagery of Dickens and Conan Doyle, still attached themselves to London as if the age of its greatest greatness was reluctant to leave the feast. And as the emperor Nero had for ancient Rome, so Jack the Ripper still did for London: terrify and excite in equal measure, imagery no cosmopolitan city could seemingly do without.

The King's Road was winding down, its restaurants closing and its last revellers heading home to waiting beds or on to some human cave of physicality where everything but the sensations of the moment could be cast aside. A few black cabs still searched for fares like jackdaws after scraps; others were aiming for the suburbs, their day's work done.

Not until Putney Bridge did Harvey feel his journey south had begun, even though the suburbs would surround him for many miles yet. And it was only after he had skirted the leafy darkness of Richmond's Royal Park that the miscellany of small shops with flats above, which lined his route like flag-waving celebrants to trade, began to fade and England's army of semi-detached homes take root, each one a little haven of repose, its red bricks a panegyric to conformity.

New Malden, Long Ditton, Chessington with its famous zoo, the names passed by dimly in the night, each hamlet the work of time and individual ambition, now princelings in Greater London's mighty court. It was true, he thought, that the kingdom's pulsing heart sucked in everything it could reach, draining centres such as Glasgow, Liverpool, Newcastle and Birmingham of their power. Like ancient

Rome, England's capital fed on its empire, sending back its template in return: its military and economic order, its justice, its priorities, its culture, a compact most seemed willing to accept until one day they did not, prompting a future Gibbon to ponder London's decline and fall.

For a while, after Leatherhead, he joined the M25, the capital's 117 mile orbital motorway, second only to the Berliner Ring. Continental competition had not died, only mutated, but at least one could now die in the comfort of one's automobile instead of a mud-filled trench in Flanders fields. The numbers were also better. He'd read that these days only 5,000 people were being killed on the roads each year, compared to the 8,000 Britons killed during the first battle of Ypres alone.

Near Mersham, he branched south onto the M23. He passed signs to Redhill, where Polish pilots had been trained to fight the Luftwaffe, followed by Gatwick, London's second airport and then Crawley, a coffee-stop for contestants during the London to Brighton Veteran Car Run. In 1896, the journey had taken Léon Bollée, the fastest contender, three and three quarter hours to complete. Harvey looked at the illuminated clock on his car's dashboard. With luck, he would cover the same distance in ninety minutes.

Night-time, solitude and travel were a cocktail designed for thought. These last years had been the most exciting of his life, even more so than the time he had spent at university. Then, a feeling of being liberated from one's background and offered seemingly limitless possibilities had been intoxicating. Now, nurtured by experience, the growing sinews of his mind no longer moved freely in the wind but were resisting it and assuming a concrete shape. Having drawn freely on the lives of others, Harvey realized that he had become himself and it was a good and powerful feeling.

Crossing the western end of the High Weald, over 500 square miles of what had been designated an area of outstanding natural beauty, running from Kent to Surrey, he begrudged the darkness. He had seen it in daylight certainly – rolling land crisscrossed with hedgerows. This was quintessentially England. The Battle of Britain had been fought in its skies. Somewhere out in the darkness, to the north, was Runnymede, now a prosperous part of the London commuter belt, where a group of nobles in 1215 had forced the king to sign a Magna Carta restricting his power: one milestone in the eternal struggle between individual and State. How, he wondered, would the battle now raging around him be thought of in 700 years?

The road dropped down from the Weald crossing the River Adur, before rising again over the South Downs, the chalk escarpment which buttresses England from the sea and guided fighter pilots back across the Channel. He wondered what the Prime Minister would have to say at her conference. The economy was slowly picking itself off the floor and her poll ratings were improving, but outside Nottinghamshire the miners were fighting on and she was loathed by large swathes of the population. Around 3 million people who wanted to work were still unemployed – 20% of all men under twenty-five and 9% of those over – and there were many in the country who felt that her government had simply taken a sledgehammer to their lives.

* * *

It was approaching 3.00 a.m. and the Prime Minister was still working on her speech. She, too, was enjoying the quiet solitude of the night. In the bedroom next door, her beloved husband was sleeping soundly. She rose and in the bathroom mirror saw herself staring back: a lady in a nightgown two days short of her sixtieth year. It had to be a good speech. She knew that. The party needed reassurance that things were on the mend. Often she felt that only her will kept Britain from sliding back into a collectivist nightmare in which every soft option taken led not just to further decline, but to a belief that more of the same, not less, was needed to reverse it.

How could so many intelligent people have thought that a country's economy could be left to organizations like an elected government, the civil service, the nationalized industries and the trades unions, all of whose leaders were more anxious to maintain their political control than meet the needs of individual consumers? She rubbed some cream into her cheeks and forehead. In a war, a nation could be run like a giant corporation because there was one overriding objective – to beat the enemy. But not in peacetime, when individuals had many objectives and a free market, under law, was the best medium through which to express and reconcile them. She gently wiped off the surplus lotion. In a few hours, her beauticians would be in attendance. She had to look her best.

In the ante-room, she sat again at the desk to look over her speech one last time. She should turn in. She knew it. The day ahead was going to be long but she was determined not to let people down. In moments of doubt, she reminded herself that Moses, often in the face of fierce protest, had led the Israelites away from Egyptian slavery.

"So buck up, Margaret," she whispered. She *would* lead her people away from the slavery of socialism.

And had Sylvia been listening from her resting place in the afterlife, she would surely have called out, 'And don't you give up, dear.'

* * *

Harvey entered the outskirts of Brighton on Preston Road. The town had a genteel, if somewhat worn-out appearance, like an elderly widow still living off what remained from an ancestor's fortune. He passed Patcham, Cliveden Close and Lansdowne Road, all solid names appropriated by the middle class. It was a privilege to have a room at

The Grand, even if his would be a small one, up in the rafters. Most of the British Cabinet would be housed there along with the movers and shakers of the Conservative Party. Although a representative of the fourth estate, George Gilder was considered a 'trusty', in prison parlance, and his deputy was to be accorded the same respect. At the Kingsway, he turned left. The famous pier lay ahead. It still had some lights shining on it and appeared to hover above the water.

From nowhere, Graham Green's novel *Brighton Rock* came into his head. Perhaps Ida Arnold was the Prime Minister, determined to bring down the sociopath Pinkie Brown, a sort of small-scale Joseph Stalin with a Catholic rather than Communist background, after a chance encounter with Hale, one of Pinkie's victims, on the Palace Pier. As he turned left again, out of the Kingsway, to confront The Grand, he glanced at the dashboard clock. It was 2.54 a.m. He had made excellent time.

The car must have been about a hundred yards short when Harvey slammed on the brakes. At first he could not make sense of it. The entire centre section of the Hotel simply fell in on itself. Then came a bang, followed by complete and utter silence. He just sat there, staring, as dust, under-lit by street lights, rose ethereally into the night sky. For a split second he could see only the destructive beauty of it all. And then his violently-contracting stomach muscles alerted him to the true horror. They – whoever 'they' were – had just blown up the British Government.

* * *

"What the devil was that?"

The Prime Minister's husband sat bolt upright in bed. There was a smell that wasn't scented polish in the air and the room looked ghostly in the pale glow of an emergency light.

"I think it was a bomb, dear," his wife answered. "You'd better get dressed quickly. We should investigate. There may be people hurt."

"We should get out, more like," he cautioned. "Oldest trick in the book: one bomb followed by another when everyone's in disarray."

He moved quickly to the bathroom.

"Heavens, Margaret! Take a look at this!"

They both stared through the half-open door. The darkened room looked as though it had been torn apart.

"I was in there moments ago," she said, aghast.

"Margaret, I'm getting you out of here, now."

* * *

Harvey stood next to his car, unsure what to do. At first the only sound came from the building as some loosened sections of masonry fell to the ground and others settled. The Grand appeared to be adjusting to its new situation like a sleeper turning over in bed. A dog began barking. Lights were coming on in buildings nearby. He heard voices and then shouts. With about as much forethought as one of the zombies in *Night of the Living Dead*, he approached the hotel. A call box on the pavement seemed intact so he went inside. He heard the familiar purr of a dialling tone and dialled 999.

"Fire service, ambulance or police?" a female voice asked.

"All of them," he answered. "There's been an explosion at The Grand Hotel."

Harvey then felt in his pockets for change, but there was none and so he made a reverse-charge call to the night desk at *The Sentinel*.

"Henry, it's Harvey ... No, I'm not in bed. Look, this is big. I need you to get a photographer down here now ... Brighton. I'm in Brighton. This is going to be front page so stand by ... There's been an explosion at The Grand Hotel. Most of the cabinet must be staying here ... I don't know. But there will be casualties ... No, I don't know if the Prime Minister is amongst them, Henry, it's just happened. Get that photographer down here and start working on a headline ... No, I don't know who or what was responsible..."

"Fair enough...," Harvey conceded at Henry's not-unreasonable plea that he would need something more to go on and glancing at his watch said, "Look, it's just gone three. I'll call you in a couple of hours. There's bound to be an agency photographer down here who'll get something up to London in time for the early editions ... I know that'll cost us. Oh, and Henry, call George in New Zealand. Tell him I'll contact him when I can."

As he emerged from the kiosk, an armada of police cars approached, their blue lights flashing and sirens blaring, followed by a line of more deeply-throated fire trucks. Normality, then the event, then silence, then the ululation of the response teams announcing their arrival like the US cavalry in a spaghetti western after the wagon train has been decimated by Indians. Within seconds, as the only living being visible, he had been bundled into the back of a police car. Who was he? What was he doing outside The Grand Hotel at 3.00 a.m.? And if that was his car in the middle of the approach road, would he get it out of the way as it was impeding the emergency services. Harvey was freed from detention, mildly punch drunk, relieved he had been neither black nor Irish.

* * *

For the next several hours, members of the fire service worked to secure the building, locate the dead and wounded and lead survivors to waiting ambulances or to safe areas nearby. Mrs Thatcher and her husband were escorted to the police station where their statements were taken and at 4.00 a.m., the Prime Minister agreed to be interviewed by the BBC's political editor, John Cole. The Conservative Party Conference would go ahead as planned, she told him with the verve the world had come to expect. The Conservative

Party treasurer, Alistair McAlpine persuaded the head of Marks & Spencer to open his Brighton store early so that all those without garments could be reclothed.

Five Conservative Party officials were found dead, four of them women, and the trade and industry secretary, Norman Tebbit, lay trapped under rubble next to his severely-injured wife. Cameras captured his dust-covered face and pyjama top and he later told reporters how comforting it had been holding the hand of a fireman while masonry was carefully lifted from his body. The remainder of the cabinet had escaped injury.

* * *

At 5.00 a.m., Harvey filed his first report under the headline, *Outrage! Thatcher Defiant.* As the only eyewitness to the explosion, his account was one of the best that morning, but he needn't have worried about photographers: they were everywhere. Much of the media was already in Brighton for the conference and now the rest had moved there en masse. The greatest difficulty was finding a free telephone. The new mobile version had not seemed that appealing until then, but he made a mental note to have a fresh look.

* * *

Frances Graham turned on her radio shortly after 6.00 a.m. The excited tone of the newsreader alerted her to the fact that an unusually newsworthy event had taken place, but its content did not become clear until after her visit to the bathroom and the word 'Brighton', which would pepper the airways like machine-gun fire for the rest of the day, had penetrated her own consciousness. Besides, she was too busy recalling the pleasure of the night before. It was the first time she had broken cover to show off the new man in her life, at least to her closest friends and family. She thought Harvey had gone down well although was not sure how much he himself had enjoyed being inspected.

But when her rekindled hopes came face-to-face with Brighton and sudden fear, the juxtaposition pulled her earlier equanimity apart. She paced around the bedroom holding the radio to her ear, hoping that, amongst the flood of commentary, speculation and editorial indignation, Harvey's well-being would be revealed. But it wasn't. So she continued her pacing downstairs, switched on the kettle and emptied two scoops of Brazilian coffee into her cafetière. While the kettle boiled, she telephoned *The Sentinel*, but only got a recording thanking her for contacting the nation's largest circulation broadsheet and informing her that the switchboard would open at 9.30a.m.

"Damn you, Harvey," she said out loud. "Don't you dare get yourself killed," and then realized that he might already be dead.

"It is believed five persons were killed in the blast and at least thirty-seven injured," the host of the morning's current affairs programme was announcing in a tone adrift from his normally measured delivery. "No names will be released by the police until next of kin have been informed," he said. "What we do know, however," he now told his listeners, in a voice of renewed steadfastness, "is that the Prime Minister escaped injury and has insisted that her party's conference will go ahead as planned."

I am not even 'next of kin,' she thought. So what am I? What are any two people who have found one another within the topsy-turvy maelstrom of life and now inhabit that private, peaceful space reserved for lovers, away from social recognition and the claim of others? She had even been wary about dinner. As nice as it was to share her happiness with those closest to her, mightn't something have been lost as well as gained?

She looked at her watch. It was only 6.30. But she called *The Sentinel* again for want of anything else to do. This time she heard no recording, just a gruff "Sent'n'l" from Jim, the cleaner, who happened to be passing and interpreted his duties rather widely in the interests of job satisfaction. "Switchboard's closed," he then announced.

"Yes, I know. Don't hang up," Frances pleaded. "I just want to know if Harvey is all right."

"Friend of yours then?" Jim enquired, alive to the sound of a lady in distress.

"He's in Brighton, you see," she said, "and with the explosion and everything…"

"Brighton's a big place, dear," Jim soothed. "Harvey, you say? Does he work here?"

"Yes, he's the deputy editor. He was supposed to be staying at the hotel that's exploded."

"Hotels don't generally explode, love. But I'll ask downstairs. If the newsroom doesn't know anything then it hasn't happened," Jim assured her with a degree of confidence she found strangely reassuring. "Now don't go away, dear. What's your name?"

"Frances Graham," she told him and at that point she would have confided her life story and thrown in a few sins, such was the unexpected power of this electronic confessional. "I am a friend of Harvey Mudd."

"All right, Frances," Jim allowed. "Now I'm going to try and put you on hold, sweetheart. It's a bit of a complicated system this–"

There was an ominous click and Jim was gone.

She hung on, and on. The act of holding convinced her she was doing something. The minutes passed, but still she held, drinking coffee with one hand, pressing the phone to the side of her head with the other until her ear hurt and arm ached. The pain was almost pleasurable, born out of sound homeopathic principles, she imagined – a little controlled pain to counteract the pain that couldn't be controlled. And then for no accountable reason, her mind wandered off to the Marquis de Sade and sadomasochism…

"Hello? Hello?"

Out of nowhere a different voice was addressing her.

"Yes, hello," she answered.

"Frances Graham?" the voice asked.

"Yes."

"Oh thank goodness you're still there. Harvey told me to call you but I must have taken the number down wrong. He's fine by the way. But Brighton's bedlam right now and every phone line's been commandeered by some journalist or newsman."

"Was he in the hotel?" she asked.

"No. He was approaching it when the bomb went off – and we do think it was a bomb now, probably another calling card from the IRA. Look, I'm most awfully sorry I didn't call you. Harvey was insistent that I should when he filed his report, but it's also pretty good bedlam inside *The Sentinel* right now, I can tell you."

"Who am I speaking to?" she asked.

"Henry Smart, the night editor, which is just a grand title to persuade some junior like me to sit up all night in the newsroom in case something turns up – which it hardly ever does. Harvey will crucify me for not having called you."

"Don't worry, Mr Smart. We're talking now. But who was that who answered my call?"

"That was Jim, our cleaner. We're forever telling him to leave the switchboard alone because we have direct lines into the news desk. But he says what if someone just calls?"

"Well, today they just did," laughed Frances. "So will you thank him?"

"You bet I will!" agreed Henry, as much now in Jim's debt as was Frances.

Suddenly she felt happy again – inordinately so.

* * *

The atmosphere in the hall was electric when the Prime Minister approached the lectern. She looked fresh and perfectly coiffed despite having endured a night in which friends had been killed or injured and she and her husband had narrowly escaped death.

She commenced by condemning a cowardly act against innocent people intended to cripple a democratically elected government. She thanked and praised the emergency services and offered up, on behalf of everyone present, her sympathies to all those who had suffered. Then it was down to business.

She praised the conference chairman's organization in spite of her having had little sleep and she praised the contributions made by party members from the floor as having been 'an outstanding example of orderly assembly and free speech'.

She reiterated her government's determination to bear down on taxation at both a local and national level and reminded conference that thirteen major enterprises had been denationalized since 1979 and said she looked forward to seeing British Airways and British Telecom soon pass into private hands.

She reminded conference of her government's support for pensioners and the National Health Service and stressed that efficient and competitive industries were needed to pay for both. Efficiency, she said, was 'not the enemy, but the ally, of compassion'.

She compared her government's stand on defence with that of the Opposition and reminded her audience of Winston Churchill's dictum that giving in to aggression merely courted more of it. Her party, she said, had no truck with Marxist notions of class warfare. What counted was not your background but what you could do for your country.

She mentioned her government's satisfaction with the terms under which Hong Kong would be returned to China and praised Geoffrey Howe's 'skill, hard work and perseverance in this regard'.

On Europe, she claimed satisfaction with the new level of Britain's contribution to the community budget, forcefully negotiated, she added, to much laughter, and stressed her government's determination to bear down on surplus food production and other wasteful expenditure. But now she hoped the European Community would 'use its energies and influence to play a greater part in world affairs'.

Turning to the still-vexed question of employment, she conceded that having 3 million people unemployed was undoubtedly bad but refuted accusations that it had been used as a 'political weapon'. She also disagreed with those who, while accepting her government's sincere wish to deal with the problem, disagreed with its method. The problem, she said, had run very deep.

In 1944, she told the delegates, a seminal White Paper had been drafted on how best to ensure full employment. And she knew this document rather well, she explained, to much delight, because as Margaret H. Roberts she had been one of those who had helped draft it.

The problem, she told them, was that successive governments had cherry-picked the easy parts and ignored those parts that were harder. Not only had the warning that government should not weaken people's resolve to be enterprising and fend for themselves been ignored, but so had the paper's warning that 'without a rising standard of industrial efficiency, you cannot achieve a high level of employment combined with a rising standard of living'. Now, of course, she conceded, this means that old industries will die as new ones are formed, not by governments, it had to be stressed, but by individuals searching for better ways to meet people's needs and improve their own standing, and all this caused disruption.

What governments could do and should do to ease these transitions was underpin redundancy payments, make payments to individuals while they looked for new work and help with the costs of retraining. What made no sense was for taxpayers to prop up uneconomic industries. Instead, government should keep taxes low, inflation tame and regulation minimal so that new businesses could form and new jobs be created, all of which, she stressed, her government was seeking to do.

"May I now turn to the coal industry?" she stated rhetorically and her audience was more than ready for her to do so.

She pointed out that for over seven months the country had been living though an agonizing strike.

"Let me make it absolutely clear," she said, "the miners' strike was not of this government's seeking nor of its making." The annual losses being compounded by the coal industry were enormous, she said. £1.3 billion in the previous year and the money had to come from somewhere. That amount, their party leader explained "is equal to the sum we pay in salaries to all the doctors and dentists in the National Health Service".

The present Executive of the National Union of Mineworkers, she pointed out, was making demands that could not be met. Why? Because, she maintained, an organized revolutionary minority within the union was intent upon the destruction of democratic parliamentary government. To those who told her to give them what they want to stop the violence, she drew on a quotation from Rudyard Kipling – "We do not pay Danegeld."

The true heroes of this dispute, she said, were those miners who still went to work each day in order to support their families and keep their mines open in spite of threats and intimidation, and the wives who had to put up with their husbands being branded scabs. 'Scabs?' she almost shouted. "They are lions!"

"The nation faces what is probably the most testing crisis of our time," she said, "the battle between the extremists and the rest. We are fighting, as we have always fought, for the weak as well as for the strong. We are fighting for great and good causes. We are fighting to defend them against the power and might of those who rise up and challenge them. This government will not weaken. This nation will meet that challenge. Democracy will prevail."

The audience rose and clapped as they had seldom clapped before. Harvey wrote at the foot of his notes: *Concluded at 3.30 p.m. Brilliant – a political master class!*

* * *

Up in Yorkshire, the mood was glum. Jack Pugh had been ecstatic when news of the Brighton bomb broke. He and Mona had been out late clubbing and were listening to the first sketchy reports as they came in. His excitement had been intense.

"This is it," he had confided to her, "the revolution is under way!"

"Did you have something to do with it?" she had asked, secretly appalled by what was being reported.

Jack had hesitated. The temptation to take credit for such a magnificent act was almost overwhelming.

"Sadly not," he had said eventually. "But I hope the bitch copped it."

"Charming!" Mona had admonished, but the organizer wasn't listening.

They drove straight to the NUM offices and Jack hadn't even thought to drop her back at their rented flat, which the union was paying for. People trickled in to headquarters throughout the morning and she struggled to keep her eyes open as the mood turned from euphoria to resignation.

When the Prime Minister's conference speech concluded and it was reported that she had left the Conference Hall to visit the wounded in the Royal Sussex County Hospital, Mona heard someone remark, with what she thought was a hint of admiration, 'That woman has the devil's luck, I'll give her that. First it was the bloody Argentines and now this. She probably planted the damn thing herself!'

The executive committee agreed to meet later that evening for a strategy meeting, but everyone was beginning to realize the same thing: they were running out of options.

"It's now down to NACODS," Jack told her as he drove them back for some much-needed sleep. Mona had heard about the power of the National Association of Colliery Overmen, Deputies and Shopfitters to close all the pits, but apart from something to do with safety, what they actually did was a mystery. Later, when Jack was nursing his misplaced hopes, she would excuse herself and call Stacy.

Part 3

CHAPTER 42

THE UNION was like a church around Wakefield. Little escaped its influence. There were fifteen pits operating in the area and the rhythm of coal played into everyone's life to some degree. The National Coal Board had already closed six pits it deemed uneconomic since 1979 and anxiety was widespread. People were determined to hold onto their livelihoods and communities.

After the start of the strike, Mabel and Stanley Preston had been coming to the town to offer what support they could. With him now retired and the beneficiary of a generous redundancy payment from his old employer, British Leyland, he felt it was the least he could do. Mabel had picked Wakefield because she liked its history and liked what she had read about West Yorkshire.

They had taken to staying with Alfie and Evie Chappel, a young couple who had purchased their council house at the start of the year under the government's Right to Buy scheme. Originally proposed by a Labour Government back in 1959, the idea had been embraced by Mrs Thatcher as a way of freeing people from their councils and forcing those councils to pay down some of their excessive debt. With Alfie earning good money from the colliery and Evie earning a reasonable wage as a beautician, their year had begun well.

The newlyweds had hoped their second bedroom would soon do for a bairn, and were pleased to earn something extra from the Prestons in the meantime. Besides, they enjoyed having an older couple in the house from time to time. Since the start of the strike, however, what had begun as a luxury was now a necessity. With Alfie earning nothing and in receipt of no state benefits because the strike had been ruled illegal, their finances were in a mess. In September, their hopes that the union and Coal Board would reach a settlement had been dashed. The Coal Board had blamed the union and their president had blamed the government. No end seemed in sight.

* * *

"Come on in, Prestons," Evie greeted. "How was thy trip?"

"Mabel here wanted to go via Peak District," Stanley told her, "so we started early an' took our time."

"That must have been grand," Evie said as she helped to get their case inside.

"Yes, you an' Archie should go sometime," Mabel enthused. "It's lovely."

"Perhaps when all this is over," Evie agreed. "Things are tight now. Car's gone."

"I am sorry to hear that, dear," Mabel commiserated.

"Yes, and that's not the half o' it," Evie replied as she manoeuvred the Prestons' case up into the spare room. "But enough o' our problems. There's folk around here in worse shape. Come down when thou're ready and we'll have us a grand pot o' tea."

"Where's Alfie?" Stanley asked.

"He's down at Institute," Evie told him. "And if he's not there, he'll be on t' picket line. There's nowt much else for the men to do these days."

Stanley sat on the chair while Mabel unpacked. Both thought back to when they had started out on their own married journey. A war might have been raging but there seemed to be prospects then and they'd never gone short, at least not *short* short. True they had probably expected less and it had been a good while before a car had come their way, but by the standards of the day, neither felt the Chappels had been extravagant. And besides, miners were well paid, compared to some; at least they were when they were working.

Stanley respected union solidarity. It had served him and Mabel well. A man couldn't support his union one minute and disregard it the next. That wasn't how the system worked. Certainly you had to trust your union leaders to look after your best interests, but how could it be otherwise? No group of men could function without discipline. He and his John had had some fierce arguments about that, for sure. What if you were being led the wrong way? That seemed to be his point. But John was back in the union fold now.

He didn't really know what to make of his other boys. Neither had followed his path. There was the runaway Billy. The invisible Billy. The Billy with a strange accent. The Billy who appeared to have money. The Billy who was always about to come home but never did. The Billy he no longer knew. And then there was Joseph…

"Penny for them, dear?" Mabel asked.

He wasn't sure his thoughts were worth a penny. The world was changing and he wasn't. That was about the sum of it.

"I think I'll go an' find Alfie," Stanley said, getting up.

"You do that, dear," Mabel agreed. "Evie an' I can have a laugh and a chat. The skint love looks as though she's carrying all the world's problems on her pretty shoulders."

Mabel carefully folded the clothes that needed folding and hung those that needed to be hung. The room was spotless. Pulling aside the net curtain, she looked across at the matching council houses on the opposite side of the street and wondered how many of them had been bought by other young couples anxious to 'get on'.

As she came down the stairs, she heard sobs coming from the kitchen and found Evie sat at the table, tears pouring down her cheeks and a stack of papers in front of her. The young woman looked up and her wide eyes signalled only desperation.

"I can't make 'em balance out, Mabel. I just can't!"

Mabel walked across, sat next to Evie and placed an arm around her shoulder.

"Why don't I brew us both some tea?"

Evie Chappel just sobbed and so Mabel set to work. She'd been dying for a cup since Sheffield.

With the tea made, she settled down next to Evie and began looking over the papers, which, in reality, were all bills. Very quickly it became clear that the biggest drain came from the mortgage, followed by the gas and then the rates the council were demanding.

"I just don't know where to start," Evie said, her sobs subsiding. "With Alfie bringing in nowt it's down to us 'n I'm barely making fifty pound a week an' that's down from eighty. Who around here has brass to waste on they looks these days? We'll have to fettle for free soon, it's that bad."

"How much of everything's on tick?" Mabel asked, looking around.

Suddenly Evie brightened up.

"All bought 'n paid for," she answered with obvious pride. "Alfie had saved up afore we wed so we could make the deposit 'n furnish the house. It were the car that caught we."

"Well done you, then," applauded Mabel. "That's a mighty sound start."

"But look at what's left," Evie moaned, looking depressed again.

"Well the gas is easy peasy," chortled Mabel. "You tell them they can have their meter."

"But there's cooking, 'n we are coming into winter."

"Not everything has to be cooked an' you can get a hot meal at The Centre."

"And the parky?" Evie asked.

"You've got a bonny fire an' you must be able to get coal around here, for heaven's sake!"

"You would have thought. But a group o' lads was arrested for trespass searching through t' slag near we pit," she told Mabel. "It's dang'rous and all. Two bairns were killed doing it somewhere, I read."

Mabel thought the 'parky' would just have to take care of itself. At least there were no young children involved. She'd bring along some of her and Stanley's old jumpers next time they came up.

"So let's think about the council an' the mortgage," Mabel advised. "I see mortgage is with the Halifax Building Society. Have you an' Alfie spoken to them?"

"No."

"Well you should. An' the council?"

"They are being right buggers, if you'll excuse us language. I don't think they liked t' fact we purchased we house."

"You can't be the only ones and they can't pick on just you, whatever they say. They will have to wait until this strike's over."

"An' t' Halifax?"

"You an' Alfie arrange a meeting," Mabel repeated. "But I can't see them wanting to repossess your home. What good would that do them? No one would buy it."

Mabel patted Evie on the shoulder and told her it might not be as bad as it looked. But Evie just dissolved into tears again.

"Dear girl. You're never pregnant, are you?"

"Three months. It wor a mistake."

"Well that's a most wonderful mistake, Evie," Mabel cooed. "Now let's get ourselves up to The Centre. I have a car chock full o' provisions."

* * *

What had now become known simply as The Centre, a Methodist hall made available for the duration, was a hive of activity. The striking men's womenfolk had decided they had a role to play. They were the ones who had to get food on the table, clothe the children, juggle the bills, deal with the bailiffs, placate the council and pep up their husbands, sons and brothers when they were down. They had even endured their share of police harassment on the picket lines and in the town. But in The Centre they had found their calling as had other Women's Action Groups, from Gateside in Scotland to the Rhondda Valley in South Wales and Chislet in Kent.

Mabel was warmly greeted when she and Evie carried in boxes of provisions from the car.

"Come on, darlin'. Bring us thy bounty!" called out Helen who appeared to be the group's unofficial leader.

"Children's clothes here 'n food yonder," directed Marge, one of her several assistants.

"Evie love," summoned Helen, who knew full well how hard it was for the younger couples, "when thee are done helping Mabel come 'n help us wi' t' soup."

In no time, Evie Chappel's tears had been forgotten and Mabel Preston was doing what she enjoyed most: helping out.

* * *

Stanley caught up with Alfie Chappel playing a game of pool with his friend Randolph, who was still earning, at the Institute. The two men were hatching a plan to take Randolph's two whippets to Kirkthorpe where some hares had been spotted. And if they couldn't get a hare, there were always rabbits. But even these were becoming scarce and Randolph was struggling to catch the six-or-so a week he needed for his dogs, let alone a few extra for the pot. He wasn't the only one scouring the countryside for food. Pheasants were thought fair game, but sheep were frowned upon: farmers had a living to make like everyone else.

"Stan, it's grand to see thee," Alfie called out as he saw Stanley Preston at the far end of his pool table. "Mabel well?"

"Mabel's sound Alf. She's with Evie. They were going to The Centre with some provisions we brought up."

"You are both stars, Stan," Alfie told him. "Now I don't think you know Randolph here. We were about to gi' 'is whippets a run. Are you game for it?"

Stanley had never seen whippets work before and said he was game, so they all bundled into Randolph's beat-up van, with Alfie squeezed in the back next to the caged animals, both in a state of excitement, and Stanley in front next to Randolph, on account of him being their guest.

"Randolph 'ere's management, although thee wouldn't have thought it," Alfie shouted to make himself heard above the clatter of the van. "'Ee gets to nip on down t' pits to make sure they will still be operational when strike ends."

"An engineer?" Stanley asked.

"Trainee," Randolph told him. "We get passes so pickets let us through without fuss most of the time. But it turned foul a fortnight back. One lad tried to return to fettle 'n were given a right going over. The police got involved 'n for a few days after we needed an escort. Tempers was running high. Some said lad had been bribed by management, but it could have been pressure from his family. But no one likes scabs roun' 'ere."

The van eventually cleared the town and Randolph started to drive slowly, looking at the fields as they passed. The angry grey clouds chasing each other across the countryside looked as though they might crash land, so low and heavy they were.

"There's one in the middle o' 'at field,' Randolph announced, bringing the van to a halt.

Stanley looked across but could see nothing.

"'ares lie flat when they sense danger so you can't see 'em," Randolph explained. "Now we need to be right quiet. We walk towards it 'n get as close as we can afore it runs 'n I let dogs loose. The dogs are faster but if they don't cop the 'are afore the end o' t' field we lose it."

The three climbed out of the van and the whippets started whining and pulling against the quick-release straps Randolph had attached to them. Only then did Stanley realize how cold it was.

"Here, Stan, put this on," Randolph whispered, handing him his old coat. "I'm used to it, really. Now take it."

The three passed though a gate into the stubble field whose crop of wheat must have been harvested only two months before. The grass the farmer had under-sown to feed stock over the winter was just visible but had been feeding the hare instead.

Randolph lined them up about 20 yards apart. He and Alfie each took a dog at one end, placing Stanley between them. The three then walked stealthily forward towards the centre of the field. Stanley pulled the borrowed coat tightly around him and looked forlornly down at his polished shoes. Then, from nowhere, snow flurries started dancing through the air like confetti. For several moments the centre of the field became invisible and they could barely see one another. But they kept their line and they continued walking.

As quickly as the flakes had come, they left. The trio were approaching the middle of the field now. But still Stanley could see no hare. Then suddenly an animal got up only a few yards ahead of him. The whippets were unleashed and he stood transfixed as the chase ensued. The speed of it was breathtaking. Both dogs converged on the hare from either side, their legs pounding the ground like pistons and the hare looked done for. But then it jinked, completely jinked, and the two dogs crashed into one another.

"Oh fookin' 'ell, they dosey 'ounds," cursed Randolph.

But the dogs recovered and got back into the race and were on the hare's tail by the hedgerow. The most heart-rending squeals reached them through the blustery squalls, indicating that the beast had not quite made its escape. The whole thing could not have lasted more than 30 seconds. Stanley looked shocked. The closest he came to nature were the robins in his back garden. Although these could be quite aggressive at times, especially to each other, they largely kept their feelings to themselves.

"Noisy blighters, 'ares," muttered Randolph. "We'd better get to whippets afore t' bugga thing's torn t' shreds."

Back at the van the dogs were caged and the dismembered animal was popped into a plastic bag. As they were about to drive off, a police car pulled alongside and the officer driving lowered his window.

"You boys wouldn't be 'are coursin' would you?" he asked when a nervous Stanley had lowered his.

"Certainly not offsa," replied Randolph, leaning across as Stanley dissolved himself into the passenger seat. "Just strollin' t' dogs."

"That's what I like to 'ear, boys. Keeping thy animals 'ealthy," the officer said. And then to Stanley Preston's surprise and relief, he drove off.

"That was close," Stan exhaled.

"Not so close," Randolph assured him. "That were Tommy Jackson. He's a great fan o' whippets. Its t' Metropolitan Police we have to watch up 'ere."

CHAPTER

THE NUM EXECUTIVE left the offices of ACAS without an agreement. Its members, however, felt that the Coal Board Chairman, Ian MacGregor, was showing signs of wanting to find a way out of the deadlock. This was just as well, because the executive knew its members could not hold out indefinitely. And with the High Court having fined the union £200,000 (and its president £1,000 personally) for contempt on 10th October because no national ballot had been called to authorize the strike, the union's ability to cover picketing and organizing costs was being degraded.

Along with all the other journalists following the talks, Harvey had elicited only stone walls of 'no comments' from both sides. However, he'd noticed from earlier disputes he'd covered that when neither side wished to rubbish the other in public, compromise was often being considered.

The Advisory, Conciliation and Arbitration Service, better known as ACAS, could trace its roots back to 1896 when the government had launched a voluntary service to help unions and employers resolve disputes. By 1976 it had become a statutory part of the nation's labour relations process. But the body had its critics and Harvey thought they had a point.

The core of their argument seemed to revolve around the basis of the body's objectivity. In order to uphold its perceived usefulness to both sides (and thus its existence), wasn't it likely, they suggested, that ACAS would opt for a strategy of 'splitting the difference' – of accepting some of what each side wanted so as to cement a deal? What this amounted to was that when a union asked for a wage increase of 20% and management offered 5%, ACAS might suggest 12.5%; the figure would be grudgingly accepted by both sides and ACAS congratulated. But, these critics wondered, how objective was that? Wouldn't such a process merely bake into the status quo an inflationary bias?

The problem, they felt, had been hatched when governments took ailing industries into public ownership at a time when market forces appeared to be making whole swathes of British businesses uneconomic so that they were closing down, shedding workers and disrupting entire communities. Had the government motive been to ease the transition from uneconomic to economic practices, then perhaps, just perhaps, these critics conceded, a period of public ownership might have been warranted; although, they added, it would almost certainly have been cheaper and more effective in the long run to have simply let the business owners go hang and to have given every displaced worker a fat redundancy cheque.

But this is not what happened, they pointed out. What happened was that business owners were bought out at a time when market forces would have destroyed many of them. Jobs were saved, certainly, but complex businesses were brought under the control of elected parliamentarians, most of whom had never run anything in their lives, on the overconfident promise that they would protect workers and their communities. What happened, of course, was that they did neither.

As organs of the state, these industries then had to be run by bureaucrats anxious to satisfy their paymasters and so fell foul of endless political cross-currents rather than commercial reality. Not only did losses mount to such an extent that even the taxpayer could no longer be relied upon to underwrite them, but the state was forced to pretend that these industries were being run at arm's length by corporate bodies like British Steel, British Leyland, British Telecom, British Rail and the National Coal Board, whose primary remit was not to build great businesses, but to reduce their cost to the government. And to preserve a fig leaf of fair play, ACAS was empowered to act as honest broker between management and unions.

The upshot of all this, the critics maintained, was that not only were jobs still lost and communities still ruined, but the process took far longer and cost far more than it need have. Furthermore, while this agonizing adjustment was being drawn out by wanton political hubris in the United Kingdom, elsewhere in the world, in parts more attuned to commercial reality, new industries were being formed and old ones reconfigured, pushing Britain further and further behind. So to these critics, a body like ACAS was not just useless, but worse than useless because it helped to sustain an unsustainable fiction. The one thing it could not say, and which needed to be said, was that the government's model of cosy deals between unions, managers and politicians, sometimes called collective bargaining, was a cruel fraud on both employees and taxpayers alike.

What Harvey also knew was that amongst these critics was the Prime Minister herself. So if the smoke coming from the chimney at ACAS was hinting at a potential compromise, she, for one, would be profoundly unhappy.

* * *

At NUM headquarters, the president was in an ebullient mood. With the support of the Trades Union Congress and the Labour

Party, the president of NACODS had just put forward a plan that would prevent any pit closures without a thorough and wide-ranging review. All of NACODS' 16,000 members were balloted and had approved strike action if their executive deemed it necessary. Although NACODS had not joined the strike initially, it had agreed not to cross picket lines. Even at the Nottinghamshire pits, where miners had refused to strike and were continuing to work, there had been some unease amongst NACODS members. But now, with NACODS behind him, the NUM President felt confident he could force the Coal Board to back down and defeat the Thatcher Government.

Jack Pugh was not so sure. He had no love for the Labour Party or the Trades Union Congress, seeing both as bourgeois bastions of the status quo. Like his nemesis, Mrs Thatcher, he wanted a total transformation of the country, but what he wanted was a communist state. This would only come about, he believed, after Britain had been brought to its knees by a total industrial stoppage. Then, just as Lenin and his Bolsheviks had in Russia, a cadre of men like himself and his president, working though the shop stewards and their works councils, could seize control amid the chaos.

So he dashed off a memorandum to his president urging him not to accept any deal. Drawing on his hero, Lenin, he wrote: *The specific feature of the present situation is that the country must pass from the first stage of revolution, in which insufficient class-consciousness and organization of the proletariat has placed power in the hands of the bourgeoisie, to its second stage in which power is placed in the hands of the proletariat through the works councils we control.*

He placed the note in an envelope and rushed to headquarters.

* * *

Peter Betsworth was verging on the apoplectic. He had just heard about the NACODS strike ballot. This was a disaster. With NACODS behind the strike, the government would be finished.

Having just failed to prevent a bomb that came close to killing the Prime Minister and key members of her cabinet, MI5 was feeling vulnerable. A half-hearted attempt to blame MI6 for the lapse, on the grounds that the bomber might have originated in the Irish Republic and so outside the country, had not even convinced themselves and so was dropped. Police incompetence in failing to secure the hotel before the Conservative Party Conference would have to do. And now he had to call the cabinet office with this news.

"Adrian, it's Peter ... No we haven't got a hard suspect yet, but at least the IRA are bragging, so we know where to start. But I am afraid something else has cropped up. NACODS have just balloted their members for strike action ... Yes, I know that's bloody awful news ... I realize the Prime Minister is not going to take this kindly ... Well we are working on Nottingham. Most of the miners there don't want to strike. A number are near retirement and face losing generous redundancy payoffs if they do. It's even possible a breakaway union will be formed ... Yes, I know that's good news. But it doesn't help us with NACODS ... Fine, but what am I supposed to do about it? I can't just intimidate 16,000 men ... That's their membership ... No, it's not a large number. But it's their executive that matters. They have the final say ... I don't think I heard that, Adrian. We don't live in a police state yet ... You mean try a capitalist approach: out-and-out bribery? ... Well you get the authorization and the bag of lucre and I'll see what I can do. But Frankly, Adrian, I'm pretty sure that would push the executive in exactly the wrong direction ... Of course there are honest men in the trades union movement ... Well don't sound so surprised. This is mostly King Arthur and his henchmen's fight. I don't believe there are too many, even within the Trades Union Congress, who want to see him anointed in Westminster Abbey ... Yes, a troubling thought that. It almost makes one want to become a republican ... Try reason, you mean? ... OK, but what exactly is anyone supposed to say to the NACODS executive? Please don't, it'll sink this government and raise Arthur to near sainthood ... I agree. What a choice to have to make!"

There was a brief pause before Peter heard Adrian's voice again.

"You've just had an idea? Well I hope to hell it's a good one ... Have the NACODS executive take their proposal to ACAS? Is that it? ... Adrian, you know what the Prime Minister thinks of that august body ... Quite! ... You mean use our dysfunctional system to devour itself? A sort of Marxist hybrid? ... You might just have something there, you know. If I recall correctly, Citizen Robespierre, the French Revolution's leading light, ultimately fell under the blade of his own guillotine ... Yes, I enjoy history, although it's a lot easier reading about it than making it ... We certainly are living in strange times, Adrian. For once, I think there will be a before and after when this battle is over. Things won't be the same ... She's had Ian MacGregor in? ... How did that go? ... He came out shaking? ... God, I hope she doesn't want to see me!"

* * *

Members of the cabinet sub-committee concerned with the strike were grim-faced. As usual, the Prime Minister was in the chair.

"What can we do about NACODS, Robert?" she asked.

"We are hoping they will take their proposal to ACAS, Prime Minister."

"You know my feelings about that talking shop."

"Indeed I do, Prime Minister, but on this occasion, it might prove useful. If the choice is between every pit having to suspend operations and a compromise brokered by ACAS, the latter must be preferable."

"If every pit suspended operations, that would save us a great deal of money," observed the Chancellor wryly, "and spare the Coal Board from having to close them!"

"How are coal stocks holding up, Peter?"

"It might be touch-and-go over the winter, Prime Minister," the Secretary of State for Energy reported. "If dock workers prevent coal imports, as they threatened earlier in the year, we would be in trouble."

"We must isolate the NUM and get the public on our side," the Employment Secretary urged. "Ian can be rather abrasive. I have spoken to him about this and suggested he consider offering bonuses to any striking miner willing to return to work. I have also told him not to mention additional pit closures, even as a negotiating tactic. Stoking up emotions again is not what we should be doing right now."

"I understand, Tom," the Prime Minister acknowledged, "but I have made it clear to Ian that only an unconditional return to work will do. We cannot have that man Scargill claiming any sort of victory."

"How successful has the High Court been in seizing union funds?" the Chancellor asked.

"These have not been that easy to locate, apparently," the Cabinet Secretary explained. "Also rumours have been circulating about the union getting funds from Moscow, or even Libya."

"Oh my goodness, Robert," the Prime Minister said. "Surely we can stop that?"

"Well, the security services are aware of the possibility," Prime Minister, "but short of inspecting every suitcase and diplomatic bag that enters the country, it will mostly be down to luck if we pick out the one stuffed with notes destined for Yorkshire."

"So back to NACODS," the Prime Minister directed. "There must be something we can do?"

"I could have a word with the chairman of ACAS," the Cabinet Secretary suggested. "He is a reasonable man."

"Then why don't you, Robert," the Prime Minister agreed. "It is about time he earned his salary."

The meeting adjourned.

* * *

The NACODS strike was scheduled to begin at the end of the coming week. Harvey had learned that some members of the cabinet were anxious to have the Coal Board settle. It was feeling like the approach of a seminal moment when events could spin off in different directions towards different futures. Friday 26th October would either go down as a red-letter day for the NUM or for the government.

Added to which, George Gilder was due back on Monday – his sister had died while he was with her, which was a blessing – and Harvey felt a need to reflect. He would visit his mother in Islington Cemetery.

She hadn't been visited as often as he had intended, but suspected that was always the case with the departed. Lethargy aside, the need to attend a person's jumping-off point into eternity was deep-seated, even if only some simple marker was there to reflect their physicality. Perhaps it was no more than the reassurance one felt from knowing that they did exist and were not just a figment of one's imagination. Whatever the strictures against graven images and the admonishment given to poor Thomas, Harvey knew he related to the power of physical objects. They might only contain the trace of long-faded notes, but they were real.

He walked briskly through Coldfall Wood. The living green had ebbed away from the leaves of the sycamore, ash and oak, leaving behind dead but lovely gold: the alchemy of nature. Some were falling in zigzag loops and he passed children trying to catch them. Away to the left, through the trees, he could see the allotments where women and those too old to fight had dug for victory when Britain needed to cultivate every patch of ground to avoid starvation, and where men now went to escape their wives.

Sylvia had fancied Hampstead Cemetery – "It's a good address,

Harve" – but it was full and so had resigned herself to Islington. Towards the end, she had even been quite enthusiastic when Harvey told her about some of those she would be joining. There was Ludwig Mond, he told her, a German Jew and chemist who had become a successful British industrialist, and his son, Alfred, who had created Imperial Chemical Industries and himself been created the first Baron Melchett. That had bucked her up no end.

She was doubly chuffed when he told her Henry Croft would be there, a working man from the East End who had founded the order of Pearly Kings and Queens and whose pearly-buttoned clothes had been delighting people since 1880.

"You see, Harvey," she had said, "you don't have to be rich to make your mark on life. You just need to have character."

She wasn't sure about having Cora Henrietta Crippen as a neighbour. The lady had been murdered by her husband, Dr Hawley Crippen, and he had been hanged in Pentonville Prison for the offence.

"I hope the poor dear has put it all behind her," she said. "Bitterness can be such an unpleasant companion."

He had tried to counter Cora's sorry tale by telling her that the famous musician, Sir Eugene Goossens, would also be there. He'd been a violinist in Thomas Beecham's orchestra before going on to conduct the Rochester Philharmonic, Cincinnati Symphony and Sydney Symphony orchestras.

"Oh dear," he had found himself saying as he read out the biography to his mother. "It seems he got himself into a spot of bother."

"Well come on, Harvey, don't just stop there," she had said. "A spot of bother is often the most interesting thing about a person."

So Harvey had to recount how Eugene had fallen head-over-heels for Rosaleen Norton, known as the Witch of Kings Cross on account of her interest in the occult and erotica. It appeared that

Joe Morris, a reporter for *The Sydney Sun*, had broken into her flat and retrieved a bundle of letters and photographs depicting their occult activities. Arrested in Sydney and facing the serious charge of scandalous conduct, Goossens pleaded guilty to the lesser charge of pornography, but his career was ruined.

"The only scandalous thing about that, Harvey dear," she had snapped, "was the behaviour of *The Sun*," before adding, with what he took to be satisfaction, "But I don't think I'm going to get bored up in Islington."

He passed the Grecian-styled Mond Mausoleum and away from the leafy walkways surrounding it into the increasingly utilitarian section of the cemetery, which lay just short of the North Circular, part of London's busy inner ring road, where more recent burials were being tightly aligned in regimented allotments of the dead. For a moment he couldn't pinpoint his mother at all and felt that unpleasant giddiness that comes with disorientation.

"You lost someone?" a passer-by enquired.

"My mother," Harvey answered.

"Easily done," the stranger acknowledged. "What year did she come here?"

"1982."

"Then she'll be over there," he said, pointing.

Harvey thanked him, recovered his bearings and soon found his mother. There wasn't much there. A simple headstone, her name, the years of her birth and death and the words: *A person of character. Much loved. Greatly missed.*

Well, Sylvia, it's Harvey. I'm sorry it has been a while. There's been a lot on. I hope your new friends have been entertaining. I am afraid you are some way from the Monds, but perhaps everyone moves around when no one's looking. You were right about Frances, of course. We are getting on well and seeing a lot of each other but have decided to keep our own homes for the time being. No, we are not married! The country continues in a mess, I'm afraid, and there has been a lot of suffering. Government policy drove thousands of companies to the wall, I now realize. Your Maggie is still going head-to-head with King Arthur and it's anyone's guess who'll win. She has pretty much beaten off his flying pickets, which is a blessing, so there have been no blackouts. It'll come down to which one can best hold their supporters in the end.

Apart from the three million souls still unemployed, most people's lives are good right now. Their general view, I think, is that the hardships being experienced by the striking miners and their families have been self-inflicted. It was one of your sayings that the milk of human kindness was like mother's milk: it didn't flow far. Of course *The Sentinel* has played its part in isolating those on strike. Most, I fear, imagine they are being asked to fight for their livelihoods, when in actual fact they are being used to fight a political war. There will be a lot of bitterness when this is over.

I told you I'd been made deputy editor, didn't I? George Gilder will be back tomorrow, which is a relief. His sister died by the way. I can't remember whether or not I told you she had cancer. It's hard to keep track of what I've already mentioned with you up here.

"So you found her then?"

The voice of the stranger jolted him from his silent monologue.

"Yes. Yes I did."

"You'll find some wild roses in the hedgerow over there, if you're interested," the man advised before going on his way.

Only then did Harvey realize he'd forgotten to bring flowers. The wild roses would have to do.

*C*HAPTER

44

THE DISCUSSIONS within ACAS were both simple and profound. Ken Sampsey, the president of NACODS, was a union man to the core as was his general secretary, Peter McNestry. Both knew well enough that at the time of the industry's nationalization after the Second World War, its 600,000 miners were the backbone of the Labour Party. But neither was blind to the fact that barely 150,000 men were now employed mining coal and that this trend, driven by cheaper and more easily accessible sources of energy, was likely to continue.

What they wanted, above all, was to bring the strike to an end on terms that would allow mining communities time to adjust to the inevitable. The pay and conditions their members enjoyed were not an issue. Even the redundancy payments being offered to miners whose pits were being closed seemed generous enough. For them the matter was how best to manage an industry in decline. They believed the Coal Board's pit closure programme was harsher than it needed to be and that this was something which could be negotiated.

They had talked these points through with the NUM executive and come up with a formula in which the interests of mining communities would have to be considered before a pit was closed. However, it had become apparent that the issue for the NUM President, as well as for the Prime Minister, was not how best to manage an industry in decline but whose authority ought to prevail when it came to managing the country. Should it be that of a Prime Minister and her elected government or that of an NUM President and a lukewarm trade union movement which had seen its own authority shredded by an outbreak of stoppages engineered by politically-motivated shop stewards and their Marxist-oriented works councils? It was a simple distinction with profound implications.

* * *

Since his bruising by the Nottinghamshire miners, Jack Pugh had been trying to put the experience behind him. So the tip-off he had just received was doubly unwelcome. John Preston, it seemed, was actively encouraging the formation of a breakaway union.

Barely able to hold back his fury, he told Mona that he needed to go and see John right away. He didn't say why because he knew she was friendly with John's girl, Stacy. However, he was less inscrutable than he realized. While Jack was fizzing his way down the M1, Mona was on the phone to her contact who was soon calling her handler.

* * *

"Betsworth."

"It's Stacy."

"Yes, Stacy. What is it?"

"I've just had a call from Mona. I think Jack Pugh may be on to Marx."

"What makes you think that?"

"He drove from York to go and see him and Mona said he was

furious."

"When was this?"

"Twenty, thirty minutes ago, I suppose."

"So we've got an hour to alert Marx," he calculated. "Why does Mona think Jack Pugh might be onto him?"

"Because he did not tell her what he wanted to see Marx about."

"Is that so unusual?"

"She thought so," Stacy told him. "There was something in his manner."

Peter Betsworth had long ago realized that it was a bad idea to ignore female intuition.

"Can you contact Marx?" he asked. "He's not due to call me for several days."

"I can try. He's working above ground at the Blidworth Colliery," she said. "If I can reach him, what do you want me to say?"

Peter Betsworth pondered the question for a moment.

"I think he should play this one with a straight bat."

"A straight bat, sir? What do you mean?"

"Oh, I'm sorry. You're probably not a cricketer. What I meant was he should just tell it as it is. He should admit that he has become disillusioned with the NUM and its objectives."

"And if Jack has stumbled upon your link with Marx?"

"Denial, of course, but I think it unlikely."

"How can you be so sure?" she asked, worried as much about her own position as John Preston's.

The answer she got was opaque in the extreme and she never did understand what her handler meant by it.

"I think it could soon be time to declare the organizer's innings over," he said.

* * *

By the time Jack made it to Blidworth, some of the steam had left his boiler. But he had nurtured his anger since leaving York by rehearsing everything he intended to say to the turncoat. The man was a pitiful prisoner of false consciousness, a quisling, a traitor to his class, an intellectual pygmy blind to the big picture. He imagined how it would be when the communist state had been established. Men like Preston would simply be taken off and shot or subjected to years of re-education, or both. He rehearsed the prospect with almost erotic zeal.

As he drove into Blidworth, he was struck by its insignificance. How could people in such a place even see, let alone understand, the big picture? Most of the houses in the village had been built for miners in the early part of the century. He'd even heard it said that Robin Hood's friend Will Scarlet was buried in the church grounds of St Mary of the Purification. What a pathetic notion! History was a fable anyway, constructed to justify the present. Soon all that would be airbrushed from people's memory save for its role in bringing about the communist state.

"I'm looking for John Preston," he announced at the pithead gate.

"You're in jam mate. 'E's jus' this minute come back from Newstead Colliery," the gateman told him. "I'll give 'e a buttle. 'Oo's I'll say wants 'e?"

"Jack Pugh. NUM organizer."

"Oh aye," the man acknowledged, with a marked degree of circumspection.

When John appeared, Jack was reminded that his deputy was better built than him. In a one-to-one contest, brain had no edge over brawn and he suspected John might have a brain in there somewhere as well, if the idiot could work out how to use it.

"We need to talk, John," he announced with a little less firmness than he'd imagined.

"What about? I am really busy roight noo, Jack. Do you wanna have a bevy later? We could go over ter the Fox an' 'ounds."

"No, I don't want a bevy," Jack replied, anxious to dull any familiarity. "I just want to ask you one question and I've driven all the way from York to ask it."

"It must be 'un 'ell of a question fer you ter come all this woy ter ask it!" John responded with barely disguised incredulity. "So what's your question then?"

"Are you trying to organize a breakaway union?"

"Yes, that's roight."

"But you can't!" the organizer exclaimed.

"And why not?"

"Because you work for me, for the NUM."

The man in the cabin looked on with growing fascination.

"I work fer meself," John countered, "jus' as the men round 'ere do. We aren't into changing t' world, just getting the best fer ourselves."

"You bourgeois idiot!" Jack exploded. "Doesn't the dictatorship of the working class mean anything to you?"

"The dictatorship of people like you, more loike," John Preston snapped back. "Now if you don't mind, I've got work ter do."

"You are done for!" Jack Pugh ranted. "You do not work for me anymore. You are fired, dismissed, ostracized, finished…"

"I never did work fer you, moy little lovely," John answered in a tone that was well frozen. "And afore you bugger off back ter headquarters, let me give you an' your NUM colleagues sum free advice: look after your members an' stop trying ter rule t' fuckin' world!"

Jack Pugh stood for several seconds, just staring, open-mouthed, like a boxer fatally winded by his opponent's last punch.

"You're not worth it," he snarled.

The organizer then turned tail and skulked off like a sorrowful mutt unwilling to defend a losing position.

"There's summat up we 'im," the gateman chuckled. "He's gorra right bag on, he has! Oh, and by the way, John, I forgot to mention: there's been a posh lass trying to get you. Says its right urgent and can you call her."

* * *

If Jack's mood on the way down had been angry, on the way back it was incandescent. To have been humiliated twice in the Midlands was twice too many. The whole region should be liquidated. The Sheriff of Nottingham had been right after all. These renegades had to be taught a lesson. Arthur would know what to do. He would go to headquarters first thing in the morning. But for now, he'd find some of his fellow travellers, talk about the coming revolution and get ratted. After that, he'd pump the living daylights out of Mona.

* * *

It was near ten when he awoke with a splitting head. Mona was already dressed and he was aware of her opening the curtains.

"I am not doing this again," she announced.

He tried to remember what he had done, but couldn't.

"I need to go to headquarters," he mumbled. "Those miners must be disciplined; they have to be. Christ, my head hurts. Make us some coffee, pet."

Mona said nothing, but went into the kitchenette and boiled the kettle.

"What the hell's that smell?" he asked when he had finally got himself dressed and joined her.

"That, Mr Trotsky, is your puke," she told him with acid precision. "There, there, all over that rug. You could at least have made it to the toilet. You even managed to wretch over me which is not the kind of foreplay a girl appreciates. And there wasn't any play. You passed out."

"We ate pizzas and drank a bit," Jack confessed like a six-year-old schoolboy caught with a pocket full of partially dissected worms and a belly-full of cheap liquor.

"I know exactly what you ate," she told him. "Now I'm going downstairs to check on the washing machine. I won't be here when you get back."

* * *

At headquarters it was pandemonium. As he waited in the anteroom he could hear Arthur shouting.

"It is a shameful sell-out. We had an agreement. What they have agreed to is non-binding. It's worthless."

Young Frank, one of Arthur's assistants whom Jack often dealt with to get funding and line up flying pickets came out to see him.

"Arthur's furious," he said, stating what was already obvious. "NACODS have settled and called off their strike."

"No, surely not; I thought we had them in the bag."

"And there's been a development, Jack," Frank told him. "I'm afraid it's not good news for you."

"What sort of development?" Jack asked, his head still pounding. More aspirin, I must get more aspirin, he thought.

Frank handed him a copy of *The Post*.

"Page five," Frank instructed, "bottom left."

Jack's fingers started to shake as he searched for page five. There he saw the headline above a small article: *Is NUM organizer an MI5 plant?* The piece mentioned him by name saying that although he was one of the striking miners' top organizers, a rumour was circulating that he might be an MI5 plant. The article added that a union spokesman had described this rumour as groundless.

"It's disinformation for sure," Frank offered up by way of encouragement, "but the executive can't take the risk. You can keep your room until the end of the week."

"But then what? And what about my pay and expenses?" Jack pleaded.

"Well, you won't have any expenses," Frank reassured him, "so that's a plus."

"I'm being fired then, just like that, with no payoff?"

"Money's tight, Jack. You know that. I'm sure you'll be able to get food at The Centre."

"But you just can't do this. I mean, after all I've done. Let me see Arthur. This has to be a mistake."

"I am sorry, Jack," Frank commiserated, "but my instructions are to have you escorted from the premises."

And with that Frank nodded towards two burly men Jack recognized as flying pickets he had once used to try and stop fuel deliveries leaving Hunters.

Back on the street, one of the men attempted to grab his car keys.

"This is my fucking car!" he protested.

"OK, Comrade Trotsky," the man laughed, releasing his grip on the keys. "No harm done. Now bugger off."

As he drove back to his lodgings, he couldn't help remembering the real Trotsky's fate. The driving force behind Russia's great Revolution, after Lenin, had been cut loose like him. His head hurt even more now and he felt like a rudderless boat on a stormy sea enveloped by darkness. He had to lie down.

He trudged up the stairs to his room. Inside he found his washed clothes from the previous evening neatly folded on the end of a made-up bed. His spirits lifted. At least there was Mona. But then he noticed that her clothes were no longer in the cupboard and that her things were not on the dresser. She, too, had abandoned him.

CHAPTER 45

THE STRIKE limped on until March of the following year. In November, cash bonuses had been offered to any miner returning to work and although the Coal Board had done its best to flatter the total, it wasn't until after Christmas that an appreciable number of men did so. Stanley and Mabel came up with a car load of provisions for Christmas and there had been a *fin de siècle* atmosphere of dark-humoured jollity at The Centre. But when Alfie confided to Stan that, with Evie due in three months and their bills mounting, he would be returning to work in the New Year, the Prestons had decided that this would be their last trip north.

The truth was that the public had lost interest in the plight of the miners. And when a Cardiff taxi driver taking one to work at the end of November was killed by two pickets who had dropped a slab of concrete onto his car from an overpass, indifference turned to revulsion. In December, the Union of Democratic Mineworkers, based in Nottinghamshire, came into existence and on 3rd March 1985, one year after it had begun, the NUM executive voted to end their strike. Three days later, Peter Betsworth accepted John Preston's request that Marx be retired.

* * *

The atmosphere inside *The Sentinel* was one of quiet satisfaction.

"Why don't you go to Grimethorpe?" George Gilder suggested, looking at his gazetteer. "There can hardly be more of a Yorkshire mining village than that: one road in, one road out and only the pit."

"I have always loved the name!" Harvey said.

"Yes, isn't it a doozy," George agreed. "Apparently it came from Grime, a Viking chieftain who set up his stall there. So perhaps the chief was a forbidding character and 'grim' came from him and the village became his alter ego. I can't pretend I've ever been there myself."

"It did experience some quite serious riots last year," Harvey told him. "Twenty-two people were arrested."

"What was the spark?" George asked, dimly recalling something.

"Two miners picking small coal from the surface near the pithead to heat their homes – pretty much an accepted tradition around there, apparently – were arrested for theft. Youths in the village took to the streets and twenty were arrested. The police, who were not local, did offer an apology later saying that they had not been aware of the custom."

"That would have made a good story," George Gilder remarked.

"Yes, it did," Harvey agreed, "but you refused to run it."

"Ah!" his editor laughed. "I knew it rang a bell. In victory magnanimity, Winston Churchill said, so why don't you go on up there and right that wrong."

* * *

Harvey needed little persuading. For over six years he had borne witness to and reported on a time of great change in his country's history. He had even played a small part in moving it along. Now the

338 • ROBERT MERCER-NAIRNE

much-mellowed journalist wanted to be in the heart of Yorkshire mining country when the men returned to work.

As he drove north, he thought about his start in life. Never once had it occurred to him that he was a prisoner of his background.

'Everything's possible, Harvey dear,' his mother would say between back-to-back cleaning jobs, and the implausibility of it never struck him. Only when he arrived at Oxford University, every penny paid for by his fellow countrymen, did origins become a concept with any meaning and even then its meaning seemed superficial.

His drift into journalism had matched his ill-formed politics. George Gilder picked up where his mother had left off as guide to his hazy opinions, which were little more than a sense of things, in the way you sense heat from a fire without much caring how it came about. But since then he had observed many things and become aware of what they meant in human terms – not just in terms of how best they could be dressed up to please an editor.

The Sentinel had a political point of view, certainly, but perhaps he had failed to notice this because that same point of view had run though his mother's blood. Even at university, where socialism was fashionable, he had not strayed much beyond wondering why such people were intent on 'helping' the less well off when the less well off he knew already had pretty good lives and could mostly look after themselves. So he had kept clear of politics and immersed himself in history. And history had taught him that individual men and women mattered, even when – or perhaps especially when – circumstances conspired against them.

He had seen inflation devour great chunks of people's livelihoods and the value of his mother's pension wither. He had watched those who could, fight back, exposing government and trades union weakness. He had been there when parts of the economy had ground to a halt and become accustomed to piles of rubbish rotting in the streets. He had witnessed the aftershocks from England's long colonization of Ireland. He had walked through industrial graveyards filled with companies put there by government policy. He had reported on race riots in Brixton and Toxteth. He had helped his newspaper wave the flag when his country had gone to war with Argentina over some sparsely populated islands 8,000 miles away. And he had almost been blown to pieces by a bomb, along with the Prime Minister and her cabinet. Now a titanic struggle, involving violence and subterfuge, between the government and members of a union whose forebears had powered Britain's Industrial Revolution, was coming to an end, along with much of their industry. It seemed as though the nation he belonged to had been at war with itself for most of his working life.

* * *

Harvey and his cameraman were muffled up against snow flurries that danced around a dilapidated town laid low by a year without income. People had gathered at the end of the High Street, men, most in their pit clothes, together with their wives and children, to hear an address by their leader. Only two had broken the year-long strike and gone to work in nearby pits and they were nowhere to be seen nor would they ever be spoken to again, not in Grimethorpe anyway. This was a community where jobs had been handed from father to son since the pit was sunk in 1896, jobs that were hard and often dangerous, but jobs that gave these families their identity.

Wearing a thick plum-coloured anorak, their leader mounted the platform. To be heard against the weather, he lifted a loudhailer to his lips. The machine emitted a plaintive whine which was carried away in the wind as had been their hopes.

"On Sunday, your executive voted ninety-eight to ninety-one for a return to work," he began, against calls of "Shame!" and "We'd have gone for another year!"

"There will be those who say that after a year of hardship, of no income and rising personal debt, that our members have achieved nothing," he went on. "But that is not what you should think. We faced not only an employer but a government aided and abetted by the judiciary, the police and people in the media."

Harvey felt a twinge of guilt. His presence was being acknowledged.

"We have been criticized for not having held a national ballot at the start of this strike. Perhaps we should have. But what we did, under union rules, was support each of our areas as they opted for strike action.

"We have been criticized for supporting strike action at the start of the year when coal stocks were high and usage was about to fall over the summer months. But that is to ignore the fact that the Coal Board had announced the closure of twenty pits and loss of twenty thousand jobs and that our members wanted to resist this. So the timing was not of our own choosing.

"We have been criticized for endorsing violent picketing. It is true that some of our members, fired by a sense of great injustice, did resort to violence. But their violence pales to insignificance when set against the violence meted out to our members by the police."

Murmurs of "Thee are reet theear!" and "An' still they didn't break we!" rippled through the thousand or so listeners huddled together for warmth like emperor penguins.

"We have been criticized for our unwillingness to sit down and negotiate with the Coal Board. But we have always been willing to sit down with the Coal Board as long as pit closures and manpower cuts, other than on the grounds of pit exhaustion, were off the table.

"The Coal Board has already announced twenty pit closures and twenty thousand job losses and the Board's own papers indicate that sixty pit closures and sixty thousand job losses are likely over coming years. What union, in its right mind, could endorse such a programme? What responsible union could agree to endorse its death warrant and the death warrant of all those communities dependent upon the mining of coal?"

Cries of "Not fra Grimethorpe, not t' NUM an' not we miners!" ricocheted around the crowd like pinballs.

"Throughout this confrontation we have been told that uneconomic pits must close. But what other jobs are there in towns like this? How is it economic to put miners on the dole and to pay them for doing nothing so that cheaper coal can be imported from abroad; cheaper either because it is subsidized or because those who mine it are paid rock bottom wages?

"One has to ask this: if market forces are allowed to override communities and to destroy people's livelihoods, what did our members fight for and die for in two world wars?"

A shout of "No fer bloody this!" said it all.

"Of course we wouldn't be where we are today if the Trades Union Congress had given us their full support," the leader thundered to the supportive sounds of an opinion widely held. "But what I would say to them is *your turn will come*. This Tory government, under Maggie Thatcher, is out to destroy the trades union movement."

The mere mention of the Prime Minister's name triggered cries of "Maggie out! Maggie out!" from a group of children and their mothers whose folklore now included stories about the wicked witch from the south.

"But let us not be despondent. Let us raise our banners, let us have our musicians strike up and let us march back to work with our heads held high. You and your families have fought for your way of life as hard as any group of individuals could have fought. Take pride in that."

The brass band began hesitantly as cold lips and chilled limbs adjusted to the challenge and people shuffled into position behind their colourful gold-braided banners – *The National Miners' Union: Grimethorpe – Fennymore Lodge. NUM: South Kirby* – and slowly started their march down the High Street which would take in as many roads as they could manage on their journey to the pit.

When the band got into its stride, the mood lifted. They passed the fish and chip shop, In Cod We Trust, they passed St Luke's with a capacity for 500 worshippers, but which had lately seen its congregation fall to as few as thirty. They marched with growing enthusiasm towards their colliery built to tap into the rich Barnsley seam, a 6-foot layer of high-quality coal and one of the country's most productive tended by miners, scientists, joiners, electricians and all those needed to sustain the town's population, which had grown from a few hundred to many thousand with the discovery of coal. Harvey couldn't help wondering what the future held for the bustling oil city of Aberdeen, now so prosperous and confident.

They passed the Red Rum public house, actually opened by the three-time winner of the Grand National, where men would unwind after finishing their shift down the mine. Along Ladywood Road were the red brick and white pebble-dash houses of White City, built by the mining company in the 1930s for an influx of miners from as far away as Scotland. These had been taken over by the council at the time of nationalization and some were now owned by mining families using the government's Right to Buy scheme; but who would purchase them if the pit was closed?

Harvey's cameraman captured the faces and some of the placards – *Coal not Dole*; *Grimethorpe Women's Action Group*; *Too much coal? Give it to the pensioners* – as the crowd, with increasing verve, every man, woman and child determined not to show any hint of defeat, approached the colliery gate. They lined up on either side. The band, which would one day attain fame after starring in Mark Herman's black comedy *Brassed Off!*, started in on the rousingly soulful tune 'Nimrod' from the great English composer Edward Elgar's Enigma Variations as the men marched away to the mine. These were people who knew their fate and the snowflakes melted on tear-stained cheeks. There were few dry eyes that day.

Postscript

POSTSCRIPT

IN SEPTEMBER 1990, the opinion polls gave Labour a 14% lead over the Conservatives and with an election due in eighteen months, Mrs Thatcher's party was restless. Over the course of her time in office as Prime Minister, her approval rating had averaged only 40%, which was the lowest for any incumbent and regularly less than support for her party. The root cause of Labour's substantial lead this time was a profoundly unpopular tax she had introduced to pay for local government.

The Prime Minister had never much liked the way local government was funded: a combination of central government grants and a tax on the value of property. The opacity of such a system, she felt, divorced the majority from how their councils were financed because most people did not own property. This, to her mind, was wholly undemocratic and encouraged some councils to be spendthrift. So her government had introduced a flat rate of tax, with adjustments for students and the poor, to be paid by everyone.

This Poll Tax, as it came to be called, caused riots on the grounds of its regressive nature. It also proved hard to collect because councils never knew exactly who was living where at any point in time. Recognizing its political ineptitude, many in the government wanted to abandon the tax, but knew this would not happen while Mrs Thatcher remained at the helm. So a succession of leadership challenges were mounted and when it became clear in November that she did not command sufficient support from her parliamentary party, she was persuaded to resign. After watching as she left the Prime Minister's residence for the last time with tears on her cheeks, Harvey set about writing her political obituary.

The Sentinel
November 29th 1990

Yesterday a political life came to an end and it was perhaps fitting that the dagger which brought this about was thrust in by a Brutus from South Wales. The Deputy Prime Minister Geoffrey Howe's resignation speech may have purported to be about the government's drift away from Europe, but in reality it was about much more: fundamentally it was a call for the ex-Prime Minister to listen more and assert less.

But he must have known that every fibre of Margaret Thatcher's being lay against consensus because it was the post-war consensus she blamed for so much of her country's ills.

Margaret Hilda Roberts was barely twenty when the Second World War ended. For five years, wartime Britain had been run by the government and with the war over, the newly-elected Labour administration set about rebuilding the country's shattered economy.

A National Health Service was established, the welfare state put in place, workers' rights improved and large swathes of industry taken into public ownership: the Bank of England, civil aviation, coal mining, the railways, road haulage, canals, telephony, electricity, gas and the production of steel. Within six years, some 20% of the economy was being run directly by the State. But, following a war during which almost everything had been directed by government, this seemed more logical than odd.

When Margaret Thatcher, as she became, entered Parliament in 1959, the conflicted nature of this State-run colossus was beginning to show, although the belief that government could do it better continued right up to the nationalization of British Leyland in 1975. The problem with such a structure, as the Soviet Union was also discovering, is that it reacts to political signals rather than commercial ones and can only be kept going for as long as there are tax revenues to support it.

With the rapid rise of oil prices in the 1970s, governments found themselves between a rock and a hard place. The illusion that 'collective bargaining' was a commercial exercise ran headlong into the reality of tax receipts that were insufficient to meet workers' inflation-matching wage demands. Because the cost of our energy had risen, our wealth, in effect, had declined. What was needed to adjust for this was either a fall in wages or employment or both, but the colossus found this politically impossible to engineer.

What Mrs Thatcher and those closest to her argued publicly, and many – even inside the Labour Party – admitted privately, was that the consensus around the colossus had to be broken. But this was a Herculean undertaking. Over thirty years' worth of structure, every bit of it precious to someone or some group, needed to be unravelled. In 1979, the British people gave Margaret Thatcher and her government the chance to try.

Her Conservative predecessor, Edward Heath, had reached for a revised consensus but this had been rejected by both the trades unions and, in 1974, by the electorate, albeit narrowly. This convinced Mrs Thatcher and those closest to her that there could be no consensus, only an entirely new structure built around market principles. What this meant was that the colossus had to be broken up into chunks which willing customers, rather than reluctant taxpayers, were ready to support.

For the next eleven and a half years, in the face of a deep recession, mounting unemployment, a war she did not seek but which she won, a terrorist campaign that almost killed her and a bitter stand-off with the National Union of

Mineworkers (which was fighting for its very existence), this remarkable woman held the line. She operated within the rule of law and our democratic system – more or less – and carried the country with her.

Way back in 1948, she had once applied for a job at Imperial Chemical Industries but was rejected after the personnel department assessed her as 'headstrong, obstinate and dangerously self-opinionated'. Well, their loss was our gain!

The country endured a great deal of pain between 1979 and 1990. Individual lives were ruined, businesses wrecked and whole industries destroyed. It would have been preferable if these great changes had been more intelligently managed, but they were not. Politicians and their civil servants cannot run everything under the sun – other than in bursts and during a war – and should not pretend that they can. A government's task must surely be to maintain a framework that enables people themselves to adapt.

How great leaders leave office is rarely pretty. The Poll Tax was certainly not Mrs Thatcher's finest hour, and I for one am pleased she has retired. But the lady did her duty. And although she may not realize it, there are a great many miners' wives out there just like her – hard-working, loyal, intelligent, honest, patriotic and proud – who did theirs. If her time in office has taught us anything it is that we must learn to manage change better.

But to do so we will have to fight one another less, face up to reality more, agree what problems we are trying to solve and be accountable for our own actions. It may have been George Orwell who said that ideology serves power, not truth, I am not sure, but having observed Britain for these last twenty-one years, I am inclined to agree.

Harvey Mudd, Editor

* * *

"Andrew, its Harvey ... Pretty good, really. And you? ... The reason I'm calling is that I was wondering if I could book the private room in your new establishment on Thursday fortnight? ... Dinner, say around eight ... Twenty-two people, give or take ... How's it going, by the way? I've read some good reviews ... That's excellent. Now, Andrew, there's one more thing. Could you be at the Chelsea Old Town Hall at 7 p.m. on that day? ... You've guessed it. Frances and I are going to do the deed. So could you? It'll just be some of her family and a few from my office ... Perfect ... No. Absolutely not! We will definitely pay ... Well I won't say no to some champagne on the house. That's really kind. Thank you ... Yes, we've become a nation of shopkeepers again! ... OK, until then. Bye Andrew."

* * *

Harvey stood in the Brydon Room with Frances on his left and George Gilder, as best man, on his right. The apprehension he and Frances had both felt was now firmly locked in the past – was it fair on her children? Weren't the two of them doing just fine as they were? She had wondered if she really wanted another husband. He had wondered if he really wanted to *become* a husband. But now their union was out in the open. The chit-chat from the small assembly had subsided and the sideways looks across the aisle given way to full attention forward.

"Harvey, will you take Frances to be your lawful wedded wife?"

"Frances, will you take Harvey to be your lawful wedded husband?"

Frances's son then stepped forward to give his mother's hand to Harvey, a simple gesture of great poignancy which Frances had assured him her son had wanted to make. Her children understood what she had been through.

Next came the rings, circles with no beginning and no end, symbols of everlasting love.

These were exchanged.

Harvey and Frances confirmed their vows and the registrar pronounced them husband and wife.

Their single selves had been transformed.

* * *

Although it was only a ten-minute walk down the King's Road to Quince, Andrew Champion's new restaurant, they all tumbled into minicabs outside Chelsea Old Town Hall and tumbled out again the other end three minutes later. Andrew was as good as his word and corks from bottles of vintage Pol Roger popped like firecrackers as restaurant staff handed round bite-sized delicacies; that is until George Gilder, who had just been made a knight of the realm 'for services to journalism', started tapping his glass.

"Ladies and gentlemen, if I could have your attention…"

The buzz reluctantly subsided.

"Before we sit down to what I know will be a culinary treat, I thought I should fulfil my duty as Harvey's best man and say a few words.

"Harvey joined *The Sentinel* fourteen years ago from the *Oxford Mail*. He landed his first job as a result of an exposé in his university paper about some goings-on between the college kitchen and a local butcher who believed that the price of his wares should be arrived at by consenting adults, in this case himself and the head chef. This happy union might have continued had our fearless cub reporter not discovered that the price covered both the meat and an annual holiday for the chef. There will be no such goings-on here!

"Now I don't think Harvey would mind me saying that back then he did not dwell on the rights or wrongs of such a situation. He just knew it would make a good story. Not only did it, but his little exposé earned him an internship at the *Mail*. And so a young man, with no clear idea of what he wanted to do with his life, became a journalist.

"I have been a newspaperman all my working life and I think I can safely say that most journalists remain more interested in what will make a good story than they are in what is right or wrong. Journalists, as a breed, are profoundly amoral, mining that seam of activity just below the surface of current convention for nuggets that will stimulate, shock or simply entertain and earn them a pat on the back from their editors, or better still, a pay rise.

"I freely admit that I have done my fair share of back-patting, although – as Harvey will corroborate – I may have been a little less than fulsome on the pay front.

"The difference between a good journalist and a great one is that a great one develops a moral sense without becoming a tiresome moralist, and Harvey here has done just that. One of my great pleasures in recent years has been to watch this side of him grow and when I retired earlier this year he was my obvious successor.

"However, I am not going to give Harvey all the credit for this. As he would be the first to admit, he owes a great debt to his mother, Sylvia, and I just wish she could have been here today. It would have given her such pleasure. Sylvia was one of those people who possessed instinctive good sense and rock solid values. Harvey was twelve when his father died and Sylvia just got on and coped. She never expected anything from life that she did not work for and she had a deep suspicion of all those who offered to make her life easier – 'They're after something, Harvey. Now you find out what it is,' was one of her favourite expressions and her son has been finding out ever since.

"A love of opera was another gift his mother gave him and it was opera that brought Frances and Harvey together. I believe she and Sylvia did meet once, after a performance of *La Bohème* at La Scala in Milan, and they got on. But Frances was married to my friend David Graham then. When tragedy struck, Frances picked herself up and got on with life, just as Sylvia had once done. So here we are.

And I have to say, what could possibly be a better advertisement for a positive attitude than today? Please raise your glasses to our lovely Frances and to my Harvey."

The best man just couldn't help feeling a little possessive.

* * *

The guests were split across two circular tables of twelve, with Harvey at one and Frances at the other. Twenty-four sat down in the end when Frances's two daughters both brought boyfriends. The initial plan had been to jumble everyone up, but tribal loyalties asserted themselves and the atmosphere was better for it. But like two planets separated by gravity, it did leave the bride and groom having to settle for amused glances at one another as the general level of bonhomie escalated around them.

"This is most awfully good, Andrew," extolled Porter. *The Sentinel's* social reporter and avowed monarchist was in his element. "Is it hard to find cooks these days?"

"They are called chefs now, Porter, and are like royalty. This one's my partner."

At the royal comparison, the duck egg tart he'd selected almost stuck in Porter's throat.

"What's the wine, Harvey?" asked Pete who had selected the crab raviolo with samphire in a bisque sauce. "It's tasty!"

"Tasty!" scoffed Porter. "Tasty is what you say about a plate of jellied eels, not a Côte de Beaune Meursault."

"How did you know it was that?" gushed Georgina.

"It's on the menu," Harvey pointed out.

"You are such a snob, Porter!" Pete growled.

The rest of the groom's table sat in silence as *The Sentinel's* boys and girl went at each other in their customary manner. In the past, it would have been George Gilder who called a halt, but today Lady

Gilder did with a firm change of subject.

"Do you think Mr Major will make a good Prime Minister?" she asked.

There were various half-hearted attempts from the Fourth Estate's junior members to express an intelligent opinion, but it was left to Lady Gilder's husband to capture the prevailing view.

"Having endured ten righteous years under Oliver Cromwell," he recounted, "the British people were hungry for a return to easier ways. I suspect much the same applies today."

When the main courses were brought – the choice had been between gilthead bream with palourde clams and under-blade fillet with Café de Paris snails, served with a Château Angélus Bordeaux for those who wanted it - Harvey and Frances changed places. He found it a relief to be out of the 'press room' for a while and could see that Frances had his boisterous colleagues quickly tamed.

By the time the blood orange sorbet with Tanqueray gin and freshly baked madeleines was being enjoyed, along with glasses of Chartreuse de Coutet Sauternes, which Frances's children appeared to be enjoying more than most, the gathering had slipped into a state of happy contentment. Even *The Sentinel*'s habitual sparring partners were congratulating one another on their respective contributions to journalism.

It was with the coffee that Andrew's partner put in an appearance in his chef's fatigues to receive an enthusiastic round of applause and to chat. Harvey had been anxious to meet Joseph Preston ever since Andrew had told him about Quince. He watched as the young man engaged with his customers with charm and an easy authority.

"Mr Mudd, it's a pleasure to finally meet you," he said after he had spoken to everyone else.

"Harvey, please. That was just the most superb meal. As Andrew probably told you I met your brother several times over these last years and your parents certainly once. How is John?"

"He's well and married now. He owns a bicycle shop in Solihull."

"To Stacy?"

"Oh no. They split up in eighty-five. I don't know what became of her. I think she was too posh for John."

"You've pretty much lost *your* accent."

"That's London for you."

"And you had another brother didn't you?"

"Yes, Billy: still drilling for oil. He's up in Alaska right now."

"Married?"

"No. I don't think he wants to risk starting a family. He's seen too many changes."

"And your parents?"

"They are both well and enjoying retirement. My father's still a union man of course."

"They must be proud of you."

"Bemused, more like!"

"Have they eaten here?"

"Once. They insisted on paying, so of course we had to doctor the bill rather substantially – and they still thought it was more than anyone should pay for a meal!"

"That's parents for you!"

"Right."

"Back then there was a Jack Pugh with your brother, if I recall. Did he ever mention him?"

"Oh, a right poser that one, John said. My brother couldn't stand him. Teaching politics at a community college near Oxford, I think he said."

Harvey smiled to himself: another generation of Marxist revolutionaries being readied for a moment that might never come.

"Well, I'm very pleased to have met you and don't think we could have enjoyed a meal more. Next time you speak to John, please tell him that Harvey Mudd sends his regards."

* * *

After their guests had gone, the newlyweds walked home together, arm in arm. The pavements were all but deserted. Winter was back in control.

A young woman approached from the opposite direction, muffled-up and in a hurry to get out of the cold.

"Stacy?" Harvey said, but his question was hesitant and the woman walked on.

"What was that about?" his new wife challenged.

"Oh, just someone I thought I recognized."

A red double-decker bus thundered by, embracing them momentarily in its slipstream while keeping warm those inside.

"Who'd have thought it?" Frances laughed. "Mrs Mudd!"

"With two Ds," he joked.

A cascade of crystals hanging from an opulent chandelier within an antiques shop blazed out the refracted light its owner was paying for to entice absent customers.

"You know, Harvey," Frances announced after they'd crossed an empty side street, "I sometimes think the present moment is all we ever have."

"It certainly often seems that way," he agreed, "but even moments must exist within stories."

"Well, you write stories don't you?" she asserted.

"Yes," Harvey admitted, "I suppose I do."

END

ROBERT MERCER NAIRNE

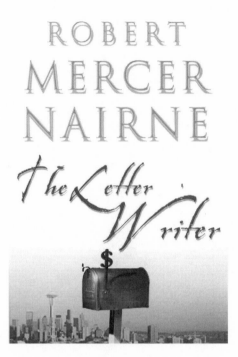

The Letter Writer

Tracing the misfortunes of four Seattle families caught up in the dot-com bubble of the 1990s, *The Letter Writer* paints a striking picture of its time. Described by the *Seattle Post Intelligencer* as wickedly funny, its moral message remains apposite!

ROBERT
MERCER
NAIRNE
LIKE
NO OTHER

This roman-à-clef covers the opening stages of the second Iraq war. With understated, sardonic humour, the clash of ideas and opinions, at every level, is laid provocatively bare.

Mercer-Nairne shows skill at capturing the ethnic and economic outlook of his characters. In the case of political leaders one may easily recognize, he's justly lampooning them, especially the 'make the decision then find a reason' cart-before-the-horse methods of the Bush administration. This is not chauvinism on his part; he shows no favouritism to the Blair government. He is also not afraid to portray a decent, intelligent character favouring the war.

ROBERT
MERCER
NAIRNE
warlord

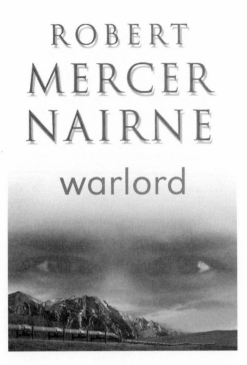

Dedicated to the murdered Russian journalist, Anna Stepanovna Politkovskaya, Warlord follows Orla Kildare, DEMOS-TV's top new reporter as she investigates atrocities carried out by Russian soldiers in Chenchia, an imaginary country on Russia's southern border.

__Warlord__ describes the often unbridgeable gap between cultures and the hard choices those in small countries lodged next to large ones, such as Russia, must make. Yours and my insatiable thirst for oil is the catalyst. You might want to ponder who the warlord in the story is. The ones we think of as backward, with traditional ways – or the Russian President? Could the Warlord even be ourselves, hiding conveniently behind the men and women we elect?